I, KRISHNADEVARAYA

(Naan Krishnadevarayan)

Ra. Ki. Rangarajan, who was with Tamil magazine *Kumudam* for forty years, left a mark on almost every genre of Tamil literature. He even wrote on the occult. He was perhaps the author with the most pseudonyms—as many as ten! He also tried his hand at translations, capturing the flavour of Sidney Sheldon and Jeffrey Archer for the Tamil reading public. His translation of Henri Charriere's *Papillon* was serialised in *Kumudam* and was a huge hit. Ra. Ki's short stories with a surprise twist in the end were compiled under the title *Twist Kadaigal*, and were inspired by Jeffrey Archer's *A Twist in the Tale*. Ra. Ki.'s magnum opus was *Naan Krishnadevarayan*.

Suganthy Krishnamachari is a Chennai-based journalist, and has written articles on history, temple architecture, Sanskrit, mathematics, literature and music. She has written a series of books for schoolchildren on mathematics and English grammar. One of her short stories, published in a leading newspaper, is being used by an educational publishing company which is bringing out two English Language Teaching (ELT) series for school students. Another story was translated into Tamil some years ago, and published by an educationist in a magazine he edits.

I, KRISHNADEVARAYA

(Naan Krishnadevarayan)

Ra. Ki. Rangarajan

Translated by
Suganthy Krishnamachari

Published by
Rupa Publications India Pvt. Ltd 2023
7/16, Ansari Road, Daryaganj
New Delhi 110002

Sales centres:
Bengaluru Chennai
Hyderabad Jaipur Kathmandu
Kolkata Mumbai Prayagraj

Copyright © Ra. Ki. Rangarajan 1998

This is a work of fiction. Names, characters, places and incidents are either the product of the author's imagination or are used fictitiously and any resemblance to any actual person, living or dead, events or locales is entirely coincidental.

All rights reserved.
No part of this publication may be reproduced, transmitted or stored in a retrieval system, in any form or by any means, electronic, mechanical, photocopying, recording or otherwise, without the prior permission of the publisher.

P-ISBN: 978-93-5702-789-2
E-ISBN: 978-93-5702-668-0

First impression 2023

10 9 8 7 6 5 4 3 2 1

First published in Tamil by Vanathi Publishers 1998
First published in English by Westland Publications Ltd
in association with Mysticswrite 2017
Published in English by Rupa Publications India Pvt. Ltd
in association with Mysticswrite Pvt Ltd 2023

The moral right of the author has been asserted.

Printed in India
This book is sold subject to the condition that it shall not, by way of trade or otherwise, be lent, resold, hired out or otherwise circulated, without the publisher's prior consent, in any form of binding or cover other than that in which it is published.

Foreword

Three praiseworthy features

This piece of historical fiction by Ra. Ki. cannot be bracketed with other historicals. Even today, historicals in Tamil are written in the style followed by Kalki, Sandilyan and Vikraman. You just have to read one or two of them to know what to expect. Long sentences, difficult Tamil, spies, horses, women, Chola kings, or failing that, Pandya kings, one or two Pallava kings (but definitely only Tamil kings), footnotes—these are the unvarying features of historicals in Tamil. Ra. Ki. has broken with this tradition. That is the first praiseworthy feature of this book.

This is the first time a historical in Tamil has been told in the first person. This story is about a Telugu/Kannada king, whose court was dominated by Brahmins. And the story begins with the king 'writing' a few short sentences in Tamil:

> This is my maiden attempt in Tamil. So this work is unlikely to have either a felicitous use of words or a lyrical style. I am writing this work in colloquial Tamil. And even that has been possible only because of my association with poets. Reading Villiputturar's *Bharatam* many times has helped. Tamil poet Veerakavi, the poet who is well known for his extempore poems, and who wrote *Harishchandra Venba*, is my friend.

It is hard to tell if these are Krishnadevaraya's words or Ra. Ki's.

There is always a debate about how much history to include in a work of historical fiction. Historical accounts are few and far between, and are not always complete. The author has to fill in the gaps. That is a great challenge. And when trying to fill in the gaps, the author must not assert 'this is what happened.' He must only suggest that this is what could have happened.

With this in mind, Ra. Ki. indicates how Krishnadevaraya could have picked up Tamil. Further exploration of the possibility of the king having learned Tamil becomes impossible, because the story picks up momentum right away. He has also managed to bring in Tirumangai Azhvar's verses and also some Sanskrit mantras and slokas.

The hero of the story was a famous king. When he tells his story, the author faces many difficulties. The author cannot keep away from the king. Even when other people have to be written about, it has to be in such a way that either the king has heard of them, or the circumstances are such that he might have heard of them. The king's descriptions of himself have to be moderate. Ra. Ki. has managed to surmount all these difficulties. His experience with the magazine *Kumudam* has helped, because its editor S.A.P. encouraged Ra. Ki. to try his hand at all genres. This is the second praiseworthy element about this book.

This is the first Tamil historical to be written in the first person. Ku. Pa. Ra. wrote a few short stories in the first person. Even in English, I think the only historical in the first person is *I, Claudius*, where the Roman emperor Claudius tells his story. It is not necessary that historicals should be told in a stilted style. As long as there are no anachronisms, I don't think an author needs to resort to an old fashioned style of writing for historicals, and Ra. Ki. has proved this through this book.

After John Fowles wrote *The French Lieutenant's Woman*, many English historicals began to follow his informal style of writing. In the same way, Ra. Ki. too is a pioneer. He has ushered in a new style of writing historicals.

> It was getting dark. Was a storm really brewing? Or was a storm of emotions tormenting me? As I put some distance between me and the battlefield, the smell of corpses that were beginning to decompose became more and more faint, and there were fewer vultures circling the sky. It was only after a long time, that I realised that I was walking along the banks of the river Krishna. The waters of the river flowed furiously, and the image of the moon in the waters quivered.
>
> I couldn't see the opposite bank of the river. But I had the illusion that I could see the village, Venkata Thathayya's matha, Chinnadevi at the entrance to the matha, welcoming me with extended hands.

We too have the same illusion upon reading this passage, and that is the third praiseworthy feature of this book.

Ra. Ki. has given us a list of the books he has consulted. He has read almost a hundred books; he has consulted many scholars; he has even seen Telugu films about Krishnadevaraya. With so much research behind a novel it is hard to resist the temptation to show off one's reading. But, Ra. Ki. has not fallen prey to such a temptation. He has brought devadasis, ministers and hundreds of ordinary people into his story and spun his tale around them. Among them, Thirumala Devi, whom the king marries out of political necessity and Chinnadevi, whom he marries for love, stand out.

By asking me to write a foreword for this book, Ra. Ki. has given me the joy of reading his well-written novel. My thanks to him for this.

Sujatha

Foreword

Readers expect novelty from an author. Ra. Ki. Rangarajan, who has written many books, is an author who has understood what readers want. He has now offered to his readers this story titled *Naan Krishnadevarayan*.

Krishnadevaraya was a genius, a king who never knew defeat. His contributions to religion, culture, to the country's progress and to economic development are immense. Inscriptions referring to him bring out his greatness. Many foreigners have given glowing accounts of his reign. A bronze likeness of this king and his two queens Thirumala Devi and Chinnadevi can still be seen in the Tirumala temple. The temple towers of Hampi, Kanchipuram and Chidambaram are testimony to his contributions.

Ra. Ki. has spun this story against a historical background. This story is unique, because it is in the first person. It is as if Krishnadevaraya is narrating his life story.

The book is just as racy as any other well written novel with unexpected twists and turns. And yet, unlike other stories, most of the incidents in his story have some history behind them.

Krishnadevaraya's period was a golden period in Indian history. There were great poets, dancers, architects attached to his court. Foreigners visited his capital. Krishnadevaraya was a man with so many achievements to his credit, that it is not easy to tell his story through a novel. And to make it appear as if the king himself is telling his story only adds to the difficulty. By writing this book, Ra. Ki. has himself created history.

The practices that prevailed at that time have been portrayed authentically in the book. All the great men who lived in

Krishnadevaraya's time find a place in this book. The roles they play in the story are in keeping with their characteristics. Krishnadevaraya's mother, Appaji, Tenali Ramakrishnan—the list of historical characters in the book is big. With most of the characters in the story being historical ones, it is hard to describe this book as fiction. It is an account of history. And yet, unlike a history book, this book isn't bland.

It wouldn't be an exaggeration to say that in future, this book will be considered the most authentic source in Tamil, for information about Krishnadevaraya. The effort the author has put in to collect information is evident from the range of information he presents. The import of Arabian horses, the introduction of paper, the coming of the Portuguese, the king's love of dance, accounts of foreigners—the book includes all these nuggets of information.

Most attempts to introduce novelty in stories result in nothing more than stories that are tasteless, useless, and what's worse—harmful to society. Ra. Ki. shows us how to blend the past with the present, how to adopt a 'novel' style to present the past. This is a great service he has done to Tamil literature. I pray that Ra. Ki. will enrich Tamil literature with many more such works.

Dr. R. Nagaswamy

Time to Express My Gratitude

Now that I have completed this book, it is time to express my gratitude to many.

It was Kamal Haasan who gave me the book *I, Claudius*, and wrote on the first page, 'Dear Ra. Ki. Translate this book to Tamil.' He told me it was a book he liked very much. He is a man with good taste in reading. So I began to read the book.

The author had written the story of the Roman Emperor Claudius, with Claudius himself narrating his story. He had presented the period before Claudius' time and also the period in which Claudius lived, and using his imagination, had spun a story that read like a modern novel. Gibbon's *Rise and Fall of the Roman Empire*, and other books must have provided him with a lot of information.

Initially, I thought I would act upon Kamal Haasan's suggestion and translate *I, Claudius*. But that seemed a difficult task. First of all, I had to acquaint myself with Roman history. Readers should also know some Roman history. Since I had my reservations about these two aspects, I was not sure an attempt at translation would be successful.

No one had written a historical in Tamil in the first person, and so I began to wonder why I shouldn't be the first to do so. (I do not know if there are such works in other Indian languages.) Many books have been written about the Cheras, Cholas and Pandyas, and I didn't want to write a book about them. I toyed with the idea of writing about Meera, Akbar and Shivaji. Finally I settled on Krishnadevaraya.

Muslim rulers held sway over North India, but were not so successful in South India. One can't be judgmental and conclude that this was either good or bad, but there is no doubt that it was the great emperor Krishnadevaraya who was responsible for this. He ruled for just twenty-one years from 1509 to 1530. But in that short span of time, he had almost all of South India under his control. No other empire had so much influence on South Indian culture, society and politics as the Vijayanagar Empire. So I chose him as my hero.

I found a lot of reference material about Krishnadevaraya. But they were all in English. If I were conversant in Telugu and Kannada, I could have avoided many mistakes in this novel.

Once I had decided that Krishnadevaraya was to be my hero, I began to gather information about him. I read whatever I could lay my hands on. I made photocopies of all the books I found in the Ayanavaram Circle Library and also in Connemara Library. All this took up to three years. The gathering of all this information gave me a lot of joy. I would show all the details I had gathered to my friends.

The next thing I had to do was to organize all the matter I had collected. I took the help of a hard-working girl called Sarala. With her help I sorted out the matter under different headings: Tamil poets of the time, Krishnadevaraya's military campaigns, the taxes he levied, the practice of sati, dance, temples, military tactics, portraits, etc. I came up with a total of forty headings. I put the matter under each heading in a separate bag, and neatly labelled each of them.

But a book called *Naan Krishnadevarayan* still remained a dream and I wasn't sure I would actually write the book.

One day I happened to meet S. Balasubramaniam, the editor of *Ananda Vikatan*, and told him about the book I was planning. 'A great idea. Start at once,' he said, and also said that the story could be serialised in *Ananda Vikatan*.

I began to write the story in *Vikatan*. The employees of *Vikatan* were very helpful. Every chapter was illustrated by Maruti. As the story took shape, I realised how difficult it was going to be for me to compete it. I also realised how many scholars there were to guide me.

Author Srivenugopalan (Pushpa Thangdurai) lent me books about the 16th century from his collection. He also gave me valuable suggestions. 'Don't forget to maintain the suspense till the end,' he cautioned. I kept that advice in mind.

Archaeologist Dr. R. Nagaswamy gave me information about the roads, inns, and food habits of the time. Dr. T. Satyamurthy of the Archaeological Survey of India and Avudaiyappan—the librarian of Connemara Library, located books I needed.

T. S. Parthasarathy of Music Academy told me about Kuchipudi and Bhagavata Mela. Padma Subrahmanyam explained some aspects of dance to me. Srinidhi Rangarajan (now Srinidhi Chidambaram) demonstrated what an *arai mandi* was.

M. Jagannatha Raja is a Tamil and Telugu scholar. He has translated Krishnadevaraya's *Amukta Maalyada* into Tamil, I found that book very useful. I have used lines from that book in my novel. He also gave me information when I met him and also through our correspondence by letter.

R. Sowrirajan told me about North Indian literary works.

Astrologer Puliyur Balu and Dr. K. Parthasarathy gave me information about astrological techniques. Author Makaram, who also knows astronomy, helped me with astronomical information.

The most difficult task was researching Vaishnavite beliefs and practices. Agnihotram Ramanuja Thathacharya and Dr. M. A. Venkatakrishnan of the Department of Vaishnavism helped me, with regard to this. I have also used my imagination a bit. But it was Venkatakrishnan who explained to me how Krishnadevaraya and Chinnadevi could marry under Vaishnava tradition.

I wanted to know what Krishnadevaraya's palace would have been like. A. V. M. Saravanan procured video cassettes of some Telugu films about Krishnadevaraya, and watching these helped me to get some idea about what the palace might have been like.

I have tried not to omit the name of any person who helped me. If I have left out any name inadvertently, I beg the forgiveness of those whose names have been omitted.

'Apart from portraying Krishnadevaraya as a great emperor, portray him also as a human being, just like anyone else. Write that his back felt itchy and he scratched his back,' my friend Sujatha suggested. I would recall his words every now and then. In one chapter, I have written that Krishnadevaraya found his throne uncomfortable to sit on.

Krishnadevaraya was a connoisseur of all the arts. He was acquainted with many Tamil poets. Using this as an excuse, I have made him sing and ponder Tamil verses.

If I had written in the first person about wars and events that took place after Krishnadevaraya's death, it would have been ridiculous. So I have taken care not to make such mistakes. In spite of my care, a few mistakes might have crept in.

I wanted to get an accurate picture of fencing. So I spoke to actors who do stunt scenes in films. None of them was able to help.

I wanted to visit Hampi. But the summer heat and my health made travel impossible. Because I have only used books and pictures as reference, some mistakes are bound to be there in the book.

Many of the towns and cities I've written about had different names in Krishnadevaraya's time. If I'd known Telugu or Kannada, I could have understood what their original names were. But since I only read English books, and these give only the modern names, I have used the names by which these places are known today. This too could have resulted in some mistakes.

Historians have documented in detail all of Krishnadevaraya's wars. But for the sake of my story I have changed a few dates here and there. But I have not omitted any of the wars, or included any imaginary wars. I couldn't find much information on his wars in Tamil Nadu, or about his travels in Tamil Nadu. Maybe if I had tried harder, I could have got some more information.

I had some other difficulties while writing this novel. In Krishnadevaraya's time, Brahmins held all the high posts. The Emperor had laid down the rule that only Brahmins were to be appointed military commanders. In his time, there was a domination of the higher castes and suppression of the lower castes. There was no religion called Hinduism then. It was called Sanatana Dharma. But keeping in mind the sensitivities of present-day readers, I have glossed over these aspects. After all, these areas are the concern of those who chronicle the history and social life of the period.

Whether it is just a joke or a novel, I follow my mentor S. A. P. But there is one area where I have not followed his advice. 'Gather a lot of information. But do not overload your book with all the information you have gathered,' he would say. I have not followed his advice. I have given a lot of information in my book *Naan Krishnadevarayan*. In fact, I have gone to the extent of thinking up incidents just to include some snippets of information. As a result, the story might get boring at times. I beg your forgiveness for this.

I wish to thank Vanathi Publishers, Dr. Nagaswamy, Sujatha, and my patient wife Kamala, who put up with my temper tantrums, while I was working on this book.

Ra. Ki. Rangarajan

PART I

One

My name is Krishnan. As a mark of respect to my ancestors, I have adopted the surname Devarayan.

Some people say I am a man with rough-and-ready manners. Some say I'm naïve. Some say I'm a Hindu fanatic. Some say I kowtow to the Muslims. Kannada-speaking people refer to me as a Telugu, and Telugu-speaking people refer to me as a Kannadiga. There are yet others who see me as belonging to the Tulu-speaking community. Some equate me with the Emperors Harshavardhana and Chandragupta. Others say I am unfit to be even a chieftain.

Every time I walk to my court, the herald calls out my titles: 'Here comes the Emperor of the Universe! Ruler in the East, West and South! The King who always keeps his word! The terror of his enemies! The one who commands many war elephants! Saviour of the Yadu race! Sun of the Tulu clan! Son of Narasabhoopalan! Devotee of Lord Virupaksha! The upholder of righteousness!'

I have many such titles. If I were to list all of them, you will stop reading further.

This is not my first book. I've already attempted some writing in Telugu and Sanskrit. If Fate and Chief Minister Appaji had not put me on the throne, I would have been a full-time poet by now. This is my maiden attempt in Tamil. So this work is unlikely to have either a felicitous use of words or a lyrical style. I am writing this work in colloquial Tamil. And even that has been possible only because of my association with poets. Reading Villiputturar's *Bharatam* many times has helped. Tamil poet Veerakavi, the poet who is well known for his extempore poems, and who wrote *Harischandra Venba*, is my friend.

Whenever there is the danger that I may not be completely

honest, I recall Chandramathi's words in the Harischandra story: 'I've lost my husband, my son, my wealth. But even if I were to face further travails, I will not utter a lie.'

Although I have a smattering of Tamil, there may be flaws in my writing. There could be factual errors; I might have got the names of people, castes and places wrong. I request readers to forgive me for these slips.

༄

That morning, when I woke up, there was a soothing breeze. Two attendants were fanning me. I signalled to them to leave. I felt depressed.

The reason—Chinnadevi.

When I finished my morning ablutions, an attendant brought me sesame oil, which is what I usually consume in the morning. I drank two cups, like an automaton, not paying attention to what I was doing.

The reason—Chinnadevi.

I'd promised to build a mosque for the Muslim soldiers in my army. I'd intended to discuss architectural plans with architects and scholars. But I couldn't think of any of this.

The reason—Chinnadevi.

I had received information that the Lahore Sultan had sought the help of Babur—the King of Afghanistan. I had sent my spies to gather more information about this. They must have returned by now. But I wasn't inclined to find out what information they had gathered.

The reason—Chinnadevi.

I did my usual physical exercises half-heartedly. I skipped the horse riding session.

Reason—Chinnadevi.

Usually the first thing I do every morning is to meditate on my guru—Vyasateertha, and recite a hymn. I forgot to recite the hymn today. And then remembering that I had forgotten to recite it, I muttered it hastily. It did not lighten my heart.

Reason—Chinnadevi.

I had to meet priest Louis, the messenger of the Portuguese Governor Albuquerque. But I could think of nothing to say to him.

Reason—Chinnadevi.

The five Bahmani Sultans on the northern boundary of my empire are constantly warring amongst themselves. A nagging worry has always been that one day they might decide to set aside their differences and join hands. But today, I didn't even worry about that possibility.

Reason—Chinnadevi.

I picked up my veena. My music teacher Lakshmi Narayana is a great scholar. He has written a book on music titled *Sangeetha Suryodayam*. He is such a good teacher that just one music lesson is enough to give the student a grasp of a raga. Last week, Lakshmi Narayana taught me the nuances of Sankarabharanam[1], and I had a firm grip on the raga then. But when I attempted Sankarabharanam on my veena this morning, all I could produce were a few discordant notes, which were an assault on one's auditory sense.

Reason—Chinnadevi.

It all began yesterday night, when I was on my usual inspection of the city. I saw her dancing in the Vittala temple.

I had searched for her for four years, and had given up hope of ever finding her. But yesterday, I saw Chinnadevi.

---

1. Sankarabharanam—A raga in Carnatic music

She didn't notice me. The audience, enjoying her dance, didn't notice me either. I was in disguise.

I wanted to run up to her, embrace her and shed copious tears.

Unfortunately, I am no longer the Krishnan of four years ago. I am now caught up in the trappings of royalty. I am the Emperor of Vijayanagar. I can no longer do as my heart bids me.

Long after I returned to the palace, I kept thinking of her. I couldn't sleep. 'Chinnadevi, Chinnadevi, Chinnadevi...' I repeated her name, *sotto voce*.

What could I do? That's when I thought of my mother. There is nothing to beat a mother's wise counsel. Who better to turn to, when a man wishes to unburden himself?

Feeling encouraged, I stepped out of my palace. A girl ran up to me, and knelt before me. It was not to pay her respects to me, because her back was turned towards me, and she was facing away from me.

'Climb on to my shoulders, Your Majesty,' she said.

I was taken aback. I noticed Veeranna standing some distance away from me. He was the administrative officer, in charge of appointing servants to the palace. He didn't seem to be surprised by the girl's gesture.

I called out to Veeranna and said, 'What is going on here?'

'This is the custom followed by the royal family. Members of the royal family are carried around the palace complex, either in a palanquin, or on the shoulders of a servant.'

'But a woman?'

'Yes.'

'Are there no men servants?'

'Men aren't allowed into the women's quarters. Whether it is the emperor, or a prince or a princess—whoever it is—they are carried on the shoulders of a woman servant. This is an old practice, followed even in the days of your ancestors. Surely you must have noticed this, Your Majesty.'

I had seen members of the royal family being carried by women servants. But those servants had been hefty, middle-aged women, not a slip of a girl like the one kneeling before me.

'What a shame!' I said angrily. I tapped the young woman on her shoulder and said, 'Get up.'

She stood up. She had an attractive face and a determined look in her eyes. She didn't seem to me to be from a humble background. 'Come along with me. I'm going to visit my mother,' I said to her. 'Let's walk to her palace.'

She was hesitant at first, but did follow me. It's difficult to explain why we choose to be friends with someone, or why we develop an affinity for someone. I can't explain why I liked the girl.

'What's your name?' I asked her.

'Gayatri,' she replied. She had a pleasing voice.

'In future, you don't have to carry anyone on your shoulders. You can be one of my personal attendants.'

'I'm honoured, Your Majesty,' she said, quite unemotionally. There was no trace of happiness in her voice. It seemed as if she was resigned to accept whatever duty was assigned to her.

I turned round. I found I was being followed by four servants. I was always surrounded by servants.

What a nuisance! One of them carried a gold plate with betel leaves in it. Another had a gold cup with areca nuts in it. Yet another carried a silver plate with chunam[2], and the fourth one had a copper spittoon. There are always five to ten men to do even the simplest of things for me. My elders believe this to be in keeping with the status of an Emperor. So I put up with it.

---

2. Chunam—Lime paste

All I did was raise my eyebrows, and the four servants came running towards me. I picked up two betel leaves. I put some areca nuts on a betel leaf, and asked Gayatri to stretch out her hands. I had a glance at the lines on her palm. They seemed to indicate that a difficult life lay ahead of her. It saddened me.

Just as I was about to put the betel leaf on her outstretched palm, I noticed Chief Minister Appaji and Army Chief Nagama Nayaka hurrying towards me. Veeranna must have told them about what had happened.

'Your Majesty,' called out Appaji. The agitation in his voice was unmistakable. He was panting for breath.

'What is it, Appaji?' I asked.

'Please come with me,' he said. He gripped my hand, as if to prevent me from giving Gayatri the betel leaf. I'd known Appaji since my childhood days. He'd never once touched me. That was his way of showing his respect for me. This was the first time he had touched me.

I followed him. Nagama Nayaka stayed behind as if to keep an eye on Gayatri.

We walked to the end of the hall. There was a proliferation of flowers in the garden beyond. The yellow champak flowers and the jasmine flowers spread their fragrance.

'How could you think of doing such a thing?' Appaji asked me.

'What have I done?' I asked.

'First of all, you should not have walked. Secondly, you should not have allowed a servant to walk beside you. And, you were about to offer that girl betel leaves. How could you do that?'

'Why not?'

'You know that when a king offers betel leaves to someone, it is to seal a pact with that person. It is to show that the King reposes trust in that person. Don't you know that?'

'I do. This too was to be a pact,' I chuckled.

My chuckle only added to Appaji's distress. 'Your Majesty, this is not a laughing matter,' he said.

'Nor is it something you should worry about,' I said. 'I'm going to appoint that girl as one of my personal attendants. Since men in the palace do women's work and vice-versa.'

Before I could complete the sentence, Appaji butted in. Holding my hands, he said, 'That's exactly what I don't want you to do.'

'Why not? I like her.'

'Rulers of Vijayanagar have no personal likes or dislikes. They do what their ministers advise them to do.'

'You're the Chief Minister. Go ahead and give me your advice.'

'I've already given you my advice. Do not appoint this girl as your attendant,' said Appaji.

'And I've already asked you to tell me why I shouldn't.'

'There is some mystery surrounding this girl. We don't know who she is, where she is from. She says she is from some village, the name of which we've never heard. She says our soldiers captured her and brought her here.'

'Ah, so she was captured, was she? That is a favourite pastime of our soldiers. Anyway, I trust this girl. I think she is intelligent and cultured,' I said.

'I know what you are afraid of, Appaji. Let me assure you, your fears are unfounded,' I whispered to him. 'And that's because…' I was about to tell him about Chinnadevi, but changed my mind. This wasn't the occasion to speak of her.

I walked back to Gayatri. I gave her the betel leaf. She seemed to know the significance of my gesture. Her eyes glistened with unshed tears. Or perhaps that was just my imagination.

'Let's go,' I said to her.

A shocked Appaji watched us leave. I had never gone against his wishes. This was the first time I had not paid heed to him. Should I have done so? Would my disregard for his advice have undesirable consequences?

Two

Mulling over Appaji's advice, I walked towards my mother's palace. I noticed Gayatri watching me intently, as she walked alongside me.

'Why are you staring at me?'

'I know what Appaji would have told you. He warned you not to appoint me, didn't he?' she asked.

'Yes. He says there is some mystery about you, about where you are from. He's justified in doubting you, isn't he? Why don't you tell me who you are and where you are from?'

'I will give you a detailed account at the appropriate time, Your Majesty.'

'Tell me something about yourself now, briefly,' I persisted.

She walked silently. Palace workers we came across moved aside respectfully. They must have been surprised to see their Emperor in conversation with a servant.

'I'm from a village called Chichil, near the west coast,' said Gayatri. 'I lost my mother at a young age, and suffered ill-treatment at the hands of my stepmother. One day your soldiers came to our village. They said a beautiful girl like me should be in the Emperor's palace. My stepmother was glad to be rid of me, and sent me along with them. That's how I came here. I live in the women's quarters of the palace. The administrative officer sent me to your palace this morning. That, in brief, is my story.'

I looked at her. I couldn't make out if she was telling the truth. There is a Telugu proverb, which says that a man's lies are transparent. You can see through them. But a woman's lies are like a thick, impenetrable wall. You can never guess if she is telling the truth or lying. I smiled to myself as I recalled the proverb.

Gayatri probably interpreted my smile as indicating my trust in her. She smiled too.

I saw a young man dart behind a pillar. He had a huge silk cloth in his hands. I recognized him as an artist I had rewarded recently.

'Come here,' I called out to him. 'What is that you have in your hands?'

'It's a… I thought I would bring it to the court… disrespectful to show it to you here,' he stuttered.

'Never mind. Let me see your work.'

He gave me the silk cloth. It was a painting—the picture of a king, who resembled me.

'Who is this in the painting?'

'Why it's you, Your Majesty.'

I was amused. 'Me? This? But I'm not so tall or well-built. I am a man of average height and average build,' I pointed out.

'It is said that a portrait of an emperor should bring out his majesty,' he said humbly.

'There's something else you've missed out in your painting. See these scars on my cheek? They are the result of small pox. You haven't shown the scars in the portrait.'

'An emperor's face should be portrayed as handsome…'

'Is your house a large one or a small one?'

He didn't understand why I was asking him the question. 'It's neither small nor big,' he said.

'Very well. If there is space in your house, keep your painting there. Come and meet the Royal Treasurer tomorrow. I will instruct him to give you hundred gold coins,' I said to him, and sent him away.

'Artists seem to like exaggerated and unreal representations,' I said and turned towards Gayatri. She looked unhappy.

'Poor man. He must have felt hurt,' she said.
'You seem to have a soft spot for artists,' I said.
'Yes, I do. My sister was a very good artist. She…'
'Yes? Go ahead. Your sister…'
But Gayatri chose not to pursue the subject further. We walked on in silence.

When my mother Nagalambika saw me enter, she tried to get up, which wasn't easy, considering her age. Since my father's death she had taken to sleeping on the floor. 'Remain seated, Mother. There is no need for you to get up,' I said, and sat beside her on the floor.

My mother had been watching a girl called Moorthyamman dance, while another called Madivilasini had been singing Jayadeva's verses. They bowed when I entered, and left.

Jayadeva was a poet who had lived four hundred years ago. He had been the court poet of Lakshmanasena, the King of Bengal. Mother was very fond of his verses, and I often teased her about it.

I decided to have some fun at her expense now. 'Mother, at your age, you still like erotic verses!' I teased her.

'Krishna! How can you talk like an illiterate person? Jayadeva's verses are about the Paramatma-Jivatma[3] relationship. You will understand the import of the verses, if you study them. Do you know which verse that girl was singing when you came in?'

'I didn't notice, Mother.'

'Beautiful lines! The nineteenth verse in the tenth chapter. Lord Krishna is pining for Radha, and says, "My love for you, Radha, is like a poison that has affected me from head to toe. Put your soft feet on my head, to rid me of this poison".'

'Oh, how wonderful,' I said half-heartedly. I was wondering how to broach the subject of Chinnadevi.

---

3. Paramatma-Jivatma—Supreme God-Individual Soul

'Those lines are very significant, Krishna,' Mother continued. 'Jayadeva wrote the lines, but had second thoughts about them. He felt it was blasphemous to suggest that Radha would put her feet on the head of the Supreme One. He decided he would rewrite the verse, and went away to have his bath. In his absence, Lord Krishna came into Jayadeva's house, in the guise of the poet, and wrote the same lines!'

Even as Mother was giving me the background to the verse, my thoughts went to Chinnadevi. I visualised Chinnadevi's feet brushing against my face gently.

Mother's description of the love between Lord Krishna and Radha seemed to provide me with an opening gambit. I thought it best to tell her about Chinnadevi without further delay.

'Mother,' I began, but noticed that she wasn't paying attention to me. She had spotted someone near the door, and called out, 'Who is there?'

Gayatri entered and bowed before Mother.

'Servant,' I said.

'Appaji was here a while ago. He told me about a servant girl. That must be you,' Mother said to Gayatri.

'Our soldiers captured her and brought her here. She is the daughter of a poor farmer. She looked forlorn, and I felt sorry for her. I've appointed her my personal attendant,' I said.

'She doesn't look forlorn,' observed Mother.

I was afraid that if the conversation continued on these lines, I would never be able to bring up the subject of Chinnadevi.

'You may leave,' I said to Gayatri.

'No, no. Let her stay. Come here,' said Mother to Gayatri. 'What's your name?'

'Gayatri.'

'My son says you are a poor farmer's daughter. Which village are you from?'

Gayatri hesitated, either due to fear or due to a disinclination to talk about herself.

'She's from a village called Chichil, near the west coast,' I said.

'Chichil. Hmm. That's surprising,' said Mother. I didn't know what prompted the remark.

'Come here and sit beside me,' said Mother to Gayatri. 'Show me your palms.'

Gayatri was still holding on to the betel leaf I had given her.

'Oh, so you've entered into some arrangement with this girl, have you, Krishna?' Mother asked mockingly. She had a close look at Gayatri's left palm. 'Palmistry interests me,' she said.

I had noticed the lines on Gayatri's palm, which seemed to indicate that she had had a difficult life. Mother had studied astrology and palmistry, and she now scrutinised Gayatri's palm, muttering to herself all the time. As for me, I was repeating to myself the name, 'Chinnadevi'.

Mother relaxed her hold on Gayatri's hand, and said to her, 'You may leave. You will stay here in the women's quarters, and attend to the Emperor, when he sends for you.'

When Gayatri was beyond earshot, Mother said, 'This girl has uttered two lies.'

'Never mind, Mother,' I said, because I wanted to talk about Chinnadevi. Mother misunderstood my impatience, and said, 'I can see that you don't like to hear criticism of that girl.'

'Nothing of the sort, Mother.'

'Then why don't you want to know what the two lies are?'

'All right, Mother. Tell me about her lies.'

'Maybe she is afraid of someone and has therefore lied,' Mother said, in an attempt to mollify me. 'The first lie is her reference to Chichil as a small village. It is not a village. It's a big town. The Portuguese bring Arabian and Persian horses for sale to a port near Chichil. One of the Bahmani sultans has been opposing this trade, and the Portuguese have sought our help many times. But, so far, we've never sent any of our soldiers to that region. So this girl could not have been captured by our soldiers there.'

Now that Mother mentioned it, I recalled these facts. But to me, what was surprising was the fact that Mother, who never ventured out of the palace, was so well-informed.

'Let me tell you about the second lie. From a study of the lines on her palm, I can tell you that she is not the daughter of a poor farmer. She is an educated, courageous, religious-minded girl, from a cultured, well-to-do family. But don't ask her to tell you about her family.'

'Why not, Mother? Are you suggesting that dishonest people should be allowed to get away with their lies?'

'At least don't ask her about her family for now. There is a line in her palm, which indicates that since the age of fifteen, she has faced enormous difficulties. It's because of her unhappy experiences in life, that she has sought refuge in the palace.'

Mother gave me a meaningful look and then asked, 'There is nothing between the two of you, is there?'

'What am I to make of that question, Mother?'

'You know what I mean. And I know that you know what I mean,' she laughed.

Sometimes, when she is in a bantering mood, Mother is much more than just a mother to me. She becomes a dear friend.

'I've already told Appaji, and let me repeat this. I am not romantically drawn to that girl. I...' It seemed the most opportune moment to talk about Chinnadevi.

'Good. With my knowledge of palmistry, I guess that she

must be from an aristocratic family, but I could be wrong. What if she is speaking the truth, and is indeed the daughter of a poor farmer? You should not become attached to a commoner.' Mother's words filled me with dread.

'Mother,' I tried to interrupt, but Mother didn't let me get a word in edgeways.

'Krishna, I don't have to tell you about the history of our empire. Since the time Kumara Kampanna crossed the Kollidam river, defeated the Sambuvaraiyars, and captured Madurai, the empire has expanded to include the kingdom of Chandragiri, Chola territory and Madurai. A total of five kingdoms are a part of this huge Vijayanagar Empire. We have vassals to the south of Madurai too, like the Tenkasi Pandyas and the Cheras, who pay taxes to us.'

I was bored, because I knew the history of the empire, and also of its present geographical spread. You, the reader, reading this account hundreds of years later, may be bored too.

'Excuse me, Mother. I have some administrative duties to take care of.'

'I want you to be able to carry out those duties more efficiently. I want this empire to become stronger. With that in mind, I have made some arrangements. Actually, I can't take credit. It's Prime Minister Thimmarasu, the man you fondly refer to as Appaji, who deserves credit. Of course, his efforts have my blessings.'

I felt uneasy. What arrangements, I wanted to ask, but was unable to. I could guess what Mother was about to say.

'I've made arrangements for your marriage to Thirumaladevi, the daughter of the King of Srirangapatnam,' said Mother.

I was shattered.

Three

How true it is that man proposes and God disposes! I wanted to talk to my mother about my love for Chinnadevi. But here she was telling me that I was to marry someone else.

All I could do was to mutter an inaudible protest.

My mother has always been worried that my interest in philosophy and temple-building would one day lead to my becoming a renunciate. The hasty marriage proposal is perhaps a result of that worry.

'This marriage has Appaji's blessings too,' she said. She might as well have said that it was Appaji's command to me. She knows I will never go against Appaji's wishes.

I left abruptly, without taking leave of my mother. I could hear her calling out to me, but I paid no heed.

Since I had made it clear that I didn't want to be carried on the shoulders of servants, a palanquin had been arranged for me. The gem-encrusted palanquin glittered. Palanquin bearers stood in readiness, waiting for me. I signalled to them I didn't want to use the palanquin.

I walked along the long corridor.

I had given up hope of ever meeting Chinnadevi again. But I had seen her yesterday… How could I forget my promise to her? How could I marry anyone else?

But on the other hand—how could I go against the wishes of Prime Minister Appaji, who had served three generations of my family?

I owe my present position as Emperor of the Vijayanagar Empire to Appaji. In fact, if I am alive today, it is because of Appaji. How can I forget the events that led to my accession to the throne?

After the death of my father Narasa Nayaka, my step-brother Veera Narasimha, son of my father's first wife Thippamba, became king. When Veera Narasimha was on his death bed, he sent for Appaji and Govindaraja—the Presiding Officer of the city. He told them that he wanted his eight-year-old son to succeed him to the throne. To keep me from aspiring to the throne, he ordered that I should be imprisoned and blinded.

Appaji was shocked.

He felt that it was essential for the welfare of the kingdom that I should ascend the throne. He made secret plans to bring me to the capital.

At that time, I was travelling around the country, incognito. Appaji found me and took me to the safety of his palace.

My mother knew nothing of Appaji's plans. When she heard of Veera Narasimha's intentions, she crossed the Tungabhadra river, and travelled to the ashram of Vyasa Teertha. She begged him to save me. He assured her that no one would be able to harm me, for I was destined to be emperor. He told her that the day I would be crowned emperor was not far off.

Eleven days after the death of my step-brother—Veera Narasimha, the Council of Ministers gathered. The ministers were in a fix. They were unwilling to put an eight-year-old on the throne, just because that had been the late king's wish. What would happen to the empire if a child were to be in charge of it? Besides, the people favoured Krishnadevaraya. But Krishnadevaraya was dead—killed upon the instructions of the late king. Even as the ministers fretted over the future of the Empire, Appaji made a dramatic announcement: 'Krishnadevaraya is not dead.'

'Here he is,' said Appaji, introducing me to the ministers. The ministers cheered. And then of course, I became the king. These were events my mother often recalled in her conversations with me, and reminded me of the debt I owed Appaji. Not that I had to be reminded... Could I now refuse to do something Appaji wanted me to do?

☙

I tried hard to sleep, but sleep eluded me.

The royal stable was a considerable distance from the palace. But I could hear the neighing of the horses. It was on a dark night such as this, four years ago, that I mounted a horse from the royal stable and rode off towards Srisailam, which is in the southern part of the Empire.

I wasn't the king then. I was only a prince.

But I didn't let on to anyone that I was the prince. I wanted to acquaint myself with the problems the people faced, and I felt I could do that better if I didn't reveal who I was. But I was wearing a ring, which had the royal insignia—a boar.

The country was prosperous under my brother's rule. People didn't seem to lack anything. It was not difficult to find food or a place to stay.

That day...

The sun had set, and twilight had fallen. I wanted to reach Kalahasti, before dark. But my horse was slowing down, possibly because it was tired. I tethered the horse to a tree, and began to look around for a place to spend the night in.

I could see some lights in the distance, and I walked towards the lights. As I got close to them, I could hear music. A man who was passing by said that the villagers had gathered to watch a Bhagavata Mela performance. I decided to let the horse rest for the night, while I watched the Bhagavata Mela drama.

I sat among the villagers. The men were clad in dhotis, and the women in saris. But the women weren't wearing blouses.

They had covered their bare shoulders with the tips of their saris. The villagers were a jolly lot. The prosperity of the land was reflected in their robust, healthy appearance. Even the elderly were strong and healthy. I could see why Vijayanagar attracted migrants from other countries. The prosperity of the country must be a major draw.

The smell of sweat, so common in huge gatherings, was missing here. Instead, there was an overpowering smell of the fragrant substances the villagers had applied before coming here for their evening of entertainment. The smell of the fragrant substances was so strong it gave me a headache. But I sat among them patiently, waiting for the dance drama to begin.

I smiled to myself when I thought of what their reaction would be, if they knew who I was. But I was dressed like any other villager. So no one guessed I was a prince.

The stage had a curtain in front, held in place by two men. The stage was well lit, and there was a heady smell from the incense that was burned near the stage every now and then. The stage had a canopy of thatch. But the audience sat in the open, unprotected by any canopy.

The drama that was to be staged was *Bhama Kalapam*. I had seen this Bhagavata Mela drama in a few other places. I knew the basics of the art form. Of course, dear readers, by the time you read my books, there would have been a lot of research about this art.

As far as I knew, this dance originated in a village called Kuchelapuri, situated where the Krishna river joins the sea. Siddhappa was an orphan who belonged to this village. He used to follow dance troupes as they travelled from place to place. One night he had a dream. In his dream he saw Lord Krishna dance on his back. And from then on, he became a devotee of Lord

Krishna. He studied the scriptures, and acquired the moniker Siddhendra Yogi. He composed the Bhagavata mela drama. His village Kuchelapuri is also known as Kuchupudi. A Muslim king who invaded the region liked the play Bhama Kalapam so much, that he gave many grants to the village.

Bhama Kalapam is the story of the Parijatha flower which Krishna gave his consort Rukmini. Angered by the preferential treatment to Rukmini, Satyabhama, who was also Krishna's wife, quarrelled with him. To pacify her, Krishna brought her a Parijatha tree from the land of the celestials. This was the story that had been dramatised by Siddhendra Yogi in his Bhama Kalapam.

Siddhendra Yogi laid down the rule that women should not perform in the Bhagavata Mela. I didn't like this injunction against women dancers. I once suggested to some scholars that the ban against women dancers be lifted, but they were aghast at what they saw as a blasphemous suggestion. And now I didn't want to draw attention to myself by such revolutionary suggestions. I settled down quietly to watch the show.

Tossed over the curtain was a long plait. That was the plait of the person playing the role of Satyabhama. It was an indication that he would soon make his appearance on stage. The plait was decorated with glittering ornaments. At the top of the plait was an ornament that resembled the expanded hood of a cobra. There were twenty-seven twists in the plait, with a gold ornament adorning each of them. The ornaments represented the twenty seven stars. The tip of the plait was divided into three sections, with ornaments for each of them. These three ornaments symbolised the earth, sky and the netherworld. Below these were nine pom-poms, one for each of the nine planets.

The head of the dance troupe came on to the stage. He had

a turban round his head. Strands of pearls and precious gems adorned his neck. He began with the usual question: 'Who are you, my girl? Tell me why you are wearing so many ornaments in your plait?'

The answer came from behind the curtain: 'These are the ornaments which Lord Krishna gave me, when he married me. This is the plait that caressed his chest. I am Satyabhama. There is no one who is as beautiful or as intelligent as I am. I am Krishna's favourite wife.'

Singing her reply, the lady who played the role of Satyabhama, emerged from behind the curtain. Yes, it was a woman. I was certain. But no one else seemed to think so. A lady seated beside me exclaimed, 'Amazing! Hard to say this is a man! He looks like a woman!'

Since there was the rule against the participation of women in Bhagavata Mela dances, it never crossed anyone's mind that the person on stage could be a woman. But right from the beginning, I had my doubts. The grace with which Satyabhama walked, the slenderness of the waist, the fulsome breasts—how could this be a man? How was I to find out if I was right? I wasn't paying attention to the dance. Of course, I could go away quietly, without checking if my guess was right. But my pride wouldn't let me do that. I simply had to know. Even as I was wondering how to find out the truth about the dancer, the drama drew to a close. Satyabhama retired from the scene. The curtain was back in place, and there was her plait, hanging over the curtain again, as it had been at the beginning of the drama. There was a reason for the plait being tossed over the curtain. It was a challenge—if anyone in the audience could match the actor's skill in dancing, then he could cut off Satyabhama's hair, as a trophy. Usually, no one in the audience took up the challenge. I decided I would.

'I'm going to dance,' I cried out, and jumped on to the stage. I had a plan. If the person who played the role of Satyabhama was a man, he wouldn't bother if the hair was cut off. After all in his case it was only an attachment of false hair. But if it were a woman, she would not want her long tresses to be cut off. I had a feeling that if the actor was indeed a woman, then my plan would call her bluff.

The crowd that was about to leave, stayed back, surprised at this unexpected development.

I was nervous. I had some theoretical knowledge about Bhagavata Mela, but I had never practised the dance. My challenge was nothing but sheer bravado.

The musicians began playing. Everyone waited for me to begin dancing. What they didn't expect was that the girl who had played the role of Satyabhama would come running from behind the curtain. Yes, it was a girl. My plan had worked.

The girl fell at the feet of the head of the troupe, and said, 'Forgive me. I broke the rule.' She began to sob and turning to me, she said, 'You too must forgive me…'

I put my finger on her chin and lifted it. There was fear in her eyes; tears rolled down her cheeks; her red lips quivered. And that was the moment when Chinnadevi took up permanent residence in my heart.

Four

Even as the dancer was apologising to me, a young man came on to the stage. It was clear that he was unwell. He was shivering. A thick blanket was draped around his body. 'Chinnadevi,' he shouted at the dancer.

'Forgive me, Brother,' she said, and fell at his feet.

The head of the troupe, who had by now recovered his composure, said to him, 'Ethiraja, your sister has gone against our rules. You know women are not allowed to dance in Bhagavata Mela dramas. How could you be a party to it?'

'Please don't be angry with my brother,' said Chinnadevi. 'He didn't know I was going to dance in his place. He has fever, and he asked me to tell you he wouldn't be able to dance today. I didn't tell him I was going to do the role of Satyabhama. The fault is entirely mine.'

But the head of the troupe was not convinced. 'Ethiraja, your sister danced like one trained in the art. Who but you could have taught her how to dance?'

'That's exactly what I'd like to know,' said Ethirajan. He gripped Chinnadevi's arms and shook her violently and said, 'Now tell me, where did you learn dancing?'

Because of the vigorous shake he gave her, some of the ornaments in her hair began to fall off. 'My dear brother, our parents died when I was only five years old. And since then you have been both mother and father to me. I have never parted from you. I've seen you practise. In your absence, I used to try out the steps and moves. I was eager to dance before an audience, and when the opportunity presented itself today, I grabbed it. I know I should never have done it. Forgive me.'

As I heard her explanation, I chided myself. How lively and bubbly she had been a while ago! And now she was miserable. I was the cause of her embarrassment. If I hadn't interfered, she wouldn't have been found out. I hated myself.

That was when Ethirajan noticed me. 'Who are you?' he asked, looking at me with suspicion.

Before I could answer him, another disaster was upon us.

Some members of the audience, who wanted to know what the ruckus on the stage was all about, had clambered on to the stage. The wooden stage couldn't take the weight of so many people. One of the planks broke. Following this, the other planks gave way, and the thatched roof came crashing down.

I heard Chinnadevi scream, and turned to find that one of the wooden reapers had pierced her forehead. Blood gushed from the wound.

I cradled her head on my lap, wrapped my towel round the wound. 'I have some medicines in my bag. There it is,' I said, pointing to the place where I had been seated. 'Get my bag. Quick.'

The bag was brought to me. In addition to my clothes, I had also brought some medicinal powders. I took out a powder, which consisted of ground myrobalan[4] and the powdered bark of a banyan tree. I removed the towel, and pressed some of this powder on the wound. This helped to staunch the flow of the blood to some extent.

Chinnadevi opened her eyes. I could tell from the expression in her eyes, that just as I was smitten by her, she too was attracted to me.

'I asked you a question. Who are you?' said Ethirajan. His

---

4. Myrobalan—A tree species the fruits of which are used in ayurvedic medicine

voice had softened, probably because of my ministrations to his sister.

He gave me an appraising glance.

'You look like a soldier,' he said.

'I'm a soldier too. I am in the medical division of the army. I am now on a pilgrimage,' I said, uttering a string of lies.

But there was some truth in my words. My education had also included a study of Siddha medicine. One of the eighteen *siddhas* was Theraiyar. Although he was a Telugu, he had written books in Tamil. I had read his *Maruttuva Bharatam* and *Theraiyar Karisal*. So when I said that I was a practitioner of medicine, there was a grain of truth in my words.

'Good. For a minute I was afraid you belonged to the royal family,' said Ethirajan. The anger and hatred in his words were unmistakable.

I was taken aback. Why should he be relieved that I didn't belong to the royal family? I couldn't understand.

Chinnadevi stood some distance from me, blushing, because I had touched her. The head of the dance troupe said to those of the audience who still remained, 'There will be a performance tomorrow. But let me assure you that today's mistake will not be repeated. Ethirajan will don the role of Satyabhama tomorrow.'

'No, no. This girl dances very well. Let her dance. Let's abandon this tradition of not allowing women to dance. From tomorrow, let women be allowed to dance too in Bhagavata Mela dramas,' said the villagers.

'All right,' agreed the head of the troupe, albeit reluctantly.

I gave myself a pat on the back. A while ago, I'd chided myself. But now I said to myself, 'I've set in motion some revolutionary changes in the Bhagavata Mela tradition.'

Ethirajan invited me to spend the night in his house. And if the brother extended an oral invitation to me, the sister extended one with her eyes.

One of the villagers said, 'This dance troupe will be here for some days. Why don't you stay too? There is no one in our village with knowledge of medicine. There used to be a man who would prescribe potions and brews, but he died some time ago. The utensils and containers in which he used to store his powders are all still in the village. You can use them.'

What had I let myself in for? Anyway, I was prepared to brave all manner of difficulties, so long as I could stay beside Chinnadevi.

'All right. My horse is tethered to a tree in the grove. Let me bring it here,' I said.

'A horse!' exclaimed Ethirajan. And then as realisation dawned on him, he said, 'Yes, a horse. Naturally. You are also a soldier, aren't you?'

In order to establish that I had some knowledge of medicine, I felt his pulse. 'You have fever. Go home and rest. I will make a potion for you, which will bring down the fever.'

He smiled.

༄

The house in which Ethirajan lived had pyols[5] at the entrance, and flowering shrubs all around. It was a pretty little house, with a tiled roof.

Whether an hour seems like eternity, or whether time flies, depends on the company one keeps. Since I was in the company of Chinnadevi, time flew by. I did justice to the role I had assumed. I went to the forest and gathered roots and leaves, to

---

5. Pyol—Platform built along the house wall that faces the street

make medicinal powders and decoctions. Luckily for me, most of the villagers I had to treat only had minor problems. My medicines proved effective, and the villagers were full of praise for me.

At home, I had the pleasure of watching Chinnadevi dance. Her brother had begun to teach her the nuances of the Bhagavata Mela dance, and as she danced, I forgot myself. I wasn't troubled by hunger: I didn't feel the need to sleep. I forgot all about the empire.

When I saw beads of perspiration on Chinnadevi's forehead, I wanted to kiss them away. I wanted to fix the anklets round her feet. I don't know whether the elderly can understand my aches and longings, but I know youngsters can.

Ours was a love that began when our eyes met. And it was a love that we nurtured carefully. I dressed the wound on her forehead every day. Sometimes the wound smarted, when I applied herbal powder on it. Sometimes Chinnadevi pretended that the wound smarted. In any case, she would grip my hand hard, as if she needed to do so because of the pain. The wound healed, and our love became stronger.

But I didn't tell Chinnadevi who I was. I didn't want to keep the truth from her. But I had to find out why her brother disliked the royal family. 'Don't even mention the royal family to him,' she said. 'I don't know why he hates them, but he becomes furious the moment someone mentions the Vijayanagar Empire…the emperors…Devaraya…the royal family. At such times, even I don't dare approach him.'

Hearing her describe her brother's anger, I was a little frightened myself. What was the mystery behind Ethirajan's dislike of our family? I had to find out. No point revealing who I was, before that. Why earn Ethirajan's wrath? Why should

I do something that might jeopardise my relationship with Chinnadevi?

So I decided not to speak of my family. Unfortunately, the truth came out, because of that unexpected incident.

Ethirajan had gone out somewhere. Chinnadevi was resting after her dance practice. 'Chinnadevi, why don't you teach me how to dance?' I asked.

'No, no. I cannot do it. I am scared.'

'Why should you be scared? Are you afraid that I will become a more famous dancer than you?'

'No.'

'Is it fear of what people will say if a woman were the teacher and a man the student?'

She smiled. 'No, that's not the reason.'

'Then tell me, what is the reason for your refusal to teach me?'

She blushed. It was clear that she wanted to say something, but couldn't bring herself to say it. But that only made me more curious about the reason for her refusal.

'If I were your teacher…' she began.

'Yes, if you were…'

'A teacher can't marry a student. Our elders have said it is a sin to do so.' She covered her face with her hands, embarrassed by the implication of what she had said. She ran out, and I followed her. 'Chinnadevi, I am prepared to sin for the sake of our love.'

I held her shoulders, and whispered, 'Chinna…' But before I could say anything more, we heard the strains of the nagaswaram on the street. It was a marriage procession.

'An auspicious sign,' I grinned at Chinnadevi. The bride and groom seemed to be from a middle-class family. The bride was wearing an inexpensive sari, and she was wearing silver jewellery, instead of gold. But what did the lack of ostentation matter? The bride and groom were beaming. What were riches beside such happiness? I laughed. 'Why are you laughing?' asked Chinnadevi.

'Look at the bride and groom. The sacred rice thrown on their heads. They haven't shaken off the grains. You can still see some on their hair.'

'It's customary to put powdered jaggery and cumin seeds on the head of the bride and groom, and look they haven't dusted that off completely either,' said Chinnadevi.

'Don't worry. When we get married, I'll dust off all the rice grains and the jaggery powder from your hair, before the marriage procession begins,' I teased Chinnadevi. I thought of what a grand wedding ours would be. The marriage of a prince of the Vijayanagar royal family was no ordinary matter.

The procession went past our house, but was stopped by two armed men, who, with their spears, looked like thugs. They stood blocking the procession. I could tell from their turbans and the way they wore their dhotis, that they were guards sent by the village administrative officer.

'Have you paid the marriage tax?' one of them asked the groom.

'A tax for marriage? How unfair!' I said and stepped forward, but Chinnadevi put a restraining arm on me.

Five

The families of the bride and groom were just as shocked as I was.

'Marriage tax…tax?' The bride's father spoke haltingly.

'Have you completed all the wedding rituals?' asked one of the guards.

One of the invitees to the wedding mustered up enough courage to ask the men who they were.

'We are Pattanna Swami's men,' one of the village guards replied. Pattana Swami was the chief of a cluster of villages.

The other village guard repeated his question: 'Have you completed all the wedding rituals?'

'Not yet,' said the groom. 'We are on our way to the temple, which is where the wedding will take place. Why have you stopped us?' He sounded defiant.

'You can't pay the marriage tax. But you go on a procession shamelessly. Let go of your wife's hand,' said the guard, and pulled at the groom's hand.

How could I be a silent witness to such unfairness? I took a step forward. But again Chinnadevi restrained me. 'It is customary in these areas to pay a wedding tax. No one can change the rules,' she whispered to me.

By now Ethirajan and others of the dance troupe, who had gone out, arrived.

'Please wait until I sell my goods in the market next month. I will pay the tax then,' pleaded the bride's father.

The chief of the dance troupe clearly wanted to help, but what could an old man do? Ethirajan, however, boldly stepped forward and said, 'Why don't you give them time until next month to pay the tax?'

'Very well. Then let them get married next month. In any case, who are you to come to their support?' asked one of the village guards and pushed Ethirajan away.

Ethirajan, who was well-built, could easily have dealt with the village guards, but he was bound by the rules of the village, and did not retaliate.

An elderly gentleman said, 'We have paid all the other taxes they demanded of us. We paid for the decorations. They wanted a tax for the musical instruments used in the procession. We paid that too.'

Another said, 'Usually, the groom is taken round on horseback. But since they asked for a tax for that too, we decided we would dispense with the horse. That is why the groom is proceeding on foot to the temple.'

'Do you know how much you have to pay as marriage tax?' asked one of the village guards.

'Yes. Five gold coins for the groom, and ten for the bride. We will definitely pay the tax.'

'Do you also know that since you have not paid the tax prior to the wedding, you will have to pay a fine of hundred gold coins?'

'A hundred?! We can't afford that!'

'If you can't, then leave this village.'

I could hear murmurs in the crowd. 'Already many people have left this village because of all these unfair taxes.'

A woman said, 'And because of the inability of parents to pay the tax, many girls remain unmarried, and are on their way to becoming aged spinsters.'

'We are taxed for everything,' complained another. 'Tax for drawing water from the well to irrigate our fields, tax for operating an oil press, tax for extracting jaggery from sugarcane. There seems to be nothing that is exempt from taxation…'

I was livid. I shook off Chinnadevi's hand, and ran up to the armed men. 'Let them go ahead with the marriage. Don't stop it. It is unfair,' I said.

'Who are you to object?' said one of the guards and aimed a kick at me. Another said, 'This happens in other districts too.'

For the first time in my life, I was unhappy with the way my family was administering the empire. The Vijayanagar Empire—sounded grand. We had divided the empire into several provinces and put a member of the royal family in charge of each of them, and had given the administrators the grand title of Mandaleswara. They in turn had divided each province into smaller administrative units and had appointed governors to administer these smaller units. The governors, in turn, had divided the units under their control into smaller units, with village administrative officers in charge of each cluster of villages.

There was no communication between the Emperor and the humblest citizen of the land. The village officers collected taxes according to their whims and fancies. All that was required of them was that they pay the requisite tax to the governors, who in turn had to pay a certain amount to their Mandaleswara. And as far as the Emperor was concerned, all that mattered to him, was whether the Mandaleswaras sent him the required number of horses and elephants every year. Who cared about the common man?

I hated myself.

When Gautama Siddhartha left his palace, he was witness to the sufferings of people. As for me, all I had done so far was to indulge myself by watching dances and dramas. And I had been proud of how well our empire was being administered. I had no idea of the darker side of our administration, no idea at all, of the burden on the common man.

Disregarding my intervention, the village guards insisted that the families that had gathered together for the wedding disperse. 'There is going to be no wedding. Go away, all of you.'

'Please don't say such inauspicious things,' an old man begged them.

'Nothing auspicious is going to take place now,' the village officer's men said.

I lost my patience. 'Let them go ahead with the wedding,' I said.

One of the guards laughed and said, 'Since you seem to care so much about this wedding, why don't you pay the tax?' He saw the ring on my finger and said, 'I see that you are wearing a ring. Why don't you sell it and…' He didn't complete what he had planned to say. He was shocked. The reason—the ring on my finger bore the royal insignia—none but those of the royal family could wear such a ring. Everyone in the kingdom knew the rule. I had taken great care to ensure that no one noticed the ring. But now my identity was going to be revealed.

The man dropped to his knees. 'Lord, forgive me…' he said, and threw away his spear.

The other man too realised who I was and threw away his spear. 'We didn't know you belonged to the royal family. Forgive us.'

But I didn't want anyone to know I belonged to the royal family. I tried to pretend that I had nothing to do with the royal family. At that moment, I heard the sound of galloping horses. I could see two men on horseback coming towards me. They had recognized me from a distance. They slowed down, and stopped before me. They alighted, and fell at my feet. 'Prince, we have been looking for you for over a month now…' said one of them.

'Prince? Prince? Who is the prince here?' I protested. But I didn't sound convincing. One of the soldiers said, 'Appaji has sent you a letter.' He handed me a silk cloth, which I unfolded, and read.

'Dear Prince, please come at once to the capital. It's urgent. Thimmarasu.'

'He is a prince,' the people whispered among themselves, and stood aside respectfully.

But Ethirajan said to me sternly, 'Tell me, are you from the Vijayanagar royal family?'

The villagers were shocked. How could Ethirajan be so rude to the prince, they wondered. No one except Chinnadevi and I knew of his hatred for the royal family.

'Ethiraja, I will explain later...' I tried to pacify him.

Chinnadevi moved close to me, and put her hand on my shoulder reassuringly. 'Come here,' Ethirajan snarled at her, and pulled her away from me. 'My family has been opposed to the Vijayanagar royal family for generations. If I had known who you were, I would never have let you into my house. And if you had tried to enter my house in spite of my objections, I would have cut your legs off.'

The soldiers, whom Appaji had sent, drew their swords and would have attacked Ethirajan, if I had not stopped them. To Chinnadevi I said, 'Do not be afraid. I will keep my promise to you.'

Chinnadevi who was now crying, said to her brother, 'I...I...'

He cut her short, and said, 'Don't say that word. Don't.' He then did something totally unexpected. He dragged her to a horse that belonged to one of the two soldiers. He lifted her and put her on the back of the horse, mounted it himself, and rode off, kicking up clouds of dust.

'Stop him!' I cried.

'Wait, Prince,' said the chief of the dance troupe. 'You are a prince…'

'And so?'

'You mustn't go against tradition. A girl's parents or the person under whose care she lives, must give her in marriage to you. That is our tradition. To take a girl forcibly, when her family is not interested in a proposal is wrong. And how can a person from the royal family break the rules?'

Some of the young men from the village said, 'Tradition! As if it matters! We'll fetch them.' Youngsters who understood the pull of romantic love.

I sighed. We could no longer see Chinnadevi and Ethirajan. As for the soldiers from the palace, they were furious. The prince had been insulted, and they had been kept from punishing the man who had insulted the prince.

I was confused. What should I do? Heed Appaji's order and return to the capital? Or start looking for Chinnadevi? I decided I would obey Appaji's summons.

I took out a gold bracelet from my bag and handed it to the groom. 'Don't stop the wedding. This is my order,' I said to the village guards. The horse that Ethirajan had taken belonged to one of the soldiers who had come from the capital. So another horse had to be arranged.

I had a final look at the places which had been Chinnadevi and my favourite haunts. While a common man could give way to his emotions, it was expected that a king should be stoical. But how could I harden my heart? The heart is a coward. It isn't made of iron, is it? It melted like wax.

We left the village, and I stopped my horse when we reached a junction of four roads. Chinnadevi, my darling, which is the road that you and your brother took? I couldn't move any further.

The soldiers mistook my hesitation and thought I didn't know the way. They pointed to the road we had to take. That was the last time they spoke to me. They were silent for the rest of the journey. They offered no answers to any of my questions. Their stock reply was, 'Sorry, Prince. We are not supposed to say anything to you. The Prime Minister's orders.'

After two days, we reached a place that was not far from the capital. We decided to spend the night in a rest house. The manager of the rest house gave us a room to stay in. And once we were in the room, one of the soldiers said, 'Prince, the king is seriously ill. He is on his death bed.'

I was shocked. 'Why didn't you tell me this earlier? I have to see my brother at once.'

'No, Prince. You have to see the Prime Minister first. He has specifically told us to escort you to his palace. And you are to travel in disguise.'

'Disguise? Why?' I asked.

'Forgive us, Prince. We do not know the reason. Here are clothes for your disguise. You may choose which of them you wish to wear.'

I looked at myself in the mirror. 'Okay. Shave off my moustache,' I said.

I knew my moustache would give the game away. I had been very proud of my luxuriant moustache and I would often tell myself that no one had a moustache like mine. Losing it wasn't going to be easy. But it had to be done. One of the soldiers shaved off my moustache. I looked so different now, I could hardly recognize myself. I didn't like the way I looked without my moustache. I chose some clothes from the bundle they had given me. 'We have to take your leave, Prince. The Prime Minister has told us that we are not to travel with you.'

'Take my horse with you,' I said to them.

'You'll have to walk a long distance to get to the city.'

'I am young. I can walk.'

They left.

I had entered the rest house, dressed like a villager. Now I was dressed in silk, with a silk turban to match. I had pearl strands around my neck, and an impressive walking stick. The manager of the rest house was surprised by my change of appearance.

I walked towards the capital. I held my head high, for I was trying to pass off as a scholar, and scholars were held in great respect in the Vijayanagar Empire. People who saw me greeted me respectfully. There was a lot that could be said against the Vijayanagar Empire, but one thing was certain—the people of the Empire had regard for the learned. I knew that even if I had entered with all my royal paraphernalia, I wouldn't have commanded so much respect. I recalled the words of poet Bhartrhari[6] that the only imperishable ornament was a man's knowledge.

I reached Appaji's palace. I asked the guard at the gate if Thimmarasu was at home.

'Please come in,' he said respectfully.

Appaji's palace always remained open to scholars and poets. Appaji himself was a scholar and poet. He had authored many books.

I sat on the cushioned seat offered to me.

'Who is it?' asked Appaji.

'Are you the poet called Thimmarasu?' I asked.

'And you…?'

---

6. Bhartrhari was a Sanskrit poet who wrote three works. The verse Krishnadevaraya is referring to is from Bhartrhari's *Niti Satakam*.

'I am the king of poets. You may be the Prime Minister, but I can point to many flaws in your work *Manorama*. I have come all the way from Kerala, to discuss these lapses in your writing.'

Appaji signalled to the guards to leave and then said to me, 'I am glad that even when the Prince was travelling, he found time to read my work.'

I laughed. My disguise had not kept him from recognising me. But when I recalled that my brother was on his death bed, I could think of nothing else. 'Is it true that my brother is dying? I want to see him…'

'Ssshhh,' warned Appaji, with a finger on his lips. He then told me about the King's order—to find me, throw me in prison and blind me.

I couldn't believe Appaji's words! Was it possible for a man to hate his brother so much?

I have already narrated how I hid in Appaji's palace, and of how he later made me King.

But the one month that I spent in Appaji's palace was sheer agony. Since I was in hiding, I couldn't send soldiers to look for Chinnadevi. I didn't confide in Appaji. I knew what his reaction would be. He would disapprove of my preoccupation with love, when so many important things needed my attention.

Appaji and the other ministers wanted a grand coronation ceremony. But I refused. I wanted no grand celebration so soon after the death of my brother.

The first thing I did upon taking charge as Emperor, was to send my spies to look for Chinnadevi. But they all drew a blank.

In the meanwhile, my duties as Emperor took up a great deal of my time. I had to bring in many reforms. I abolished many unfair taxes, like the one on marriage. I had to deal with the conspiracies of the governors. And there was trouble from the Bahmani Sultans.

The people were curious to know who my queen would be. My mother and ministers were all anxious to see me married soon.

I was, however, determined to find Chinnadevi. Sometimes, I worried that I would forget my promise to Chinnadevi, because I had other pressing responsibilities.

But now I knew she was somewhere close to the capital. And just when I thought that all I had to do was tell my mother about Chinnadevi, she says I should marry the Princess of Srirangapatnam.

☙

I could hear the bell being rung, indicating that it was midnight. I couldn't go to sleep. Memories kept me awake. How could I go to sleep when I knew that Chinna, who I had pursued for four years, was here, close to the palace?

I got up from my bed, changed my clothes, and took the secret passage that led out of the palace.

I had seen Chinna dance at the Vittala temple the previous night. I walked towards the temple. The street where dancers lived was close to the temple. My guess was that Chinnadevi would be in one of the houses there. I had the feeling I was being followed. Appaji had made arrangements to have me watched all the time by one of his trusted men. My safety was a matter of concern to him. I presumed I was being followed by one of them.

Six

I had assumed that Chinnadevi would reside in the street in which dancers resided. But as I made my way into the street, my heart was heavy with worry. I didn't want her to be there. I prayed that she shouldn't be in that street. 'Oh Lord Virupaksa! Lord Venkateswara of the Seven Hills! Please, let not Chinnadevi be a resident of this street'—this was the prayer I kept repeating.

The reason was that although the street was home to many dancers, it was also home to women who offered their favours to men, in return for money. Funds had been provided to take care of the needs of dancers who were attached to temples. But some of them had taken to immoral ways either because they felt what they received from the temple was inadequate, or because of their desire for a more ostentatious life.

Many of these dancers were also great musicians. They could play the veena. They could give religious discourses. They could play chess. They even understood the intricacies of statecraft. When a man visited them, they knew how to hold his attention. Wherever his interest lay—music, politics, or chess—they knew how to entertain him.

In course of time, this practice of dedicating women to temples, and then pushing them into prostitution might end. Who knows if this system will still be in existence, when you read this record of mine? But, now, in my time, there is no doubt that despite the fact that they make money through immoral means, they are held in great regard. Kings and rich merchants pride themselves on their liaisons with these women. Even married men take pride in their association with these dancers. It is seen as a status symbol to have a relationship with a temple dancer.

Many rich men even go to temple festivals, and to fetes with their favourite paramours. They are not ashamed to do so.

Many of the dancers who live on this street have the privilege of visiting the women's quarters in the palace. They are treated on par with royal princesses.

Be that as it may, I didn't want my Chinnadevi to live in this street. I knew she would never have gone astray, but still, I didn't want her to be here.

The silence of the street was in sharp contrast to what it is like in the evenings. In the well-lit street, one can see the huge houses that dot the street. The railings at the entrance are plated with silver, and vie with the flowers in the garden for our attention. The young dancers on the swings are as fresh as emerging saplings. Older dancers, grandmothers of the younger ones, keep a watch over visitors who come in. They are clever at assessing whether a man is wealthy or not. A wealthy one is welcomed in; the man of frugal means is mercilessly expelled. There is no poet who has not cursed these old grandmothers. The street is a hive of activity in the evenings. But it was midnight now and the street was silent.

Where was Chinnadevi's house, and how was I to find it? I was angry with myself. How could I be so foolish as to have come here myself? I could have enquired about Chinnadevi discreetly through servants.

It was a long street. When I had reached the end of the street...

One of the houses was well-lit, and the people there hadn't gone to bed yet. Even as I stood wondering who lived there, an old man came out of the house and asked, 'What do you want, young man? And why have you come now? Could you not have come in the evening? There was so much dancing and merry making here.'

'And what was the reason, may I ask?' I said.

'It is only natural that there should be merry making when a wedding is about to take place.'

His words filled me with dread. A wedding? It was at a wedding that Chinnadevi and I had parted. And now…

I was assailed by doubts of a different kind now. A temple dancer would sometimes 'marry' and on those nights when a client didn't turn up, the husband would get the privilege of enjoying conjugal rights. Was something like that about to happen in the life of Chinnadevi?

'Tell me, please, who is getting married?'

'Why the bride, of course,' he laughed.

'Yes, that is obvious. But who is the bride?'

'Nagalakshmi,' he said. Even as I heaved a sigh of relief, I heard a girl's voice calling out to the old man. I was about to follow him, but on second thoughts, I stayed back. I was sure to be recognized, and if I were to be recognized, then my excuse that I was on a night inspection of the city wouldn't sound convincing. Even as I hesitated, the old man came out again, and said, 'I have been asked to tell you that tomorrow, at the palace, you will get answers to all your questions. Are you employed at the palace? I didn't know you were employed at the palace. Please forgive me if I have said something wrong.'

'Never mind. Who was the girl who called you in?'

'Don't you know that when a wedding is about to take place, there will be a lot of people visiting? How can you expect me to know the names of all the people who visit? How can you expect me to know who the girl is or where she is from?' said the old man, and proceeded on his way.

Soon after he had left, I entered the garden, and looked round. I could hear someone running off. It was dark, and I couldn't see anyone. I turned in the direction from which I could hear the sound of running feet. I stretched out my hand, to try and stop whoever it was. All I could lay my hands on was a sari. I pulled at it, but it tore, and all I was left with was a bit of the sari. The woman who had worn it had made good her escape.

I made sure I would be able locate the house the next day. I then left for my palace. I looked at the piece of sari I had torn off. It was a few inches long. It could be silk. Or it could be finely woven cotton.

I tried to recall the voice of the girl who had called out to the old man. It didn't seem like a familiar voice. But I was certain that the girl had changed her voice so that I should not recognize her. The girl to whom the voice belonged knew me. That was why she had said that I would get my answers the next day at the palace.

And as I said to myself, 'The truth will be out tomorrow,' tomorrow had arrived, for I could see the sun rising!

I went to sleep as the sun began to rise. I only slept for a few hours. But I was a disciplined man, and whatever my worries, I was determined that I would adhere to my routine. So I played the veena for some time. I wrestled for some time. I rode a horse for some time. I swam for a while. I read *Vidura Neethi*[7]. I meditated for some time. I wrote for some time. (I had started writing when I had been hiding in Appaji's palace.)

I was late for the morning session at the royal court. Appaji, Madhanna, Lakkanna and other ministers, and army generals were waiting for me. I apologised for being late, and took my seat. One of the deputy ministers read out my agenda for the day.

'Let us first discuss our losses at the Ummathur battle,' I said.

Many of our vassals in the Ummathur region, had rebelled

---

7. Vidura Neeti is part of the Mahabharata.

against our Empire, even in my brother's time. They had assumed all kinds of grand titles—'Uncrowned King', 'Unequalled Hunter of Elephants', 'Avatara of Hanuman' and so on.

They hadn't been paying their taxes to the Vijayanagar Empire. My brother Veera Narasimha had not been able to quell these vassals. And I had received intelligence reports from our spies, that these small chieftains were planning an attack on our empire. I could not be patient with them any longer.

At that time, I was engaged in fighting the Bahmani Sultan Muhammad Shah. So I had to send another general to deal with the troubles in Ummathur. Ummathur fell to my army. Sivasamudram Fort and Srirangapatnam Fort, which were under the control of the rebels came under our control. The ruler of Ummathur, Gangaraja, drowned when he tried to escape. I entrusted the conquered territory to Chikkaraja, who had been opposed to Gangaraja, and once again our flag, bearing the emblem of the discus and conch, began to fly in the region.

When I summarised these events, the minister said, 'We all know of these events. What is there to discuss with regard to these battles?'

'There is a lot to discuss,' I said. 'The losses we incurred, and our expenses because of the Ummathur campaign, have just come to my notice. We have lost many horses. Why did that happen?'

General Kondamarasu said, 'I wish to draw your attention to something. But you must first promise that you will not be angry with me.'

'Your preamble suggests that you are going to say something that will make me angry. Anyway, go ahead.'

'Seventy years ago, Emperor Virupaksa made a wrong decision.'

'Tell me about it without any hesitation. Virupaksa's Sangama dynasty was replaced by the Chaluva dynasty and then that in turn was replaced by the Thuluva dynasty to which I belong. So let me assure you that I will not lose my temper.'

'Arabians used to bring excellent horses from their land and also from Persia, and all the kings would buy horses from them. Those were sturdy horses, unequalled in strength and speed.'

'And what is the connection between what you are saying and Emperor Virupaksa?'

'The price the Arabians fixed, when they sold their horses to us, was much higher than the price they fixed when they sold to Muslim kings. When Emperor Virupaksa heard of this, he took an army to Goa, where they brought their horses. He destroyed their ships, and killed many of them. You must forgive me, Emperor. I am only stating facts.'

'And what happened after that?'

'The Arabians were afraid to come to the West Coast for their trade. We could no longer buy horses from them. So we couldn't get strong Arabian horses. And we were forced to make do with the weak horses we could buy locally. We still continue to buy horses locally…'

Is it possible for a man to think of two things at a time? It seemed possible in my case. On the one hand I was Emperor Krishnadevaraya worrying about matters of state. On the other hand I was Krishnadevaraya, the man in love.

Yesterday night, a lady had sent word to me that I would get an answer to my question in the palace. Why was I being kept waiting? What was the answer to my question? I was wearing rings of precious gems and as I rested my hand on the arms of the throne, the rings chafed my fingers. But this discomfort was bearable. Worse was the nagging in my heart. Why had no one brought me information about Chinnadevi? Lovelorn fool that I was, the incongruity of such a message being brought to me when I was at a meeting of the Council of Ministers didn't strike me.

'But now the situation has changed,' said Lakkanna, in his stentorian voice. 'At present the people in control of the West Coast are not the Arabs but the Portuguese. The Portuguese have chased away the Arabs and the Portuguese sell horses brought from Arabia and Persia. We can buy the horses we need from them.'

'I remember that I am to meet someone from Goa today,' I said.

I looked at the notes he gave me, and even as I was studying them, Gayatri entered. She had a tray with glasses of fruit juice on it. How did she gain access to the place where the ministers were in discussion with the Emperor? Had my mother given her permission? She went round serving juice to all the ministers. She came to me with her tray, and signalled to me with her eyes. It was clear that she had something to say to me. It must be about Chinnadevi. Was it Gayatri who had told the old man that there would be a message for me the next day at the palace?

Seven

Gayatri left, after serving juice to the ministers. But I was distracted.

'Shall I continue, Your Majesty?' asked the Deputy Minister.

'Yes. You were telling me about Arabian horses.' I noticed that Appaji was staring at me.

The deputy minister continued: 'The Portuguese Governor of Goa, Albuquerque, has sent an emissary. His name is Father Louis. He has brought fifty Arabian horses as a gift to you from the Governor. He is waiting outside with the horses, to meet you.'

I had been waiting for an opportunity to find out what Gayatri had to say. This seemed like a godsend.

'Why didn't you tell me this earlier?' I said, and rose from my throne. The other ministers stood up too. 'It is wrong to keep guests waiting. And you tell me he is a man of God. It is much worse to keep such men waiting. I must meet him at once,' I said, as I exited the hall.

I summoned a guard and said to him, 'Fetch the girl who brought us fruit juice a while ago.'

Appaji and the other ministers were surprised, and waited for me.

Gayatri arrived. 'Have you no manners? Do you not know that protocol prevents anyone from entering a meeting of the council of ministers? Has no one taught you how to conduct yourself in the palace?' I said loudly. This was for public consumption. I then said to her *sotto voce*, 'You signalled to me. What did you wish to say to me?'

'I am new to the palace, Your Majesty. I will learn the rules of the palace in time,' she said loudly, again for public consumption and then whispered to me, 'I can sing.'

What kind of answer was that?

'You must learn the rules from the Palace Administrative Officer,' I said, again loudly, and then whispered, 'What does your answer mean?'

She merely repeated what she had said: 'I can sing.' She then bowed before me and left.

And then I had an idea. I said, 'Stop! I am told you sing well. Is that true?'

'I am not an accomplished singer. But yes, I can sing,' she replied.

'In that case, this evening, when the lamps are lit in the palace, come to my room and sing for me,' I said.

She gave me a knowing smile and said, 'As you command, Your Majesty.'

A palanquin was brought for me. I refused it. As I left the hall, the ministers followed me. 'You are far too lenient with that girl,' Appaji said to me.

I laughed. 'So long as I don't let her sit on my lap, you don't have to worry,' I said.

'And that's what I am afraid of—that one day she will also be given that privilege.'

'And the reason for your fear?'

'She has some connection with the street in which the dancing girls reside. She makes many visits to that street.'

'Really? But many dancers from that street are frequent visitors to the palace. So what's wrong with Gayatri's visit to that street?'

'Let her visit the women's quarters in the palace. Is it right that she be allowed to come to your private rooms? How can you allow that?'

'I heard she is a good singer. It's been a long time since I heard good music. Some people claimed they were good singers, but the moment they started singing, I wanted to run away to some other country,' I laughed. But Appaji was not amused.

By now we had reached the royal stables.

I could see a priest there. I guessed he must be the priest Louis, sent by the Portuguese governor. Another white man stood beside him, and next to him stood a translator. Behind the priest I could see fifty wonderful horses.

The priest came forward, took my hand in his, and kissed my hand. He said something in his language, which the translator translated for me: 'I was told that visitors should kiss the Emperor's feet. But I am a priest, and so it would not be proper for me to kiss your feet.'

I laughed. 'No one kisses my feet. I don't let anyone do that. People fall to the ground before me, and the head, knees, and elbows touch the ground. To those watching from a distance, it seems as if they kiss my feet. Foreigners like you think people kiss my feet. I was shocked to read such an erroneous observation in the records of the Persian Ambassador Abdul Razack. I pointed out his mistake to him and told him to correct it.'

When the translator translated my answer, the priest smiled. He showed the horses to me and said, 'Look at these horses, which the Governor has sent for you as his gift.'

The horses were tall and well-built. They had all the features which Manumanchi Bhatta had listed as the features of good quality horses in his *Hayalakshana Sastra*.

'Have the horses branded with the royal sign, and then take them to the royal stables,' I said to an army general.

'What is he saying?' the priest asked the translator. (I will not bore you by recounting my words and then the translation thereof and then the reply from the priest and the translation of that. It will be tedious. I will just recount the conversation.)

'Every year, we buy 30,000 horses. Each horse is put under the care of a soldier. He is paid to look after the horse. He also receives a certain amount every month for maintenance of the horse,' I said.

'And if a horse dies, all that a soldier has to do is to bring the skin of the dead horse, bearing the royal sign, and we will give him another horse,' said Appaji.

'We do something similar. Kings order horses, and we bring them the horses they ask for. If on the way a horse dies, we cut off its tail, and throw the carcass into the sea. We show the king the tail of the horse, and we are compensated for the dead horse,' said the priest.

The young man who had accompanied him was silent. These white men never speak until they are formally introduced.

'This is Nicholas. He is an Italian. He is a man with knowledge of medicine. He has come here to learn the medical practices that prevail in your country,' said the priest. The young man kissed my hand.

'I am glad to hear that. In our country we follow Siddha medicine. You can study Siddha,' I said.

'I don't think it is right to allow so many white men to stay in the capital. Many of them are the Bahmani Sultans' spies,' said Appaji to me in a low voice.

Minister Ayyapparasu said, 'If we are careful, no one can harm us. I think this man should be allowed to remain in the capital. It would help us learn their medical practices too.' It was his habit to oppose whatever Appaji said.

But I could see the logic in Ayyapparasu's words. Our empire was making strides in all fields. Why should medicine lag behind?

'Let him stay here for some time,' I said, and ordered that arrangements be made for his stay.

Although I was talking to the visitors, and carrying out such other duties of mine, my thoughts were on what Gayatri would tell me that evening. I could hardly wait.

☙

Evening. I was overwhelmed by worries. At such times, I would think of Hanuman, of the determination with which he had sought out Sita. Determination and unflagging enthusiasm for the task undertaken would lead to success. Enthusiasm…

The hour was late and Gayatri wasn't here yet. I was trying hard to quell my agitation. And at last there was Gayatri, with a veena in her hands.

'Come in Gayatri. Now you are caught,' I laughed.

'Me? What makes you say so?'

'Well, you lied that you could sing. And now you are in the sorry position of having to prove you can sing,' I said.

She didn't reply. She tuned the veena, and sang a Tamil verse in Ananda Bhairavi raga. Since I was familiar with the verses of the Azhvars[8], I could identify the verse she sang as Thirumangai Azhvar's composition. Her soulful singing was mesmerising, and I forgot myself.

I had underestimated her. I didn't know she could sing so well. 'Since you sing Tamil verses so well, you must be a Tamil-speaking girl. Am I right?'

'You asked me if I could sing. I said I could. And I've proved that I can,' she said, not really answering my question.

I pointed to the bit of the sari I had torn off the previous night. 'Have you seen a sari of this kind before?'

---

8. Azhvars (Alvars)—Vaishnavite saints, who composed verses in Tamil, in praise of Vishnu

She was not in the least surprised. 'That's my sari. That's the sari you pulled at yesterday night. It tore when you yanked it.'

'So you were the one who shadowed me yesterday night? And you were the one who spoke to the old man?'

'Your Majesty, I have been a servant in this palace for a long time now. I noticed that you go out for an inspection of the city every night. And so I've been following you every night.'

'And who gave you permission to follow me?'

'Why, your mother, of course,' she said. 'She asked me to play chess with her. I defeated her.'

'Really?' I gasped, in amazement. No one could beat my mother at chess. I had lost many times to her.

'I am speaking the truth, Your Majesty. Your mother was very pleased and she said, "You are a very intelligent girl. I want to reward you. Tell me what you want." And I said, "I want your permission to move freely about the palace and also in the women's quarters of the palace." She granted me permission to move about freely, and also instructed all the servants of the palace that they were not to stop me.'

'So, it was because of the permission my mother gave you that you followed me, is that right?'

'Your Majesty, a couple of days ago, the palace administrative officer asked me to be your personal bearer, carrying you on my shoulders to the women's quarters. But you refused to allow any servant to carry you. That was the first time you saw me. But I have been a servant in this palace for a long time. And since the day I came to the palace, I have been following you every night, when you go on your inspection of the city.'

I was shocked. 'Why do you follow me?' I asked.

'Just as an Emperor cares for his subjects, should a good subject not care for the welfare of her Emperor?'

'There are five lakh people in the capital. There are three crore people in my empire. Do you mean to say that you have some special interest in my welfare that none of them has?'

'I have a special reason. But this is not the time to talk about it. I will tell you when the time comes.'

How much longer is this girl to remain so mysterious?, I wondered.

'So, you have taken upon yourself the task of protecting the Emperor of Vijayanagar,' I mocked. 'Since you have set yourself up as my guardian, I am sure you know why I was in the dancers' street yesterday night.'

'Yes, I know, Your Majesty. You came there looking for Chinnadevi.'

'How did you know that?'

Gayatri laughed. 'For the last four years, you have sent your spies throughout your Empire, looking for Chinnadevi. I know many of your spies. I too was doing my best to find her. Chinnadevi has been in the capital for over a month. She has been dancing in all the temples in the capital. I have known this for a month. But you found out only recently.'

'Did you see her?'

'Not only did I see her, but I observed her at close quarters, while she was dressing up for the dance.'

'Gayatri, since you know so much, I am going to seek your help,' I said. I forgot that I was an Emperor, and that I was begging a servant to help me. A man who is hungry thinks of nothing but assuaging the pangs of hunger. A man in love is also like a man whose hunger has to be satiated. And that is why I was begging a servant to do me a favour.

'You want to meet Chinnadevi. Right?'

'Yes, yes,' I said.

'I can arrange that. But you must be prepared for a shock. When I saw Chinnadevi dressing, I noticed that her arms had impressions of the conch and discus.'

'And so?'

I knew what that meant. But I couldn't bring myself to say it.

'She has dedicated herself to some Vishnu temple. She has married the deity of that temple too. She has become the wife of the deity. She has become a Devadasi[9]. She will never marry anyone. She will never touch a man.'

---

9. Devadasi—dancer dedicated to a temple

Eight

A devadasi? What kind of madness was this?

My first reaction was anger. But anger soon yielded place to amusement.

Gayatri said, 'I don't think I said anything amusing.'

'I will tell you why I laughed. Do you know how many foot-soldiers there are in the capital of the Vijayanagar Empire?'

'No.'

'One-and-a-half lakh soldiers. And if you were to add the soldiers of the various governors and those of our vassals, then the total comes to five lakhs.'

'Oh?'

'Do you know how many horses there are in my army?'

'No.'

'Fifteen thousand. And if you add those of the vassals, we have a total of fifty thousand horses.'

'Oh, I see.'

'Do you know how many war elephants I have?'

'No, Your Majesty.'

'A total of two hundred elephants, including those belonging to our vassals.'

'I see.'

'The figures I've mentioned only refer to the current strength of my military. If there were to be a war, I can add to my forces. I just have to pass an order, and my forces will swell. Do you know why I am telling you all this?'

'No, Your Majesty.'

'I, Krishnadevaraya, the one with such military might, can I not marry the woman I love? In just a second, I can have her brought to me by force.'

'You mean like Ravana abducting Sita?'

She had gone too far, and I was beginning to lose my temper. 'How dare you speak to me like that?'

'It's courage that comes from knowing that I am on the side of justice,' Gayatri said, without losing her equipoise. 'You command a huge army, and you reel out figures about the number of horses, elephants and soldiers your army has. You have no difficulty remembering these figures. But you've forgotten something very important.'

My anger against her was growing. With great difficulty I restrained myself and said, 'What have I forgotten?'

'That you are a Sri Vaishnava. For generations, members of your family have been adherents of the Sri Vaishnava religion. Your family has made huge contributions to Vaishnava temples.'

'I won't accept your last observation. We donated liberally to Siva temples too. And I continue to support Siva temples and Saivite mathas too.'

'Maybe, Your Majesty. I am not denying your catholicity. Religious tolerance is the hallmark of your family. Not only have you donated to Siva temples, you have donated to mosques too. And you have imposed no restrictions against the Christian missionaries either. I know all of that. But there is no denying that you are, by conviction, a Vaishnavite. A staunch Vaishnavite. A devotee of Vishnu. Your spiritual gurus are Vaishnava Acharyas.'

'And so?'

'Therefore, for you to forcefully capture a woman dedicated to a Vishnu temple would be unthinkable. If you were to do so because of your love for her, then that would make you a sinner. And people will lose their faith in you. Your vassals and the governors and your subjects believe that this empire came into existence to protect our religion from the onslaught of people professing other faiths. And that belief is your strength. Is it right that you should think of doing something that will destroy that belief?'

No one had ever presented such lengthy arguments to me before. And I am not sure I would have had the patience to listen, if they had. I don't know why I heard her out. I suppose it must have been because I could see the truth of her words.

I paced up and down the room. My room was beautifully decorated with sculptures and paintings. I would often enjoy the work of the artists, and lose track of time. But in my current state of mind, nothing gave me joy.

Gayatri continued: 'Your Majesty there is a way for you to attain your goal—that of marrying Chinnadevi, without using force. And that's what I am thinking of now.'

The moment she said this, my anger vanished. 'Gayatri, will I marry my love? Will you help me?' I asked shamelessly.

'I was thinking of how to help you. Unfortunately, Chinnadevi and her brother Ethirajan left the city early this morning.'

'Where have they gone? Why? And I didn't get an opportunity to talk to her!'

'You will be able to spend the rest of your life in her company, Your Majesty. I promise I will help you find her.'

I was at a loss for words.

Gayatri continued: 'If a devadasi visits a place, the rule is that she must dance only in temples and maths. She should not dance in anyone's house. Not even in the king's palace. And if a devadasi goes on a tour, then within a year, she should return to the temple to which she has dedicated herself. I think Chinnadevi has been away from the temple she is dedicated to, for close to a year. That is why she has hurried back.'

'But which temple is that?'

'I was told that she travelled towards Madurai. The most famous Vaishnavite centre in that region is Srivilliputtur. My guess is that she is a devadasi attached to that temple…'

'In that case, I will go there at once.'

'You don't have to. I will leave tomorrow morning for Srivilliputtur.'

'Alone? Let me send some soldiers with you.'

'Not necessary, Your Majesty. I know horse riding and elephant riding. Most importantly, Lord Jagannatha, the God I worship, will protect me. It may take a month or two for me to return. Please be patient.'

The mention of Lord Jagannatha made me wonder if she belonged to Orissa. But I was too preoccupied with thoughts of Chinnadevi to think about anything else, and thoughts about where Gayatri could be from, soon yielded place to thoughts of Chinnadevi.

'Gayatri…Gayatri…why are you prepared to take such risks for my sake? Why should you?'

'Your welfare is of paramount importance to me, Your Majesty. There is something I seek from you. I will ask for it, when the time comes.'

Was this the girl who, not so long ago, had bowed before me and offered to carry me on her back? No, no! Here before me was a modern woman.

'Long live the Emperor,' said the guard at the door. He came in, bowed before me and said, 'The Finance Minister Chellappa Dandanayak is here with the collections.'

This was the last ritual for the day. 'Ask him to wait,' I said. And then I said to Gayatri: 'I pray that you are successful in your mission to find Chinnadevi. I shall repeat on your behalf, Hanuman's prayers when he went looking for Sita. I will pray that the sages of this land bless you. I shall pray that Agni, Vayu, Indra, the Moon, the Asvins, and Vishnu, who is the Lord of all, will bless you. I don't know what else to say to you.' I turned away from her, for I couldn't let her see the Emperor of Vijayanagar crying.

She fell at my feet, picked up her veena and left.

I controlled my emotions. I was now the Emperor who had masked his emotions. And then I said to the guard outside, 'Ask the minister to come in.'

Chellappa Dandanayak was followed by four men, with huge boxes on their heads.

We crossed my room, went past a narrow corridor, and reached the treasury. Four armed men stood guarding the entrance to the treasury. When the Finance Minister gave the key to one of the guards, he opened the massive door to the treasury, and held up a torch for us, as we made our way into the room. We went down steps that led to a huge room. The guard put the torch in a bracket in the wall and left the room. The room had no ventilation, and it was stifling. The four men, who had come with Dandanayak, put down the boxes they had carried on their heads, and left. Only Dandanayak and I were now in the room. There were thirteen huge iron chests in the room, each of them so huge, that four well-built men could sit comfortably in each of them. The first twelve chests contained the treasures that my predecessors had saved. The thirteenth chest was mine.

Every Emperor of the Vijayanagar dynasty had an iron chest of his own. This contained the Emperor's share in the government revenues.

When an Emperor died, his successor would seal the chest belonging to the previous ruler, and would bring in one of his own. The rule was that no sealed chest was to be opened.

Once when Appaji had been in the treasury with me, he had said, 'Although we have tried our best not to let anyone know about the existence of our treasury, our enemies have somehow found out about it. Most of the wars we have had to fight have been on account of the desire of enemy kings to lay their hands on our treasury.'

'Yes, there is so much here, that naturally, they want to take it all away.'

'I have calculated the total worth of what our treasury contains. One would need 550 elephants to transport all the gold and precious gems here. And what is all this wealth doing here? Nothing. Would it not be better if it were put to productive use, for the welfare of the people?' Appaji had asked.

'That is a good idea. But the rule is that we should not open the chests of the previous kings. I am ready to spend my own treasures for the welfare of the people. Why don't you draw up a plan for spending it?' I had said.

And here I was with Dandanayak, for the daily ritual of depositing the day's collections in the treasury. 'Today's collections come to 27000 gold coins, Your Majesty,' he said.

If this were to be taken as the average daily collection, then in a year I would have one crore gold coins!

Dandanayak began to fill up my chest with the day's collections. The clink of coins did nothing to make me happy. I had so much wealth at my disposal, but all I ached for was Chinnadevi. Ethiraja, please bring Chinnadevi back to me. You can have all my wealth.

Dandanayak locked up the door to the treasury, and retired for the night.

It was too late for dinner. So I just had a glass of milk. I was drifting off to sleep, when I woke up with a start. What had I done? How could I send Gayatri alone to Madurai? There was a lot of political disturbance in Madurai. That was the scene of conflict between Veerasekara Chola and Chandrasekhara Pandya. I had sent an army under the command of Nagama Nayaka to the area. If a woman travelled alone to an area which was a battleground, could she come back unharmed?

There was still time to stop her. She would depart for Madurai only at dawn. I would send for her in the morning and tell her that she was not go to Madurai.

How foolish I had been to think that an Emperor could have what he wanted. I didn't know then, that in a few days I would have to step down from my throne!

Nine

As usual I was up before sunrise. I prayed to my favourite deity for a few minutes, and then put my foot on the footrest. But I didn't get up. I was tired of life in the palace. The room looked dull. I got up and pulled forward the wicks of the lamps. The flames were brighter now. The room looked better now, like a patient who has had some medicine. I too felt better.

I picked up a book at random from my collection. It was my habit to pick up a book, any book, just turn the pages and read from it. It so happened that the book I picked up today was *Jnaneshwari*. It was a work written by Saint Jnaneshwar, who was born on the banks of the Godavari, and spread a fiery bhakti all over the country.

I began to read the page I had randomly chosen.

'You say you want to run away from your home, because you find your responsibilities burdensome. But will you not find your own body burdensome? Will it not accompany you? You say you will run away from your parents, your brothers and your relatives. But your arrogance, your anger, your desires, will these not come with you, wherever you go?'

It seemed as if the lines had been written for me!

I continued to read. Saint Jnaneshwar had written that one should carry out the duties God had assigned, that all one's actions should be surrendered at His feet, and that one should perform one's duties whole-heartedly.

His words shook me up. For the last few days, I had not given a thought to my many duties. Instead, I had let my thoughts wander in other directions. I decided I would henceforth concentrate on my duties as Emperor.

I got up from my bed, had my daily dose of sesame oil. I lifted weights. I couldn't lift heavy weights as I had in the past. This came as a shock to me. When one's spirit is weak, the body is weak too, isn't it?

I added some more weights to the bar, and was going to try to lift it, when I saw a palanquin arrive. I saw my mother alighting from it. I welcomed her. 'What is the reason for this early morning visit?' I asked.

She kissed my head, and said, 'I don't know why, but I was anxious to see you at once, Krishna.'

'Mother, if you had come a few minutes later, you would not have been able to embrace me,' I said.

'Why, Krishna? What is the matter?' My mother was agitated.

'Because, Mother, the next thing I have to do is to cover my body with oil, and then exercise, until I sweat profusely. You won't even want to touch me when I begin to sweat, leave alone wanting to embrace me,' I said.

My mother smiled, and said, 'Krishna, even if you were to wear someone's entrails as a garland, like Narasimha, who wore the entrails of Hiranyakasipu like a garland, I would still not hesitate to embrace you. Whatever your appearance, you will always be dear to me. I couldn't sleep the whole of yesterday night, Krishna.'

I wanted to say, 'Neither could I, Mother,' but I checked myself, and said to her, 'Why, Mother? What was the reason?'

'There are two things I want to talk to you about. Your father appeared in a dream yesterday.'

'Nothing unusual about that, is there?'

'There were tears in his eyes, and it seemed as if he was asking me for a favour. I sat up the whole night and thought about what troubled him, and then it dawned on me.'

'What do you think was troubling him?'

'You have imprisoned your step-brothers Rangan and Achyuthan and your nephew, and housed them in the Chandragiri fort. Is this fair? I think your father wanted to remind me that they should all be set free. Tell me, Krishna, when are you going to set them free?'

'You have got the facts wrong, Mother. First of all, I didn't imprison them. Appaji did. Whatever Appaji does is for the welfare of the Empire. You know that as well as I do.'

'I don't care who did it. I don't like it, Krishna. Rangan and Achyuthan may be my husband's sons through another wife. But I think of them as my sons too.'

I didn't know what to say to this. When Appaji put me on the throne, he wanted to ensure that I would face no challenges from my step-brothers. He had, therefore, arranged for them to stay in the Chandragiri fort.

'Another erroneous impression you seem to have, Mother, is that they are prisoners. They are not. They are in the palace in Chandragiri. We have just posted guards outside the fort, so that they cannot leave the fort. But they lack nothing in the fort, and continue to live like princes. If you have any doubts on this score, please visit the fort yourself, and check for yourself.'

My mother was not satisfied with my reply.

Although I prided myself on my courage, there were moments when I was afraid. Some years ago, I had overheard two old men talking about the royal family. One of them had said to the other, 'There is no guarantee that a son of the Emperor will ascend the throne. Study the history of the royal family over the last two hundred years and you will see what I mean.' And since then, I had always felt a little unsure of myself.

And the old man was right. The history of the Vijayanagar

Empire showed that he was right. That is why I mistrusted my relatives and my generals. I did not trust anyone completely. Not even Appaji.

I didn't tell my mother about my fears.

'You said you wanted to speak to me about two things. What is the second item on your agenda?' I reminded her.

'The Krishnaswami temple needs some repairs. Palace officials tell me that it is difficult to find carpenters, sculptors, masons, because they are all working in that new city you are going to establish. Tell me about this new city. I can tell from your smile that you have something up your sleeve.'

'It's no secret, Mother. It is true that I am building a new city. It will have all facilities—good roads, supply of potable water, temples, bazaars. I have also been urging the rich men of the capital to build some mansions for themselves there. When the city is ready for occupation, I want you to declare it open, Mother.'

'Me?' asked my mother in disbelief.

'Yes, you, Mother. The new city is going to be named after you, Mother. It is going to be called Nagalapura. It is my way of showing my regard for my mother.'

'There is another way in which you can show your regard for your mother,' she said.

'And what is that, Mother?'

'I told you that I wanted you to marry Thirumala Devi, the daughter of the King of Srirangapatnam. But you have not given your consent to this proposal. Agree to marry Thirumala Devi, and then I will tell you whether I want this new city to be named after me or not,' said my mother angrily.

I was a coward. I didn't have the courage to tell her of my love for Chinnadevi.

'I told you I wanted to speak to you of two things. Actually, I wanted to speak to you about three things. The third is Gayatri. She left suddenly yesterday night, saying she had to leave the capital and go on a long journey.'

Oh dear, had Gayatri left already? And I had wanted to stop her from going to Madurai.

'How do I know anything about Gayatri, Mother? She is with you most of the time. You told me you didn't want her to be my personal servant. But then I find that she has your permission to move freely about the palace.'

'Yes, I did give her permission to move about the palace without hindrance. I had underestimated that girl. She defeated me thrice in chess. She can sing. She can dance. She knows astrology, astronomy, medicine. An amazing girl!'

And what would Mother say if I told her that Gayatri also knew horse-riding, elephant-riding and archery?

'I have a strong feeling that she will bring prosperity to our empire. And while it is true that I gave Gayatri permission to move about freely in the palace, I was surprised when she told me she wanted to leave the capital. She said she wanted to visit some temple. Do you know anything about her visit?'

'I have no idea,' I lied.

My mother got into the palanquin. A short while ago I had determined not to think of Chinnadevi, but when Mother left, my mind went back to Chinnadevi.

☙

That afternoon, when the priest Louis and the translator came to meet me, many of my ministers were present.

The priest was stunned. Perhaps, he had never seen such a grand hall before. He must have been astounded by the sculptures, the gleaming floor, and more importantly, my gem-studded throne. I had to mount twenty steps to get to my throne. It was so big that three people could easily have been seated on it.

The priest Louis stood before me and brought his palms together in order to wish me. Clever priest! He had already learnt our way of greeting others.

A palace attendant brought a Kashmiri shawl and a Thanjavur plate and placed them before me. 'Take them, priest Louis. They are for you,' I said.

It was a time-honoured custom in Vijayanagar, that gifts would not be handed over by the Emperor to anyone. They would be placed on the floor, and the recipient would have to pick them up himself. The palace attendant placed the shawl and plate on the floor, and Father Louis, who seemed to know our custom, picked them up. Appaji then unfolded the shawl and draped it around the priest's shoulders.

The priest then said, 'The King of Portugal has asked Governor Albuquerque to sign a treaty with you. I am here to talk to you about the treaty. The Muslims in Kozhikode prevent us from doing business there. In Goa, the soldiers of the Vijayapuram Sultan harass us. We need your help to drive the Muslims out of Goa and Kozhikode. Our king requests your help. And in return we will give you Arabian and Persian horses. We will give you cannons, and weapons. We will help you defeat the Vijayapuram Sultan.'

'I will first have to consult my ministers before I take a decision,' I said.

It was true that I had waged war against the Bahmani Sultans, whenever there had been trouble from them. But I couldn't think of them as foreigners. They had settled in this country, had married here and were never going to think of any other place as home. And they were not going to take away the wealth of this country. But I was not sure I could think of the Portuguese and the other white men who came after them as people who would live here.

The priest had expected that I would agree to the Portuguese king's request with alacrity. He was disappointed with my lukewarm response. 'Is that Italian physician who came with you doing well?' I enquired.

'Nicholas? I haven't seen him since the day I brought him to you,' replied the priest.

After he had left…

'I have some news for you, Your Majesty,' said Appaji.

'What is it?'

'The priest doesn't have any information about Nicholas. But I have some information about him. Our spies saw him leave the city yesterday night.'

'He might have wanted to see the other cities in our empire. So he might have gone on a tour of the cities. I don't think it was necessary to have him watched by our spies,' said Minister Ayyapparasu.

'Let him go where he pleases. Who has any objection to that? But why did he have to take a girl with him?' asked Appaji.

'A girl…?' I asked.

'Yes, Your Majesty. A girl. A girl you know.' He paused for a minute, enjoying my anxiety, and then continued, 'That servant girl Gayatri…'

I was shocked. 'Gayatri!'

'They took the road that passes through Kalahasti, Tirupati, Kanchi, Tiruvannamalai and Chidambaram to Madurai. By now they must have reached Kalahasti or Tirupati…'

Even as Appaji was telling me about where Gayatri was headed, I heard voices outside. Someone was trying to get in. I could hear a woman's voice saying to my guards, 'Let me go in, I must meet the Emperor at once. Please allow me to go in…'

Ten

It was getting noisier outside the conference hall.

Appaji got up angrily. 'What is happening outside the conference hall? Are rules not followed any more?' He went out to see what the matter was.

I have always held that the greater the distance between the king and his subjects, the more shaky is the king's position. In fact I had even been suggesting to my ministers that we should have a bell outside the royal court, such as the one the Chola kings used to have, so that if anyone had any grievance, he or she just had to ring the bell to gain an audience with the king.

And now Appaji had gone out to check what was happening. He was sure to have that woman, whoever she was, punished. I had to stop him.

The guards outside had not expected me to come out. They moved aside. Just as I had feared, Appaji was about to order that the woman be punished. She was wearing a purdah. I was afraid that it might be a spy in disguise. So I did something that I, as an emperor, should not have done. I moved aside the veil. The moment I saw the face behind the veil, I wished I hadn't suspected her. She was a young Muslim woman, and she must have been in great distress, for she was weeping.

'Your Majesty, my husband was arrested a couple of years ago, and was imprisoned. And now he and many other prisoners are being taken to the new city you are building…'

'What for?'

'They are going to be offered as sacrifice,' she said.

'What?' I was horrified.

I had heard of goats and hens being offered as sacrifice. There were many village temples where such sacrifice was common. I never interfered in the religious observances of my subjects. But human sacrifice? I had heard people talk about it, but I had never believed them.

'What is all this about, Appaji?' I asked. Appaji didn't approve of my taking an interest in anything except entering into trade agreements, welcoming foreign dignitaries and going on official processions. 'If you keep analysing trivial things, you will only end up wasting time,' he said.

'This is not trivial, Appaji. It's very, very serious. She says human sacrifice is going to be offered. Is it true? Tell me.'

Minister Kondamarasu, who was in charge of irrigation, said, 'Your Majesty, a lake is being built in Nagalapuram. One of its walls keeps collapsing. The workers believe it is because of the curse of some evil spirit. And so they must have thought human sacrifice would help get rid of the curse.'

'If a wall collapses, then that means that the construction is faulty. It means you have not appointed the right men. I have heard that there are excellent architects in Goa. I have heard it said that a particular architect called Joe Ponty is very good. Tell the priest Louis to fetch him. Instead of doing something sensible, you just stand by while the workers talk of evil spirits and human sacrifice. It's terrible!'

'Your Majesty, you have forgotten to consider something very important,' said Appaji.

'And what is that?'

'The people who are going to be sacrificed are not law-abiding citizens. They are all people who have been in prison for crimes they committed. They are people who are going to die anyway.'

'All of us are going to die one day, Appaji—you and I included. Let the prisoners die when the time comes for them to die. Let us not arrogate to ourselves the role of God.'

'You are absolutely right, Krishna,' said a voice endorsing my words. The voice belonged to my mother. Someone had told her of the disturbance outside the conference hall, and so she had come to the hall.

'Why are you here?' Appaji mumbled. My mother never went against Appaji's advice; perhaps Appaji was upset because my mother was now opposing him.

The woman who had come to complain to me had been a silent spectator when these arguments between me and my ministers had been going on. My mother put her arm round the woman and said, 'Don't worry, my child. The Emperor will send some officers to Nagalapuram, and save your husband.'

'No, Mother. Some tasks cannot be assigned to officers. They may be indifferent. This is something that requires my personal attention. I am going to go to Nagalapuram myself.'

'That is not necessary. We will take care of everything,' said Appaji, Nadendla Gopa, Chaluva Govindarasu, Rayasam Kondamarasu, Ayyapparasu and all the other ministers.

'Get me a horse. And make arrangements for this woman to come with us,' I ordered.

A child is cute even when it is dirty. Nagalapuram, a city that was taking shape, was like a dirty, naked child, but still it did have its appeal. Streets, bazaars, the mansions of the rich, the more humble dwellings of the poor, market places…And there was no dearth of temples either. I could hear Vedic chants and Tamil verses being recited. In some places, ad hoc markets were functioning. The landscape was dotted with parks. The traditional designs called *kolams* drawn at the entrance to some houses showed that they were occupied. Elephants and horses ambled along, as if they had all the time in the world.

There is a poem about the ancient city of Poompuhar, which

talks of its importance as a trade centre. The poet records that one could find in Poompuhar gold and gems from the North, pearls from the South, corals from the East, produce from the Gangetic plains, yields from the river Cauvery, food from Lanka, and products from Kaazhagam[10]. And I wanted my new city of Nagalapuram to be like Poompuhar. That was my dream, and I could see my dream taking shape.

Not many recognized me. But one man did, and he seemed to have some complaint to make, for he fixed the branch of a poovarasa[11] tree on a staff and ran up to me.

This was the practice in our empire. If a person, who had a grievance, saw the king on horseback, all he had to do was to approach him with a poovarasa branch fixed to a staff, and the guards would make way for him. The king would then listen to him and instruct his ministers on what they had to do to help the complainant. If the king happened to be riding an elephant, then a person with a complaint would have to lie down on the road. The king would then stop the elephant and ask him what his complaint was. But now, although this man obviously had a complaint, I had to give up the usual practice of stopping my horse to listen to him. I was in a hurry to save the Muslim woman's husband. She was accompanying us too.

Human sacrifice…human sacrifice…

Before I had become the emperor, I had travelled extensively all over the empire, and had been witness to many trials and many cruel punishments handed down. I had seen people being hanged. I had seen people being trampled by an elephant.

And I have seen a person being judged guilty or innocent

---

10. Kaazhagam—probably Burma (Myanmar)

11. Poovarasa—Tamil name for the Portia tree. The botanical name is *Thespesia populnea*.

on the basis of the most irrational and cruel considerations. To prove his innocence, a man is asked to lick a heated iron rod. Or he is told to walk for twenty feet holding the red-hot rod in his hand. If he remains unscathed after such cruel treatment, then he is given the benefit of doubt. Or he is asked to dip his fingers in boiling oil. His fingers are then wrapped in cloth, and the bandage is sealed with wax. At the end of three days, the bandage is opened. If the fingers show signs of the burn injuries, then the man is declared guilty and punished.

I always ask myself how such barbaric practices can continue. I have often thought of consulting my ministers on how to end such barbarism. But what stays my hand is the fear of the consequences of my interference. Each region has its own ways of dispensing justice, and if I were to interfere, it might be like stirring a hornet's nest. The people may resent my interference. And that is what keeps me from putting a stop to abhorrent practices that still prevail in various parts of my empire.

Appaji was pointing out the various streets in the town to me. When we got to the street where the dancers resided, Appaji said, 'This is where the devadasis reside. They are dancers, but they also…'

'Can't we do away with the practice? Can't we punish the practice of prostitution?' I asked testily.

Appaji laughed. 'What? Do away with the oldest profession in the world? No one can abolish prostitution, and no one should try to.'

'Why not?'

'Because one-third of our revenues come from the tax paid by Devadasis. Besides, the Devadasis spend a lot of money on charitable activities. They build temples, tanks, rest houses—they do a lot of good. And this means, that the government doesn't have to spend on all these things.'

He was candid, and I couldn't refute his arguments.

A soldier guided us to the top of a small hill. There was an abyss between this hill and the next and that is where we were trying to build a lake. Rain water from the two hills would flow into the lake. In addition to this, pipes were to be laid, which would bring water from neighbouring villages to the lake.

From where we stood, the workers working on the lake looked like ants. The sun was setting, but the workers hadn't called it a day. They had lit up lamps, and continued to work. The workers couldn't see us, because it was dark on the hill top. But we could see them because of the lights they had lit. The Muslim woman was on edge.

At the foot of the hill, was a foot high stone. It was decorated with flowers and kumkum. A goat had been sacrificed, and women were dancing around the goat. The right leg of the goat was cut off, and stuck in its mouth. Water mixed with turmeric was sprinkled on the goat. 'If the goat opens its mouth when water is sprinkled on it, then that means it has given the go ahead for the next sacrifice,' Kondamarasu explained to me.

I had killed many men in war. I had maimed many in battle. Never once had I worried about this. The flow of blood from the wounds of enemies had never bothered me. I would go to every battle telling myself that it could well be my last one, for I might be killed in the fighting. And once the battle was over, I would be concerned only with analyzing my victory or defeat, as the case may be. I never worried about the people I killed. I never saw it as murder. I saw it as my duty, a king's duty to kill enemies, to protect his land. But what I was witness to now, the wanton killing and the blood and gore, was disturbing. That I was a silent witness to all this filled me with self-loathing.

I turned to the Muslim woman and said, 'I don't see your husband anywhere.'

'Maybe they have killed him already,' said Thimmarasu, and the Muslim woman began to wail.

'They first sacrifice hens, goats and buffaloes, and get to human sacrifice later.' Even as one of my generals was explaining, the Muslim woman cried out, 'Look! Look!'

I looked in the direction in which she pointed. Some people were being escorted out of a tent.

'There! That's my husband,' she said.

I couldn't make out which of them was her husband, but bringing up the rear was a woman.

A woman…My God, yes it was she!

Shocked, I shouted, 'Gayatri!'

None of us had expected to find Gayatri there, and Appaji and the other ministers were too shocked to say anything.

'That is the woman who sent me to you,' said the Muslim woman.

'Gayatri…how did she…'

'When my husband and the other prisoners were taken away from prison, I asked the soldiers where they were being taken. They replied that the prisoners were going to be sacrificed. I begged them to release my husband, but they kicked me aside. This woman was passing by, and when she came to know the cause for my grieving, she offered to speak to the soldiers. She argued that the soldiers should not sacrifice human beings. They then said, 'You dare to protest, do you? All right. We will sacrifice you too.' And they took her away too. But she said to me, "Go to the palace, and ask for an audience with the Emperor. He will come in person to rescue us. Or he will send someone to save us." That is why I came to the palace…'

Even as she gave me this account, in between bouts of weeping and sobbing, I ran down the hill towards the lake.

Eleven

I left the horse in the care of a soldier and ran up to Gayatri. I could hardly recognize her. Water, turmeric powder and vermilion powder had been sprinkled upon her, as in the case of animals about to be sacrificed.

No one had expected to see me there. And when the workers working on the lake, the men who were sharpening their scimitars, the priests and those striking the drums before the sacrifice, saw me, they stopped what they were doing and stood frozen like so many statues. And when they got over their shock, they fell at my feet. The prisoners, who were bound in chains, cried out to me to save them, and they too fell at my feet.

'Remove the chains,' I ordered. The chains that bound the prisoners dropped to the ground noisily. But Gayatri didn't ask me to save her. Nor did she fall at my feet.

I gave her my shawl and asked her to clean her face.

I could see that Appaji and the other ministers felt that this was most unbecoming of an Emperor. But I couldn't care less. Gayatri wiped her face with my shawl. Her face gleamed like a mirror that had just been cleaned.

'You said you knew how to wield a sword. You boasted that you knew archery. You said Lord Jagannatha would protect you…But ultimately it was Krishnadevaraya who had to come to your rescue,' I said.

'I didn't want to save myself. I wanted to bring this barbaric practice to your notice, Your Majesty. I knew that if I brought this practice to your notice, you would come here at once. I deliberately picked up a quarrel with these men, so that I too would be taken prisoner. I was wondering how to get word to you, when this woman arrived. So I sent word to you through her,' Gayatri explained.

'Whether something is barbaric or not is not for you to decide. That is for the Emperor to decide. Now I have a question to ask you. Answer my question. Why did you leave the palace in a hurry?' asked Appaji angrily.

'I had to leave on an official trip, Prime Minister...'

Appaji looked at me as if waiting for me to clarify. With a shake of my head, I indicated to him that I would tell him about it later. Appaji was unhappy with the importance I gave Gayatri. He didn't relish being defied in public by this slip of a girl. He was not prepared to let her off the hook. 'What happened to the Italian physician you took with you?'

'I didn't take him with me, Prime Minister. He was on his own, and I was going ahead with my journey. It so happened that our paths crossed. He told me that he wanted to see the cities in the south of our Empire, and so I took him along with me.'

'Isn't that what I told you?' asked Ayyaparasu.

Ayyaparasu's words did nothing to mitigate Appaji's anger. Appaji had never liked Ayyaparasu, and resented his interference now.

'I admit that I lack your prescience and your sharpness of intellect,' he said caustically to Ayyaparasu, and then to me he said, 'The Italian said he wanted to study our indigenous system of medicine. Why did he not stay on in the capital then? Why the urge to visit other cities?'

'It is possible that there might be people with knowledge of medicine in other cities too,' I said.

'Where is the Italian?' I asked Gayatri.

'There he is, among the prisoners,' she pointed out.

And there indeed was Nicholas, his face covered in dust, and his body smeared with vermilion powder and turmeric powder. It was clear that he had not got over his fright. His body still shook with fear.

Nicholas murmured something in his language. Gayatri volunteered to translate for me. Is there no end to this girl's abilities, I wondered. She gave me a mischievous smile and said, 'I was the one who was included among those to be sacrificed. This Italian had not been taken prisoner. He could as well have just gone on his way. Instead he argued with them to release me. They couldn't understand his language. And they didn't know who he was. So they took him prisoner too. Poor man…' Gayatri explained.

'Ensure that these people are released and are on their way to their villages,' I said to Ayyapparasu.

Gayatri and Nicholas took leave of me. I could see tears in Nicholas' eyes. He was telling me something. I couldn't understand what he was saying, but I could guess what he meant to say: If not for Gayatri, I wouldn't be alive today.

I told the guards to arrange for food and change of clothing for Gayatri and Nicholas. 'Shall I send some soldiers with you?' I asked her. I wanted to warn her that as she journeyed to meet Chinnadevi, she would have to pass through places where the Pandyas and Cholas were engaged in battle. But I couldn't, because Appaji was beside me.

She declined my offer to send soldiers for her protection, leaving me worried about what further harm would befall her on her arduous journey.

Appaji waited until she had left, and then said, 'What boldness! She goes on a long journey in the company of a white man. I ask her where she is bound, and she says audaciously that she is on official duty.'

He had hoped I would tell him what that 'official duty' was at least now. But I was silent. I was worried because she had been delayed in her search for Chinnadevi.

The workers waited for further instructions from me. I told them that I would get an architect from Goa, and that they were to entrust the work of building the lake to him. I warned them that there should be no human sacrifice there or anywhere else in my empire.

Appaji laughed softly. He was experienced and knew that changes in society can never be brought about through royal decrees.

༄

Dawn was breaking when we departed for the capital. We had to pass through a village where the temple festival was in full swing.

'Let's take some other route. Otherwise you will be mobbed by the villagers,' said Appaji, and took an alternate route.

'Thank God your favourite daughter isn't here for the temple festivities,' he said.

'By daughter, do you mean Gayatri? I am glad you have given her such an exalted status. But what would have happened if she'd been here?'

'She is here to change age-old practices. She might have objected to the chariot festival of the temple.'

'Why would she do that? Is human sacrifice offered at a chariot festival?'

'Not human sacrifice, but one can witness suicide at a chariot festival.'

'I don't understand.'

'There are people who throw themselves under the wheels of the chariot, and die. They believe that if they do that, their prayers will be answered. They also believe that this will ensure their place in heaven. Now Gayatri might want to change this practice too.'

'I think she is a woman born before her time,' I said. 'If she had been born three hundred years later, people might have understood her reasoning. But now her arguments will sound insane to them.'

Appaji didn't like my speaking up for Gayatri every time he criticised her. I wasn't concerned about Appaji's reaction. My thoughts were about Gayatri's journey and Chinnadevi.

☙

Time is like an untamed horse. No one can control its galloping away.

Even as I write these accounts, battles, peace treaties, successes and defeats are taking place. But I have not mentioned many of them.

In the North, when Babar tried to capture Delhi, he learnt war techniques from the Uzbeks, the use of cannons from the Mongols, the use of rifles from the Afghanis, archery from the Persians and the management of equestrian forces from the Turks. When I was told that he was a great warrior because of his training, I tried to make the military forces of Vijayanagar up- to- date too, with training in various aspects of warfare. I haven't mentioned that.

I haven't talked about how Adil Shah—Sultan of Vijayapuram, Qutub Shah—Sultan of Golconda, Nizam Shah—the Sultan of Ahmednagar, Farid Shah—the Sultan of Bidar and Imad Shah—Sultan of Berar kept asking for my help. I haven't mentioned that acting upon Appaji's advice, I made friends with them in turns, now with one, then another, and thus successfully played them off against each other.

I haven't recorded any of these things, because I know that future historians will write pages and pages about all this.

But who will tell my story? My personal story? No one. Who will talk about my dreams, my yearnings, my desires, my disappointments, my sorrows, my love, my heartaches…? That is why my record has only some mention of historical events and a lot about my personal life.

Spring had arrived. Trees and bushes, laden with flowers and fruits, swayed in the breeze. On the outskirts of the city preparations were on to stage *Jamabavati Parinayam*, a drama I had written.

I set off on my elephant, to watch the drama. My subjects lined both sides of the streets, and cheered me. I was preceded by my equestrian force, which was under a Muslim general. The drum-beaters and the ones who blew the horn rode on camel back. Women dancing traditional folk dances accompanied the procession. Women from the royal family were carried in ornate palanquins, with servants fanning them. White umbrellas swayed here and there…

The cushion on the elephant's back was not placed properly, and I felt uncomfortable. I tried to make myself more comfortable.

I could see Allasani Peddanna walking along. He had followed in the footsteps of the great poet Srinath, and at a time when the only literature in Telugu was what we had through translations, he shook off the domination of Sanskrit, and wrote his *Manu Charitram*. He was my court poet. How could I allow him to walk?

'Stop,' I called out to the mahout. He stopped the elephant. I asked him to make the elephant kneel, and invited Allasani Peddanna to sit with me on the back of the elephant.

'Your Majesty, how can I sit beside you? How can I think of myself as your equal?' Peddanna objected.

'The proper thing to do would be for you to ride on the elephant and for me to walk. Please sit beside me. You will do me a great honour, if you sit beside me.'

After much persuasion, Peddanna agreed to ride on elephant back.

The procession resumed. Peddanna was a genial soul. But today he looked forlorn. 'You have been granted the privilege of travelling by palanquin. Why then did you have to walk?'

'I felt dejected…' He did not explain why he felt dejected. I waited for him to tell me, but he was silent.

After some time, he said, 'I sent you a work called *Kavikarna Rasaayanam* written by poet Narasimha. Did you receive it?'

'Oh yes, I did. I also read it.'

'Thank God,' he said and heaved a sigh of relief.

'Why, what's the matter?'

'I was accused of keeping you from reading that book. It was said that I was afraid I would lose my position as court poet, if you read that book, and liked it. That poet has been spreading this tale everywhere.'

I laughed out loud. So poets had many problems too!

'King of Poets, do not fear…it was a mediocre work. It is not a patch on any of your works. Such jealousies are common in the literary world. I took so much trouble to write *Parijata Parinayam*. But people say that you wrote it, and allowed me to claim authorship.'

'My poetic abilities are no match to yours,' said Peddanna, even as we crossed the Vittala temple.

Proximity to the temple brought back memories of Chinnadevi. Unaware of my emotional turmoil, Peddanna said, 'The whole of last month a devadasi danced in this temple. I watched one of her performances. What a beautiful woman! What a wonderful dancer!'

My heart began to beat fast. 'Oh, really? What was her name?' I asked, trying not to show my excitement.

'I was told her name was Chinnadevi. She has a brother, who kept watch over her. And a very vigilant bodyguard he was too…'

'Oh, really?' I said again.

'At the end of the performance, I complimented her on her wonderful dance, and told her brother that she should dance before the Emperor one day. I extended an invitation to him without consulting you…'

'So what? You invited her, because you knew of my interest in the fine arts. And what did he say?'

'Ethirajan was livid. He said, "My sister is a temple dancer. She will never dance anywhere except in a temple. No one can insist that my sister should dance in his house. I was sure of that, and that is why I brought my sister here." I asked if he would not come even if the Emperor were to invite him. He said, "We are avowed enemies of the Vijayanagar Empire. Who cares for the Emperor? We think it is a sin to even see him," he shouted angrily.'

'And what is the reason for his hatred of me?'

'That's what I wanted to know and I asked him the reason for his hatred.'

'Did he tell you?'

'Yes, he did. It's a long story.'

By now we had reached the place where the drama was to be enacted. Peddanna alighted from the elephant, and merged with the crowd. The celebrations began. Dance, music, games and fireworks marked the celebrations.

But my eyes scanned the crowds for Peddanna.

Twelve

I wondered why Peddanna had left so abruptly, and I now had the answer. Appaji was coming towards me, and Peddanna was scared of Appaji.

Appaji had many duties as Prime Minister of the Empire. But in the midst of all his duties, he found time to author many tomes. He had written a commentary for Agastya's *Bala Bharatam*. There were eight poets in my court and whenever the poets met, Appaji presided over the meeting.

But there's something I want to clarify. Actually I don't know how people got this count of eight poets. I've never seen all of them gathered together. Allasani Peddanna, Nandi Thimmanna, Durjati, Tenali Ramakrishna—these were the poets I met often and discussed literature with. Other poets would visit me now and then. Which of these were added to the list to bring the number of court poets to eight, I do not know. I sometimes wonder if this number eight is the handiwork of my admirers, who had come up with the number to add to my reputation. My admirers wanted me to be respected as the equal of the Maurya king Chandragupta. And so they gave me the titles he had been given. There had been eight poets in Chandragupta Maurya's court and they wanted me to have eight court poets too.

Be that as it may, I had never once taken Appaji with me on the royal elephant. Appaji would not relish the special treatment I had given Allasani. That is why Allasani must have slipped away when he saw Appaji approaching. But Appaji didn't mention Allasani.

'I have something to tell you,' he said.

'Go ahead.'

'The administrators of the Tirumala temple want a bronze likeness of Your Majesty to be placed in the temple. They have sent some bronze image makers to meet you, so that they can finalise the measurements and proportions of the image.'

'Ask them to come some other time.'

A disappointed Appaji left. I immediately summoned a palace servant and asked him to find Allasani Peddanna. 'He is somewhere in this crowd. Find him, and bring him to me,' I ordered.

When Peddanna arrived, I said, 'Where were you? You disappeared suddenly. Now tell me about Ethirajan.'

༺༻

I have given here an account of what Allasani Peddanna told me, and I have also included other details known to me.

It is said that the pontiff of the Sringeri Math was worried about the turmoil in the land. He wanted to find a suitable king for the land. His choice fell upon Bukka. Bukka was the Yadava youth who used to bring milk for the pontiff everyday, when the latter did penance in a cave on the banks of the Tungabhadra river. Thus began the rule of the first Vijayanagar dynasty—the Sangama dynasty. This is one version of the origin of the Vijayanagar Empire. There are those who doubt the veracity of this account.

They have another story. According to this version, two brothers—Hakka and Bukka were generals under a Muslim king. One day in a place called Anegundi they saw a rabbit chase away a hunting dog. They felt that there was something about the place which must have made this possible. So they felt this would be the ideal place for them to establish their kingdom, and thus began Sangama rule.

The incident that I am going to narrate took place long after the time of Hukka and Bukka. In fact it took place after three other kings had succeeded them. When this incident took place, the king was Immadi Devaraya.

Immadi Devaraya was a great king and his rule may well be described as the golden period of the Vijayanagar Empire. He marched to Gulbarga and defeated Sultan Alauddin. The kings of Orissa, Kanauj, Kambhoj, and Nepal paid taxes to him. It was a king who fanned him. Another held up his royal umbrella for him. Another had the duty of handing betel leaves to him. When he realised that Muslim generals visiting him had religious reservations about bowing before him, he did not insist that they should.

But Immadi Devaraya, whose fame had spread beyond the boundaries of his empire, had an enemy—his nephew, Vikraman, the son of his sister Harima.

Mallanna was a general in Immadi Devaraya's army. He was also a close friend of Vikraman. Mallanna, who had married recently, was away in Lanka. Vikraman, who had been waiting for an opportunity to usurp the throne, built a palace for himself in Anegundi. It was a very ornate palace. He invited the king to a feast in his palace.

'I am your uncle. Do you have to address me as "Your Majesty"?' asked Immadi Devaraya.

'I am grateful for your affection. But how can I use terms of familiarity to address you? I am not old enough to address you so. Nor do I have the stature to do so,' Vikraman said with false humility.

'All right. When is the feast?'

'I have invited all the ministers and generals too to the feast.'

'They will not feel free in my presence. So I will come to your palace after they have partaken of the feast, and left.'

Vikraman was pleased, because he had made no arrangements for a feast for anyone. His plan was to provide a feast to the God of death—Yama.

He had arranged for musicians to play their instruments at his palace. The ministers and generals were seated in the pavilion outside his palace. It was uncommon for people of different ranks to eat together in those days. Why, it is not common even now!

So Vikraman invited one general or minister at a time for dinner, and as each of them entered the palace, Vikraman's men, who were in hiding, killed them.

The feast lasted the whole day, and a total of hundred officials of the Court were slaughtered. All that remained was for him to kill the king too. Vikraman went to the king's palace and said to the guards there, 'Please go, all of you. A feast awaits you in my palace.'

They hesitated, but Vikraman said, 'Are you worried about the king? I am here. Will I not take care of him?'

The guards felt the king would be safe while his nephew was there to protect him, and so they left the king's palace. They met with the same fate that had befallen the other officials. All the guards were killed.

Immadi Devaraya was now alone in his palace. Vikraman approached him, with a plate of betel leaves. Concealed beneath the plate was a sword.

'Your Majesty, everyone has departed,' he said, punning on the word 'departed'. 'Now it's your turn.'

The king either saw the sword, or caught the pun. Or perhaps his knowledge of astrology came to his help. He declined Vikraman's invitation and said, 'I will not come to your palace today. I don't feel well. I will come another day.'

Vikraman could sense that the king suspected him. He pulled

out the sword and attacked the king. The king toppled over. 'Behead him,' he said to his men.

He then went out into the balcony of the palace and called out to the people on the street below. 'Dear citizens of Vijayanagar. I have some good news for you. I have killed the generals, court officials and ministers of the king. I have also killed the king. Now I am your king. Long live your new king, Vikraman!' shouted the traitor in glee.

But his plans went awry. When attacked by Vikraman, the king had fallen off his throne, but he was not dead. When Vikraman's guard approached the king to behead him, the king summoned all his strength and pushed the man down. One of the guards loyal to the king had been witness to the gory scene, and he killed Vikraman's guard. Immadi Devaraya slowly made his way to the balcony, where Vikraman was proclaiming himself king. He pushed Vikraman down and shouted, 'My dear subjects. I am alive. I am not dead. Vikraman is a traitor. Kill him.'

Vikraman was already injured by the fall from the balcony. The enraged citizens who had gathered, trampled him to death.

The King Immadi Devaraya was seriously injured, but Vikraman's plan to kill him had been foiled.

༄

At this juncture, I interrupted Allasani Peddan's narration. 'What is the connection between these events and Ethirajan's hatred of the royal family?' I asked.

Peddanna smiled. 'Why would I narrate all these events, if there is no connection between Ethirajan and these events? You might remember I told you about Vikraman's friend?'

'Yes. You said his name was Mallanna.'

'A few days after all these incidents, he too was killed.'

'But you said he was away in Lanka when Vikraman put his murderous plan into action.'

'That was the tragedy. If he had been there, he might not have lost his life.'

I couldn't understand what Peddanna's cryptic observation meant.

The festivities before commencement of the drama were in full swing. An elephant was dancing, following the movements of the mahout's moving hand. Fireworks rent the air. Religious discourses attracted some sections of the crowd. There were women dancing. And once these celebrations were over, it would be time for the staging of my drama, Jambavati Parinayam. But I wasn't interested in any of this. All I wanted was to hear the rest of Peddanna's narration.

Thirteen

Allasani Peddanna was amused by my interest in Ethirajan's story. Just to tease me, he would stop the story at an interesting juncture and watch my anxiety to hear him continue with the story.

In the middle of his narration, he would stop and say, 'Your Majesty! Look at that girl in a yellow sari. Doesn't she dance beautifully? See how flexible her limbs are!'

'I haven't been paying attention to anything…your story…your lively narration… I was absorbed in your story. I marvel at your story telling ability, and wish I could tell a story so well,' I said.

Allasani was shrewd. He knew my praise was to make him get on with the story. 'I forgot all about the story. Now where was I?'

'You were telling me about Mallanna, Vikraman's friend, who was in Lanka when the attempt to kill the king took place,' I said.

Peddanna gave me a brief account. But I could imagine the conversations that would have taken place between the various people in the story. So I have used my imagination to give you the following more colourful and lively account of what happened.

༄

When Mallanna returned from Lanka, he should have gone to meet the king, and told him about his trip. Or he should have met one of the ministers. Had he done that, he would have known of Vikraman's betrayal. But he went to his palace. He was anxious to see his young wife Kadambari, who was pregnant at the time. Mallanna had brought a strand of rubies for her, and he wanted to give his gift to her at once. When Kadambari heard him enter, she ran up to him, and threw her arms around him. But she was also agitated because of all that had happened in his absence. She wanted to tell him about the attempt on Immadi Devaraya's life. She wanted to warn her husband that the king was in a dangerous mood. But even as she opened her mouth to tell him what had happened, he sealed her lips with a passionate kiss.

Before he ended the long kiss, the king's guards arrived to arrest him. Mallanna, who was besotted with his wife, did not hear the men enter. Just as he was about to put the rubies round Kadambari's neck, the guards surrounded him.

'Let him go,' beseeched Kadambari, but the guards pushed her aside and took him to the king. Mallanna was too shocked to even speak. Why had he been arrested? He was a general in the army. That being the case, why was he being treated like a prisoner? Mallanna still had the rubies with him. 'Please stop. Let me at least give my wife the gift I have brought for her,' he begged. But they ignored his pleas.

Mallanna thought the guards had made a mistake. They must have arrested him instead of someone else. Mallanna thought that the moment the king saw him, he would chide the guards and ask them to release him.

But Mallanna's expectations proved wrong. Immadi Devaraya smiled at Mallanna and said, 'Welcome, general. Have all your treacherous plans been successfully executed?'

'Your Majesty, what are you saying? What treachery? Planned by whom? I can't understand what you are saying.' Mallanna fell at the king's feet. His rubies slipped from his hands, fell on the lap of the king. The sight of the rubies exacerbated Immadi Devaraya's anger.

'Oh, so this is the reward you received from your friend for treachery,' he said.

'I repeat, Your Majesty. I have committed no act of treachery. I have just returned from Lanka.'

'Of course. You were clever. You drew up the plan, and then conveniently went away to Lanka,' said Immadi Devaraya, who was in no mood to show Mallanna any mercy.

'Drag away this dog! He must be beheaded at sunrise tomorrow,' ordered the king.

Immadi Devaraya was a man who usually did not lose his equipoise. But he had just had a narrow escape. He was like a man who has been bitten by a snake, and who therefore mistakes even a rope for a snake.

Mallanna thought of putting forth his defence again, but then thought better of it. His self-respect kept him from demeaning himself further and begging the king to spare his life. He thought that there was no point arguing with a king, who would not even listen to what he had to say, and who had unfairly labelled him a traitor. Death was preferable to further humiliation, Mallanna thought. He prepared to embrace death bravely, although he still didn't know the reason for the king's anger.

It was only on the way to prison that he heard the story from the guards who were taking him away. He learnt of Vikraman's treachery and that he himself was suspected to have had a hand in the plot too, because he was Vikraman's friend.

But if Vikraman had cruelly killed all the ministers, Vikraman's uncle was no better. He had killed all of Vikraman's relatives, and friends. Even the man who took the invitations to the various ministers had been killed, although he was innocent of any wrongdoing. And now Mallanna had been sentenced to death, and he had not been given an opportunity to prove his innocence. What a cruel king! Mallanna was ashamed that he had fallen at such a cruel monarch's feet.

What a shame! Mallanna could not get over it. He kept striking the walls of the prison with his fists. His clenched fists began to bleed.

The silent night was the only witness to this pathetic scene. A faint sound broke the stillness of the night.

Two of Mallanna's dear friends entered.

'How did you get here?' he asked.

'Sshhh! We have bribed the guards to let us in. Come with us,' they said.

But Mallanna would not budge. His response to their suggestion was a bitter laugh.

'Thank you for your efforts, my friends. But I do not want to escape. I have already been labelled a traitor. Should I be further be labelled a coward too? I will not come with you.'

'Don't be foolish, Mallanna. How can you call your escape cowardice? You have been unfairly sentenced. To escape an unfair sentence is by no means an act of cowardice. Surrendering meekly to such a sentence would be cowardly. Some day you will get an opportunity for revenge against this kingdom.'

'There will be no need for that. This kingdom will collapse. There are enemies waiting to strike. And when they do, all the ostentations and vanities so characteristic of this kingdom, will come to an end. We don't have to do anything. However, there is something you can do for me.'

'Tell us what it is, and we will carry out your wishes.'

'Can you bring my wife Kadambari to the prison? I want to see her before I die. I want to tell her to be brave.'

In half-an-hour, Mallanna's friends brought Kadambari to the prison. She was nearing the end of her pregnancy, and Mallanna couldn't stop the tears that came to his eyes, when he thought of leaving her to fend for herself. As for Kadambari, she thought of what a loyal official her husband had been to the king, and yet here he was, wrongly accused, and awaiting death. She put her head on his lap, and sobbed.

'You mustn't cry, Kadambari. You are the wife of a general. You are soon going to be the mother of a brave son.' He kissed her forehead; he ran his hands through her hair soothingly.

'Kadambari, this royal family which has unfairly sentenced me to death will be our enemy always. Keep that in mind. Tell your son this, and tell him to tell his son and then his son's son too. Let future generations not forget the injustice that has been done today.'

'What should I do?' she asked, calmly.

'My grandfather was a loyal servant of the Vijayanagar Empire. My father too served the king. And I followed in their footsteps. Enough is enough. Future generations of our family should have nothing to do with this royal family. No one in our family must have any truck with this royal family. Tell my son that,' said Mallanna.

The friends who were waiting outside warned that it was getting late.

Mallanna kissed Kadambari and took his leave of her.

The next morning Mallanna was executed. At the same time, Kadambari gave birth to a boy. A death in one place. A birth in another. Here the last cry of a human being. There the first cry of another.

༄

'Ethirajan is the grandson of the grandson of Mallanna,' said Allasani Peddanna, bringing his long narration to an end.

The spring festival was drawing to a close too. More oil was being poured into the lamps, to keep the flames alive. This was how the family of Mallanna had kept the flame of anger alive, I told myself.

'Very nice performance,' said my minister Vallabha.

'Which one?' I asked.

'The staging of your drama Jambavati Parinayam. Excellent performance,' he said. He studied my face and said, 'I think Your Majesty is not happy with the performance.'

'Not at all. The actors did very well. Bring the gifts set aside for them. Let me give them their gifts. I want to return to the palace.'

Allasani mistook my thoughtfulness and said, 'I think my narration was too lengthy.'

'No. I was thinking of how Devaraya's act of injustice has led to successive generations of a family nurturing such hatred against the royal family.'

'Ethirajan, especially, is very adamant. Rank stupidity! With just a snap of your fingers, you can have him and his sister captured and brought to the palace.'

'What is the need for that? Is it necessary that I should take so much trouble to see the two of them?'

'That is true. The loss is theirs,' said Peddanna.

And what about my loss? Who will compensate me for my loss? Who can understand my agony—the agony of one who cannot openly talk about his love?

※

The next morning, I did my exercises. I went horse-riding. But my heart was not in it. I paced up and down the long corridor in my palace. The story of Mallanna's execution and his curse disturbed me. I could understand Ethirajan's hatred for the royal family. I was no longer angry with him. But given his hatred for my family, how was I to make friendly overtures to him? How was I to marry Chinnadevi?

I detested the very sight of the gleaming floor I was walking on. I had been told that many years ago, this was where executions took place. I had also been told that the king would be witness to beheadings. How many of those people had been innocent like Mallanna?

I thought of the blood and gore that must have once marked the place where I was now walking. I was haunted by images of headless torsos. Walking on the corridor filled me with revulsion. Can the stains of sin ever be removed?

I was reminded of Vidyapathi. He was the court poet of King Sivasinga. He was the poet who made out a copy of the entire *Bhagavatam*. One day he had a dream, in which he saw himself being carried by four men. He realised that this was an indication that his end was near. It had been a long-standing desire of his to die on the banks of the River Ganga. So he took his daughter with him and set off towards the river. But he was old and he could not walk beyond a certain distance. He knew he could walk no further and he was sorry that he couldn't die on the banks of the Ganga.

And that was when something unbelievable happened.

The river flooded, broke its banks and washed over Vidyapathi. Even today, villagers show visitors the marks left by the river, when it burst its banks.

Could something like that not happen now?

'Oh River Tungabhadra! River Krishna! Mother Godavari! Will not all of you breach your banks, flow into the palace and cleanse it of the sins of the kings?' I prayed.

But how foolish I was! The Ganga came to bathe Vidyapati's body, because he was a virtuous man. Will any river come to this palace, which had been the abode of sinners? Will rivers not change course and flow away from this palace?

I wondered what I could do by way of atonement for the sins of the royal family. And then I had an idea! I sent for my minister

Venkaiyya. 'Appaji told me that a sculptor is here to make my image for the Tirumala temple. Bring him to me at once.'

'As you command, Your Majesty,' said Venkaiyya.

'Also bring the dance guru Lakshmi Narayana.'

I stared at the corridor. Here I could…

My imagination ran riot.

Fourteen

I paced up and down the palace corridor, as I waited for the temple architect. I was mulling over the treachery of Vikraman and the cruel killing of innocent Mallanna. I must atone for the sin of Immadi Devaraya. The wives of scores of innocent men who perished here would have cursed the royal family. In a place where cries of mourning were once heard, pleasing music must be heard henceforth.

Even as I wondered what was keeping the architect, Appaji arrived, and said, 'I am very happy.'

'What are you happy about?'

'I was told you had asked the sculptor to meet you. Here he comes. He can take your measurements and we can go ahead with the making of your likeness in bronze for the Tirupati temple.'

'Wait a minute, Appaji. What have I achieved to merit a bronze image? And besides, do I have the stature to have my image in the Tirupati temple?' I could see that Appaji was disappointed. 'Moreover, I do not want just my image there. It is our tradition that even when a man goes to the temple for worship, he goes with his wife. So what is the hurry to make my image for the Tirupati temple? Why don't you wait till I am married?'

Appaji smiled and said, 'So your thoughts lie in that direction, do they? Don't worry, Your Majesty. I've made arrangements for your marriage. I have your mother's approval. I am going to send word to Srirangapatnam.'

'Appaji, in matters of state, you are never hasty or impulsive. Your decisions are well-thought-out. But when it comes to making decisions about my personal life, you make the wrong decisions. Is this fair?' My mention of marriage was prompted by thoughts of Chinnadevi, but Appaji was keen on my marrying Thirumala Devi.

My mind went to Chinnadevi, who was now in Srivilliputtur. Chinnadevi! What are you doing now? Will you draw a kolam that has my name hidden in it somewhere? Will you keep whispering my name, when you string flowers? Or will you be like the heroine in Pothanna's poem—the one who did not even know how to chase away the bee that was annoying her? Are you pining for me as I pine for you?

No, I don't think you are. I think you have forgotten me. If you still had thoughts of me, would you not have sent word to me, when you were here? Why did you not try to meet me? Ethirajan didn't keep you chained, did he?

'Then why did you send for the sculptor?' asked Appaji. Before I could answer Appaji, the sculptor arrived. He was a young man.

'Come here,' I summoned him.

At first he hesitated, and then moved closer to me.

'What is your name?'

'Muthu Manicka Rajendran.'

'That's a mouthful!' I laughed. 'Do you mind if I call you Muthu?'

Muthu was surprised that the Emperor could converse on such familiar terms with a commoner. It was clear that Appaji disliked my being familiar with a commoner. But how many masks can I wear, just in order to please Appaji?

'Whatever pleases the Emperor is acceptable to me,' said Muthu.

'Do you only make bronze images? Or do you also know how to make stone sculptures?'

'I am from a traditional family of sthapathis. My ancestors

built the Pallava temples in Kanchi and Mamallapuram,' he said proudly.

'Good. Listen to me carefully. I want this hall to be transformed into a hall of beauty. I want this to become a place where princesses and girls from rich families learn dance. Do you know *Natya Sastra*?'

'A little.'

'That is not enough. Dance guru Lakshmi Narayana will clarify your doubts about dance. He has been honoured with the title of Bharatachariar. He will teach you what you don't know. Look at these walls. I want sculptures that will explain Bharata Muni's *Natya Sastra*. I give you the freedom to choose as many assistants as you want, to help you with the work. Remuneration to them will be no constraint.'

'As you command, Your Majesty.'

'All the sculptures must be clad in gold. Appoint goldsmiths also. I want a total of eighty pillars, and in each of them I want you to sculpt the figure of a dancer depicting a mudra[12]. The sculptures should be so perfectly done, that a dancer practising here can consult the sculptures, if she has any doubt. Do you understand what I want?'

'Yes, Your Majesty.'

'You can do it, can you not?'

'Certainly, Your Majesty.'

'I would like to see the dancers practise. So I also want you to make seating arrangements for me at one end of the hall. At the other end, I want an idol of Lord Krishna installed. So I want you to build a small mandapa to house the idol.' I still wasn't sure he understood what I wanted. I asked for a piece of coal, and drew out my plans for him on the floor.

---

12. Mudra—a mudra is a hand gesture in Indian classical dance.

'I also want the ceiling to be decorated with paintings of trees, birds, deer, horses and elephants. So appoint artists to do the painting.'

I turned to Appaji and said, 'Appaji, please help this man carry out my orders. Tell the dance guru Lakshmi Narayana about my plans.'

'Please wait outside,' Appaji said to Muthu, and then to me he said, 'May I know the reason for your sudden interest in dance?'

'I was thinking of the unjust killings of Immadi Devaraya's time. I was disturbed. I conceived of this dance mandapa as atonement for past sins.'

I wondered if I should tell Appaji that this was only part of the reason, and that the other reason was my obsession with a dancer. I thought better of it, and held my silence.

༄

That night, the court hall was packed to capacity. All my ministers, generals, important administrative officers—were all there, because I had sent out a royal order for their presence there that night. But they didn't know why I had summoned them.

Work on the dance hall had begun, and we could hear the sculptors at work. Since the sound of the chisels would be distracting, I had arranged for the official meeting to take place in the Venkata Vilasa Mandapam. The ministers had taken their places, according to protocol.

The visiting royal guest—Chandrasekhara Pandya was seated beside me. Sorrow and shame were writ large on his face.

Appaji spoke on my behalf. 'Greetings to the generals, ministers and officials gathered here. I am sure you all know that our honoured guest, Chandrasekhara Pandya has been in our capital for the last ten days. I am sure you also know why he is here. A portion of the Pandya kingdom was captured by Veerasekara Chola, and as a result there were frequent disturbances and skirmishes in the region. Our Emperor sent Nagama Nayaka to the area to deal with the situation. Nagama Nayaka defeated Veerasekara Chola, and recaptured the lost Pandya territory. Unfortunately, instead of handing over the recaptured territory to Chandrasekhara Pandya, Nagama Nayaka has set himself up as king…'

'What a shame! Nagama Nayaka should be a taught a lesson'—those in the august gathering expressed their shock and disapproval.

'Quiet, please,' said Appaji. 'The Pandya King is here to complain about the conduct of Nagama Nayaka. We have sent many messages to Nagama Nayaka, but he continues to give evasive replies. It seems as if he wants to establish a kingdom for himself in Madurai.'

I could no longer contain myself.

'Traitor! Is there no one here to question this traitor and to teach him a lesson?'

'I shall do it, Your Majesty,' said a voice. The voice belonged to a young man seated in the last row.

'Come here,' I said.

His name was Viswanathan. He was one of the minor generals. 'You…you are Nagama Nayaka's son, aren't you?' I asked.

'I am, Your Majesty. But if you give me permission, I will lead an army against my father.'

I should not have said what I did, but I couldn't help saying it. 'So you are planning to use this opportunity to join forces with your father, are you?'

Viswanathan pulled out his sword from its sheath and ran towards me. Everyone in the court stood up stunned, afraid that he would do me harm.

But the young man placed his sword in my hands, bowed before me and said, 'If you suspect my motives, please kill me now, Your Majesty.'

'Get up,' I said. 'Let your name be remembered in history as the man who imprisoned his own father in the service of his country.'

Viswanathan accepted the sword I placed in his hands. He brimmed with confidence, and I was sure he had a bright future, and that he would revive the glory of Madurai.

'How many soldiers are there under your command?' I asked.

'Six thousand, Your Majesty.'

'This is an opportunity for you to prove your greatness as a commander. You must manage with the six thousand soldiers under you. You must not expect any further help from me.'

'I can manage with my forces, Your Majesty.'

'Prepare to leave tomorrow,' I said to him.

I then said to those assembled in the court hall, 'Let us all wish Viswanathan.'

'Jaya Vijayi Bhava[13]!' they all shouted in chorus.

I was anxious to have a private conversation with Viswanathan. I wanted to tell him that my beloved Chinnadevi was in Srivilliputtur, near Madurai. I wanted to ask him if he would tell her about my anguish upon being separated from her.

These thoughts were sheer agony, and I suppressed my feelings.

☙

Darkness had enveloped the palace. The Treasury Officer Chellappa Dhananayaka arrived as usual. I went with him to

---

13. Jaya Vijayi Bhava: May you be victorious!

the treasury. He opened the chest allocated to me and put the day's collections into it.

I watched the proceedings disinterestedly.

I looked at one particular chest intently. The fourth one, the one which had the words—Immadi Devaraya etched on it. I knew that the chest would be full of diamonds and gold and silver. And in the midst of all that there would also be that ruby strand which Mallanna had brought from Lanka for his dear wife.

Allasani Peddanna had told me that when the guards brought Mallana to the king, the strand had slipped out of his grasp and onto Immadi Devaraya's lap. What had happened to it? It must have found its way into Immadi Devaraya's treasure chest.

'Chellappa, who has the key to Immadi Devaraya's chest?' I asked.

Fifteen

I stared at the name 'Immadi Devaraya' etched on the chest. I didn't even notice Chellappa Dananayaka standing next to me.

This chest would be full of jewels. And in this chest I was sure I would find the ruby strand which Mallanna had brought for his wife. It shouldn't be difficult to find it in this chest. Since the ruby strand had been made in Lanka, it would be of a distinctive style. I could easily get goldsmiths to identify it.

And once I found the ruby strand, all I had to do was to send for Ethirajan, and tell him, 'Here is the strand that your ancestor brought from Lanka. I have atoned for the injustice meted out to your ancestor by Immadi Devaraya. Give this jewel to your sister, Chinnadevi. Let her wear it. Let the enmity you have nurtured for generations against the Vijayanagar royal family come to an end. Let whatever happens henceforth be auspicious.'

Ethirajan would be so moved, he would fall at my feet. I would then tell him that he was not to fall at my feet, for he was going to be my brother-in-law. I would then embrace him.

Chinnadevi would blush, and would steal a glance at me. We would both experience a frisson of delight.

Some of you who read this may laugh at my foolishness. If you do, then either you have never known what it is to be in love. Or you must be middle-aged people, who have forgotten their days of romancing. But young men in love will understand my feelings.

'Your Majesty, you asked me a question.' Chellappa's voice shook me out of my reverie.

'Yes. I asked you who had the key to this chest. Did you not hear me?'

'I did. I thought you had mistakenly asked me for...'

'Do you think I asked you for something I should not have asked for?'

Chellappa looked confused. 'It's just that...I mean...' he stuttered, not knowing what to say. 'I'll get the key, Your Majesty.'

When he left, the men who had accompanied him also left.

Immadi Devaraya's chest was at least three feet high and six feet in length. It was a beautifully carved chest, inlaid with gold in the corners. Even as I stood admiring the chest, Chellappa was back and with him was Appaji!

And neither of them had the key to the chest. I also noticed that Rayasam Kondamarasu, and Chief Accountant Mangarasayya too were with them.

'Your Majesty, we were told you wanted a key...'

'Yes. I want the key to Immadi Devaraya's chest. I want to open it.'

'Open? Chest?' Appaji was so shocked, that words failed him.

After a few seconds he said, 'Your Majesty, those are chests that belonged to previous Vijayanagar Kings. Successive kings have their own chests, but they have never opened a chest of any previous king. And it should not be done.'

I didn't relish Appaji questioning my decision, but I controlled my anger and said smilingly, 'Why not? Will I be letting out some demons and ghosts?'

'Your Majesty, what is the need to open this chest now?'

'I will tell you about that later. Give me the key.'

'Please listen to me, Your Majesty,' Appaji pleaded. 'There is a hitherto unbroken rule that whatever the need, chests that belonged to earlier kings should not be opened...'

'In the last century, during the rule of King Virupaksha, there was a drought and a severe famine. Thousands of people died of hunger. Wherever you looked, you could see skeletons piled up. People were afraid to venture out of their homes, because cannibalism was rampant. Parents would throng the ports to sell their children to sailors from foreign lands. And yet, Emperor Virupaksha did not open the chests of his predecessors. He only spent the wealth he had accumulated and also spent the money in the state treasury. He did not break the tradition even in such times of distress.

'You call this a tradition. What are traditions? They are man-made, are they not? And that means they can be changed. They are not laws laid down by God,' I said adamantly.

Appaji could see that arguing with me would be futile. So he gave me the key, with a final word of advice that I should rethink my decision.

Just as I was about to open the chest, 'Krishna! Stop,' cried my mother Nagalamba, who must have been sent for by Appaji.

I was taken aback. 'Mother, it is important that I open this chest. It concerns my life…my happiness. My future…'

My mother spread her arms before the chest and said, 'Krishna, you will have no future if you open the chests of your predecessors. Are you faced with a financial constraint? Please tell me, if you have a financial crunch. I will give you all the jewels I was given at the time of my marriage. Your father too later gave me a lot of jewellery. I can let you have all my jewels now. I have them with me in my palace. Come with me now and you can take all of them.'

'This is not a financial crisis, Mother. It is the hand of destiny. You cannot understand my motives. Nor am I in the mood to explain to you. Just don't stop me, please.'

'I will stop you,' said my mother sternly. 'You studied under Vyasa Teertha and studied the *Dharma Sastras*. Appaji took great risks to save you and put you on the throne. And is this how you repay them? If I had known that you would do something so improper, I would have disowned you…' If it is possible for a person to tie up one's hands with harsh words, my mother's words were proof of it. In the face of such stiff opposition from my mother, I did not know what to do.

I felt someone exert pressure on my arm, and turned to find Jangamaiah. Jangamaiah was not a high-ranking official. He was chief of those who guarded the city at night. He had no ministerial status. How dare he touch me? There was seldom any need for him to meet me, and even when he did, he would stand some distance from me, never getting close to me. He didn't have the status to stand beside me. And yet he had dared to touch me. What presumptuousness!

I was so angry that I would have cut him up with my sword. But Lord Venkateswara, the Lord I worship, stopped me in time. If an ordinary official had exceeded his limits and had pressed my arm, there must be a reason for it. There was a beseeching look in his eyes. I could see that he wanted me to follow him.

I had to worm my way out of the embarrassing situation which was my own doing. I gave Appaji and my mother to understand that I was still very upset at being thwarted. 'Mother, you and Appaji have spoken very harsh words to me. I have never done anything to displease you. For now, I will obey your command. But at some later date, I will not only explain why I want this chest opened, but I will open it. That is certain,' I said, and left the treasury.

༄

I lay in a golden swing, which was suspended with silver chains. I had removed all my jewellery and I was glad to be rid of the burden of the jewels. But I could do nothing about the thoughts that oppressed me.

As I waited for Jangamaiah, I was reminded of the day I had waited for Gayatri's message. A girl was playing the veena in my room. An old man played the kanjira[14].

I was in no mood for music, but I didn't want to hurt the feelings of the artistes. So I listened for some time, and then told them to leave. But I was not left undisturbed. The chief cook of the palace, Dharmapalan came to tell me that dinner was ready.

'Just send some food to my room,' I said.

A gold stool with castors was wheeled up to me. Food was served in silver bowls. There was a lot to choose from—both vegetarian and non-vegetarian food. As a Sri Vaishnava, I wanted to give up non-vegetarian food. But I was a King, and a strict vegetarian diet was unsuitable for a warrior.

A eunuch sprinkled rose water in the room. A girl brought fresh flowers—jasmine and roses and put them in vases. I took out some flowers and was enjoying their fragrance, when Jangamaiah entered.

'I must first apologise, Your Majesty. I pressed your arm. I should not have done so…'

'I could guess that there was something important you wished to say to me.'

I noticed that he had a cylindrical brass container. He opened it and pulled out something mildly yellow in colour. It wasn't like the silk cloth used to write on. But it could be rolled up and stuffed into the container. There was something written on it too.

'Your Majesty, this is called paper. It is made using dried grass, wood pulp and cotton. The Chinese knew how to make paper,

---

14. Kanjira—percussion instrument

and they had kept it a secret for many years. The Arabs learnt it from them. At present the Europeans use this paper instead of palm leaf to write on,' explained Jangamaiah.

I lost my patience. 'Did you keep me waiting for so long just to tell me this?'

'If you knew where this came from…'

'Where did it come from?'

'Srivilliputtur.' Before he could finish, I grabbed the paper from him. There were a few lines written on it. But I couldn't make out what language it was. It seemed as if the lines were in Odia.

I knew many Dravidian languages and also North Indian languages. But I had not learnt Odia, although it was the language in use in the neighbouring country of Kalinga. I had tried to learn Odia, but I had given up the attempt, because in Odia the same word can have several meanings, and I found it very confusing.

I looked at the paper again.

'You said this came from Srivilliputtur. Who sent it?'

'Gayatri,' he said. 'A soldier on horseback brought it to me and said Gayatri had sent it with instructions that it should reach you.'

'Gayatri? Do you know her well enough for her to entrust something confidential to you?'

'Your Majesty, I am in charge of security in the capital. Naturally when I saw Gayatri leave the palace often at night, I questioned her. I came to know that she was working for you. She told me that I was not to tell anyone about her nocturnal trips. There is an additional reason for my regard for that girl…'

'And what is that reason?'

'My daughter used to live in Shivasamudram with her husband. My son-in-law lost his life on the battlefield. My daughter, unable to bear the shock, threw herself into the

Shivasamudram falls and died. This girl Gayatri is about the same age as my daughter. She even looks a little like her. So I have a soft spot for her...'

The details about Jangamaiah's daughter didn't interest me. Gayatri had sent word. That was all I could think of. Gayatri, who used to say, "Your Majesty, I want you to be healthy, happy and prosperous," had sent word. It must be about Chinnadevi.

What was it? What was it? What was it?

Sixteen

I looked at the scroll which Jangamaiah had referred to as 'paper.' What was written on it? It did look like Odia. I was happy that Gayatri had sent me a message. She was also right to have written it in Odia, because the paper was going to travel through Tamil Nadu and the possibility of someone in Tamil Nadu being able to read Odia was remote. She was right to have taken such precautions. But why had she overestimated my knowledge? Why had she assumed that I could read Odia?

I also asked myself how and when Gayatri had learnt to write Odia.

Jangamaiah was still waiting for me to say something. And here I was, lost in thought, oblivious to the presence of a junior official in my administration. I was ashamed of myself.

'You may leave,' I said. 'And do not tell anyone about this message.'

Jangamaiah could not conceal his agitation. 'Your Majesty, my family and I have served your family for generations. I will reveal no secrets.'

'You said that the Arabs and the Europeans have learnt how to make paper. I would like our people too to be trained to make paper. Tell the Commerce Minister that I instructed him to ensure that people are taught how to make paper. It will help us in our commercial activities. It will provide employment to people.'

'As you command, Your Majesty,' said Jangamaiah and took leave of me.

I had often worried about great poems being written on palm-leaf manuscripts. Sometimes silk cloth was used. Silk too had the same limitations as palm leaf. Copper plates and stone inscriptions helped to record government orders, but they were of no use when it came to writing poems. I was happy that we had something called paper, which promised to be a good substitute for palm- leaf and silk. A small consolation when I was in the middle of myriad worries.

That night, I placed the paper with Gayatri's message, under my pillow. Silly of me to think that this might somehow help decipher the writing. As was the custom, two guards came into my room, lit two torches, bowed before me and went out to the balcony. They waved the flaming torches. This was called the 'Salute of the Torches'. I don't know when the practice originated. It is my guess that it was a custom borrowed from the Mughals. It was to indicate to the people that the king was safe and well. If the torches were not waved, that meant the king was unwell.

The guards waved the torches to let my subjects know that I was keeping good health.

The King was indeed in the pink of health. But how could I tell my people that my mind was in turmoil?

Dawn was ushered in by the chanting of verses from *Sanjaya Niti, Vidura Niti, Chanakya Niti*, and Bhartrhari's *Niti Sataka*. Singing these verses was the everyday duty of a poet called Chandrayya. He had a voice that had an excellent timbre. But today his voice sounded weak and tired. I looked out. I saw a twelve-year-old boy singing in place of the poet. When he saw me, the boy fell at my feet and said, 'My father has fever. So he has sent me to sing instead.'

'You sing well. Don't be diffident,' I said encouragingly to the boy, and gave him a pat on the back.

The boy had not expected me to talk to him. My kindness only seemed to make him more nervous. He fell at my feet again and again.

At the ministerial meeting that day, there were very serious discussions on various matters.

'We have to check the Sultan of Vijayapuram, Adil Shah. He is getting more rebellious by the day,' Appaji set the ball rolling.

'I beg to differ,' said Nadendla Gopa. 'Adil Shah is the only one of the Bahmani Sultans we can trust. It is said that in Vijayapuram or Bijapur as his capital is called, a temple for Balarama has been built. He is reputed to be a fair man…'

'Besides, there is a treaty of friendship between us and Adil Shah,' pointed out Rayasam Kondamarasu.

Appaji ignored him. 'Read the terms of the treaty. It says that if a person who has indulged in any activity against the Vijayanagar Empire seeks shelter in Vijayapuram, he should not be given refuge by the Sultan. The Sultan should hand over traitors to us. But Adil Shah has not done so. We sent forty thousand gold coins through a trusted official called Siddhi, and dispatched him to Goa, to buy Persian horses. Siddhi has been a loyal servant of the Empire. But he fell prey to temptation, and instead of going to Goa, he went to Vijayapuram and sought refuge there. The Sultan not only allowed Siddhi to stay there, but has granted him special privileges in Vijayapuram. We have sent word several times, asking the Sultan to hand over Siddhi to us. But the Sultan has not acceded to our request.' Appaji panted for breath after his long-winded speech.

Accountant Mangarasayya forgot that he was in the presence of his king and laughed out loud. 'How will he hand over Siddhi to us? The information I have is that Adil Shah has killed Siddhi and has taken the forty thousand gold coins.'

'Whatever be the case, the fact remains that Siddhi was not handed over to us and Adil Shah is in possession of our money. We must declare war against him,' said Appaji.

I too wanted to declare war against Adil Shah. In fact I had come to the conclusion that if I managed to defeat Adil Shah, then bringing the other four Sultans under my control would not be difficult. I had even been thinking of the best persons to appoint as generals for the various divisions of my army. However, instead of announcing my decision right away, I just said, 'I will think about it and come to a decision soon.'

There was a reason for my decision to defer my announcement. When two ministers, both of them senior ministers, are in disagreement, whose side should a king take? In fact I have myself written in my works, that in such a case, the king should not take sides. The person whose side the king takes will become smug and the other will feel he has been slighted.

I thought of paying a visit to my mother. There were many things I had not told her. I wanted to bare my soul to her. I felt I was as foolish as a man who keeps putting off the laundering of his clothes indefinitely. I too had kept postponing the moment when I would have to confide in her.

Even as I turned towards my mother's palace, I noticed two men entering the hall. One of them was the sculptor Muthu. The other was dance guru Bandam Lakshmi Narayana.

I was not inclined to converse with either of them. But Bandam Lakshmi Narayana was my music teacher. Out of respect for him, I waited. 'Well, Muthu, is work towards construction of the dance hall progressing satisfactorily?' I asked.

'Yes, Your Majesty,' said Muthu. The pointed look he gave Lakshmi Narayana suggested that they had some problem, and that Muthu was waiting for Lakshmi Narayana to tell me about it.

'Is there some problem, teacher?' I asked Lakshmi Narayana.

'Yes, Your Majesty. There is a small disagreement between us. If you will come to the dance hall and have a look…' His voice was as gentle as the strains of a veena, an instrument he was accomplished in playing.

'Certainly,' I said and followed him.

The dance hall was buzzing with activity. Dozens of sculptors were transforming stone into art. The sound of their chisels was music to my ears. As I had suggested, pillars with dancing girls depicting various karanas[15] were being sculpted.

Lakshmi Narayana took me to the last pillar and said, 'You said that the last pillar should show a dancer's pose when she has finished dancing. Now if that were to be the case, then this sculpture is wrong. It is against the natya sastras.'

'What do you say to that, Muthu?'

'The dance guru is right. I just thought this sculpture would look more aesthetic.'

'Muthu, I understand and appreciate your fertile imagination. But this dance hall is being built to be instructive to those who are learning dance. So the sculptures have to be in accordance with the Natya Sastra. Please change the sculpture to one which Lakshmi Narayana will approve of.'

Muthu was disappointed. But he said, 'I will do as the dance guru tells me, Your Majesty,' said Muthu.

'I have heard it said that education gives humility. You are both intelligent and humble,' I complimented Muthu, and left the dance hall.

Lakshmi Narayana walked with me, and said, 'Your Majesty. My wife and family are in Katak[16]. I want to bring them to Vijayanagar.'

'Yes, yes. You have been living alone here for a long time,

---

15. Karanas: In Indian classical dance, a karana is a coordinated action of the body, the hands and the feet. There are 108 karanas.
16. Katak—Cuttack

haven't you?' I said. Lakshmi Narayana was from the Kalinga country, the capital of which was Katak.

This kingdom on the east coast was a wealthy one, enriched by its trade. For some time it had been under the control of the Vijayanagar Empire. It had also been an enemy of the Vijayanagar Empire for some time. At present, territories that belong to us are under their control, and so for now we have to think of Kalinga as an enemy kingdom.

In the past the Kalinga kings had been vassals of the Chola kings. When they refused to pay tax to the Cholas, Kulottunga Chola dispatched an army under his general Karunakara Thondaiman, who defeated the Kalinga king Anantavarman Cholaganga. This Chola victory was praised by the poet Jayamkondar, in his *Kalingathuparani*. For every verse of his, the poet received as a gift a golden coconut!

But today's Kalinga is not the Kalinga of the Chola period. Today it is ruled by the Gajapatis. They claim they are of the Solar Dynasty. They say they are descended from Lord Rama. I have no idea which of them tamed an elephant, but every one of them proudly calls himself by the title Gajapati—the one who conquered an elephant.

The current ruler of Kalinga is Prataparudra Gajapati. He is an intelligent man. A well-read man too. But he gave short shrift to Telugu and Odia and promoted Sanskrit. Many Telugu poets therefore left Kalinga and made their home in Vijayanagar.

One of the scholars who left was dance guru Lakshmi Narayana.

It has taken me a long time to write all this history, but I recalled all of it in a flash. And then I had an idea. Lakshmi Narayana was from Kalinga. He should be able to read Odia. Why shouldn't I ask him to read Gayatri's message to me? But would this be wise? Jangamaiah already knew of my love for Chinnadevi. Should Lakshmi Narayana also be let in on the secret?

I was steeped in thought and was shocked when Lakshmi Narayana said, 'Your Majesty, there used to be a girl in the palace called Gayatri. I haven't seen her for a long time. Where is she?'

'Do you...She...I mean...'

'Gayatri is from Kalinga. She belongs to the family of Prataparudra Gajapati. I have often wondered why she worked here as a servant. I even asked her why she was here as a servant,' said Lakshmi Narayana, rendering me speechless with shock.

Seventeen

'Are you sure?' I asked Bandam Lakshmi Narayana. I had guessed Gayatri was from a high-class family. My mother too had guessed as much. But I had not expected her to belong to the Kalinga royal family!

'Your Majesty knows I am from Kalinga. I used to be the court poet of Prataparudra Gajapati. I wasn't treated with respect, which was why I left Kalinga and came to Vijayanagar. When I lived in Katak, I used to visit the palace, and I have even been to the women's quarters…'

'You mean you have seen Gayatri there?'

'Yes. I have seen her there. She is Prataparudra Gajapati's niece—either his sister's daughter or brother's daughter. Since I felt it would not be right to enquire about women of the royal family, I didn't probe further. When I saw her here, I was surprised. I wondered why she had come here and how she had come here.'

'Did you ask her why she was here?'

'I did. She said she was here because there was something important she had to do, and that she would tell me later about it. She also requested me not to reveal her identity to anyone here. I felt sorry that a woman of a royal family was here as a servant. So I didn't mention who she was to anyone. It was wrong of me not to have told you. Please forgive me.'

'You don't have to apologise. I don't think you did anything wrong.'

So Gayatri was from Kalinga—an enemy country. She was also related to the King of Kalinga.

Appaji had repeatedly warned me not to trust her. He suspected she was a spy. Was he right?

But I had appointed her my personal servant and to worry about it now would do me no good. In any case she had often said to me that she wanted a favour from me, and that she would ask for it at an appropriate time. Would someone who wanted a favour of me, harm me?

'Will you come with me?' I asked Lakshmi Narayana.

'Certainly, Your Majesty.'

I went to my room and took the paper which I had been given.

'I know what this is. It is called "paper",' Lakshmi Narayana said.

'I want you to read what is written on this paper. It looks like the script of the Odia language. So I thought you might be able to read it,' I said.

'It is Odia. But it looks different from the usual script.'

'Don't worry. It's not important. I chanced upon this paper and I was curious to know what was written on it,' I said. Lakshmi Narayana looked relieved, and left as quickly as he could. When an intelligent, well-read person finds he cannot understand something, he feels embarrassed. I thought Lakshmi Narayana was ashamed that he couldn't decipher the script.

It was two days since I had received the paper. I knew Gayatri had sent me a message which I had to act upon at once. But what had she said in her message?

The third day. I got up early in the morning and recited Aditya Hrudayam[17], even as I watched the sun go up. From my room I could see my mother's palace.

The palace guards were there in their places, but someone was going in stealthily, and the guards didn't stop them. They looked like priests of village temples.

And after some time my mother came out and hurried them on their way.

---

17. Adtiya Hrudayam—a hymn in praise of the Sun-God

My mother was generous to a fault, and would never send anyone away empty-handed. Appaji and I too had told her countless times to give only to the deserving, but she didn't exercise discretion, when it came to giving. Appaji and I had stopped advising her, because giving gifts to people made her happy.

I smiled to myself when I thought of my mother's innocence. My mother noticed me and began to walk towards my palace. The palanquin-bearers ran up to her with the palanquin, but she dismissed them. I welcomed her to my rooms. She held my hand, and I helped her up the steps. She had held my hand many times in the past, but I noticed that her grip was weak today. A sign that she was aging. It made me sad.

'Why did you smile at me, Krishna?' she asked.

'You know why I did, Mother. Your secret is out,' I laughed.

'There was nothing secret about the visit of those people. They came to me for help for temple worship.'

'People are clever. They know that if they use the name of God, they can cadge money out of people.'

'Don't make frivolous remarks about people's faith, Krishna,' she chided me. 'They had come from a village near Chittoor. They wanted money for the finger festival.'

'Finger festival? What is that?'

'It is a festival…No. I will not tell you.'

'So what if you won't tell me? I will send my guards and bring those men here, and get an answer to my question from them.'

'No, no. Please don't do that. I will tell you myself. But only upon one condition.'

'And what is that?'

'You have stopped human sacrifice. But you can't change people overnight. It will take time for them to give up their beliefs and practices. You cannot get them to give up their beliefs through legislation. Now you must promise not to start interfering in this village festival.'

'All right, Mother.'

'There is a Kala Bhairava temple in the village to which those men belong. And the finger festival is in fulfillment of a vow. If the rains are good…'

My mother hesitated.

'If the rains are good…' I prompted.

'The men will offer their wives' fingers—the little finger and the ring finger, as a sacrifice.'

'How unfair, Mother! If the men have vowed to offer two fingers to their God, why should it be their wives' fingers? Why not their own fingers? What right have they to cut off the fingers of their wives?'

'Now this is what I was afraid of. How do we know the women are being forced to cut off their fingers? What if they willingly offer their fingers?'

'You have an answer for everything. But why were the men here to see you?'

'There are temple employees in the Kala Bhairava temple, to help the men carry out their vow. There is a goldsmith, a barber, a priest, a physician and a guard. There are people to bandage the hands of the women whose fingers have been cut. They also apply medicines to help the wounds heal. Now all of these people receive rice as their pay. The temple has lands but the rice from the lands is not enough to pay all the temple employees during the finger festival. The people you saw are devotees from that village. They were here to ask me for more land to be donated to the temple, to meet the expenses of the festival.'

'What a wonderful practice!' I said sarcastically. The city

was coming to life, and the streets were getting noisy. I looked down from the balcony. Soldiers from my equestrian forces were queuing up for their daily allowance. Palace servants were being paid their salary. In the bazaar, merchants were engaged in bargaining.

From the end of the street came the sound of singing. 'Hari Narayana, Hari Narayana, Hari Narayana enu manave,' sang a voice.

'Dasa is here. Come Krishna,' said my mother. She went hurriedly to a box of gold coins I had in my room. She took out a handful of coins, and hurried out to meet Dasa. I followed her.

Dasa's full name was Purandara Dasa. I am sure you are familiar with the story of Puranadara Dasa. He was a rich diamond merchant, whose original name was Cheenappa Nayaka. He earned so much money that he came to be known as Navakoti Narayana. Lord Panduranga had brought about a change of heart in rich Navakoti Narayana. Cheenappa Nayaka gave up all his wealth and took to the life of a wandering mendicant.

He had taken the blessings of Vyasa Teertha a few years ago, and had left on a religious pilgrimage. He had travelled from the Himalayas to Kanyakumari and had returned only last month. He, his wife and four sons live in a matha. Every day, their morning bhajans take them through different streets in the city. I was lucky, for today, they had chosen to come to the street housing my palace.

When we reached the entrance to the palace, we could see Purandara Dasa with a tambura and with his cymbals. His wife had a copper bowl, into which people respectfully dropped grain. Purandara Dasa was followed by his four sons, who were writing down their father's songs on palm leaves.

My mother and I fell at his feet. He put his hand on my head and said, 'Panduranga Vittala.' I was moved by his blessing. My mother's servants washed his feet, and Mother sprinkled the water on my head and hers. She dropped gold coins in the copper bowl. It was the people of Vijayanagar who were stunned into silence by the respect their monarch had shown Dasa, but Dasa himself remained placid and unmoved. He continued with his singing, and moved on.

'It is a matter of regret, Krishna,' said my mother.

'What is? Dasa's giving up all his wealth?'

'No, no. He chose to give up everything. I am not talking about his wealth. I am talking about the thousands of songs he has composed. He must have composed at least 300,000 songs, don't you think?'

'Perhaps.'

'That is why everyone calls him the father of Carnatic music. Do you know that it was he who realised that Mayamalavagowla Raga was the most appropriate one in which to begin music lessons for beginners?'

'Really?' When it comes to music, I'm not a patch on my mother. As in the case of Bharatanatyam, and discussions on the Sastras, when the discussion becomes serious, I slip away.

'You mentioned a matter of regret. What was that about, Mother?'

'Yes, it is a matter of regret that his songs are being written on palm leaves. How long can you preserve palm leaf manuscripts? We have already lost knowledge that should have been preserved for posterity, because our records were palm leaf manuscripts. These songs of Dasa too will be lost in the course of time.'

'A substitute for palm leaves has been discovered, Mother,' I said. And even before I knew what I was doing, I had taken out the paper I had under my pillow. 'This is called paper, Mother. If we begin to use paper, then it will be easy for us to preserve the works of our poets and scholars.'

But my mother wasn't paying attention to what I was saying. She was more interested in what was written on the paper. 'This looks like Odia.'

And that was when I realised that in my enthusiasm I had done something foolish. Mother knew many languages. What if she knew Odia? She would then be able to read Gayatri's message!

'Yes, this is Odia. But it's written cleverly. Come with me. Let me show you,' said my mother, and took me to the next room.

She stood before the mirror in the room, and held the paper before it. And now the letters appeared in reverse. 'See? I was right. This is Odia. The letters have been written in reverse.' But she said nothing more. She read the lines on the paper, and looked sternly at me.

'Krishna, what is the meaning of this?' she asked me.

'Mother...I...' I stuttered.

'You haven't been honest with me, Krishna. Your activities have, of late, been very mysterious.'

A couple of days earlier, I had resolved to unburden myself to my mother. But now when opportunity presented itself, I developed cold feet.

'I asked you a question, Krishna. What is the meaning of this?'

'What does the message say, Mother?' I asked.

'I will tell you about that later. You tell me about all those things you have been keeping from me. Can you not confide in your mother?'

I broke down, when she said that.

Eighteen

When my mother asked me why I had not confided in her, I didn't know what reply to give her.

'Krishna, will you not tell me what it is that troubles you?'

I turned to face her, but I didn't have the courage to look into her eyes. I averted my gaze, and said, 'Mother, this is not something a son can talk to his mother about. It is my problem and I will have to tackle it myself.' I said.

'Do you think so? And I was all along under the impression that a son was close to his mother.'

I looked round. There was a man with a stylus and a palm leaf in his hands. It was his duty to record the visits of those who came to see me and also to record the conversations I had with them. Later in the day, I would check his records for accuracy. He was reliable and loyal to me, and that is why he had been appointed to this post. Sometimes, I would not want to carry on a conversation in his presence and would ask him to leave. This was one such occasion. I signalled to him to leave.

After he had left, I said, 'Mother, it's a long story.'

I told her about how I had met Chinnadevi, about my love for her, of the fact that Gayatri belonged to Gajapati's family, and about what Lakshmi Narayana had told me.

Mother listened to me without displaying any emotion, except when I told her about Mallanna's curse, that one day the Vijayanagar Empire would be reduced to ashes. She shivered when I told her about Mallana's curse, and murmured 'Hari, Hari,' and reverentially pressed her garland of tulsi seeds to her eyes.

When I finished speaking, she was silent for a few minutes

and then she said, 'So that is why you wanted to open Immadi Devaraya's chest!'

'Yes, Mother. I wanted to give Mallanna's strand of rubies to Ethirajan. I wanted to try to pacify him.'

'So you are determined to marry Chinnadevi…'

'Yes, mother,' I said. 'The…I…have…for…'

'The love you have for her, why don't you express it openly? All right. Now I will tell you what this paper says.'

I could hardly contain my excitement.

Mother read from the paper: 'Chinnadevi is not here. I will give you all the details in person. Gayatri.'

I was devastated. But before I could respond, a palace servant peeped in. She had a silver basket full of flowers. 'We'll continue this conversation later. Come with me to the temple. I prayed for a son, and to fulfil my vow, I had an image of the Snake God installed at the foot of the Matanga hill. And since your birth, I have been visiting the shrine every month. Why don't you come with me today to the shrine?' my mother said.

My mother's face betrayed nothing. I could not tell whether Mother approved of my love for Chinnadevi or not. Gayatri's message that she couldn't locate Chinnadevi added to my anxiety.

When Mother and I stepped out of the palace, Appaji arrived and said, 'Your Majesty, how can you leave without any guards?' Turning to my mother, he said, 'And how can you travel on foot? Where is your palanquin?' Appaji disapproved of members of the royal family moving about like commoners, but my mother and I liked it.

'It doesn't matter. Let us have a walk, please,' said Mother. Appaji subsided into disapproving mutters. A soldier on horseback was telling the people to make way for us. The people moved aside to let us pass. Some fell at our feet.

When we reached the exit gate of the fort, we saw a small crowd gathered there. There was a poor girl there, and a circle had been drawn on the ground around her.

The girl was weeping. When she saw us, she covered her face with her hands, and continued to weep. But she did not move out of the circle drawn around her.

If a person could not repay a loan, the creditor had the right to treat the defaulter in this manner. Until the defaulter repaid the loan, he or she would have to remain inside the circle.

'Mother, I had assumed that such practices were prevalent only in villages, but here it is being practised in the capital city, right under my nose,' I said in disgust. A palace official, who had been witness to the proceedings, stepped forward when he saw us. 'Settle this girl's dues from the palace treasury,' I ordered.

'At once...' added Mother.

There was a grateful expression on the girl's tear-stained face.

My mother and I walked on.

We walked past the Krishna temple, the Veerbhadraswami temple, the Narasimha idol and the Ganesha idol. Mother was silent. We reached the foot of the Matanga hill. The idol of the Snake God had been installed in a place where a neem tree and a peepul tree grew side by side. After we had offered worship to the Snake God, Mother sent away the guard on horseback and the maid servant from the palace. 'There is a small temple on top of the hill. It's been a long time since I visited the temple. Let us go there,' my mother said.

The Matanga hill isn't a big one. But it is steep.

People claim that this is the Matanga mountain mentioned in the Ramayana. It is said that the city of Kishkinda was close by. When Sugriva was chased by his brother Vali, he is supposed to have taken shelter here. Vali had been cursed by the sage

Matanga. If Vali ever set foot in the Matanga mountain, his head would shatter into a hundred pieces. That was why Sugriva took shelter here, knowing that Vali would not dare to venture here. Hanuman met Rama here, and it was here that Rama and Sugriva became friends. When Ravana abducted Sita, she flung her jewels, to mark the path through which he was taking her. The place where Sugriva hid her jewels is known as Sugriva's cave. A small mound is pointed out as the place where Vali was cremated. There are lots of monkeys here, all of them said to be the descendants of Vali and Sugriva.

It was getting dark, and there was a nip in the air. The place was desolate. The temple built centuries ago was in a state of disrepair. Thinking I would have to repair it, I turned round and to my shock I found that Mother was climbing another mound.

'Mother,' I called out.

She didn't respond.

There were steps only up to some distance on the mound which she was now climbing. Mother was putting her toes in little gaps between the rocks and climbing up.

'Stop, Mother. Why are you climbing up further? There is no temple there,' I said loudly, even as I followed her. I had climbed these rocks umpteen times as a boy, and my ascent and descent would be faster than that of the agile monkeys that jumped from rock to rock, screeching shrilly. It is quite possible that my mother too might have played here as a child. But, now…Oh my God!

'Mother, what are you going to do there?' I shouted, but my voice was drowned by the noise of the strong breeze that was blowing.

I raised my voice and called out again, 'Mother.'

'Are you scared?' my mother asked, and gave an eerie laugh.

'Mother, your laugh fills me with dread,' I said. 'What are you going to do at that height, Mother?'

A few minutes ago, she was at a height, where with some effort, I could have touched her feet. But now she had climbed much higher, and she looked smaller from this distance.

'Vijayanagar is a beautiful city, Krishna. I can see our palaces and temples and gardens from here. What a lovely sight!' She laughed again.

I had a horrible feeling in the pit of my stomach.

'Mother, please come down. If you want to admire Vijayanagar, there are a dozen safe places from where you can do so. I will take you to a safer place.'

It was now very dark, and I couldn't make out how she had climbed. So I didn't follow her. There was a very strong, cold wind blowing. I shivered. I tried to wrap my shawl round my shoulders to keep out the cold. But the wind whipped it out of my hands. The shawl twisted and turned in the wind and drifted down, until I could no longer see it. The monkeys were retiring for the night. I saw each monkey as an avatar of Hanuman and prayed to each of them to keep my mother safe.

My mother was now at the top of the mound. I have heard it said that sometimes people lose their sanity all of a sudden. Had something like that happened to my mother? The blood froze in my veins.

'Mother, stay right where you are. I am coming up. I will help you down,' I said.

'Don't come here, Krishna. I can climb down myself. Stay there!' Mother commanded.

'All right, Mother. Come down yourself. But why do you play such games at your age, Mother?' I asked, although something told me that this was no game, and that something serious was about to happen. It seemed as if she was swaying in the wind. I became more panicky. I wondered if I should run to her and hold her, lest she fall down. But she was on such a narrow ledge, that one misstep was all it would take for her to go hurtling down.

'Mother, please come down. Why do you torment me so?'

'I will come, Krishna. I will, once you give me a promise,' she said.

'A promise? What promise, Mother?'

'Promise that you will forget Chinnadevi.'

It seemed as if my whole world had come crashing down. 'Mother, Mother. What are you saying? Please come down.'

'I asked you for a promise. Give me your word and I will come down. You cannot marry that dancing girl. Tell me you will forget her.'

'And if I don't promise?'

'Can't you guess what will happen if you don't promise? I will jump from here. Very easy.'

'Mother,' I screamed. 'Is this why you brought me here?'

'Yes, Krishna,' she admitted. 'I knew that I could never get you to make such a promise under any other circumstance. That is why I ask you now. Tell me. Will you promise? I am old. I cannot stand here for long. You were the one who worried about my age a while ago.'

'What do you want me to say, Mother?'

'How many times do you want me to say it? Promise that you will forget Chinnadevi. Do you want your Mother or Chinnadevi?'

My lips twitched in anger. 'I gave her a promise long before your demand for a promise. I promised that I would marry her.'

'I do not want to hear about your promises to her. Your mother, or your lover? Make up your mind.'

I couldn't believe what my eyes were seeing or my ears were hearing. It must be a nightmare. I would soon wake up from this nightmare. I would hear music in Mother's palace. I would watch dance dramas there. 'Listen to this song, Krishna. This is Jnaneshwar's composition. He was a great saint born in a village near the Godavari river,' Mother was going to say. A servant was going to place a golden plate full of pomegranates before me. Mother and I would savour the fruits. Now, now…

But no, nothing of the sort happened. There was my mother standing precariously, after having put such an unfair proposition before me.

There was a story that thousands of years ago, the Matanga hill had been a tall one, and that an earthquake had shattered the hill into dozens of small mounds. It seemed to me that I was experiencing such an earthquake.

Nineteen

I was in torment. 'Will you give up your love for Chinnadevi, or shall I jump from here?'—that was Mother's ultimatum.

What was I to say? What could I say?

On the one hand was my mother, who had carried me in her womb for ten months, and who doted on me. On the other hand was my love Chinnadevi, whose affection I had been the recipient of for ten months. On the one hand was my affection for my mother. On the other hand was my unshakeable love for Chinnadevi.

'Krishna, have you made up your mind?' my mother asked.

I gritted my teeth and decided to tell her what my decision was.

'Yes, Mother. I have made up my mind.'

'I know you are an obedient son. So I know you would have decided to give up Chinnadevi, in order to save your mother,' she said. Darkness had enveloped us, but I could see her face brighten in anticipation.

'Your guess is wrong, Mother,' I said.

'What?'

'I do not want this empire, or the luxuries of the palace, gold, jewels, wealth. There is nothing I want in this world. I only want you and Chinnadevi,' I said.

'Are you sure?'

'Yes, Mother,' I said, and closed my eyes, unwilling to witness what was going to happen.

I also closed my ears, because I wanted to shut out the last shout of my mother, as she leaped to her death.

But…but…the next second…

I saw my mother climbing down from the mound. I ran to her, and embraced her.

'Mother,' I cried in relief.

'Krishna.' My mother too embraced me. She was old and yet I could feel the strength in her arms, and I knew the reason for it—her love for me.

'You've won, Krishna. You have passed the test,' she said, and kissed my forehead.

I was confused. I thought she had developed cold feet, and had therefore abandoned the idea of suicide, but, here she was, talking of a test and of my having passed it!

'Yes, Krishna. Romantic love has become a pastime for rich young men, especially those of royal families. I came across several such young men in my youth. I wanted to know if you were one of those men who toy with women, or whether your love for Chinnadevi was strong. I know how much respect you have for me. So I decided to gamble on that. And you, my son, are a gem! Unalloyed gold!' Mother was holding my hands and we made our way down, and reached the foot of the hill.

'Mother!' I exclaimed, and pressed her hands to my eyes, reverentially. I was no longer worried about whether my love for Chinnadevi would lead to marriage.

Still I had to ask: 'Mother, were you speaking the truth when you were on top of the hill? Or were you speaking the truth after you descended? I don't know what to believe.'

There was a small ledge on the rock, which could comfortably seat two people. Mother sat on it and asked me to sit beside her. 'I want to talk to you, Krishna,' she said.

The village was a scene of great activity. Children were throwing coloured powder at one another.

'I think they are celebrating Holi—the festival of colour.

Different places celebrate Holi on different days. There used to be an ogre called Holika. She used to swallow up children. A sage told the children that if they shot jets of coloured water at her, and made fun of her, she would die. The children followed the sage's advice and Holika died. It is to celebrate the death of Holika, that Holi is celebrated.' Some of the village children ran up to us, and shot jets of coloured water at us, and ran off laughing.

'Children will be children. They treat emperor and commoner alike,' Mother said, and wiped her face and mine with her saree. But the only effect this had was to spread the colour all over her face, so that she looked worse now. I was sure I looked funny too.

'You asked me whether I was speaking the truth when I was at the top of the hill, or whether I was speaking the truth after I descended. What I said to you after I climbed down is the truth, Krishna. From now on, I shall be on your side. I will find Chinnadevi and get her married to you. Don't ask me how I will accomplish this. Just trust me, I will,' my mother said.

Mother's words were as sweet as honey to me. How foolish I had been! Why would someone look for driftwood to take him across the sea, when a ship with sails is available?

A girl with a basket of steamed peanuts asked us if we would like to buy some from her.

Mother spread the tip of her saree and said, 'Give us some.'

'Mother, I haven't any money. Have you brought any coins?' I asked.

'I had some with me, but I dropped them into the collection box in the temple,' Mother said.

'Will you come to the palace tomorrow and collect the money for your peanuts?' Mother asked the girl. 'Tell the official in charge at the palace that the Queen asked you to collect your payment from him, and he will pay you.'

'Listen you old hag, do you know what will happen to me if I go to the palace and tell them the Queen sent me? I will be killed. I don't want your money, old woman. Take my peanuts for free!' the girl said and left in a huff.

'Poor thing. She doesn't know who we are. I should have given her my bracelet.'

'That would have placed her in danger, Mother. If she had taken it to a goldsmith to sell it, it would have been identified as belonging to the royal family. It would have been assumed that she had stolen it, and the poor girl would have been killed.'

My mother laughed and we began eating the peanuts. Every day, we ate all kinds of delicacies in the palace, specially prepared for us. But nothing seemed to equal these peanuts in taste. I even picked up a peanut that slipped from my hand onto the ground, and put it into my mouth.

'Krishna, did you have to pick that up?' Mother laughed.

'Mother, when one is happy, even mud is tasty. And now I am very happy,' I explained.

'You are an Emperor. Open your mouth, Krishna,' she said.

'Mother, you keep reading the *Bhagavatam*, and the *Divya Prabandham* all the time and I think you have come to think of yourself as Krishna's mother Yashoda. When Yashoda asked Lord Krishna to open His mouth, she saw all the worlds in His mouth. Don't expect to find anything like that in my mouth. All you can see in my mouth are my tongue and my teeth, and even they are not attractive,' I teased her.

My mother waited for me to finish speaking and then said, 'Krishna, you really are very happy.'

'And it's not surprising that I am happy, Mother. I was afraid you wouldn't consent to my marrying a devadasi, but you have consented. Isn't that reason enough for me to rejoice?'

I recalled Gayatri's message that Chinnadevi was no longer

in Srivilliputtur. But I was certain I would find here wherever she was and marry her.

The moon cast its light on my mother's face. The light from torches and lights in the distance also illumined her face. The coloured powder had settled in the wrinkles on her face and she looked funny. I wondered if I looked funny too. But Mother looked serious, not amused.

'What are you thinking about, Mother?' I asked.

'I too am a dasi. You are a dasi's son,' she said.

'Mother! What are you saying?'

'Yes, Krishna, I too was a dasi, that is a servant. I was one of many hundreds of serving girls in the palace.'

I couldn't believe my mother. I had always seen her in the palace, and had only known her as a Queen. My mother—a servant?

'I know you find it hard to believe. Your step-mother, Tippamba, your father, Narasa Nayaka, and Appaji are the only others who know the truth. It is, of course, possible that Tippamba might have told her son Veera Narasimha the truth.'

I was shaken. My breath came in short bursts.

'If you are interested I will tell you my story,' my mother said.

'Go ahead, Mother, I have become accustomed to being shocked. One more shock is not going to make any difference.'

'There is a need to tell you my story now. Otherwise, I would never have mentioned my past to you,' said Mother. 'The Empire was running to seed after the death of Devaraya. His sons Virupaksha and Mallikarjuna took their duties lightly, and when they died, there was a lot of internal strife in the land. This situation lasted for fifty to sixty years. That was when the administrators and ministers crowned your father. Your father put things on an even keel. He made the Empire strong and restored to it its lost glory. He earned the affection of the people…'

I knew all these historical facts. I was anxious to know more about mother's revelation that she was not of royal blood, and that she had been a servant. Mother's statement, that there was now a need for her to reveal the truth, made me uneasy.

'Your father married Tippamba, who was from a royal family. While she was pregnant, the Emperor and Tippamba went to Tirumala. On the way, they spent the night in a palace. I was a servant in that palace. My duty was to carry a torch to light the path whenever the queen ventured out.'

My mother paused, and looked at me to see if I was paying attention.

'I am listening to you, Mother. Go on with your narration,' I urged.

'One day, I was carrying the torch, while the Emperor and the Queen followed me. A spark from the torch fell on my saree, which caught fire…'

'My God! And?'

'Your father took a blanket that he had thrown over his shoulders, and draped it round me, and put out the fire. And that's when…'

Even after so many years, my mother still blushed when she recalled the past.

'The Emperor stayed in the palace for two months. And he and I…' Mother hesitated and then continued. 'He and I became close to each other. Tippamba came to know of our relationship, but she could not do anything about it. Your father made her promise that she would not tell anyone that I was only a servant. We then returned to the capital city, and everyone was told that I belonged to a royal family. Your father then married me. Your father had great regard for Prime Minister Appaji. So he told him the truth.'

It was clear from the silence around us that it was very late in the night. We had been away from the palace for long, and soon palace officials would come looking for us. And then I would not be able to hear the rest of the story. 'What happened then, Mother?' I asked, unable to contain my curiosity.

'Tippamba gave birth to Veera Narasimha. I gave birth to you. Your father married a third wife—Obamba. She gave birth to Achyutan and Rangan. Obamba was from a royal family. She was a very gentle lady. She was very affectionate to me, and treated me like an elder sister. But Tippamba hated me. "A servant has become a queen," she would say in anger, when I was within earshot. She died shortly after your father's death, but till the end she never forgave me. Appaji said that when she was on her death bed, she made her son promise that he would rule Vijayanagar, and that after him, his son would rule the Empire. She said that on no account should you—the son of a servant—ever become king. That is why your step-brother Veera Narasimha instructed Appaji to blind you. But Appaji didn't want a child to be put on the throne. He wanted you to become the Emperor. You had travelled extensively, as a representative of the royal family. You had fraternised with the common man. You had earned the respect of the people. The generals and important palace officials wanted you to become king. For these reasons, Appaji felt you were the right choice.'

I found myself at a loss for words. My poor mother had undergone humiliation and had suffered silently. When I thought of all that she had had to face, my heart felt heavy

'There was nothing wrong with Tippamba's wish, Krishna. I too think along the same lines today.'

'Mother, what do you mean?'

I could guess what she was about to say.

Twenty

Mother was silent for a few minutes. She then said with a sigh, 'The people will never accept Chinnadevi as their queen.'

'Mother, how can you dash my hopes? Just a while ago, you said you were on my side, and that you would find Chinnadevi and get her married to me. Have your words been blown away by this strong wind?'

'No, Krishna. I will not go back on my word. I will keep my promise to you. I even have a plan to make your dream come true. With your permission, I can put the plan into action,' she said, and spat out the peanut she had been munching, and said, 'People say that the last peanut you put into your mouth is bound to be rotten, and they are right!'

'I have some peanuts left. Here—have one,' I said, and gave her a nut. She put it into her mouth. I waited for her to finish munching it, and then said, 'All right, Mother. Now tell me what your plan is.'

But before she could tell me about her plan, we spotted a group of people approaching us, with torches in their hands.

'Palace officials, coming in search of us. We have lingered for too long, Krishna. Let us return to the palace. We will continue our discussion tomorrow,' said my mother.

The palace officials had brought two palanquins with them. One was small, and could seat only one person. The other was larger, and could easily seat two people, facing each other.

'Lets us take the bigger palanquin,' Mother suggested. I moved the cushions around a little, and made myself comfortable in the palanquin. It was carried by eight men, four on each side. They carried it without a jerk. Mother closed her eyes in prayer, as the palanquin bearers chanted 'Hare Rama, Hare Krishna.'

'Tell me, Mother. You spoke of a plan. I agreed to travel by this palanquin, only in the hopes of hearing your plan.'

'Shh! It is said that even walls have ears, and a palanquin doesn't even have walls.' She silenced me.

I had always wished I hadn't been an Emperor, and the feeling was never stronger than on the morning after my trip with Mother to the shrine of the Snake God. If I were a commoner, I would not have to have an elaborate bath. I wouldn't have to exercise. I wouldn't have to wait for servants to fill up the tub, to sprinkle it with rose water, to put rose petals in the water and to massage my body. I wouldn't have to be choosy about my clothes. I wouldn't have to burden myself with jewellery. I wouldn't have to greet so many people. I wouldn't have to go for mandatory morning prayers. I wouldn't have to wait patiently, while the Brahmin priests chanted mantras.

But I wore the mantle of kingship! I had to go through all the rituals required of a king, before I could get away to meet my mother. I wanted to run to her quarters, but this again, was something I could not do. I had to walk decorously, as befitting my status.

Appaji was in my mother's quarters, when I visited.

'Welcome, Krishna,' Mother greeted me warmly. Appaji paid his respects to me formally. He was silent. I guessed that Mother must have discussed my affairs with him. I felt as if a burden had been lifted off my shoulders.

Mother smiled. 'The Prime Minister is angry with you,' she said.

'Nothing of the sort,' mumbled Appaji.

'All right. Let me put it differently. He is upset with you. He is sorry that you did not confide in him…'

Appaji then said, 'It's not just that he didn't confide in me. I've been loyal to the Emperor for years. But instead of confiding in me, the Emperor chose to confide in that girl, who is a newcomer to the palace. And to make matters worse, she is from an enemy kingdom. The Emperor has trusted her with his personal matters.'

'Appaji, it's not that I didn't trust you. But it would have embarrassed me to tell you. I can discuss affairs of the state with you. I can talk about my plans for war. But I thought that to discuss my personal matters with you would be disrespectful to you…'

'Never mind…' said Appaji. He looked a little more relaxed now. 'Your mother just told me everything. To help you is my duty…'

'Appaji has an idea,' said my mother Nagalamba. Usually, Mother referred to Appaji as Prime Minister. I guessed that her reference to him as Appaji, was to show that he was close to the royal family.

I had been nervous since waking up, and now I was even more edgy.

'Mother, didn't you say you had a plan?' I knew I could handle Mother, but Appaji wouldn't be easy to handle.

'My plan and Appaji's plan are the same, Krishna,' my mother said, with a smile. Her words did nothing to ease my tension.

Mother and Appaji gave each other a meaningful glance. 'I too am a poet, Your Majesty,' said Appaji. 'I have written poetry. I have enjoyed poetry. I know that romantic literature has greater appeal than any other kind. I can understand how you feel. I can understand your romantic feelings. It is ridiculous to lay down a rule that an Emperor should not fall in love, or that if he does, it must be with a princess. So I have no objection to your love for Chinnadevi, or your desire to marry her. There's nothing wrong with your desire…'

Appaji hadn't got to the point, but stopped after this lengthy prelude. I didn't say a word. I knew that he was preparing me for the blow that was to come.

'But there is nothing wrong with your mother's argument either. The people will not want a dancer to be their queen…'

I noticed that he didn't refer to Chinnadevi as a devadasi, but only as a dancer.

'So the point I am trying to make is…'

'Yes?'

'You should marry a princess first, to keep the people happy. We don't have to go looking for a suitable princess…'

'I know what you are going to say—"Marry Thirumala Devi, the Princess of Srirangapatnam." I knew it. I knew that you would say that. Mother, let me tell you. There is no place for anyone in my affections, but Chinnadevi.'

Appaji smiled.

'Did I say you had to give Thirumala Devi a place in your affections?' he said, not in the least perturbed by my outburst. 'I only asked you to marry her and make her your Queen. Let her be your first wife. You can then marry Chinnadevi, or anyone else of your choice. Who is going to object?'

'Appaji, I am not willing to a part of such dramas. I cannot love one woman, but marry another.'

'Krishna, listen to Appaji patiently,' Mother chided me.

'You also have to think of the welfare of the Empire,' said Appaji.

'Are you trying to tell me that the welfare of the Empire lies in my marrying Thirumala Devi?'

'Yes, Your Majesty,' said Appaji. 'Qutub Shahi, the Sultan of Golconda, and Nizam Shahi, the Sultan of Ahmednagar, have sent word to Adil Shah, the Sultan of Vijayapuram. Our spies tell me that they are planning to sink their differences and enter into a pact of friendship. In a few days, Farid Shah, the Sultan of Bidar and Imad Shahi, the Sultan of Berar, too are likely to join them. The Kalinga King, Prataparudra Gajapati may join them too. In order to prevent all this, we have to march against Adil Shah. War is impending, Your Majesty, and in this war, we will need the help of many minor kings, including that of the ruler of Srirangapatnam…'

I laughed angrily. 'After the Ummatur expedition, Sivasamudram and Srirangapatnam came under our control. We appointed some of our relatives as our representatives in the conquered territories. Have those insignificant people now become kings? Has the Vijayanagar Empire been reduced to the pathetic state of having to beg them for help?'

'Your Majesty, you are talking of the situation four years ago. Today, none of those rulers is insignificant. There still remain some vestiges of loyalty in them. But each of them is an important and powerful ruler in his territory. If you add up the armed forces at the disposal of each of these small rulers, it will surpass the numbers in our army. So it is important that we enlist the support of every one of these rulers. This is a marriage of convenience, of necessity. You have to marry Thirumala Devi, for the good of the Empire…'

I got up, even as Appaji was explaining the situation to me. The truth was bitter.

☙

Ever since I had met my mother and Appaji, my mind had been in a state of upheaval, like a lotus pond an elephant had stepped into and caused havoc. I felt I would go mad, if I didn't turn my thoughts towards something else.

I thought I would visit the dance hall and see the work in progress. As I walked towards the dance hall, I remembered that for the last few days, I hadn't heard the sound of men at work there. I used to be woken up by the sound of the chisels. And I would go to bed, to the sound of stones being moved. I had been so preoccupied with my worries, that for the last three or four days, I had not wondered about the silence in the dance hall.

As I walked towards the dance hall, I met dance guru Lakshmi Narayana. He greeted me.

'I am the one who should pay respects to you. You are my guru,' I said, trying to be cheerful. I've heard it said that one should try to be cheerful when one felt miserable, and that the pretense would soon result in one becoming really cheerful.

He gave me a sad smile. 'Are things proceeding according to my plan?' I asked him.

'Yes, yes,' he said disinterestedly.

I thought he was upset about something. With a view to cheering him up, I asked, 'Where is your disciple, Muthu? Is he asleep?'

'Your Majesty, I was on my way to meet you, to tell you about Muthu,' said Lakshmi Narayana. I could tell from the sadness in his tone, that something was amiss.

'Why? What is the matter? What has happened to him?' I asked.

'In the temple where Lord Siva dances...'

'You mean Chidambaram?'

'Yes. It is said that Kulottunga Chola had his sculptors carve many dance sculptures in the Chidambaram temple. Muthu felt that if he visited Chidambaram, he would get some ideas for our dance hall.'

Why was Lakshmi Narayana talking in the past tense about

Muthu? I was worried. I didn't want to interrupt, and waited for the dance guru to continue.

'I told him that if we told you, you would make arrangements for us to go to Chidambaram and that I too would accompany him. But he said that he didn't want to trouble you.'

Past tense again!

'What has happened to him? Tell me,' I said, forgetting for a minute that he was my teacher and that I should speak more respectfully to him.

'He left for Chidambaram last week, without even taking leave of me.'

'Alone?'

'No. There were a group of merchants and pilgrims bound for Chidambaram. He went along with them.'

'That was a wise thing to do...' I said.

'That was wise of him. I agree. But he did something foolish. He took his wife with him. She's very young. They've been married for a year.'

He then called out, 'Solai, come here.'

Only then I noticed a girl in the corridor. She had been standing behind a pillar, half hidden by it.

'Come here, Solai. Don't be afraid,' said Lakshmi Narayana. She was weeping. She fell at my feet, and sobbed, without raising her head.

'Get up. What happened? Please tell me,' I said. But instead of answering me, the girl ran back to the pillar behind which she had been hiding.

'Solai, wait.' Lasksmi Narayana said to her. He dragged her from behind the pillar. But she averted her gaze.

I was shocked when I saw her hands. She had been branded with hot iron rods. There were two lines crossing each other, like the multiplication sign. And that added to my shock, for that was how a woman who had committed adultery would be branded. If a woman were believed to be immoral, people of her caste would cast her out from their clan and brand her in this fashion.

But this girl, Muthu's wife, what had she done?

Twenty-one

I was anguished when I saw the unhealed wounds on the young girl's hands, and thought of the implication of those marks.

Muthu was an energetic young man, respectful towards his elders. The fact that he was missing was bad enough. But why had his wife been tortured so? She looked like an innocent child…

Lakshmi Narayana was as upset as I was.

'What is happening here?' I asked him.

'I had a very difficult time getting this girl to tell me what had happened. As far I as I could gather, this girl and her husband, together with a few others, set off for Chidambaram. Somewhere between Kanchipuram and Thiruvannamalai, they were set upon by bandits. It was early in the morning. It was still quite dark. I don't know why they had to leave Kanchi so early…The bandits were armed with knives, spears and scythes. As for these travellers they were unarmed. Yet, they put up a brave fight using whatever they could lay their hands on—stones, sticks…'

Lakshmi Narayana paused for breath. The girl, meanwhile had run off to hide behind the pillar. But I could hear her crying.

'The bandits took away the belongings of the travellers. Muthu and a few others gave chase, while the rest decided to return home. Muthu asked his wife to go back home, telling her that he would come after capturing the thieves. But he hasn't come back.'

'But what about these marks on her hands?' I felt very bad about asking him why the girl had been branded.

'When the elders in her community heard that she and her husband had been attacked by robbers, they suspected her morality. They felt she might have had a liaison with the robbers. So they've branded her and cast her out of their clan…'

I was furious. 'Is it possible for every girl to prove her chastity by walking through fire, the way Sita did?' I asked. I said to her, 'Don't worry. I will find Muthu and bring him back to you.' I asked the palace administrator to give the girl some work in the women's quarters of the palace.

Solai fell at my feet again, and took leave of me.

Lakshmi Narayana too took leave of me.

I sent for Jangamaiyya. 'Are our roads so unsafe for travel? How wonderfully you administer the Empire! Even if you can't make the journey of travellers easy, can't you at the very least make their journey safe?' I asked angrily.

'Don't be angry, Your Majesty. We do our best to keep the roads safe for travellers. But these bandits are very clever. They mingle with the travellers, and it becomes difficult to tell who is a bandit and who is a genuine traveller...' said Jangamaiah.

'These are the sort of lame excuses given by incompetent people,' I said. 'The Vijayanagar Empire is capable of waging war against powerful kings, and defeating them. But it is a matter of shame that it is incapable of capturing a few bandits.'

'Your Majesty... It is...I mean...'

'Please go away.... Let me think of a solution to this problem.'

I paced up and down pensively. The words of Appaji and my mother kept haunting me. They had argued that for a king to place his love above the welfare of his kingdom was wrong. But then to give up one's love for the sake of enjoying the advantages of kingship, was worse.

I looked out through the window. A squirrel was running up a tree, and a bird came swooping down. The squirrel scampered to safety, and when the bird flew away, the squirrel climbed up the tree again. But the bird came back, and again, the squirrel raced down the tree. I felt my position wasn't very different from that of the squirrel. If I tried to banish thoughts of Chinnadevi, I was troubled by thoughts of Thirumala Devi. If I tried to forget Thirumala Devi, thoughts of Chinnadevi began to torment me. And if I stopped thinking of either of the two women, then thoughts of the Bahmani Sultans came to the fore.

A guard entered my chambers and said, 'Your Majesty, minister Vadamalaiannan is here. He wants to know if he can have an audience with you now.'

I was about to say, 'Not now,' but checked myself.

Vadamalaiannan was a Tamilian from Thondai Nadu. I wanted to give some representation to Tamil Nadu in my administrative set-up, and for that reason, I had made Vadamalaiannan a minister. He kept me informed about the situation in Tamil Nadu. He was a scholar, who, in his spare time taught me Tamil literature.

But...

Vadamalaiannan was one of Appaj's close friends. So I was afraid that he might have been sent by Appaji to try and convince me to marry Thirumala Devi. At the same time, I couldn't summarily dismiss one of my ministers. And it was certainly not right to send him a message through a guard, refusing him permission to meet me.

So I decided that I would listen to him patiently, and then do just as I pleased.

'Ask him to come in,' I said to the guard.

Vadamalaiannan was accompanied by his brother Haridasa, who was a Tamil poet. A few days ago, Haridasa had given me a book written by him titled *Iru Samaya Vilakkam*—an explanation of two religions. He had asked me for my opinion about the book.

This poet had been taking up a lot of my time recently. That was a result of the respect with which I treated the poet, Allasani Peddanna.

Allasani was the author of the brilliant work, *Manucharitam*. It was an adaptation of the *Markandeya Purana*. He had dedicated the work to me. When he came to the palace, to show me his work, I honoured him. I fell at his feet and took his blessings, and adorned his wrist with a diamond-studded bracelet. I asked him to get into a palanquin and I was myself a palanquin bearer, carrying the palanquin some distance. One day, I seated him beside me on the royal elephant. This was my way of showing my appreciation for his contribution to Telugu literature.

As a result, Telugu poets, Tamil poets, Sanskrit poets—why even Arabian and Persian poets—began to come to me to show me what they had written. Since I had the reputation of being a monarch who promoted literary endeavour, I wanted to live up to the reputation. So I never sent any poet away empty-handed. I gave every one of them a gift.

Haridasa was one such poet. He had the added advantage of being the brother of a minister.

At first, I thought I would just talk to him for a few minutes, out of courtesy, and then send him away with a gift. But I changed my mind, and thought I would share my thoughts on his work with him. I saw this as an opportunity to forget my worries for a while.

I am sure those of you who are now reading my account, would have heard of Haridasa's work. It has more than 2000 verses, and it sets forth the tenets of both Saivism and Vaishnavism. It takes the form of a debate between two young women.

One of the girls is called Aranavalli. She is a Saivite. The other is called Agamavalli, and she is a Vaishnavite. If the Saivite girl completed her verse with a praise of Siva, the Vaishnavite girl completed her verse with a praise of Vishnu. They indulged in friendly arguments about their respective faiths.

'Tirumalaiyappa, I read your work. It was easy to understand. It wasn't like reading poetry, but was like reading simple prose,' I said. Tirumalaiyappa was Haridasa's real name. Haridasa was a moniker he had acquired because he served in Vishnu temples.

The poet was very happy that I had used his real name. He was even more happy to hear his work praised. 'I am honoured to receive such praise from the Emperor,' he said.

'But I want to make a point. Although your title gives one the impression that you are talking about two religions, there is an unmistakable tilt towards the Vaishnava religion,' I said.

The poet gave an apologetic smile, and said, 'Maybe…I am a Vaishnavite, who serves in Vaishnava temples. So naturally…'

'I also suspect that it might have been an attempt to please me, since I am a Vaishnavite myself,' I teased. But I didn't tease him further, because I felt it was wrong to treat poets disrespectfully. So I changed the subject and said, 'I suppose you have come to ask for donations for some Vaishnava temple. Am I right?'

Vadamalaiyannan laughed. 'This time my brother has not come to ask for any donations.'

'I have been here for a long time. I want to return to my village. I have come to take leave of you,' said Haridasa.

'If I remember right, your village is Arikandapuram in Thondai Nadu,' I said. Haridasa beamed. I've noticed that whether it is a king or a commoner, mention of their village or town makes them melt.

'I'm not going directly to Arikandapuram this time. I plan to go to Srirangam first,' said Haridasa.

The moment he mentioned a long journey, my thoughts went to Muthu and his young wife Solai.

'Will you be passing through Kanchi, Thriuvannamalai, Chidambaram…?' I asked.

'For now, that remains the best route to take. We are in the process of planning bigger roads,' explained Vadamalaiannan.

'I heard that travellers on that route are attacked by bandits,' I said.

Vadamalaiannan could not deny it. Haridasa said, 'There is nothing to fear, if you travel in a group.'

'Really? How many of you plan to travel?' I asked.

'Five,' replied Haridasa.

'You are a special poet. So I suppose you are going to travel by palanquin?' I asked. Special poets were the only ones who had the right to travel by palanquin.

'No. When all the others are going to be walking, it wouldn't be right for me to take a palanquin.'

'When are you leaving?'

'Tomorrow evening.'

'Fifteen people will join your group,' I said.

'Who are they?'

'I don't know who they are. But they came to me asking me if I could suggest suitable escorts. I told them that if someone travelled, I would let them know. They will join you tomorrow. But you mustn't ask them any questions,' I said.

Minister Vadamalaiannan looked at me suspiciously. He could guess that I had some secret plan. I didn't want to give him a chance to ask me any question. So I said, 'I suppose you will be leaving from the rest house in the capital. They will join you there.' I rose. They knew that that was my way of telling them that they had to leave. They took leave of me.

After they had left, I sent for Jangamaiah.

'Tomorrow evening, fifteen people are going to take the Kanchi, Tiruvannamalai road. I will be one of the fifteen. You will be one. The remaining thirteen should be strong young men,' I said.

'Your Majesty, you…why?' Jangamaiah said hesitantly.

'Don't ask me questions. Do as I say. Every one of the men should carry huge sacks. It must seem as if the sacks contain vessels and clothes. But the sacks should have swords, knives, scimitars and spears. Choose reliable men. We will all be in disguise. Keep this a secret.'

He understood the reason for my secret arrangement. 'Why should you trouble yourself to capture the bandits, who waylay travelers?' he asked.

'It doesn't seem as if the Emperor's men are troubling themselves to go after the bandits. So the Emperor has to do it himself,' I said.

Jangamaiah did not fail to notice the sternness in my voice.

'As you command, Your Majesty,' he said.

'Tell only the Queen and the Prime Minister about our trip. If they object, tell them that I am adamant. Don't tell anyone else,' I warned him. He left to make arrangements for our trip.

I had been telling myself that morning, that if I did not turn my thoughts towards some work, I would go mad. And now here was something I could do.

Twenty-two

Jangamaiah said that we would have to leave at least by noon the next day, so that we would be able to cross the Pennar river before nightfall. We were to spend the night in a rest house, and take the Kanchi-Thiruvannamalai road the next morning.

'It's a tiring journey…If you were to fall ill, I will be blamed. You don't want me to tell anyone about the trip, and that too is worrying,' said Jangamaiah.

'My health will not suffer, and if it will set your mind at rest, I am prepared to give you a signed disclaimer that in case the Emperor falls ill, Jangamaiah is not to be held responsible. Will that do?' I laughed.

Since I had to leave by noon, I had to finish all the pending work in the morning. The official who kept track of my appointments said that the Governor of Ikkeri was to be flogged that evening.

'Is he an important man?' I asked.

'Yes. Apart from the fact that he is an influential governor, he is also the brother-in-law of Minister Ayyaparasu,' the official said.

'All right. If he hasn't arrived yet, then reschedule the flogging for another day. I have something important to attend to this evening. In fact, I don't want to be disturbed for the next four or five days,' I said to the official.

These floggings were embarrassing. Governors who did not pay taxes, especially the ones who were suspected of having plotted against the empire, would be sent for, with the message that the Emperor wished to see them. They would come expecting a warm welcome and gifts from the Emperor. The governors would arrive in style, in a palanquin, surrounded by men on horseback, with musical instruments announcing their arrival.

There is a part of the palace grounds, where there is a pavilion set aside for the purpose of flogging offenders and defaulters. The governor would be taken there and asked to take off his clothes, and a man would pick up the whip. Realising what was to follow, the governor would fall at my feet, apologise and promise to pay taxes. No one would be present at the pavilion, except me and the man with the whip.

If the person to be whipped was not a man of high status, then he would be whipped by the palace servant appointed for this purpose. If he was an important personage, then it would be disrespectful if a servant were allowed to whip him. In such cases, I would execute the punishment myself.

I never relished whipping anyone. But the welfare of the Empire is at stake and it would be improper of me to shy away from punishing those who act against the interest of the country. My predecessors had followed the tradition of flogging offenders, and I could not go against convention. But I was glad that my pending trip had for the time being saved me from this onerous duty.

Jangamaiah came to my room and gave me clothes for my disguise. I sent away the servants, closed the door and began to put on the disguise. I stuck on a false moustache and false beard. There is a secret passage that leads from my room to the road outside the palace. I took this passage and reached the main road.

Jangamaiah, the handpicked guards, Haridasa and his friends also came to the rest house.

There were a few others already in the rest house, and three of them were women. Two of the women said they were going to visit their sons. The third woman was there with her husband, who told me why they were going to Thiruvannamalai.

'Last week, my wife picked up betel leaves with her left hand. That is a great sin, isn't it? So to atone for that, she has to bathe in the temple tank in Thiruvannamalai,' the man said.

Some people may dismiss this as silly superstition, but I was surprised at the hold such beliefs had over people.

There were twenty-three of us at the rest house. Except for the men whom Jangamaiah had brought along, the rest were middle-aged.

There was an orthodox old man in the group. He had a bag made of silk, which he hugged to himself. Even when we rested, he didn't let go of the bag, but used it as a pillow. I wondered what precious thing it contained, for him to be so careful about it.

It was time for us to depart. A man came running towards the rest house, calling out to us 'Please wait for me. I heard that a party of pilgrims was bound for Tiruvannamalai. Please let me come with you.' It was obvious that he was a devotee of Lord Siva.

'Is this your first visit to Thiruvannamalai?' Haridasa asked him.

'I go to Thiruvannamalai once a year. I've been there many times. But I've never travelled alone. I always join a group of pilgrims,' the newcomer said.

'Are you familiar with the route to Thiruvannamalai?' one of the men in our party asked.

'Of course. I can show you the way,' the newcomer said.

We all left the rest house. One of the pilgrims said, with a smile, 'I am glad there are so many of us. No bandit will dare attack us.'

'That's what he thinks,' Jangamaiah whispered to me. 'Your Majesty, I don't trust the man who joined us in the last minute. Even the rudraksha beads he is wearing are fakes.'

'Do your eyes have some special power to be able to detect all that? Please come quietly,' I warned him.

'Another thing I notice, Your Maj...' he remembered my warning and checked himself. 'Another thing I notice is that he hasn't spoken much since we left. I think he is afraid that he will be caught out if he speaks too much.'

I was now worried because of Jangamaiah's warning.

I slowed down a bit, because I was deep in thought. Jangamaiah turned to see what was keeping me. 'You keep walking. I'll catch up with you,' I said to him. The three women were carrying the luggage they had brought along, while their husbands walked unhampered by any luggage. They thought, perhaps, that it was beneath their dignity to carry their luggage.

༄

We were entering the city of Kanchipuram. There was a Jain matha there. Irusappa, who built a Jain temple in Vijayanagar, constructed this matha too. The matha was called the Vardhamana temple. Next to the matha was a house, where we saw quite a crowd. Enquiries revealed that a widow was starving herself to death.

I peeped into the house. A very young girl was lying on the floor. She was on the verge of death.

Some Jains follow this tradition. It is like Sati, but here the widows starve themselves to death. They don't think of death as something unavoidable, but as something one should welcome. For the first few days, after they decide to give up their lives by starving, they eat as they usually do. Then they switch to liquids. After sometime, they take only water. Then they give up water too. They believe that if they die through starvation, moksha is guaranteed.

I was surprised by the look of determination I saw on the girl's face. Further down the street, a group of girls was playing.

They must have been about fifteen years old. They had colourful sticks in their hands. Two girls would team up, striking each other's sticks. One girl hit her companion's stick so hard, that it flew out of her hand and came whizzing towards me. I caught it. The girl came running to me and laughed, and said, 'I am sorry.' She took the stick from me and went back to her game.

I couldn't get the song sung by the girls out of my mind, and along came an idea, about how to confirm my suspicions about the Saivite devotee who had joined us at the last minute.

We went to Ekamabareswara temple, Varadarajaswamy temple and Kamakshi Amman temple. I determined that I would soon visit these temples as Emperor, make generous grants to the temples, and initiate construction activities in the temples, and also carry out repairs.

We then proceeded towards Thiruvannamalai. We spent the night in a rest house. 'I will wake you all up early in the morning, so that we can reach the Thiruvannamalai temple before noon,' said the Saivite.

'All right,' said all the other pilgrims.

We sat down for dinner. Food was not served on plantain leaves or on plates. There was a smoothly polished stone platform. Holes had been scooped out in the platform. Those who could afford to pay more chose to sit before the larger holes. Those who couldn't, sat before the smaller holes. Vegetable curries, gravies and curd would be served in the larger holes. The poorer travellers would be served only rice and a gravy in the small holes.

Jangamaiah had brought a lot of money. So he could afford to pay for a 'big holes' dinner. I am a good eater, and so I always eat a big meal. Jangamaiah watches me sadly, when I eat in these rest houses. He cannot bear to see his Emperor eating such simple fare. On such occasions I console him with just a smile.

After dinner, we sat on the pyol. But we didn't go to sleep. Some people talked about themselves. Some people sang songs. I treated both the Saiva and Vaishnava religions with equal respect, but because I was a Vaishnavite, I knew more of the works of the Azhvars, and knew only one or two of the more popular verses of the Nayanmars. Now was the time to put my plan into action. I sang one of the verses of the Nayanmars that I knew, but didn't complete it. I said I had forgotten the lines. One of the women pilgrims offered to complete the verse, but I said I would prefer to hear the Saivite recite it and also explain the meaning of the verse.

'Please, explain the verse to me,' I requested the Saivite.

He laughed and said, 'It's ages since I read these verses. I can't remember now.'

'You are a young man. I am sure if you try, you can recall the verse.'

'No, no. I am unable to recall the verse. Why don't we all go to bed? We have to get up early tomorrow,' he said, and turned abruptly away from me.

'All right. You complete the verse,' I said to the woman pilgrim.

She completed the verse. 'Exactly. Those are the lines. Now I too am able to recall the lines,' I said.

Anyway, my plan had worked. The verse I had pretended I couldn't recall completely, was a very well-known one, and if I, whose mother tongue was Telugu, knew it, how could a Tamilian and that too one who claimed he was a staunch Saivite not know it? This was enough to confirm my suspicion that the man was a fraud.

Jangamaiah looked at me and I gave him a meaningful smile.

We all went to bed, and soon we were fast asleep.

'Get up. Get up all of you. It's going to be dawn soon. We have to leave,' that was the impostor's voice.

Everyone got up and prepared to leave. I looked out. It was very dark. I could tell by looking at the stars that it was not dawn yet, but midnight. So why was the man saying it was dawn? He was up to some trick. I could see that and so could Jangamaiah. He signalled to his men to be ready for any eventuality.

Twenty-three

There is a Telugu proverb that says, 'Don't believe everything you hear. Don't talk about everything you believe.'

Jangamaiah and I had not mentioned our suspicions about the Saiva devotee to anyone. We kept our suspicions to ourselves. Jangamaiah's men loosened the ropes tied around the mouths of the sacks they carried. All they had to do now was to give the ropes a tug, and the sacks would open, making it easy for them to pull out their weapons from the sacks.

'I know of a short cut. If we take that short cut, we will reach a rest house, where we can have our bath and have some food. If we leave now, we will be able to reach Thiruvannamalai by noon,' said the impostor. The path he pointed to was a narrow one lined with dense bushes on both sides.

We all followed him along this path.

'This path is very dark,' complained one of the women.

'All the paths will be dark now. Just be patient for a while. It will not be dark, once the sun comes up,' the man said.

I looked up at the sky. It was obvious that dawn was several hours away.

'Yesterday night, a man from this village met me. He said that some travellers employed archers, to protect them on their journey. The archers lead the way, with their bows in readiness. If bandits see the armed men, they won't attack the travellers. He asked me if we needed the help of some archers, who, if we pay them, will accompany us till Thiruvannamalai,' said Haridasa.

'And what did you say to that?' I asked.

'I told him that we didn't need archers to protect us, because the people in our group were not rich, and that we possessed nothing of value to interest the bandits.'

The impostor said, 'Why should you be afraid when I am here to protect you? Don't be afraid. I will escort you all safely to Thiruvannamalai.'

Jangamaiah and I smiled to ourselves. There were palm groves on both sides. It was a starry night and the path was clear in some places. In the city, only the wealthy wore footwear, but because we were walking a long distance, all the travellers had footwear. Most of them were wearing footwear made of wood. My men and I and a few others were wearing footwear made of leather.

Jangamaiah and I were bringing up the rear. 'How can one man dare to attack so many of us?' I asked Jangamaiah.

'This man is not operating alone. He is part of a big gang,' said Jangamaiah. 'He will deliberately lead us along the wrong path. When he reaches a particular place, he will whistle to announce our arrival there. His accomplices will come out of hiding and attack us. He is now taking us along the wrong path.'

I looked round. If we were approaching Thiruvannamalai, I should have been able to see a small hillock and a temple on it. I had travelled around these parts many times, as a soldier. I didn't know what that hillock was called, or what temple it was. But the path this man was taking us along was away from that hillock, for I couldn't see any hillock from where we were.

'Sometimes governors themselves organise groups of men to attack travellers,' Jangamaiah said.

'I think I should not be lagging behind. I should be in the first row of pilgrims,' I said.

'There are so many of us. Why should you?'

'Jangamaiah, you must have seen me when I led our troops. My tent is always the first one, and all the tents of the generals are put up behind mine. That is not just to prove that I am not a coward. It is also because I want to know the movement of the enemies, before others do. In the same way, I now want to be the one to lead the group,' I said, and before moving forward, I told Jangamaiah that his men were not pick up their weapons until I gave them the signal to do so.

I walked alongside the impostor. He was very dark, and he had applied a lot of holy ash on his body, perhaps to keep people from suspecting him.

'We know nothing about you. What was your name before you became a Saivite mendicant?' I asked.

'What does it matter what my name was? People call me Sengodan. You can call me that, if you want to,' he said.

'How did you know of this short cut? Do you have relatives in this area?'

'To a mendicant everyone is a relative,' he replied evasively.

'That is true,' I said, pretending to agree with him. The path was surrounded by rocks and bushes, which could easily conceal the robbers.

When we reached a place where the vegetation was dense, Sengodan stopped, and gave a shrill whistle.

The travellers panicked and said, 'Who was that who whistled? What is happening?'

'Stop, all of you,' shouted four men, who rushed from behind the bushes.

Sengodan pretended that he didn't know who they were. 'Who are you?' he asked the men. 'I am afraid they are robbers. I am afraid I have brought you all along the wrong path,' he said to us.

'Oh my God! Thieves! Robbers!' shouted one of the women, and her husband put his arms round her and told her not to be afraid.

Jangamaiah came close to me waiting for me to give a signal.

'I suspect that there might be more men in hiding. We must flush them all out,' I whispered to him.

'Move out of the way. We will give you nothing,' I said to the bandits.

'Oh you won't? We will make you give us all that you have,' said one of the robbers and whistled. Four more men came out from behind the bushes.

The orthodox man who carried a silk bag with him said, 'Let me take the picture of my favourite deity and the vessels I use for worship. You can have everything else.'

I was moved by his devotion.

Haridasa and a few others flung their bags into the bushes, hoping to retrieve them after the robbers left.

One of the pilgrims said, 'Please don't harm the women. We will ask them to remove all their jewels and give them to you.'

The women were wailing. Some of the more timid men were also begging the robbers to spare them. Some others looked behind them to see if they could run away, but the path was so dark, they couldn't see clearly. One of the women said, 'How can you attack innocent people? Your families will pay for your sins.'

Of what use were such curses? As if such curses would deter the bandits!

'Don't be afraid. Don't run away. I will deal with these men,' I called out.

The bandits had assumed that the travellers would be too scared to put up a fight and would hand over their possessions to the robbers. Hearing my challenge, they pounced on me. I signalled to Jangamaiah, and in a trice, my men were upon them, wielding swords and spears. Jangamaiah also joined the fight.

The robbers numbered nine, and they were untrained. My men were fifteen in number and were all men trained in handling weapons. They were expert swordsmen. They ensured that none of the robbers could escape. The robbers were cut to pieces, and the path was red with their blood. I noticed Sengodan running away.

I didn't want to let him get away. So I asked Janagamaiah to take care of the remaining robbers and I ran after Sengodan.

Chasing Sengodan wasn't easy. Night was yielding place to dawn, but it still wasn't bright enough for me to see the path clearly. Sengodan was used to the area, but I was new to the place. He was familiar with all the paths. He was able to put some distance between us. But I didn't give up. I didn't lose sight of him, and continued to run after him.

After I had run for some distance, the path joined a broad thoroughfare. We had reached some town. Which town was this? Where did this road lead to? It was too early in the morning for anyone to be out on the road. So I could ask no one about the town.

I went down this road, and found a smaller street branch off from the broad road. This street was lined with trees. There were no houses on the street, except a huge mansion at the end of the street. I saw Sengodan run into the mansion.

'Sengodan is a man who leads innocent, unsuspecting travellers to a place where robbers can rob them. It is impossible for him to live in such a huge mansion. If he takes refuge in this mansion, then it means that the owner of the mansion is the mastermind of the attacks on travellers,' I thought. I too ran into the mansion. The man on guard at the entrance was still half-asleep. I pushed him aside and ran into the house.

Lamps lit the previous night had used up all the oil and the flames had died down. The ante room with its curtains, and mirrors and teak doors proclaimed the wealth of the owner of the mansion. There were two doors on either side of the ante room. I opened the door to the left. I expected that Sengodan or someone else would be lying in wait for me. So I had my sword ready.

I opened it just a little, and saw that it was a bedroom. There was a young man on a cot. A woman was resting her head on his chest. I couldn't see their faces.

In any case, I felt I had no business being there. It may be the house of an enemy, but even so, to disturb two people who were enjoying an intimate moment seemed indecent. So I closed the door silently, and opened the door to the right. That too was a bedroom. There was a sixty-year-old-man on the cot there. He must have heard me enter. Or perhaps he didn't sleep soundly, on account of his age.

The moment I entered, he asked, 'Who is it?' and tried to pick up his sword which was beside his cot. But I didn't allow him to lay his hands on it. I pushed him down, and put my foot on his chest. 'Where is your man, Sengodan? Tell me now. Otherwise...'

It was only then that I saw his face, and cried out, 'You?' I was shocked, for he was a governor. His name was Singapiran. He had been appointed to oversee the maintenance of temples and temple tanks, and also to maintain peace in the area. Every year, on New Year's Day, he would come to the capital and pay his respects to me.

I remembered what Jangamaiah had said about some governors themselves organising bands of men to rob travellers. I was so taken aback, that for a minute I lowered my guard. He used that fraction of a second to push me off. I landed on my back, and he picked up his sword and would have cut off my head. But I was saved by a young man who ran in, pushed Singapiran down and said, 'Your Majesty, cut off his head now.'

When I heard the words, 'Your Majesty,' I turned round and saw Muthu there! The sculptor Muthu!

Where had he come from, and how? But before I could find answers to my questions, I wanted to kill the governor. I drew my sword to cut off his head. But the governor, who now knew who I was, begged me to spare his life.

'I cannot spare your life,' I said angrily to him.

'Your Majesty, if you spare my life, I can tell you something you want to know.'

'I do not need your help.'

'Your Majesty, I can tell you where Chinnadevi is!' he said.

I dropped my sword.

Twenty-four

When I heard Singapiran mention the name that occupied my thoughts every second, I dropped the sword. Now Singapiran was going to tell me about Chinnadevi! Now! My very life—my Chinnadevi! In my excitement, I forgot that the hand of Fate is sure and unfailing. I was a fool, who forgot that all things happen according to the plans of the Almighty.

Life is cruel. It never lets foolishness go unpunished, and my foolishness too was punished. The moment I dropped my sword, a hard blow fell on Singapiran's head. 'You rogue, Singapiran. How dare you try to attack the Emperor?' Jangamaiah! He dealt Singapiran another blow.

'Stop! Stop!' I said and pushed him aside, and if I hadn't done so, the third blow would have killed Singapiran. Jangamaiah's blows hadn't killed him, but blood was pouring out of a deep gash on his head. He fell unconscious. Singapiran was an old man and Jangamaiah was a trained warrior.

I tore off a curtain and bandaged the wound.

'Muthu! Is there a physician nearby? Quick. Lift him and take him to a physician,' I said.

Jangamaiah realised that he had done something wrong. But he didn't know what it was.

It was wrong to blame him. He had killed all the robbers, and coming here in search of me, he had seen Singapiran about to strike me. Naturally, he had feared I was in danger, and had dealt Singapiran a huge blow.

I looked at Singapiran. His eyes were closed. The bandage was drenched with blood. He was still breathing. But I wasn't sure how long he would be alive.

It was now morning, and the events of the previous night seemed like a nightmare.

Even a person who is on his death bed feels a little better when the darkness of the night yields place to dawn. I too felt more energetic now. Besides, the servants in the mansion attended to our needs respectfully, now that they knew who we were. Since they knew I was the Emperor, it was more fear than respect that they felt. There was a girl in the ante room. I guessed that she must have been the girl I had seen in the company of a young man. But where was the man who had been in bed with her? He must have run off! The coward!

Singapiran was carried away by four able-bodied men.

Haridasa could take some liberties with me, because he was a poet. He said softly to me, 'You said some pilgrims would join us. And I believed you. I didn't for a moment think that you yourself would accompany us. Should you expose yourself to such danger?'

I was moved by his affection and concern for me. 'Isn't this my duty?' I asked him.

'Tell the men here to make arrangements for our stay,' I said to Jangamaiah.

Jangamaiah still didn't know why I had been so keen that Singapiran's life be spared.

Muthu stayed back, in case I needed some help. I decided that I would ask him the question that had been bothering me for some time. 'Muthu, who was that girl standing in the ante room?'

'Singapiran's wife. He is an old man, but has married such a young girl.'

I was taken aback. 'But I saw her in bed with a young man,' I said.

'That was…that was…'

'Yes?'

'Your Majesty, it is not something I can talk to you about,' Muthu said.

'There is nothing that an Emperor should not know. Tell me, who was that man?'

'That was I.'

'What do you mean? Your wife is crying her heart out for you. She has been cast out by the elders in your community, and she has been branded an adulteress. And here you are in the embrace of another woman. And that too another man's wife! Aren't you ashamed of yourself?' I asked angrily.

'Your Majesty, please listen to me patiently. I adore my wife Solai. I swear on the love I have for her, that it is not as you imagine.'

'Then what was this drama all about?'

'It was indeed a drama, Your Majesty. I too took the same path that you took today. Singapiran's men surrounded me. When Singapiran knew that I was a sculptor working in the palace, he asked me all sorts of questions. He wanted to know about your palace—where your rooms were, where the rooms of the others were, where secret passages in the palace were. He said he would let me off if I gave him all these details. I know nothing about the layout of the palace. And even assuming I did, would I tell an enemy? I refused to answer his questions. So he locked me up in a room here.'

'Still, what is the connection of Singapiran's wife with this story?'

Muthu bent his head down, and looked at me through the corner of his eyes. 'It's not something Your Majesty can't guess…'

'There are lots of things I don't know. So go on and tell me…'

'You know what happens when young girls are forced to

marry older men. They ache for the embrace of a young man. I am not good-looking. But, but…she was attracted to me. She set me free without the knowledge of her husband. I pretended to reciprocate her feelings, because I thought I could somehow escape from this mansion. I am speaking the truth. I swear. That was when I heard your voice…'

'And you came and saved me,' I smiled. I was sorry that I had misjudged him.

'Please don't say I saved you. You are the Emperor who protects thousands of people.'

Muthu took leave of me. I guessed he wanted to ask Jangamaiah about his wife Solai.

I sent for the officer in charge of security in that area. He was responsible for enforcing law and order, and for arresting criminals. These security officers were paid by the local governors. He had as much power and responsibility here as Jangmaiah had in the capital.

By now news that the Emperor had come in person to deal with the robbers and had also arrested the governor, who was the chief of a gang of robbers, had spread in the city.

The security officer came in with great trepidation. Although I wasn't in my royal robes, I had removed the false moustache and beard. So he could recognize me.

'Your Majesty! Forgive me,' he said, and fell at my feet.

'Get up. What have you done wrong? Nothing,' I said. But he did not fail to notice the mockery in my tone. He shook with fear.

'You have done nothing wrong. As the master, so the servant. You were your master's partner in crime. You waylaid unsuspecting travellers, and robbed them of their belongings. You gave the governor his share and took your share too. That is not wrong at all.'

I was not prepared to forgive him. I summoned Jangamaiah's men and said, 'Deal with him appropriately.' That was enough for them to carry out the usual punishment. They would either cut off his head. Or cut off a leg and a hand.

He screamed as he was dragged away. 'Your Majesty, please spare me. I admit I did wrong. But the road from Kanchi to Thiruvannamalai is not a good one. There are not enough men to patrol the road. Nor are there enough buildings to house security men on that road.'

'People should be able to travel without fear, even in the absence of any kind of security. People should feel safe in my country. The Persian ambassador told me that even at midnight women could walk alone in the streets of Vijayanagar, even if they were wearing jewellery. Do you know how proud his words made me? If this country has governors like Singapiran and security officials like this man, what will happen to this country?' I said to Jangamaiah.

The village physician to whom Singapiran had been taken, came to meet me. He was about eighty years old. 'I have stopped the bleeding. But I don't know if he will survive. I think it is advisable to take him to the capital and let the physicians there have a look at him,' he said.

'Arrange for a bullock cart for Singapiran,' I said to Jangamaiah. Singapiran could not be taken on horseback. The Pandyas and Cholas had used chariots for travel. But now these had been dispensed with. People either used horses, or bullock carts. Bulls and mules were used to carry heavy luggage.

The cart arrived. I gave instructions that Singapiran be taken to the palace physician.

Singapiran's words, 'I know where Chinnadevi is,' kept echoing in my ears. I prayed to all the gods that they should spare his life, so that he could tell me where Chinnadevi was.

Haridasa said he would return with me to the capital. He felt the trip had had an inauspicious beginning, and so he called off his journey. The others had left for Thiruvannamalai.

'You and Jangamaiah can ride on horseback,' he suggested.

'No. Let me walk back. This has become almost a pilgrimage.'

'People are gathering to see their Emperor,' said Jangamaiah.

'Never mind. Send out a couple of guards and tell the people to make way for me,' I said.

Jostling crowds lined both sides of the street. They were grateful that the bandits had been killed and their chief captured. Some of them fell at my feet. I greeted them and walked on.

We reached the main road. I told Jangamaiah why I had not killed Singapiran. He apologised for having spoilt everything by hurting Singapiran.

The road was in good condition, but it was a desolate area.

'It is because the area is so deserted that robbers are emboldened to waylay travellers. There is no one to come to the rescue of travellers, even if they shout themselves hoarse, calling for help,' said Muthu.

'The security officer was not far off the mark, when he said that the lack of enough men to patrol the area was a reason for robbery on this stretch. We must build more security centres and appoint more guards,' said Jangamaiah.

'Where should we build shelters to house security men? Do you have any suggestions?' I asked.

'I have an idea,' said Haridasa.

'What is it?' I asked.

'Nothing is possible without the blessings of God,' he said.

'Please elaborate.'

'Three or four years ago, I went on a pilgrimage to temples on the banks of the Tamiraparini river. The river often breached its banks and the resulting floods destroyed crops. It was also a waste of rain water. So they built dams in several places. They told me something about the dams.'

'What was that?'

'A rich man called Kanadiyan from Tirupati visited the temples in the area. He wanted to know how best to spend the money at his disposal. A sage told him to build dams that would benefit the people in the area. The sage also gifted him with a cow.'

'A cow? What for?'

'The sage told Kanadiyan to allow the cow to run along the banks of the Tamiraparani river. The sage said, 'Mark out the places where the cow rests. Take them to be God's signs about where to build dams.' The people in the area said that the rich man took the sage's advice and built dams in the places in which the cow rested,' said Haridasa.

I found the account amusing. But I didn't think it was wrong to try and find out what God's will was. So I asked Jangamaiah and Muthu to find a cow for me. They brought a girl to me and told me that she had a cow. The girl was a little afraid because she was before the king. But she was proud of the fact that her help had been sought by the Emperor himself.

The cow ambled along. The girl followed the cow and we followed her.

Wherever the cow rested, we rested too. Haridasa, Muthu and Jangamaiah marked the places where it rested. They summoned the villagers in the nearby areas and asked them to mark the place with stones. On the way, I met many villagers, but we faced no problems from them.

When we reached the capital, Muthu's wife, who had heard of our arrival, was the first to greet us. She didn't feel inhibited even though I was present. She embraced Muthu and wept copiously.

The burn injuries on her hands hadn't healed. I wanted to make some arrangements for her. But I wasn't going to talk about it now, because there was something else that I was anxious to know. I went to meet the royal physician, to find out if Singapiran had regained consciousness.

But...

Twenty-five

I said that I hurried to the physician's house. But actually, I was delayed by many things.

The city is surrounded by a fort, with seven gates to be crossed to reach the city. I made my way from the city towards the physician's house, which was in the fourth street. I had just reached the first gate, when my mother called out to me. 'Krishna,' she said and gave me a hug. Jangamaiah must have informed her of our return.

'I returned her hug and said, 'Mother, why do you sound so agitated? I have returned safe and sound.'

'I was told that a governor tried to kill you, and that Jangamaiah knocked him down.'

'I will come to your quarters later today and tell you all about my trip. Let me go now, Mother,' I said, and put her in her palanquin and sent her away.

But by then a crowd of people had gathered, with cries of 'Long live the Emperor!' An old man pushed aside the others and came to me, and said, 'For the last ten days, I've been trying to meet you. There's something important I want to tell you.'

I'd seen him in my mother's palace many times. He was an astrologer.

'Later. I don't have the time to listen to you now,' I said to him.

'Your horoscope indicates that you are going to face difficult situations…' he said, and someone from the crowd jeered, 'Old man. Why don't you check your horoscope?' The people laughed. I could hear them laugh, even as I kept walking towards the second gate.

But when I crossed the second gate, I saw Appaji and a few other ministers coming to meet me. Appaji looked worried.

The other ministers stepped aside, because they could guess that Appaji had something important to tell me. They also chased away the people who had assembled. Appaji and I were alone. This was the first time an important meeting with the Prime Minister was taking place on the streets of the city!

'What do you have to say to me, Appaji?' I asked.

Appaji lowered his voice. 'I have already discussed this with you. It is about the Sultan of Golconda and the Sultan of Ahmednagar. They had sent messengers to Vijayapuram, to propose a pact of friendship with Adil Shah, the Sultan of Vijayapuram. I think they have been successful in their mission. The Sultan of Ahmednagar is bringing his forces close to the Bheema river. When he reaches Vijayapuram, the two Sultans will establish a military camp in the place where the Bheema river joins the Krishna river. Forces from Golconda are also coming to join them. They have strengthened their forts on the borders. They have also stocked up on grains, anticipating a prolonged siege.'

I realised that Appaji's worry was legitimate.

'All right. Please proceed to the palace. I will just make a brief visit to the physician's house and join you presently,' I said.

He knew that I was anxious to find out from Singapiran where Chinnadevi was. He must have wondered why Krishnadevaraya, the king of all kings was making a fool of himself over a woman. He must also have been angry at what he must have seen as a dereliction of duty.

But what did he know about romance? He knew how to write a commentary for Agastya's *Bala Bharatam*, but he knew nothing about romance.

I crossed the fourth gate and reached the physician's house. He was waiting for me.

'Welcome, Your Majesty,' he said.

'How is Singapiran?' I asked, as I entered his house.

I couldn't find Singapiran there.

An old man, whose head had been shaved, was seated on a stool. A girl was pouring oil on his head.

'Where is Singapiran?' I asked angrily.

'There he is,' said the physician, pointing to the man on the stool. 'I am treating him.'

I was shocked. Was it really Singapiran? Yes, it was. I could hardly recognize him, because his head had been tonsured.

My second shock came when I saw his eyes. His eyes were unseeing. He just stared ahead, unaware of what was happening around him.

'His wound? What is…'

The girl, who had by now used up the oil in the cup, picked up another cup of oil, and poured that on his head.

'Your Majesty, the external wound was not a serious one. But there seems to be some internal injury.'

'And so?'

'He is not aware of what is happening around him.'

'You mean he has lost his sanity?' I asked.

'No. Not exactly. This is a different kind of problem. He isn't violent. He doesn't attack anyone. He is like a child. He has regressed. He can't talk. He seems to have lost his memory. He is unable to recall anything. He walks if we tell him to. He follows us to wherever we take him. He sits where we tell him to,' said the physician.

It seemed to me as if the pain in my heart upon hearing the physician's words, was more serious than Singapiran's wounds.

'How long will it take for him to regain his memory?' I asked.

'Hard to say. It might take a month. Or even six months.'

If it had been anyone else, I would have said the man was being punished for his sins. But I couldn't say that now. I must have committed some sin, for God was punishing me! When was Singapiran going to tell me about Chinnadevi?

When I walked to the door, I found Nadendla Gopa, Saluva Govindrasu, Ayyapparasu, Mangarasayya and other ministers waiting for me. They had come to take me to the palace for an emergency meeting of the council of ministers.

Some distance away stood Muthu and his wife, Solai. 'Both of you come to the palace this evening,' I said to Muthu.

What a disappointment my visit to the physician's house had been! Chinnadevi! Where are you? What are you doing at this moment? I am tormented by thoughts of you.

The ministerial meeting was attended also by army generals, provincial chiefs, and other officials. Everyone participated in the meeting enthusiastically.

Appaji cleared his throat, and said, 'We have to first check how many horses and how many foot soldiers we will need. We have to think of possible allies.'

I turned my face away. I knew that the moment the discussion turned towards possible allies, the ruler of Srirangapatnam would be mentioned, and Thirumala Devi, the Princess of Srirangapatnam would also be mentioned.

Luckily, there was an interruption. A servant came in and said, 'Muthu and his wife are here.'

'Did they have to choose to come now? Send them away and tell them to come later,' said Appaji angrily.

But I vetoed him and said, 'I asked them to come. Send them in.'

Muthu and Solai came in.

I asked a servant to bring a plate of betel leaves and areca nuts.

I placed betel leaves and areca nuts on Solai's palm. That was an indication that I was going to appoint her to an important post.

The people assembled for the ministerial meeting stood up surprised at my gesture.

'Vaiyappa Nayak is the Chief of Senji. But he does not have able assistants. It has been ably administered since the time of Vendrumannkonda Sambuvarayar. But now highway robbers have free rein there. So I appoint you as the official-in-charge of the area between Kanchipuram and Thiruvannamalai,' I said to Solai.

'What!' That was the unanimous voice of disapproval of all my officials and ministers.

'Your Majesty, what are you trying to do? How can a woman be in charge of an area?'

'I haven't broken any tradition. There are many instances when women were given important positions. Proudha Devaraya appointed his sister Harimadevi in an important position. Bommala Devi's daughter Kalala Devi served as an official representative of the kingdom. Why, even in our time, Basavappa Udayar's mother administers many villages. The wives, sisters and mothers of many of our provincial chiefs have important administrative positions. Kallarasiyamma, Ramadevi, Savamma, Peria Narasamma, Balammadevi…so many.'

I had stated facts. So all the men, who had risen to state their objections, sat down, without voicing their dissent.

But Solai and Muthu were overwhelmed by my words, and they fell at my feet and begged to be relieved of such a huge responsibility.

'I am uneducated. I know nothing about administration,' said Solai.

'Don't worry. I will send educated, experienced people to assist you,' I said reassuringly.

'Muthu, you stay on here in the capital. Complete construction of the dancing hall, and then join Solai.'

Solai bowed before me and left. The scars from the burns inflicted on her hands could be seen clearly.

'Appaji, did you and the others see those scars on this girl's hands? She was falsely accused and punished. Now things will change. I have given her an important position. With it comes a lot of power. So the very people who disowned her will want to be friends with her. All the upper castes will begin to treat her respectfully,' I said.

'Maybe,' acknowledged Appaji, half-heartedly. 'Can we now get back to our discussion about possible allies in our war?'

We debated the matter for four days. Everyone emphasised the need to enlist the support of as many kings as possible. They said that it was especially important to have the ruler of Srirangapatnam on our side, and that the only way to ensure this was for me to marry Thirumala Devi. They said that if the ruler of Srirangapatnam turned against me, then it would embolden other kings too to oppose me.

I suffered in silence. In whom could I confide? To whom could I talk about my love? I fretted.

On the fifth day, there was some hope.

Gayatri had arrived.

Twenty-six

When a palace servant told me that Gayatri had arrived, I knew she would be in my mother's palace. The news revived hope in my heart. Although I knew that she had returned with no news of Chinnadevi, still her very presence at the palace was enough to fill my heart with hope.

I could see a sparrow seated on the window-sill. It just sat there quietly. But to me, it seemed as if the bird was flapping its wings. I could hear *stotras* being sung by the palace singer. He wasn't at his best that day, but his voice was pleasing to me. I suppose when one is happy, everything takes on a pleasant appearance.

I was sorry that Gayatri hadn't come to meet me first, but had gone to meet my mother. But I consoled myself with the thought that since she was employed in the women's quarters, it was only proper that she should report there first.

I finished my usual duties, and left for my mother's palace.

But Gayatri was not there. I was irritated. This had become a routine—my looking for Gayatri and Gayatri doing a disappearing act.

Mother was reading something. I wondered if my eyesight would be as good as hers, when I got to her age.

'Come here, Krishna,' she called to me.

I could see that she wanted to discuss what she had been reading. Out of respect for my mother, I sat down beside her. My eyes searched the room to see if Gayatri was there.

'Krishna, a great man called Kabirdass has lived in our times,' she said.

I had heard of Kabirdass. There used to a yogi called Ramananda, who had travelled to Kanchi and obtained *deeksha* there. Kabir was his disciple. Mother read a few lines of Kabir's in the Avanti language. But I did not have the patience to listen. 'Mother, where is Gayatri?' I asked.

'Can't you be patient?' Mother asked me with a smile. 'The moment I start talking about religious matters, everyone runs away. Even the serving girls manage to find some excuse to leave. You are the only one who is trapped into listening every now and then. Now if I let you go, who will I talk to?'

'All right, Mother. What do you want to talk to me about?'

'I want to answer the question you put to me a while ago. Kabirdass passed away a few years ago. There are many stories about his family. But the one thing that we do know is that he was respected by everyone—Hindus and Muslims. When he died, there arose a dispute about whether he should be buried or cremated. But when the blanket that covered him was moved aside, it was found that there was a heap of flowers in place of the body, putting an end to all the arguments about what to do with his body—bury it or cremate it!'

'Mother, you said you would answer my question. But what is the connection between your story and my question?' I asked.

'What is the connection between Gayatri and your story?'

'I mentioned a heap of flowers, didn't I?'

'Yes, and so?'

'Where would you find heaps of flowers?'

'In a garden,' I said.

'Go to the garden. I asked Gayatri to get some flowers from the garden for my morning worship. You will find her there.'

I left at once for the garden. The garden was bigger than the palace. Where should I start looking for her, I wondered. Hearing someone laughing, I turned to find Gayatri conversing with a young man. A closer look revealed that the young man was the Italian physician Nicholas. He was wearing a dhoti and a towel. Gayatri and he were looking at the plants and seemed to be enjoying themselves. Gayatri smelled a flower, and the pollen caused her to sneeze. The two of them laughed. I recalled that they had travelled together to Srivilliputtur and had returned together. It must have been a long journey, and there would have been many opportunities for them to get close to each other. I envied them.

Seeing my shadow, they turned and greeted me. The Italian greeted me in Tamil. 'So you have learnt Tamil,' I said.

'Yes. I can now speak fluently. I have a request. You are the Emperor, and I am not a royal personage. I am also a young man. There is no need for you to treat me so deferentially.'

His Tamil was impeccable, and I was surprised that he could speak so flawlessly. 'You speak like a native speaker of the language,' I observed.

'That is because I have lived in this country for many years,' he said.

'Really?' I was surprised.

'Forgive me for lying to you. The priest Louis told me that newcomers from foreign lands are accorded special respect in Vijayanagar. That is why he introduced me to you as someone who had just come from Italy. Actually, I have been here for ten years.'

'Ten years? And what have you been doing here all these years?'

He narrated his experiences, and his story was a fascinating one.

Nicholas was the son of a poor labourer in Italy. He became interested in the practice of medicine. He also managed to find a teacher. The teacher and Nicholas dissected dead bodies, to study human anatomy. To do so was against the law, and also against the Christian religion. They would exhume bodies from graves and carry out their research. One day, they were discovered, while exhuming bodies. The old teacher was burnt at the stake. Nicholas managed to escape and made his way to Portugal. There he became a sailor in a Portuguese ship and sailed to Goa.

'Your story will make a fascinating fictional account,' I said. I looked at him admiringly. He was perhaps twenty-five or twenty-six years old. That meant that he had been adventurous from the age of sixteen!

'There is a proverb in our country that says that when one is in Rome, one should do as the Romans do. Now that I am here, I have changed my speech and my clothes, to look like a resident of this country. I usually wear clothes similar to the clothes your people wear. It was only when the priest brought me to you, that I made an exception, and wore Western attire.'

'Does you research continue?'

'Here too there is objection to exhuming bodies,' he said.

'You will never be able to get bodies of Hindus, because we cremate the dead,' I interrupted.

'Not all Hindus do that, Your Majesty,' said Nicholas, and went on to give me more interesting details.

Nicholas had wandered all over North India. In Varanasi, he found that the dead were cast into the waters of the Ganga river. There is a belief that those whose bodies are thrown into the Ganga, will be liberated from further births and deaths. Nicholas would retrieve those bodies that had not begun to putrefy, and would carry out his research using these bodies. No one objected. In fact many traditional physicians even helped him in his work. He stayed in the houses of these practitioners of traditional medicine and learnt Siddha methods of treatment and Ayurvedic methods from them.

Nichloas narrated his adventures and experiences without a trace of pride. But I noticed that Gayatri was listening to him wide-eyed, and her pride in his achievements was evident.

Minister Lakkanna and other officials were watching us from a distance. They must have wondered what Nicholas and Gayatri had to say to me that I found so absorbing. And I asked myself what I was doing, listening to an Italian's story, instead of finding out about Chinnadevi.

'I am glad you research continues. But why are you digging in the palace garden? I can assure you that you will find no dead bodies here,' I said.

'Your Majesty, he is trying to find some herbs that will keep a certain man from becoming a dead body.'

'What are you saying?'

Nicholas explained: 'The governor Singapiran is unable to understand anything we say to him. I have read that certain herbs will help him regain his memory. I am looking for them here.'

'You continue to look for the herbs. When you find them, make arrangements to prepare the medicinal oil. I have something to say to the Emperor,' Gayatri said to Nicholas, who, before taking leave of me, said, 'Your Majesty, if the governor has any relatives, please send them with me,' said Nicholas.

'What for?'

'*Caraka Samhita* and *Sushruta Samhita* say that when a physician enters a patient's house, he should ensure the presence of family or friends of the patient. The physician should speak kind words. He should speak confidently to the patient.'

I gave him a pat on the back and said, 'I am glad you are so well-read. But we mustn't waste time talking. You go ahead with your treatment of Singapiran. I don't think he has any relatives here. That man you see there is Minister Lakkanna. Ask him for help. He will send someone with you.'

Gayatri kept staring at Nicholas, as he moved away. When he turned the corner and could no longer be seen from where we were standing, I said to Gayatri, with a laugh, 'All right. I hope you can bring yourself to talk to me, now.' She blushed.

'Now tell me what happened at Srivilliputtur.'

'My story isn't as interesting as the doctor's,' she said. This was the first time I was hearing the word 'doctor'. I understood that it was a word used for a physician. Just as Nicholas had been learning Tamil, Gayatri had been learning his language!

'I received that scrambled message in the Odia language that you sent me. Have you anything to add to that message?'

'Not much. We learnt that Chinnadevi and her brother had not come to Srivilliputtur. The doctor and I made enquires in many places, and made sure of this. We kept making enquires on our return journey too. It was when we reached Thiruvannamalai that we heard that you had dealt with the highway robbers and had also brought the governor here. You mustn't mistake me, Your Majesty. But I think you made a fundamental mistake.'

'And what was my mistake?'

'You should have brought the governor's young wife with you. She might know where Chinnadevi is.'

'Of course!' I admitted. 'Did you meet her?'

'I did, but it wasn't easy to find her. She was so afraid, she went into hiding. But I did track her down.'

'And?'

'I found her and also found out where Chinnadevi is. Chinnadevi is now in Bijapur, that is in Vijayapuram. Therefore it becomes imperative that you lead your army to Vijayapuram, to rescue her.'

'Gayatri, you have no idea what that would mean.'

'I know, Your Majesty. You will need the help of the ruler of Srirangapatnam, and to get his help, you will have to marry his daughter Thirumala Devi. Marry her, Your Majesty. By all means, marry her,' said Gayatri.

Twenty-seven

I was so shocked by Gayatri's suggestion that I marry Thirumala Devi, that for a few minutes I was unable to say anything. It seemed as if the usual sounds around me in the palace had ceased and there was a deathly silence in their place.

'Gayatri, how could you say make such a suggestion? You know how much I love Chinnadevi, and yet you suggest that I marry someone else,' I said.

'This marriage will not in any way mean the end of your love. I promise you that,' she said.

'How can you give me such an assurance?'

'I have an intuition that things will work out. You make arrangements for the war. Also be prepared to marry Thirumala Devi. I don't have to tell you that as an Emperor, you must put the welfare of your people above all else. You have protected the southern part of the peninsula from invasions. Should you not ensure that your reputation is protected? I will go to Srirangapatnam today and meet Thirumala Devi,' she said.

'Why should you go there? Appaji and my mother have already made all arrangements. All that remains is for me to fall into the trap they have laid for me and to be bound by the shackles they have readied for me,' I said dejectedly. I had never expected that Gayatri would take their side.

'That is not a trap, Emperor. Those are the bonds of love, of affection,' she laughed.

'Anyway, how do you know Chinnadevi is in Vijayapuram?' I asked.

'I happen to know she is there,' Gayatri said with a smile. 'When Chinnadevi and her brother and their Bhagavata Mela troupe were nearing Thiruvannamlai, some of the Vijayapuram Sultan's spies happened to be there. They watched the Bhagavata Mela drama. They decided to kidnap Chinnadevi. They pleaded with Ethirajan to come to their town and stage dramas there. But they did not tell him where they were from. Ethirajan told them that he had to go to Srivilliputtur. They assured him that he could leave for Srivilliputtur after a few days. The governor, Singapiran, was a co-conspirator. Singapiran's wife gave all these details,' Gayatri said.

I sighed and said, 'All right. Go to Srirangapatnam.'

'Thirumala Devi will come here and marry you,' she smiled. 'I have to take leave of your mother now.'

Gayatri usually looked radiant when she smiled. But now her smile seemed to lack charm.

For a long time after she had left, I paced nervously up and down in the balcony.

I could see a beggar in the street below. He knocked his head with a stone and cut himself with a knife, and people shaken by the sight of the blood from his self-inflicted wounds, tipped him generously. What was the difference between this beggar and me, I asked myself. I too was hurting myself. I too was begging an insignificant ruler to send his army to help me. I was betraying my sweetheart Chinnadevi.

Suddenly a thought struck me, and I shuddered in fright. Chinnadevi was the prisoner of the Sultan. And was she…could it be possible that she…

I could not contemplate such a possibility.

I decided that I could not postpone the declaration of war.

My Chinnadevi was somewhere in Vijayapuram. If I could find her, if I could embrace her, all my sorrows would end!

I had a meeting with my ministers that day. I could tell by looking at them that they had heard I had agreed to marry Thirumala Devi. They looked extremely pleased.

Even before I could open the discussion, the Prime Minster congratulated me on my forthcoming marriage.

I thanked him and said, 'Appaji, I have a doubt. During the Ummathoor expedition, we captured the Sringapatnam and Sivasamudram forts. We appointed Kempe Gowda, Veerappa Gowda and Chikka Raja as our representatives, didn't we? Now how did this ruler of Srirangapatnam called Kumara Veeraiyya suddenly materialise?'

'Those representatives of ours have accepted Kumara Veeraiyya as their sovereign. He is related to you through your mother. So he too, is in a sense of royal blood,' said Appaji, stressing the words 'royal blood'. Although he was glad that I was going to marry Thirumala Devi, he was unhappy about my attachment to a dancing girl.

Since this was to be a meeting about our military campaign, all the generals were present. One of them said, 'Your Majesty, the Bijapur Sultan and his forces have crossed the Krishna and have entered our territory. They have pillaged and plundered the villages in the border areas.'

Our enemies always had an eye on the area between the Tungabhadra and Krishna rivers. When there was water in the Krishna, they kept respectfully to their territory, but when there was little water in the river, they would cross over to this side and cause havoc in the bordering villages. Vyasaguru had told me several times to drive them out permanently. It was my fault for not having stationed troops there.

'I will lead the army,' I assured my generals. 'Who will be the chief general?'

'I will be the chief, Your Majesty,' said Pemmasani Ramalinga Nayak. He had accompanied me on many military expeditions, and so his suggestion met with approval from all those assembled.

'I have a plan, and I will tell you about it when we are on the battlefield,' said Ramalingam.

After the meeting ended, everyone left, but Appaji stayed back. Usually at the mention of war, he would be energetic like a twenty-year old. But for some reason, he was silent today.

'Appaji, you are unhappy about something, aren't you?' I asked.

'Yes,' he said.

'Why are you sad?'

'Your mother and I told you many times that you should marry Thirumala Devi, but you paid no heed to us. But the moment that girl made the suggestion, you agreed. Not only did you agree, but you have sent her as an emissary. I feel humiliated.'

I didn't know what to say to him. 'You have misunderstood me. Your arguments and mother's efforts were beginning to bear fruit, because I had mulled over your words. When finally Gayatri made the same suggestion, naturally I was receptive. In any case, Gayatri also suggested that I do what you have been urging me to do.'

Appaji didn't argue any further. 'Your mother wants to meet you. You must get her blessings first.'

☙

Poet Tenali Ramakrishna was in my mother's palace, when I visited my mother. Although he was a court poet, I hardly saw him in the palace. That was because he was always travelling.

'Poet Ramakrishna has come to give you his work,' said Mother, and placed the manuscript in my hands.

'I wanted to give you this before you left on your military campaign,' he said.

He had given his work the title *Panduranga Mahatamyam*. I gave it a cursory glance but even that was enough to tell me that it was a scholarly work. 'I don't have the time to read it now. You must forgive me. But there is one thing that surprises me,' I said.

'What is that, Your Majesty?'

'This work reflects your great scholarship. Why do people refer to someone like you, capable of writing such a work, as a court jester?'

'When I am in the company of poets, I behave like a poet. But when I am in the midst of the uneducated, I am like one of them. I tell them funny stories. That is why people refer to me as a jester.'

'Continue to be both scholar and jester,' I said.

After the poet left, I fell at mother's feet and took her blessings.

There were tears in her eyes. 'Krishna, I don't know if I should rejoice that you are going to marry, or whether I should worry because you are going off to fight,' she said.

൞

The next day, I went to Vyasateertha's matha and took his blessings. No one had arrived as yet from Srirangapatnam. Pemmasani Ramalingam sent some soldiers to the other side of the Tungabhadra river. Their task was to take the grains and cattle there, and bring them over to this side, thereby ensuring that nothing was left for the enemy to take away. They carried out the appointed task efficiently.

Still no sign of the Srirangpatnam people.

The date of our departure was decided and announced by astrologers.

Still no sign of anyone from Srirangapatnam.

Special yagnas were conducted for the welfare of the kingdom. Still no sign of the people from Srirangapatnam.

I went to the Vittala, Virupaksha, Ranaganatha, Krishnswami and Ramaswami temples, and worshipped in all the temples.

Still no sign of the people from Srirangapatnam.

'We need not wait any more for the Srirangapatnam army,' I said to Appaji. 'All the other kings whose help we sought have sent their armies. If we add up all these forces and our forces, we have 200,000 foot soldiers, 10,000 horses, and 500 elephants. That should be enough. Let us leave.'

Appaji too felt there was no point in waiting any further.

As was the custom, three caparisoned horses and eleven elephants stood in the palace courtyard. The decorated cushions on the backs of the elephants and the gold ornaments they wore glinted in the sunlight. As the elephants swayed from side to side, the bells they were adorned with, tinkled.

Horse and elephant worship began. A Brahmin priest brought a gold vessel with rose petals in it. He sprinkled the petals on the horses and the elephants. He then sprinkled rose water on them. He gave me the rose water and I too sprinkled some rose water on them.

'Long live the Emperor,' went up the cries from the people.

At the same time, I could hear people saying, 'They are here. They have arrived.'

The King of Srirangapatnam—Kumara Veeraiyya and his daughter Thirumala Devi got down from a palanquin. Hundred servants carried Thirumala Devi's dowry. Appaji informed me that they were being followed by 8000 foot soldiers, 400 horses and 20 elephants.

I saw Thirumala Devi for a fleeting second. The moment she got down from the palanquin, she joined the women of the royal family, and I couldn't spot her among them. Gayatri smiled at me.

Kumara Veeraiyya apologised to me for arriving so late. He said the waters in the Cauvery had risen and that they had to wait till the waters had receded.

I liked his politeness and gentle disposition. 'Never mind, I am glad you have arrived before our departure.'

'There is no hurry to celebrate the wedding now. It can wait till you return from your military campaign,' he said.

But Appaji was anxious that the wedding should take place immediately. Perhaps he was afraid that I might change my mind. He consulted my mother and said to me, 'Today is a very auspicious day. We have to leave tomorrow morning. So I think it will be ideal if the wedding takes place today.'

I wanted to prove that once I had made a promise, I would not go against it. So I agreed.

༄

That evening, I married Thirumala Devi. But my thoughts were of Chinnadevi.

The people were very disappointed, because the wedding had not been on a grand scale.

That night, Thirumala and I were alone in my bedroom. I didn't know what to say to her.

She was adorned with jewels—head to toe. She had a pleasing countenance. She also had a look of determination. There was a smaller cot some distance from mine. If Mother or other elders from the royal family visited me when I was in my bedroom, they would usually sit on this cot.

Thirumala Devi fell at my feet. She then picked up a blanket and pillow and moved over to the smaller cot.

'Princess…' I said, taken aback.

She smiled. 'Your Majesty, until you find your Chinnadevi and marry her, I will sleep alone. Please don't worry.'

PART II

Twenty-eight

Thirumala Devi's resolution left me thunderstruck.

'Chinnadevi...how did you get to know about her?' I don't know how I managed to get the words out.

'I know, Your Majesty,' said Thirumala Devi. Her voice suggested a girl just out of her teens, approaching youth. It had a certain gentleness about it. 'Gayatri told me about Chinnadevi. I resolved never to be a stumbling block in the path of your love. And it was with this resolve that I agreed to marry you.'

'Thirumala, what was the need to marry me? You could have told your father that you did not want to marry me.'

'I think God has created you in order to keep this huge empire together. Enabling God's will to be carried out is also a way of serving God. Smaller kingdoms can be safe only if the Empire is safe,' said Thirumala. A while ago I had thought of her as an immature child. But now her foresight amazed me.

'Did you have to sacrifice yourself?'

'It is possible that your mind may change in course of time. What seems like a sacrifice now may turn sweet. I don't know how long that will take, but I am prepared to wait.'

She spoke gently, and yet every word of hers was like a barb, hurting me.

What a wicked man I was! What a sinner! What a selfish man! Here was a woman who deserved to marry someone who would be true to her, who would not be a dissembler in matters of the heart. She should have married someone more suitable than me. I had ruined her life. Society still treated women like slaves. And yet, what right had I to destroy this woman's life?

'Princess...' I said. My voice broke. 'I have done you great harm.'

'Your Majesty, please don't say that,' she said agitatedly.

'I'm speaking the truth. So far there has been no one in my heart except Chinnadevi. But I will try to give you a place there.'

'You don't have to try, Your Majesty. Let Chinnadevi be the only one in your heart. If at some time she decides to allot some space to me in your heart, I will gladly take it. I will not tell anyone about this conversation of ours. You mustn't tell anyone either. It is late. You must go to sleep. Great responsibilities await you. Have a good night's rest,' she said, and lay down on the small cot.

But I didn't lie down. I kept staring at Thirumala Devi, who went to sleep as soon as she lay down. I could still hear fireworks being let off by the people, who were celebrating my marriage, not knowing that my marriage had become a mockery.

I was at first angry with Gayatri for having told Thirumala Devi of my love for Chinnadevi. But I knew that this arrangement that Thirumala Devi had suggested, of our being husband and wife only in name, must also have been Gayatri's idea. I felt grateful to Gayatri.

Thirumala Devi was fast asleep. Her hair had been parted in the middle. A small pearl strand decorated her hair. Turmeric and vermillion powder had been applied to her feet. I picked her up and put her on my cot. She looked very pretty. But why did I not feel a thing, even when I lifted her and held her close to my body? It was surprising. I suppose my love for Chinnadevi is an armour that protects me, I told myself.

☙

My army and I crossed the Tungabhadra. I am not going to go into the details of the various battles. You will read about them from the works of historians. I am only going to record the internal battles I fought, in my mind, and also a few details that I think might be of interest to you.

Portuguese scholar Barbosa expressed his surprise at the crowd that followed the army. 'In our country, only the army goes out to fight. But here an entire city moves out with you,' he said. Barbosa was planning to write on the life of the people of my empire and also about the battles we fought. So he was accompanying us.

He wasn't exaggerating when he said that an entire city moved with us, when we went out to fight.

Let me first describe my tent. All around is a barbed wire fence. Inside the tent I have all the facilities I enjoy in the palace. There are separate enclosures for my bath, for my daily worship, an enclosure where I can watch dance programmes and listen to music concerts, a dining hall and a bedroom. When this tent comes up, it is an indication that the king has set off on a military expedition. Outside my tent are armed guards. Next come the tents that house members of the royal family. Princes, princesses—all of them stay in these tents. I have objected many times to their accompanying us. But I am told that it is the practice to do so. Right behind the tents of the royal family are tents in which precious gems and pearls are sold. The tents of the goldsmiths lie next to these. There are also shops that sell aromatic substances and knick-knacks.

Then come the tents of the ministers and army chiefs. Then come the tents of the soldiers. Behind this stand the horses, elephants, mules and buffaloes.

Then again there is a row of tents selling essential commodities like rice, pulses, tamarind, salt, clothes and even fodder for the animals. The Empire never paid the soldiers, whether it was the foot soldiers, or those in charge of the horses or elephants. It was the responsibility of the vassals and the governors to pay them. This was because in times of peace, the local administrators and vassals collected taxes and administered the areas under their control.

And last of all are the tents of the carpenters, washermen and the ones who dig trenches.

So what was wrong in Barbosa talking of a city on the move? If you added up all the people who moved from one place to the next, there would easily be a million people. Every time the army moved, all these tents had to be moved too.

I had made a good decision to exclude many of the women of the palace. But Gayatri and Thirumala Devi had come. However, I had asked my mother to stay back. She was unwell, and I had left behind many people in the city to take care of her. But there were many distant relatives in the tents meant for the royal family. I didn't know many of them.

I had also insisted that the wives and children of the soldiers should not accompany us.

Many of the ministers disapproved of this. 'It was a sensible arrangement. If the soldiers have their families with them, they will fight ferociously, to protect their families. That is how the practice of taking the families of soldiers with the army began,' said Minister Kondamarasu.

'There is another way of looking at it. A soldier should not be distracted by worries about the family. He should concentrate on fighting and not worry about his family that is following him. That is why I said the families should not accompany the army,' I said, and put an end to the controversy.

☙

The sun was up, and my thoughts were of Thirumala Devi. I liked her childlike innocence. My concern for her was like that of a mother for her child. Here was Thirumala, following the army, when she had had no such experience before.

I looked out of my tent, and for a minute, it seemed as if the entire city of Vijayanagar had arrived there. The only things that were absent were the palaces and buildings. But the noise and buzz was the same as in the city.

Thousands of men with leather bags slung over their shoulders had already started moving, even before the army had. It was their responsibility to fill the bags with water. They would supply water for the army, whenever it was needed.

I watched them for a few minutes and then went to Thirumala Devi's tent. The guard on duty outside her tent was about to announce my arrival, but I put a finger on my lips and indicated to him that I didn't want to be announced. I stepped inside quietly. Gayatri and Thirumala Devi were playing pallankuzhi[18]. They didn't see me enter.

I stood watching them play. I could have had the pleasure of watching them at play for some more time. But when I saw Thirumala Devi about to drop two beads in the same hole by mistake, I said, 'Thirumala, you've dropped two beads in one hole.'

Both women jumped when they heard my voice. Gayatri had had many conversations with me, and so she did not feel uncomfortable in my presence. But Thirumala was every inch the new bride—she was bashful. There was a small slit in the tent, to provide ventilation. The rays of the sun came in through that slit and fell on her face, giving a red tint to her fair skin.

Many poets had accompanied my army. Sculptors had come too. But I felt that none of them could do justice to Thirumala's

---

18. *Pallankuzhi*—a traditional board game

beauty through their creations. And even assuming they could, they would only be able to show her external beauty. The beauty of her soul, the goodness of her heart, the co-existence in her of an iron will and the softness of flowers—these no poet would ever be able to capture. Of this I was certain.

I began to feel guilty. I felt that if I thought more of Thirumala Devi, I would begin to think less and less of Chinnadevi. So I deliberately turned my thoughts away from Thirumala Devi.

We were all three of us preoccupied with our own concerns, and so for a while there was silence. Gayatri was the first to break the silence. 'I was told that Your Majesty departs tomorrow. I am not old enough to bless you. But let me wish you all success,' she said.

'You are silent, Thirumala,' I said.

'I want you to return safely. I pray to Lord Ranganatha, my family deity,' she said.

'In future pray to my family deity as well—Lord Srinivasa of Thirumala. Remember you have the name Thirumala Devi,' I said. Suddenly the sound of skin instruments rent the air. The sound was deafening. String instruments and percussion instruments together made a big sound.

'What's the matter?' the two women asked and ran out of the tent.

I followed them calmly, and said, 'That comes from our army. Don't worry. It is the rule that every two hours these instruments must be sounded. It will stop now.' The sound was so loud, that no one could hear anyone else. Every one was using signs to communicate. I too used gestures to assure the two women that there was no cause for worry.

It was eerie to hear so many instruments all being sounded together. Birds resting in trees were frightened and flew away, screeching. Some of them died of shock. One dove fell down in a state of shock, but it wasn't dead. It dropped into Thirumala's hands. She rubbed its back gently. Observing how gently she handled the bird, I wondered how she would be able to witness the bloody battles that were to follow. Severed legs, hands and heads would float in a river of blood. Would she be able bear watching such a scene?

༄

That evening, men who were to check if the omens were good for our departure, arrived from the capital.

Appaji and the other ministers came to my tent and we had a discussion. Army Chief Pemmasani Ramalingam was also there. 'You said you had a secret plan. What is it?' I asked him.

He smiled, but refused to divulge the plan. 'Initially, there will only be small skirmishes. The big battle will begin only when we come face to face with the army of the Bijapur Sultan. I will tell you my plan then,' he said.

'All right. Keep your secret,' I said and laughed, and the other ministers joined in the laughter. But Appaji didn't. He looked stern. He didn't seem to like those who ranked below him making independent decisions.

I spent the night dreaming about Chinnadevi. At sunrise, I mounted my favourite horse, Parvatinathan, and accompanied by a few ministers and generals, I moved forward. I had a spear in my hand. I would throw the spear and whichever direction I threw it in would be the one in which the army would proceed.

This morning, I threw it in the north-western direction. The army prepared to move in that direction.

My spies told me that the Bijapur Sultan's army was stationed on the bank of the Krishna river. It was a considerable distance from where we had our camp. There were many forts small and big on the way to the place where the Sultan was camping. These were forts that were under the control of the Vijayanagar Empire, but they had been captured by the enemy. We would have to regain control of these forts before proceeding further.

As we approached the first fort, I asked for a musical instrument called ekkaalam. This is a wind instrument. I would have to throw it into the fort, and after recapturing the fort, I would have to fetch this ekkaalam. That was the usual practice. Just as I was about to throw the ekkaalam, I heard Appaji's voice. 'Your Majesty, not now,' he said. The court astrologer was with Appaji. It was the same astrologer who had stopped me on my return journey from Thiruvannamalai, saying that he had something important to tell me.

Twenty-nine

Soldiers about to mount their horses stopped, one foot on the ground, one on the stirrup. Those who were tying spears and swords on the trunks of elephants stopped what they were doing. Soldiers who were getting together their bows and arrows paused and turned in the direction from which the voice came. Those who were playing musical instruments stopped. Servants who had been working inside tents wondered what the reason was for the sudden silence, and stepped out of the tents to have a look.

If it had been anyone else calling out 'stop,' no one would have paid heed. But it was Prime Minister Appaji who had lifted his hands and asked us to stop, and so everyone stopped doing whatever it was that they had been doing.

Appaji and the astrologer came towards me. The astrologer was an old man. He was panting from exertion.

'Just a while ago he told me something important. If he had told us this earlier, we need not have made these preparations,' Appaji said accusingly.

'Please do not blame him. The day I returned from Thiruvannamalai, he came to me and said he had something important to say to me. But I assumed it wasn't important, and so I didn't probe further,' I said.

'He's told your mother what he wanted to tell you then. Your mother sent for me. I went to the palace and found out what it was. I've also brought the astrologer along to tell you what he told your mother.'

'Please don't give me these preambles. Get to the point, Prime Minister,' I said sternly. I was aware that the two million eyes of one million people were on me. That was the reason for my sternness.

'In two days, Guhu Yogam[19] begins. That means it will be a trying time for Your Majesty. There will be a threat to your position…'

'What is this Guhu Yogam? I've never heard of it.'

'Not many have heard of it. It is the coming together of eight planets. Since this is happening during the Emperor's astrological star, there is a danger to your position…'

I could see that he was afraid to elaborate.

Appaji said, 'I consulted other astrologers too. They said that only once in five hundred or thousand years does this happen. It happened during the Kurukshetra war. The one in power then was Duryodhana…' he said.

'It is said that even inauspicious periods last only for some time. How long will this last?' I asked.

'The planets will be in that position for three days at the most.'

'Is that all? Then we will postpone the military campaign by three days.'

The astrologer looked worried.

'The danger is not for just three days. The Sastras says that whoever is in power during those three days will have to face a long period of distress,' he said. By now the army generals and other important officials had joined us. Appaji didn't like them listening to our conversation.

'Let us move away and have a more private conversation,' he said.

We stood outside a tent. We peeped in to make sure no one was inside.

'This man is a very good astrologer,' Appaji said. 'His

---

19. Guhu Yogam—An astrological period that results in bad luck for a particular star sign

predictions never go wrong. But he is not wise. Instead of coming directly to me, he approached your mother.'

'I agree. He should not have added to my mother's worries.'

'That's not all. He has told your mother that if someone else is placed on the throne for those three days, and then you resume charge, there will be no danger to your position or life.'

'That is a good idea,' I said.

'It is a dangerous suggestion!' Appaji said. 'Even assuming it is a good idea, he shouldn't have spoken of it to your mother. Your mother wants me to bring one of your step-brothers and make him king for three days.'

'Oh my God!' I exclaimed. Appaji had put both my stepbrothers Achyutharayan and Thirmalairayan in Chandragiri Fort, to prevent multiple claims to the throne. Also in the same fort was the son of my step-brother Veera Narasimha, who had been king before me. They enjoyed all the comforts they were entitled to as members of the royal family. Yet, for all practical purposes, they were prisoners.

My mother, who didn't understand palace intrigue, often asked me to release them from the fort. Now she must have seen the astrologer's suggestion as a good opportunity to release them. My mother was too innocent to realise the consequences of misplaced kindness.

Appaji could guess what my thoughts were.

'If Achyuthan or Thirumalai were to be placed on the throne even for three days, they will cause so much damage, that we will be unable to dethrone them for the next thirty years. It is impossible to predict what they will do in our absence,' said Appaji.

'True, but what else can we do?'

'I can't think of anything either,' said Appaji.

'Forgive me, Prime Minister,' said a voice. We turned to find Gayatri there.

Appaji was furious. 'We are having an important discussion. Go away,' he said to Gayatri.

I knew that taking her side would make him angrier. Moreover it would be like undermining Appaji's authority. So I had to be careful.

'Look here, Gayatri. Since you helped me with some of my personal affairs, I have been lenient with you. But I do not like the way you take advantage of that. And I certainly do not like your interference in important matters that concern my duties,' I said to her, but also indicated to her with a wink, that I was not serious. Since Appaji was facing the other way, he did not notice my wink.

Gayatri was an intelligent girl. She understood the reason for my harsh words.

'You must forgive me. I happened to hear what the palace astrologer said. I thought I would tell you about my idea…'

'I don't want to hear what you have to say. Here is my Prime Minister. He is a man with foresight, with experience in guiding me. There is no need for me to listen to your half-baked ideas. Vijayanagar is not faced with a dearth of intelligent people. You may go.'

'All right. I will go away, Your Majesty,' said Gayatri, and pretended to move away.

My praise of him had pleased Appaji and he had mellowed down a bit. 'Whatever it is you have to say, say it. But make it brief,' said Appaji to her.

'Guhu Yogam is bad for those in power,' she began.

'We know that already,' I said.

'So if we put someone else on the throne for those three days.'

'We have already thought of that…'

'The one who occupies the throne temporarily should be one who has renounced worldly ties and who cares for the welfare of the Empire.'

'True,' said Appaji.

'The person who sits on the throne for three days must also be one who will not be affected by any danger. He will be protected by the powers of his penance,' she said.

'That means…that means…' said Appaji

'Yes, Prime Minister. I think Vyasa Teertha should be king for three days. I think we should implore him to accept kingship for three days to save the Empire and the Emperor,' she said.

'Wonderful idea,' I was about to say, but I checked myself, not wanting to annoy Appaji. I wanted him to give his wholehearted approval for the idea.

'Seems like a good idea,' he said.

I felt it was no longer necessary for me to keep up the pretence of disapproving of Gayatri. 'All right. Then let us return to the palace. What shall we do with the armies?' I asked.

'Let them remain here. If we tell them to disperse, it will be difficult to gather them all together here again,' said Appaji. 'Let your queen Thirumala Devi come with us. We will take some ministers and generals with us. We will return the moment we have anointed Vyasa Teertha the king,' said Appaji.

The next day we re-crossed the Tungabhadra river and returned to the capital. Thirumala and I were alone in a boat. 'I told you not to accompany me. But you didn't pay heed to me. Now you have another opportunity. After making Vyasa Teertha the king, we will all have to return. You stay back in the capital. Gayatri will keep you company,' I said to Thirumala Devi.

But she was adamant. 'It is said that wherever Rama is,

that place is Ayodhya for Sita. I too want to be where you are. Whichever place you are in, that will be the capital city of Vijayanagar for me,' she said.

She had been selfless and had given up so much for my sake. How could she sit here before me as if she hadn't done anything significant? I suppose great people are unaware of how much they do for others.

☙

Vyasa Teertha was in the capital. A Yoga Varada Narasimha idol was to be installed in the Vittala temple. Vyasa Teertha was there to install it. Appaji, Thirumala and I met him and prostrated ourselves before him. Mother was unwell, and couldn't accompany us.

Appaji told him the purpose of our visit. Vyasa Teertha burst out laughing. With him was his prime disciple Vadiraja Swami. He was collecting funds for a golden roof for the Udupi Krishna temple. Vyasa Teertha said to Vadiraja Swami, 'Did you hear that? You and I are people who have renounced the world, and here is a whole empire coming into our hands! Who can understand Lord Krishna's plans?'

To Appaji, he said, 'I do not have the kind of powers you think I have. But since you say that you are making this request for the welfare of the nation, I agree.'

On the day when Guhu Yogam began, Vyasa Teertha came to the palace. The procession of the seer was as grand as that of the Emperor.

He sat on the throne. All the people who had gathered shouted, 'Long live Vyasaraja!' Until then he had been known as Vyasa Teertha. It is said that he acquired the name of Vyasaraya from that day onwards.

A sacrificial fire was lit. Seven mantras from the *Taittiriya Brahmana*[20] were recited. Appaji and the other ministers had cups full of gold coins and precious stones. I poured the coins and stones over Vyasa Raya's head, gently, so as not to hurt him. There were heaps of diamonds and rubies at his feet.

He picked up diamonds and precious stones and distributed them to those assembled. My army had many Muslim generals. They were the first to receive these expensive gifts from Vyasa Teertha. Usually an Emperor, upon being crowned, makes donations to various temples. Vyasa Raya too announced such gifts. He then sang one of his compositions, invoking Lord Krishna's blessings. When he finished singing, there were tears in our eyes.

For three days he was Emperor, and I served him like an ordinary servant. Thirumala Devi fanned him. My mother sat at his feet. On the fourth day, Vyasaraya stepped down from his position as Emperor. I became the Emperor again. He blessed me and returned to his matha. I felt rejuvenated.

This time when I crossed the Tungabhadra River, chief of the army Pemmasani was with me.

'You said you had a secret plan. Will we have to put that plan into action in the first battle itself?' I asked him.

'Your Majesty must forgive me. The small forts here are not going to be difficult to bring under our control. Our main enemy is waiting on the banks of the Krishna river for our arrival. When we start fighting them, I will tell you about my plan,' he said.

---

20. Taittiriya Brahmana—part of the corpus of Vedic texts

Thirty

Pemmasani Ramalingam was right. The first three or four forts were taken over easily. When the guards of the forts saw the huge Vijayanagar army advancing towards the forts, they surrendered. The forts had been well-stocked with grains, in anticipation of a prolonged siege. But there weren't enough armed forces to defend the forts. I threw the ekkaalam into the fort and within a few minutes, all the generals and prominent citizens of the city came out, with their hands held above their heads, indicating that they were surrendering. The fort came under our control in a matter of minutes.

The soldiers and horses and elephants in the fort joined us in our march against Adil Shah. Even civilians joined us in our march and so the forces of Vijayanagar became bigger and bigger as we approached Adil Shah's camp. We also kept adding to our stock of food and water.

Every time a fort fell, there would be a celebration, which included dramas, dances and music. Thirumala Devi would sit beside me, and I was amused to see her childlike enjoyment of these performances.

But she wasn't present for the celebrations following the fall of the Mudgal fort. Gayatri came to me and said that Thirumala Devi would join me later. But there was no sign of Thirumala. I was worried. I was afraid that the rigours of the journey had taken a toll on her health. I went to her tent to check.

She had lit a lamp and was reading some verses. They were verses about Lord Krishna. I didn't want to disturb her. So I signalled to Gayatri to leave quietly, and stood there listening to Thirumala reading the verses. The flame of the lamp swayed to the breeze and there was a play of light and shadow on her face.

It was only after she finished reading the verses and tied up the palm leaves together, that Thirumala noticed me. 'Your Majesty, when did you arrive?' she asked, and drew up a stool for me to sit on.

'What was it that you were reading?' I asked.

'Vyasa Guru wrote some verses for me and asked me to read them every day. He said that this would assure happiness in my life.'

'In other words, you are not happy now. Happiness in your life is yet to be experienced. Is that right?' I asked.

I was teasing her, but Thirumala Devi thought I was serious. 'Your Majesty, you mustn't say such things. Even if I were to do penance for a thousand years, I will not find a husband like you.' she said. 'Your Majesty. I have a doubt.'

'What is it?'

'Wouldn't Vyasa Guru be at least 70 years old?'

'He must be older than that. Do you think he doesn't look his age?'

'I used to stand close to him when I fanned him, and I noticed that he was active and energetic.'

'There is a story about his visit to Srirangam. Some Saivites blocked his way and said, "This is the place where there is a temple for Jambulingesvara. You are a Vaishnavite. You cannot enter." Vyasa Guru said, "This place belongs to both of us. Anyway, let us enter into a pact. I will hold my breath and run. The place where I let out my breath will mark the boundary of Srirangam. Beyond that, will be the land that belongs to the Jambulingesvara temple." It is said that he held his breath and ran, and marked the boundary of Srirangam. I don't know if this is a true story or an apocryphal one. But this is a story that I have heard.'

Thirumala Devi showed no sign of disbelieving this account.

'It must be true, Your Majesty. It is said that when one does penance, one's body becomes strong.'

When I found how much regard she had for seers, I was a little ashamed, because I had often doubted the veracity of stories about them. I suppose it is because of people like Thirumala Devi, who believe unquestioningly, that faith in God remains unshakeable in our country.

'All right. You join me later,' I said to her and came out of her tent. I found Appaji outside the tent.

'Appaji, it is time for us to eat. Have you eaten?'

'No. For some time now, I have been eating only once a day.'

'What is this denial of food for? Is it a religious vow?'

'What is wrong in my taking a vow, when Your Majesty has taken a vow of bachelorhood?' he asked with a mysterious smile.

'What are you talking about, Appaji?'

'I noticed, since our departure from the capital, that you never went to the Queen's tent at night, but stayed in your tent. I guessed that you must have vowed not to indulge in such pleasures until you had defeated Adil Shah. If you, a young man, can deny yourself such pleasures, why should not an old man like me deny myself some food?'

I didn't know what to say. The person who had taken a vow was Thirumala Devi. But Appaji was giving me credit for it!

I wanted to change the topic and said, 'Appaji, our next big attack will be against Adil Shah's forces. I want my Muslim generals to lead the attack.'

'Your Majesty, we are going to attack a Muslim king!'

'Don't worry. My Muslim generals are loyal. The others in our army may turn traitors. But the Muslims generals will never turn against me. That is what the chief Pemmasani also says.'

'Any other reason why they should lead?'

'The Sultan's men will be confused when they see Muslim generals on our side. Taking advantage of their confusion, we can rout the enemy forces. If we lose, we can always withdraw, without much loss. If they lose, there is no place for them to withdraw, for behind them there is no land, but only the Krishna river.'

I had complete trust in my Muslim soldiers and generals. Once, someone asked Guru Nanak who could be termed good people—Muslims or Sikhs. He replied that he who helped others was the one who qualified to be called a good person. I too believe that to be true.

My maternal grandfather was a great wrestler, and I was told that in his youth, he defeated many wrestlers. However, I only remember him as a pious old man, who did nothing much except eat, sleep and visit temples. He used to play chess with me. He was not an expert in the game, but he was very good at narrating history.

One day he said to me, 'There are people who say that the fights between the Bahmani Sultans and the Vijayanagar Empire are religious wars. Don't believe those who say so.'

'Why not, grandfather?' I asked.

'There have been many wars in this country between kings. They have all been fought for economic reasons. These wars with the Muslim kings should also be viewed that way. The need to expand the empire, the urge to acquire more territory—that is the reason. The Cholas and the Pallavas fought many battles. The kings of Kalinga and we have waged many battles against each other. Hundred years ago, we conquered Lanka, where our co-religionists reside, and gave ourselves the title "Kings of the Southern Oceans". Was religion the cause of those wars?'

He was right to some extent. When the Vijayanagar Empire

was established, there were no fights between us and the Bahmani Sultans. Many kings who had managed to throw off the yoke of Muhammad-bin Tuglaq, had established small kingdoms, and they were interested only in expanding the area under their control. They had dismissed the Vijayanagar Kingdom as an insignificant one.

Trouble first arose when Jaffer Khan, also known as Muhammad Shah, defeated the Telangana king, Kappaiah. Kappaiah made peace with Muhammad Shah and gifted him a throne embedded with sapphires. Even today the Bahmani Sultans use that throne.

Even before the upheaval caused by this battle could subside, trouble arose again. When Muhammad Shah was the Bahmani Sultan, the wedding of his Prime Minister Shahabuddin Ghori was celebrated. Three hundred musicians and dancers had come down from Delhi for the wedding. Muhammad Shah insisted that the Vijayanagar king should meet the expenses of the musicians and dancers. The Vijayanagar King refused, and a battle ensued. Since then, defeat of the Vijayanagar King by the Bahmani Sultan and the vice-versa had been occurring now and then.

So I felt that my maternal grandfather was right when he said that these fights were not because of religious differences. But things had changed, and perhaps that was God's will.

The Bahmani Kingdom had split into five small ones. If this had not happened, then it could have been a force to reckon with. Many of the Bahmani Sultans had been able administrators. The founder of the Bahmani dynasty—Bahman Shah was a man who treated everyone fairly. He abolished the unfair jaziya tax imposed on non-Muslims. He built many orphanages and when there was a famine, he helped the poor, without discriminating on the basis of religion.

There was a poet in the Bahmani court, whose handwriting was supposed to be beautiful. Once every four days, he would write sixteen pages of the Holy Quran. If women were captured during war, he would treat them with respect, and send them away. Another king called Allaudin Ahmed built a place where people could go for treatment and here again there was no discrimination on the basis of religion. Once an eight-year-old boy called Ahmed Khan ascended the throne. His mother ruled on behalf of her minor son. The Queen and her Prime Minister Muhammad Khan were also known for their catholicity.

The jealousy and squabbles among their generals led to the decline of the Bahmani Sultanate.

The Bahamani Sultans had come to India three hundred years ago and had made this country their home. There were also others who came from Afghanistan and Persia and after successful battles, returned with their booty to their respective lands. There were fights between the Bahmani Sultans and the others who came in now and then. That too was a reason for the decline of the Bahmani Sultanate.

Adil Shah, against whom I was now leading my army, had earned the respect of the people. He treated people of other faiths with respect. It is said that he welcomed the Vaishnavite preceptor Venkata Thathayya with honours.

He did make forays into our territory. He had also given refuge to Siddhi, who had run away with our money, meant for buying horses. These were reasons enough for me to have declared war against him long ago. And yet I had hesitated. But now that I knew that Chinnadevi had been captured by the Sultan's men, I could no longer postpone the war.

༄

We were now getting closer to Adil Shah's camp. All the forts on the way fell one by one.

One fort was surrounded by a moat. We cut little canals for the water to flow out of the moat. After that, walking across the moat was easy.

Another fort had very high ramparts. The enemy was attacking us and he had the advantage of attacking from a height. So I had a platform built to the height of the fort walls. Now we were on level with the enemy, and so the advantage they had was lost. This victory was entirely due to the Muslim archers in my army.

Another victory came in the most bizarre fashion. One of our elephants ran amok. The enemy general took fright at the charging elephant and jumped off his horse and ran away. The horse returned to the enemy forces. Seeing the horse returning without the general, the soldiers assumed that the general had been killed. There was no one else to lead them and they all just ran away!

Appaji and the other ministers were generous with their praise. 'Your tricks work out. Luck is also on your side. Not only are the enemies defeated, but their armies have come under our control too,' said Pemmasani Ramalingam. Gayatri came to me with a garland of tulsi beads.

'Queen Thirumala Devi placed this garland before her favourite deity and prayed for your welfare. She requested that you wear this when you go out to fight,' she said, and gave the garland to me.

Pemmasani Ramalingam said, 'Your Majesty, for a long time I have considered starting a separate division of women soldiers in our army. If that idea materialises, then it would be a good idea to appoint Gayatri the chief of that unit.'

'Yes. Even brave generals will be felled when they see that their opponent is a woman,' Appaji mocked.

But Ramalingam was not offended by Appaji's remark. 'Prime Minister, this girl is very intelligent. She knows the tricks of warfare. She has even given me ideas, which have yielded favourable results,' he said.

'You have been talking about a secret plan for a long time. Was that secret plan this girl's idea too?' Appaji asked.

'Not at all. That was my idea.' But Ramalingam still did not elaborate on what the plan was.

A little after midnight, Ramalingam was preparing to leave with two thousand soldiers. He met me and Appaji and said, 'We will proceed silently. As soon as we throw up torches and shout, treat that as the signal for our army to attack.'

The men advanced stealthily, and Appaji and lakhs of soldiers followed them…

Suddenly thousands of torches lit the sky…

When we all pounced on Adil Shah's army, Pemmasani's plan became clear. The two thousand men who were with Pemmasani, cut off the ropes of the tents in the enemy camp. The tents collapsed on those who were sleeping inside. Before they could crawl out from under the tents, and see what had happened, we were upon them. We routed Adil Shah's forces.

When the next day dawned, the scene before my eyes…

As I had told Appaji, many drowned in the Krishna, while trying to escape. A few managed to escape. The elephants of the Sultan which entered the river, refused to come out of the river. Since it was summer, they found the water refreshing and soothing, and they began to play in the water and enjoyed themselves. Nothing that the mahouts did made them budge. Finally, the mahouts gave up trying and ran away. So now the Sultan's elephants too became ours, thereby adding to our elephant force. We also captured thousands of horses.

I had expected all this.

But something else that I had not anticipated happened too.

As I walked round looking at the bodies strewn around, I heard a voice call out, 'Your Majesty.'

It was a familiar voice. I looked in the direction from which the voice came and there lying on the ground was Ethirajan—Chinnadevi's brother!

Thirty-one

There is a demon inside me. He is asleep most of the time. Suddenly he wakes up. At such times, my good qualities, if I have any, disappear.

I was on the battlefield, where the cries of those at the door of death, and the shouts of joy of those celebrating victory could be heard. And there before me lay Ethirajan. The demon inside me was now becoming active. 'Let him die! Isn't it because of him that your love remains unfulfilled? He is the stumbling block in your love life. If you let him die, then you will be rid of the shackles with which he has bound your love.'

But this wicked wish died soon after it made its appearance. There were three reasons why it was short lived. First of all, Ethirajan was pleading with me to save him and to ignore him was wrong on humanitarian grounds.

Secondly, I didn't want to draw a blank here as had happened with Singapiran. All I knew so far was that Chinnadevi was somewhere in Vijayapuram. But where was she in that vast kingdom? I had no idea. I had come with my army, assuming that I would be able to find out where she was. But here was Ethirajan! He would know where Chinnadevi was.

Thirdly, Ethirajan had addressed me as 'Your Majesty'. That meant he no longer hated me.

Although I gave a lengthy account here, these conflicting thoughts occupied my mind for only a few fleeting seconds.

I bent down to have a look at him. He had been hurt by two arrows, one on either side of his chest. The bleeding from the wounds seemed to have stopped. The arrows had to be removed. If they were removed slowly, the pain would be unbearable, and the pain would kill him. And the moment the arrows were removed, the wounds would start bleeding again. If the bleeding was not stopped immediately, he would bleed to death.

'Move over, Your Majesty. Let me take care of him,' said a voice from behind me.

A familiar voice. I turned and found the Italian Nicholas there. There was a horse with him, and a man stood holding the reins of the horse.

'When did you come here?' I asked.

'When you returned after making Vyasaguru the king for a brief period, I too came here. I felt I could be of use to you,' he said. He wasted no more time talking.

When he bent towards Ethirajan, I thought he was going to lift him on to his horse and take him away for treatment. But he did not lift Ethirajan. He took a long rope that his assistant handed to him. He tied the rope to the two arrows. His assistant pressed down the horse's head. Nicholas tied the other end of the rope to the horse's bridle.

I watched, curious to know what he had in mind. 'The arrows will have to be yanked off in a second. That cannot be done by us,' he explained. Then to his assistant he said, 'Release your hold on the horse's head.'

His assistant lifted his hand from the horse's neck. The horse jerked back its neck, and the moment it did so, the two arrows came out. Blood flowed from the wounds. Nicholas didn't delay even for a second. He pressed some herbs on the wounds, and bandaged the wounds tightly. Ethirajan must have been in great pain and the herbs would have caused his wound to burn. But Ethirajan did not cry out in pain. He bore his pain patiently and silently. Not surprising, considering he was from the family of the great warrior Mallanna!

Two or three of my generals had joined us. 'Take this man to the tent where the wounded are treated,' said Nicholas. Four men carried Ethirajan to the tent.

'This is one way to pull out arrows. The usual method is to hold down the branch of a tree, and to tie the rope to the branch. The branch is then released suddenly and the force of the branch bouncing back pulls out the arrows. There was no tree nearby. That is why I used the horse,' explained Nicholas.

'You seem to have learnt some unique methods of treatment. Unfortunately, you have not done anything for Singapiran.'

'You are wrong, Your Majesty. I have been trying my best to cure Singapiran. I have prescribed oils to be applied on his head. A bath in waterfalls might help. So I have sent him to Tirupathi, to bathe in a waterfall there. In a month he should regain his lost memory. But we don't have to wait for him to get back his memory, because Gayatri has gathered a lot of information. She must have told you.'

'She seems to be smarter than you,' I teased.

I also noticed that at the very mention of Gayatri's name, his face became radiant. 'All right. Go and attend to Ethirajan. Send word to me when he is able to talk,' I said and sent Nicholas away.

The whole of that day I was busy organising my army and also bringing some order among the forces I had captured.

I was anxious to see how Ethirajan was doing. Would he have shed his hatred for me? Why had he joined Adil Shah's army? If he had joined the army out of compulsion, I shuddered to think what would have happened to Chinnadevi.

༄

All the generals and army officials were outside my tent, celebrating our victory. And it was no ordinary victory, for we had defeated the combined forces of Vijayapuram, Golconda and Ahmed Nagar.

The joy of victory helped me forget my worries for a while. Poets were singing verses celebrating our victory. Tenali Ramakrishna had brought along his latest work for my perusal. Even as he was about to present his manuscript to me, another poet called Durjati sang a verse in praise of me. 'The enemy's elephants refused to come out of the water. Aeons ago, their ancestor Gajendra had been saved from a crocodile by Lord Mahavishnu, and so the elephants would not turn against Krishnadevaraya, who is the incarnation of Lord Vishnu,' went the verse.

I laughed. 'So you've made me an incarnation of Lord Vishnu!' But it was true that my victories were making me arrogant. Every day I prayed to Lord Venkatachalapathy to help me conquer my arrogance.

I honoured Pemmasani Ramalingam. In order that Appaji should not feel left out, I asked him to present the shawl to Pemmasani. My father-in-law had headed a force of 400 horses, 20 elephants and 8000 foot soldiers, and had scored a great victory. I honoured him and all the other generals, and then said: 'We must not let slip this opportunity. Let us cross the Krishna and proceed towards Vijayapuram. Make preparations for our advance.'

Appaji interrupted. 'There is a lot of water in the Krishna river. So much, in fact, that I saw some elephants being washed away this morning. Let us wait until the water recedes, even if it takes a week or even a month,' he said.

How could I tell him that I wanted to leave at once, for the sake of my Chinnadevi?

'What happened to Adil Shah? Has he returned to Vijayapuram? Or did he die in the battle?'

'He could not have crossed the river. He is not dead, because we did not find his body. Some people said that he rode off towards the east. The other two Sultans have returned to their respective kingdoms,' said Minister Kondamarasu.

'My guess is that Adil Shah would have taken his army and gone to the Raichur fort. Since all our forces have been engaged in this battle, Raichur remains unprotected. So taking the Raichur fort would have been easy for him,' said Ramalingam.

Appaji bristled. 'For generations, Raichur has been a part of the Vijayanagar Empire. We cannot allow anyone else to step into our territory,' he said.

'Let us first capture Vijayapuram. All opposition to us will then die a natural death. What we have to do is wait for the waters of the Krishna to recede,' I said.

I waited for all the generals and ministers to leave. I could hardly contain myself any longer. I was anxious to meet Ethirajan. How could anyone know how eager I was for that meeting?

On my way to the tent where soldiers were being treated, I had to pass Thirumala Devi's tent. She must have seen me as I made my way to meet Ethirajan. She came out with a silver basket full of flowers, and with a container containing rose water.

'Long live the victorious king!' she said, and sprinkled rose water on me and put some rose petals on my feet.

I found it hard to resist her childlike affection. 'Sometime ago a poet described me as an incarnation of God. Now here you are worshipping me,' I laughed.

'You are my God,' she said, and then noticing a wound on my shoulder, she said, 'There is a wound there.'

'It is a very small wound. I am on my way to the physician to get that wound treated. You go and rest in your tent.'

I felt my wound. Thirumala Devi was right. There was a

small wound on my shoulder. That was when I realised how merciful God had been to me. What a battle it had been! I had been on horseback and had wielded my sword, killing many of the enemy force. And yet, except for this one small wound, I had no other wounds.

☙

That tent was like a huge hospital. Many soldiers lay on the ground, with their arms and legs and heads bandaged. Some of them recognized me and greeted me. Most of them were in such great pain, that they did not notice me. I comforted as many of them as I could, and then finally went to Ethirajan.

'He is much better now. There is no danger to his life,' said Nicholas, and left to attend to other patients.

Ethirajan looked pale, because of loss of blood. He tried to sit up. 'Please…you don't have to strain yourself,' I said.

We looked at each other in silence for a few minutes. I was tormented by a thousand memories.

My first meeting with Chinnadevi, in a village near Kalahasti…my pretence that I was a physician…my stay in Ethirajan's house…my dance lessons with Ethirajan…When it seemed as if the love Chinnadevi and I had for each other had met with his approval, the truth about my identity being revealed… Ethirajan speeding away on a horse with his sister…That village, that house, the garden in that house, where the breeze carried with it the fragrance of all kinds of flowers…

I was choked with emotion. I cleared my throat, and said, 'How do you feel now, Ethirajan?'

'You saved me in time. I feel better now.' As if he could read my thoughts, he added, 'And Chinnadevi is fine too.'

'I was told that you and Chinnadevi had been captured by the Vijayapuram Sultan…How can she be safe?' I asked in disbelief.

'Adil Shah is a cruel man. He punishes his enemies cruelly. He is a dictator. He killed many potential claimants to the throne. He has also imprisoned some claimants. All of this is true. But when it comes to women, he treats them with respect. His men took me and my sister to Vijayapuram and took us to the Sultan. They thought they would be rewarded. But all they received was punishment from the Sultan,' said Ethirajan.

Noticing that I had still not got over my surprise at his narration, he said, 'An important reason for the treatment we received was Venkata Thathayya's influence,' he said.

'Did he put in a word for you with the Sultan?' I asked.

'The Sultan treated us well, even without Venkata Thathayya's intercession. When we were taken to Vijayapuram, Venkata Thathayya was already there. All the members of the drama troupe were sent by the Sultan to Venkata Thathayya's matha. As usual we continue to stage dance dramas. Chinnadevi takes care of the day to day administration of the matha.'

I was moved when I thought of God's kindness, and I wiped the tears from eyes. 'So is Chinnadevi still in Vijayapuram?'

'No. She is not that far from where we are now. She is on the opposite bank of the Krishna river, where Acharya Venkata Thathayya has a matha…'

'Is Chinnadevi so close to us?' I asked excitedly. 'Now tell me, how did you come to fight against us?'

'When the war was announced, some men went round all the villages announcing the war, and they said that all able-bodied men above the age of twenty had to join the Sultan's army. They forced all the men to join the army. All of us at the matha had no choice but to join the army. I am alive. But who knows what has happened to the others?' Ethirajan became emotional when he thought of his friends.

'Ethirajan, I trust you no longer hate me for being a member of the royal family. Poet Allasani told me why you hate the royal family.'

'I was wrong, Your Majesty. Do you remember the elderly gentleman who was the chief of our troupe?'

'Yes, I do.'

'He is dead. One day I told him my story. He said to me, "Your ancestor Mallanna was killed by a king who belonged to the Sangama dynasty. Mallikarjuna and Virupaksha were the last kings of that dynasty. With them, that dynasty's rule came to an end. So there is no connection between Krishnadevaraya and the dynasty you think of as your enemy." I wasn't totally convinced. But…'

'But?'

'The Sultan's generals told us that you were leading an army to Vijayapuram, expressly for the purpose of freeing my sister. I realised how much you loved her, and that too played a role in changing my mind. And finally, today, on the battlefield, whatever doubts were left, disappeared. I was the one who had stood in the way of your love. You could have killed me. But you didn't. Instead, you saved my life.'

'That was God's doing. Anyway, you are weak. You mustn't talk so much. Take rest,' I said and came out of the tent.

I mulled over many things, as I walked along, aimlessly. One of my generals came up to me and said, 'Your Majesty, you mustn't go alone anywhere. Our enemies might still be lurking somewhere. I will send some soldiers with you.'

'No need to. I will be careful,' I said, and continued with my walk.

It was getting dark. Was a storm really brewing? Or was a storm of emotions tormenting me? As I put some distance between me and the battlefield, the smell of corpses that were beginning to decompose became more and more faint, and there were fewer vultures circling the sky. It was only after a long time, that I realised that I was walking along the banks of the River Krishna. The waters of the river flowed furiously, and the image of the moon in the waters quivered.

I couldn't see the opposite bank of the river. But I had the illusion that I could see the village, Venkata Thathayya's matha, and Chinnadevi at the entrance to the matha, welcoming me with extended hands.

I don't know what came over me. I took off my royal robes and ornaments, and left them near a rock. I tied a dhoti round my waist and entered the river.

Thirty-two

I don't care what you think of me. Scoff at me, and say, 'At a time when his focus should have been on how to use his courage and skills to make his military campaign successful, here was an emperor whose thoughts were of romance.' Ridicule me as the king who ruled over the entire area from the river Krishna to the Tamiraparani river, but who was a slave to his passion. I don't care.

When I entered the Krishna river, there was only one thought in my mind. I had to see Chinnadevi, who was on the other side.

It seemed as if the Gods were on my side. The water had receded a little. Where there was knee-deep water, I found a small coracle and an oar. I had been worried about how I would swim across the river to reach the opposite bank. Now I didn't have to worry about that, for here was a coracle I could use. I jumped into the coracle, and began to row.

After some time, I could see the opposite bank. It also seemed as if I was getting to a shallower part of the river. So I guessed I must have crossed three-fourths of the distance. I jumped out of the coracle and swam the rest of the distance. But I didn't let go of the coracle, but held on to it with one hand, even as I swam across.

When I reached the shore, I dragged the coracle out of the water and cast it on the sand, and ran towards the village. Was this the Nagaravedu village Ethirajan had spoken of? I spotted a goatherd. He had removed his dhoti and had rolled it up and with his head resting on this makeshift pillow, was fast asleep. I woke him up and asked him where the matha was.

He pointed a path to me, and then went back to sleep.

I walked in the direction indicated by him. I didn't know how many doors I would have to knock on, before arriving at the right place. Luckily, the first building in the street was the matha. It was an old building. It was painted in stripes of red and white, and the Vaishnavite symbol painted on the wall indicated that it was a Vaishnava matha.

I knocked on the door. I was about to call out too, but checked myself in time. How could I call out Chinnadevi's name? Or call out to Thathayya Swami? I didn't know whose name I should call out. So I just knocked, at first gently, and when there was no response, I wondered what I should do. The door was an old one and wouldn't take much knocking.

I could hear someone from behind the door. I was on tenterhooks. Who would open the door? What would I say to him or her?

The door opened.

Chinnadevi! Chinnadevi, with a lamp in her hand!

Since she now lived in the matha, she was dressed in very ordinary clothes, and wasn't wearing any jewellery. And yet she looked more beautiful than ever.

'Who is it?' she asked, but soon recognized me. I was dripping wet, and was not in my usual clothes. And yet, how could she have forgotten me? I was the one whose image was enshrined in her heart!

'Chinnadevi…Chinnadevi…' I said, and stepped forward.

Her hands shook. It seemed as if she might drop the lamp she was holding. She moved the lamp from her left hand to her right and held on to it tightly. It was midnight, and she didn't know if this was a dream, or was real.

Why hadn't she embraced me? Why hadn't she shed tears of joy? Why hadn't her tears drenched my chest?

'Chinnadevi,' I said and again tried to get close to her.

She stepped back, and said, 'Stop. Don't enter.'

'Chinnadevi, do you not recognize me?' I asked.

'Do you not realise where you are?' she asked.

'I know. This is a Vaishnavite matha. Your brother told me you were here. That is why I swam across the river. Nothing mattered to me—not the darkness or the difficult crossing of the river. Look at me. I saved your brother. He was wounded in the battle…'

She betrayed no emotion. 'Is that so? Thank you,' she said.

'Do you know that your brother has given his consent for our marriage? He has also realised that it was wrong of him to have thought of me as an enemy,' I said.

'Glad to hear that, Your Majesty,' she said, but she still stood blocking my way, as if she didn't want me to enter.

I was not prepared to be patient any longer. I tried to push her aside and enter.

'Do not enter. I swear upon your mother—you are not to enter. This is a place where renunciates live. Therefore, even if you are the Emperor, you cannot enter,' she said emphatically.

'Why? Why, Chinnadevi? Isn't our love more sacred than any sacred place? Is there any force that can stand in the way of our love?'

'Yes there is. Look,' she said, and lifted the lamp, and shone it on her arms. She had the Vaishnava emblems of the conch and discus branded on her arms. I wasn't surprised. Gayatri had already informed me about this.

Chinnadevi said calmly, 'Your Majesty, I am now a slave of God. I am a dancer attached to the Srivilliputtur Vadapatrasayee temple. I have lost the right to love any man.'

'No you have not. I will get you back your right to love.'

'You cannot, although you are the Emperor. Only one person can give me that right.'

'Who is that?'

'Acharya Venkata Thathayya!'

I laughed. 'Is that all? I will get his permission. Where is he?'

'He has gone to the North on a pilgrimage.'

'Which town has he gone to?'

'Hard to tell. A renunciate should not stay in one place for long. So it is hard to say where he is now.'

'When is he expected?'

'That too is hard to predict. It may even take a year or two.'

'Chinnadevi! This is cruel! This is torture! This is hell!' I shouted.

'Sshh! The employees of the matha and renunciates of the matha are asleep. I will send word to you, when the Acharya returns. You can talk to him…' she said, and smiled, as she was about to close the door.

'Oh, I forgot, Your Majesty,' she said.

'Forgot what?'

'To wish you. I heard that you have married the Princess of Srirangapatnam. I pray that you and Thirumala Devi should have a happy marriage!'

I was stung by her words. So that was the reason for her anger. She was angry that I had married another woman, and was showing her anger in this way. What a fool I was, not to have realised that!

'Chinnadevi, that was not a love match. That was a marriage of convenience. A marriage I had to go through because of political expediency. I haven't touched Thirumala Devi. She has told me that I should not touch her, until I have married you. We have not lived as husband and wife,' I explained.

I expected that when Chinnadevi heard my explanation, she would embrace me in joy. But how foolish I was to have had such expectations!

She gave me a sad smile. 'Your Majesty, please don't torture Thirumala Devi.'

'She is the one who made the decision. She is the one who decided that there should be nothing between us.'

'Whoever made the decision, I am the cause, am I not? Your Majesty, I do not want a beautiful, young princess to lose her marital happiness because of me. Please make her happy. She is far superior to me. She is the right match for you. She too is from a royal family. Do not treat her so.'

By now she had almost closed the door. A strong wind put out the lamp she was holding. 'Our love is like this lamp, isn't it?' I laughed dejectedly.

'No, Your Majesty. Our love is safe here,' she said and indicated her heart. 'The lamp of our love will never go out. No one can put out this lamp. I will guard this lamp till Acharya Venkata Thathayya comes and gives us permission to marry.'

'And if he doesn't?'

'If he doesn't, then I will live as I have lived the last four years. Why, I might even become a renunciate myself. Is there any rule that says only Jain women can become renunciates?'

My anger was increasing minute by minute.

'Very well, Your Majesty. I don't think it is proper for us to continue this conversation any longer.' She bowed before me, and closed the door. But I could hear her sobbing. After some time I heard her move away.

I walked back. I don't know how I reached the bank of the river, or how I found the coracle, or how I rowed, or how I reached the other side.

I was simply unaware of how I accomplished all this. I was in the grip of an inexplicable fury. I didn't know in which direction I should walk. Even as I hesitated, I saw a woman running towards me.

Thirumala Devi!

I didn't know what to say to her.

'Why have you come here?' I asked.

'Every night before retiring to bed, I used to come to your tent to check if everything was in place, so that you could rest well. As usual I went to your tent tonight. You were not there. I made enquiries and was told that you had come towards the river. That is why I...I...' she said.

'Have you been waiting here all this while?'

'Not for long. Since I couldn't find the coracle here, I guessed that you must have taken it to cross the river.'

'Do you know why I crossed the river?'

'I believe that you cannot do wrong, Your Majesty.'

I looked at her, without batting an eyelid.

I was moved by her loyalty to me, her comforting words, her trust in me...

'Thirumala...' I said, and embraced her.

It was not just my loneliness and the darkness. It was also my disappointing meeting with Chinnadevi. It was the rejection that I, an Emperor, had met with at the hands of a woman. I had begged for her love, but had been spurned. The shame of it! And here was this innocent girl—Thirumala—punishing herself. And here was I, a virile man, starving myself of physical pleasures...

All of these factors combined to make me aggressive.

'No, no, Your Majesty,' Thirumala protested. But she could not stop me, and after a while, her protests became feeble and she yielded to my passion.

Later on, thinking of my behaviour, I felt quite ashamed of myself. Wasn't it foolish of me to think that by forcing myself on Thirumala Devi, I was taking revenge on Chinnadevi? Would this one night make any difference to the love I had for Chinnadevi? Certainly not…

The next morning, Kondamarasu said, 'Your Majesty, I have some good news. Our men have brought word that the waters of the Krishna are receding.'

'What about marching against Raichur?' asked Appaji.

'That can be taken care of later. Right now, it is more important to march towards Vijayapuram. Once we cross the Krishna, we can subdue all the Sultans. This is the appropriate time…' said Kondamarasu.

'I too think that this is what we should do,' I said.

'I will inform the chief of the army,' said Kondamarasu and took leave of me.

'Let me have dinner. We need to have some important discussions after dinner,' said Appaji.

'I thought you told me that you had given up having dinner, because of a vow,' I said.

Appaji didn't reply, but gave me a mysterious smile.

'Why are you smiling?'

'Since you have put an end to your bachelorhood, I too have decided to give up my vow,' said Appaji.

'What is that supposed to mean?'

'Early this morning, I saw you and Queen Thirumala Devi coming together to the camp. Servants told me that the two of you spent the night on the banks of the Krishna river and returned only this morning,' Appaji laughed.

I didn't join in. 'It is true that I did slip from my resolve yesterday night. But that does not indicate that I have given up my resolve. However you don't have to continue with your vow of not eating at night,' I said sternly.

Appaji was about to leave, but I stopped him and said, 'Wait,

Prime Minister. When we march towards Vijayapuram tomorrow, I don't want any of the members of the royal family to accompany us. Send all of them to the capital.'

'What about the Queen Thirumala Devi?'

'I meant her too,' I said.

Thirty-three

There was a lot of excitement before our departure for Vijayapuram, also known as Bijapur.

Thirumala Devi came to my tent, and without raising her head to look at me, she said, 'I apologise for my mistake. Blame the weakness of my sex for it. I will be careful that it never happens again.'

'You did no wrong, Thirumala. It was my male arrogance that was responsible for what happened,' I said.

'Why do you punish me then? Why have you said that I am not to accompany you?' she asked, and I could tell how unhappy she was over my decision.

'Forgive me, Thirumala. I have to fight many battles. I do not want any distractions.'

She paid her respects to me and was about to leave, but she lingered for a moment to say, 'I hope that you will soon be united with Chinnadevi. I pray to Lord Ranganatha every day, so that your wish is fulfilled. Chinnadevi's presence beside Your Majesty, will bring auspiciousness to you.'

'My dream is destined to be just that—a dream,' I said, without giving her any details.

For a long time after she left, I paced up and down my tent. I had to plan for the battle that was imminent. But the irony was that I could make no plans for my personal life.

That afternoon, when the drums and other instruments were played, the Italian physician came to my tent. He no longer dressed like a foreigner. Why, even his dietary habits had changed and he was like one of us.

Whenever I see Nicholas, my thoughts go to my step

brothers—Achyuthan and Rangan, who are in the Chandragiri fort. They have no worries about the kingdom; they do not participate in any military campaigns; they live a life of comfort. But here was this Italian, Nicholas, who was risking his life for the sake of the soldiers of a country that was not his own.

'Nicholas, we are leaving for Bijapur. I suppose you are going back to Vijayanagar,' I teased. I knew that he had no such intention.

'Your Majesty, how could you say that? Some doctors from Europe are here. There are Indian physicians too. I have formed a medical unit consisting of all the European doctors and Indian ones. I have also employed many men to help us in our work. Our medical unit will also travel with your army,' he said.

I was choked with emotion when I heard him affirm his resolve to come with me. All I could say was, 'I am glad to hear that, Nicholas.' In order to mask my emotions, I teased him again. 'I suppose you know that Gayatri isn't coming with us. She is going back with the other women,' I said.

'Yes, Your Majesty,' said Gayatri, who was stepping into my tent. 'I have come to take leave of you.'

Although I said Gayatri would go back with the other women, actually I wanted her to come with us. I felt her presence would be a tonic when I felt worn out and her advice would be of help when I was confused. But I hesitated to express my wish.

I hid my disappointment and said, 'Good decision, Gayatri. You will be of help to my mother and to Thirumala Devi.'

'I will be there only for a few days, Your Majesty. The doctor has assigned a task to me. Once that is completed, I will be back here.'

'What task? Has he asked you to gather some herbs?' I laughed.

'Yes, Your Majesty,' she said, and showed me some herbs. 'He has asked me to look for these herbs on Matanga Hill,' she said. I laughed again.

'On Matanga Hill? Instead why don't you go to the desert, which they say is called the Sahara? Why don't you look for herbs there?' I then said to Nicholas, 'Matanga Hill is rocky, with no vegetation. If you plan to build a temple, you can use the rocks there,' I said.

'Gayatri is the one who said that there were herbs on Matanga Hill,' said Nicholas, before leaving to attend to some work he had.

'Gayatri, if you want to go to Vijayanagar, why don't you say so? Why give these excuses, and why deceive poor Nicholas?'

'I have something to do on Matanga Hill, Your Majesty. I am not going to look for herbs, but for something else.'

'Don't tell me it is a treasure hunt,' I said.

'In a sense, it is,' she said and gave me a mysterious smile.

'I never get straightforward answers from you. If I ask you a question, all you say is, "Your Majesty, I want you to lead a happy life, because there is a favour I plan to ask you".'

'That's exactly what I say now too,' she said, and left.

I have already told you about Matanga Hill.

Kishkinda was supposed to have been nearby. When Ravana carried Sita away, she cast off her ornaments, and her ornaments fell there; Rama and Sugriva met here; there is a cave called Sugriva cave, and there is a mound which is supposed to be the place where Vali was cremated.

There are many stories about hidden treasures in Matanga Hill. Some foolish people, believing these stories to be true, have searched the hill for hidden treasures. But no one has ever found anything here...

But Gayatri's smile, her determination, made me suspect that she was indeed going to look for some treasure on the hill.

She wasn't going to find anything on the hill. That was certain. And even if she did, what was she going to do with it? What did she need a treasure for?

This was one more unresolved mystery about Gayatri. Appaji's voice broke in on my thoughts 'We have a good omen now,' he said.

'What?' I asked.

'I had to ensure that the omens were good before we left. I heard a washerman's song…'

'And what was that song about?'

'This is our land! The one nearby is also ours. And if anyone questions us, then to them we shall say Delhi too is ours!' went the song. Appaji sang the song for me! If the old man was enthusiastic, he would not just sing, but even dance!

'An auspicious song indeed!' I said. But, although I agreed with him about the omens for our departure being good, the mention of Delhi took my thoughts elsewhere. If I had to release Chinnadevi from her vow, I would have to meet Venkata Thathayya, and he was somewhere in the North.

A new dynasty, known as the Mughals, had come to Delhi.

I had heard that the founder of that dynasty was a man with no formal education, but that he was a brilliant man. I had heard that he knew Persian and Arabic. But apart from this, I knew nothing much about the northern kingdoms. I didn't know the names of the rulers of all the little kingdoms up north… So how I was going to find Venkata Thathayya?

Perhaps it was all for the good, I thought. Let me think of the kingdom for a change, and not of Chinnadevi, I told myself. Let the romance of Krishnadevaraya be consigned to the flames of war!

I stood outside the tent. A cavalcade of palanquins, carrying the women of the royal family, and the soldiers who accompanied them, went past me. Thirumala Devi was in a palanquin. As she crossed me, she took leave of me. 'Best wishes,' I said to her. She turned and kept looking at me, even as the palanquin moved away, and I felt sorry. But only he who bears sorrows, has the right to enjoy happiness. I reminded myself of a Sanskrit proverb that says that he who refuses to eat that which is sour, has no right to savour that which is sweet.

༄

By God's grace, and because of Appaji's incomparable guidance, I won against Bijapur. We overcame resistance in the forts of Athangi, Vinukonda, Bellamkonda, Rajukonda, Devarakonda, Mudgal, Nagarjunakonda, Thangedu and Kethavaram. We captured Golconda, Ahmednagar, Bidar and Berar.

All these small Muslim kingdoms had their origin in the Bahmani Sultanate. That dynasty had three heirs. They were imprisoned in the Gulbarga fort. I rescued them and installed Muhammad Shah, the eldest of them, as the Sultan.

'We have to ensure that there is no unity among our enemies. So we have to make one of them king,' Appaji advised. But I also felt this would be a magnanimous thing to do. So I agreed. I was given the title *Yavana Rajya Sthapanacharya*—the one who had established the Yavana kingdom. (Yavana was the term used to refer to Muslims.)

Whichever direction I went in, I heard cries of victory! But I faced setbacks too. During the Vinukonda battle, I saw my men take to their heels, unable to face the enemy attack. I cut up as many of the deserters as I could.

'If anyone tries to run away, this will be his fate. You have one life. You must give up your life for the Vijayanagar Empire.

Don't lose it because of your cowardice,' I shouted, and those who were attempting to run away, returned to fight. After that, we did not face defeat anywhere. Wherever we went, I built pillars to mark our victory, and made grants to temples. I ensured that the Muslims were given protection. I also gave them some special rights. I appointed Bhaskarayya, Veerabhadrayya, Ayyavaiyya and Chennamma Naidu as my representatives. My final stop was Raichur.

I had been informed that Adil Shah, the Sultan of Bijapur was there.

The battle in Raichur was severe. Those inside the fort had gathered enough food and water to withstand a five year siege. We had with us seven lakh foot soldiers, an equestrian force consisting of 32000 horses, and 150 elephants.

It was during this war that I saw a weapon called 'musket'. Some Portuguese who had come under the leadership of Christovao had brought it with them.

Their aim was to protect their trade interests in Goa from the Muslims. So they had offered to join me. Theirs was a small force. But that weapon they had, which they called musket, inflicted a lot of damage on the enemies. If a man peeped from behind the walls of the fort, they would take aim at his head, and a bullet would be released from their muskets, and would fell the enemy.

Adil Shah had cannons on the walls of his fort. But the cannons could only attack targets that were a long distance from the fort. Since we had camped near the fort, the cannons posed no danger to us. We broke down the walls of the fort.

I had planned to have peace talks with Adil Shah, and restore his kingdom to him. I had, therefore, sent word to him. I had even waited for him. But he did not turn up.

'Adil Shah will not come. He has many enemies in his

kingdom. They will not allow him to make peace with you. They have told him that if he wanted peace with you, you would insist that he kiss your feet. Our spies have given me this information…' said Appaji.

Appaji was right. Adil Shah did not come out of the fort. He fell victim to the Portuguese musket, and he could not be traced among the thousands of bodies that piled up. Once again, Raichur became a part of the Vijayanagar Empire.

ఌ

I returned to my capital, after two years. And during those years that I was away, I kept receiving news from the palace that all was well. Even if no information had come, I wouldn't have had time to worry about it. I fought battle after battle, with victory as my only goal.

Only now had I begun to think about others.

People lined the streets of the capital, to welcome me. There was nothing unusual about this. Every time I returned from a successful military campaign, people cheered me. But this time it seemed as if they were more joyous than before. Many pointed to me and said something to each other and smiled.

It was only when I reached the palace that I realized the reason for those smiles.

My mother welcomed me. She was holding a child in her hands. The child was dressed in silk and was wearing a lot of jewels.

'Your son, Krishna. The heir that Thirumala bore for our Empire. I've named him Thirumalai…' said my mother and handed the child to me.

Thirty-four

I took my child in my arms, hugged him, and looked at him. His face looked like a lotus carved in gold. He grabbed my moustache and gave it a tug.

My mother laughed. 'You little rogue! He may be your father, but he is my son! Don't tug at his moustache. You will hurt him,' she said.

I experienced a gamut of emotions.

Should I pat myself on the back, for having provided an heir for the throne of Vijayanagar? Or should I hang my head in shame because I had succumbed to a momentary weakness on the banks of the Krishna river one night?

'Mother, how could you have kept something so important from me? Is it fair?' I asked.

'What do you expect me to do? I am no longer the Queen. I am only the former queen. Who pays attention to me any more? There is the Queen. She is the one who makes decisions. Ask her why she didn't let you know,' said my mother.

I noticed Thirumala Devi standing at the entrance to the women's quarters of the palace.

I put Thirumalai down. He held on to my finger. I felt the rings on my finger would hurt his tender fingers. So I removed them and wore them on the other hand. Usually it is a father who infuses a son with confidence. But in my case, it was the other way round. It seemed as if I was drawing strength from him. Thirumala Devi was only a few feet away from me. But as I walked towards her, I wished the distance was greater, so that I would walk for a long time with my son holding my finger.

I stood before Thirumala Devi. I picked up my son and made him lift her face with his little fingers.

'Thirumala, servants from the palace kept coming to the battlefront almost every day. Why did you not send word through them about the birth of our son?' I asked.

'You were focused on defeating the enemy. I did not want you to be distracted by anything. That is why I didn't inform you. Forgive me, please,' she said.

But I knew that that was not the reason. She did not want to remind me of that night, when I became a victim of my passion. That is why she had not told me about the birth of the child. I was moved by her thoughtfulness, and I moved closer to her, and said, 'Thirumala…'

She stepped back. I realised that she did not want me to repeat my 'mistake'.

'Ethirajan has been telling your mother and me that you would definitely bring my elder sister, with you. Haven't you brought her along?' she asked.

'Your elder sister?'

'She means Chinnadevi,' said my mother. By now Ethriajan had also arrived.

I had last seen him during the Bijapur battle. I had asked Nicholas to send him to the capital. But I hadn't expected that he would be staying here in the palace or that he would be on such friendly terms with my mother and with Thirumala Devi!

'How are you, Ethiraja?' I enquired.

'By your grace, I am doing well,' he replied. 'I have been making enquiries of all the people who came from the battlefield, if they had met a lady called Chinnadevi. They all said that there was no one called Chinnadevi in our camp. Why? Wasn't she in the place I mentioned?'

I sighed.

'I found her. I spoke with her. But she said that she could not accompany me without permission from Venkata Thathayya. And the Acharya is on a pilgrimage to the North,' I said.

'Yes, the Acharya's permission is important,' Ethirajan admitted sadly. 'He was the one who helped my sister and me, when we were faced with a problem. Actually, my sister is more indebted to him than even I. Give me permission, Your Majesty. I will scour all the villages in the North, and find him.'

'Don't be in a hurry. There is going to be a debate between the Jains and Sri Vaishnavas soon. The Acharya will be here to preside over the debate. We can talk about Chinna to him then,' said my mother, vetoing Ethirajan's suggestion. 'Just make sure Chinna is safe till then,' she said to me.

Before I could respond, I heard some commotion outside the palace. 'Long live the Emperor! Long live the Prince!' the people shouted.

Minister Kondamarasu said, 'The people want to see you, the Queen and the Prince together. Everyone knows that an heir has been born. But no one has seen the Prince so far.'

I stepped out on to the balcony, with Thirumalai in my arms. I made him bring his palms together and greet the people. The people were delighted and shouted their approval. The child too was pleased with all the adulation.

When we came back into the palace, we found ministers, kings and generals waiting for us. They greeted Thirumala and me, and presented gifts to us. Soon there was a huge pile of gifts beside us.

And suddenly I saw him—Viswanathan!

The scars on his body bore testimony to his courage. 'What happened, Viswanatha?' I asked.

'With your blessings, I defeated Nagama Nayak in Madurai, after a fierce battle. I captured him and he is now a prisoner.

What punishment should he be given?' Viswanathan asked me.

I was astounded.

Not once did he refer to Nagama Nayak as his father. When he had volunteered to go to Madurai, to fight against Nagama Nayak, I hadn't been sure he would succeed. But he had! And it was not just an achievement. It was an act of selflessness.

For a minute I forgot that I was the Emperor and that he was but the chief of a small division in my army. I embraced him and said, 'Viswanatha! What a great warrior you are!'

Minister Mangarasaiya said, 'Your Majesty, I have a request.'

'What is it?' I asked.

'I met Nagama Nayak in prison. He says it was never his intention to turn against you. He says he wanted to entrust Madurai to his son. In any case, he says he will apologise to Your Majesty,' he said.

I looked at Viswanathan. He was silent. He didn't utter a word in defence of his father. I knew then how I should reward him.

'Viswanatha, release your father and take him with you to Madurai, and fulfil his wish,' I said.

He was shocked.

'What does that mean, Your Majesty?'

'It means that Madurai belongs to you and your descendants. You will be an independent ruler there, of course with allegiance to the Vijayanagar Empire.'

'Your Majesty, I...I...'

'You have all the necessary qualities,' I reassured him. I put my sword on his head and blessed him.

I told Mangarasayya to tell Appaji to prepare the documents needed to install Viswanathan as the ruler of Madurai.

I gave Viswanathan an encouraging pat, and said, 'It is your responsibility to make Madurai another Vijayanagar. Your loyalty to your king will help you succeed in this task.'

He still hadn't recovered from the pleasant shock. 'Wait,' I said to him. I summoned a palace servant and said, 'Ask the palace administrator to bring an expensive garment.'

Vijayanagar Emperors wore a garment only for a day. They had to wear new clothes everyday. There was an official whose task it was to take charge of the discarded clothes everyday. He had to keep a list of all the clothes. When ambassadors, scholars and merchants visited, the discarded clothes would be given to them as gifts. Since the clothes were very expensive ones and because they had been worn by the Emperor himself, they would gladly accept them.

The palace official brought a discarded robe of mine. I draped it around Viswanathan's shoulders. The robe had silver and gold foil and pearls stitched on to it. Viswanathan accepted my gift humbly, and went his way.

I didn't know if I would be alive to see it, but I knew that either during his reign or during the reign of his descendants, a famous dynasty was going to grace Madurai.

Mother gave gifts to all the women servants of the palace. I realised that Gayatri was nowhere to be seen. 'Mother, where is Gayatri?' I asked.

'She spends most of the day in Matanga Hill,' Mother replied.

'I suppose she is looking for herbs.'

'There are no herbs on that hill. Maybe she has joined the ranks of those who hunt for treasure in the hill.'

'All right. She spends half her time on the hill. What does she do the rest of the time?'

'She spends the rest the time in the palace library, reading old manuscripts. Maybe she plans to write something, like

Madura Vijayam which was written by Ganga Devi, the Queen of Kumara Kampanna. All I can say is that she is a girl whose ways are mysterious.'

So far I had been the only one who had made the observation that Gayatri was a mysterious girl. Now Mother too was making the same observation!

'I have to perform an abishekam[21] in the Balakrishna temple. Once that is done, I can relax,' said Mother.

'In that case, let us leave now,' said Appaji.

There were many temples in Vijayanagar, which had lovely sculptures and which also attracted many devotees. And yet Mother had chosen this old temple. I didn't know why.

I was seated before the sanctum sanctorum, with my son on my lap. My mother and Thirumala were seated beside me. And behind us were seated the ministers.

'Krishna, look at the idol, for which the abhishekam is being performed,' Mother whispered to me.

I could see nothing special about it.

'That is not the original,' Mother said.

'What!'

'This was once a prosperous temple. When the Gajapati kings of Kalinga invaded our country, they took away the Balakrishna idol that was in this temple. A new idol was installed here in its place.'

I looked at the idol. It was shorn of all ornamentation. It did look more recent than the temple.

'Where is the original idol?' I asked.

'In Udayagiri.'

'Udayagiri? That comes under the rule of the Kalinga king Prataparudra Gajapati.'

---

21. Abhishekam—special puja

'Yes. I want you to retrieve it and bring it back to this temple. I cannot rest in peace until you have done that.'

༄

The next day, at the ministerial meeting, I suggested a campaign against Udayagiri, but there was a lot of opposition to my suggestion. Appaji was the first to object.

'Your mother's desire is legitimate. But to capture the fort of Udayagiri, we will have to fight against Prataparudra Gajapati. We have just returned from a long war. The soldiers are all tired. Another war now? No soldier will be willing.'

Even the general Ramalinga Nadiu, the author of our victory against the Bahmani Sultans, said, 'There is another danger too, Your Majesty. The Bahmani Sultans are waiting for an opportunity to have their revenge on us. If we proceed towards the East, the Sultans will regroup, and enter our Empire. They will try to recapture the territories they have lost. We might even lose Raichur to them.'

'Forgive me for barging in,' said a voice.

That was Gayatri at the entrance to the hall.

I was furious. 'You seem to think that all you have to do is say, "Forgive me for the intrusion." You seem to be under the impression that if you say that, it gives you the license to interfere in everything. Get out!'

'It is enough if Your Majesty has a look at this,' she said, and placed before me a bundle of manuscripts, and left the hall.

Thirty-five

What did these manuscripts contain? Why did Gayatri bring them to me? I looked at my ministers to see if they could throw some light, but they were just as clueless as I was.

'This girl knows no etiquette,' Appaji said angrily.

Minister Nadendla Gopa took the manuscript bundle from me and untied it. 'It is written in Sanskrit. It is titled *Dynasty of Katak*,' he said.

We all sat up waiting for him to tell us more. We could guess that it was about the dynasty of the Gajapati kings.

'I've heard that the history of the Katak kings has been written in three languages. The one in Odia is called *Madala Panji*.'

'What a novel name!' I said.

'Panji means a palm leaf manuscript. It has details about the Puri Jagannath temple, the accounts of the temple, details about the Gajapati kings who are the administrators of the temple—the work gives innumerable details.'

'All right, you have explained "Panji". But why "Madala"?'

'The manuscripts are rolled up and preserved in the temple, and the roll looks like a maddalam[22]. Hence the name Madala Panji. It is a huge bundle of manuscripts. It cannot be brought out of the Jagannath temple. One is not allowed to note down any details from it. Another work that records the history of the Kalinga kings is in Telugu. It is called *Jagannatham Kaifiyat*. But no one knows where the manuscript of the Telugu work is. The third account is in Sanskrit, and is called *Katakaraja Vamsavali*, and it is a copy of that Gayatri has brought here. The copy must

---

22. *Maddalam*—a percussion instrument

have been there in our palace library, and she must have brought it from there,' said Gopa.

Appaji lost his patience.

'That servant girl is always doing something secretive. What is she up to now?' he asked.

Nadendla didn't pay attention to Appaji. He kept studying the manuscript.

'What do these manuscripts contain?' I asked. I recalled my mother telling me that Gayatri was busy in the library, researching something.

'We have gathered to discuss an expedition against Udayagiri. What is the connection between this manuscript and our mission?' Appaji asked.

I lost my temper. Appaji found fault with whatever Gayatri did. As for me, I felt that whatever Gayatri did was well-intentioned.

'I am sure there is some connection. You go ahead, Gopannna,' I said.

'If I read out every line, it will take a long time for us to finish. I will read a few portions and summarise them for you,' said Gopanna. Everyone waited eagerly to hear what he was going to say. Appaji could do nothing but sulk.

'The Kalinga Kingdom was ruled at first by the Gangas. Their empire extended up to Bengal. The last king in that dynasty was Bhanudeva. He had no children. He prayed to Lord Jagannatha for a son, and the Lord appeared in his dream and told him to go to the temple of Vimla, and that he would find a baby at the entrance to the temple. The king did as directed and found a baby boy. He named the child Kapileswara and made him his heir,' said Gopanna, who stopped at this juncture and gave a wry smile.

'What is the matter, Nadendla?' I asked.

'This work says that Kapileswara was discovered outside a temple. But the people have a different account. They say that Kapileswara belonged to the lower strata of society, and that he usurped the throne, resorting to trickery, and that such stories were intended to mask his treachery.'

When Nadendla said this, I was reminded of my own lineage. I too was the son of a serving girl.

'How does his birth matter? I've been told that he was great king,' I said. I spoke to him harshly, and Gopanna didn't know the reason for my annoyance. He got over his discomposure and continued: 'Waging wars became a way of life with the Kalinga kings. On the one hand, they fought the Bahmani Sultans; on the other, they fought the Sultan of Bengal; They also fought the Reddys of Rajamahendravarma. However, for a long time, they were friendly with us. Once they asked for a princess of Vijayanagar to be given in marriage to one of their princes. But we refused, and since then they have been our enemies.'

'Why did we refuse? They are royalty and we are a royal family too,' I said.

'Maybe so. But during the Puri Jagannath temple chariot festival, the Gajapati kings sweep the roads. They consider it an honour to do so. But some people have spun a story that the Gajapatis were not a royal family at all and that they belonged to the serving class. So the Vijayanagar Empire spurned their offer of marriage.'

'Again and again it is this wretched caste system,' I said angrily.

Minister Mangarasaiyya said, 'What else do these manuscripts contain? Let us be done with these manuscripts soon.'

'The manuscripts repeatedly talk of the battles we fought against the Gajapatis. The unpalatable truth is that most of the time we were defeated. They have captured a lot of our territory. Udayagiri is one of the places we lost to them.'

I looked at Appaji and smiled. 'See? Udayagiri is ours. So we would be justified in trying to retrieve it. It is to make us aware of this that Gayatri must have brought these manuscripts,' I said.

'We know this history. There was no need for a serving girl to educate us. If your mother tells you to capture Udayagiri, it makes sense. But why should this girl evince an interest in this? I think she has some personal enmity against the Gajapatis,' said Appaji.

'But Appaji, sometime ago, you said that this girl might be a spy working for the Kalinga kingdom,' I reminded Appaji.

'What is this?' exclaimed Gopana. 'There is another manuscript along with the one on the Gajapati dynasty.'

His words kindled our curiosity.

Gopanna was silent for a few minutes, as he scrutinised the manuscript. I couldn't contain my curiosity, and peered over his shoulder. 'Gopanna, this manuscript is in Telugu,' I observed.

'Yes, this one is in Telugu. It is written by one of your ancestors—the Saluva king Narasimha.'

'Written by Saluva Narasimha? Let me have a look,' said Appaji and snatched the manuscript from Gopanna. 'Yes, it is written by Saluva Narasimha. It bears his royal emblem.'

'All right. Read what it says,' I said, annoyed at the frequent interruptions.

'This is a request by me—King Saluva Narasimha—to the Vijayanagar Emperors who succeed me. Udayagiri has belonged to the Vijayanagar Empire for a long time. But I have lost it today. The King of Kalinga—Purushottama Gajapati has entered Vijayanagar and has plundered the city. On his way back, he has captured Udayagiri. By losing Udayagiri to him, I have besmirched the name of our Empire. I cannot fight against him. I am too old, and I do not have the wherewithal to fight him. It is the duty of my successors to retrieve Udayagiri. It is especially important to retrieve the Balakrishna idol, which Gajapati has taken from our temple and re-install it here. Only then will my soul rest in peace and Vijayanagar's honour will be restored.'

After reading the manuscript, Appaji said, 'Saluva Narasimha has signed this manuscript and also affixed the royal seal.'

Army General Ramalinga Naidu was excited. A while ago, he had objected to the Udayagiri expedition. But now he said, 'The Queen Mother has already expressed her desire that the Balakrishna idol be brought back. And now we find that was Saluva Narasimha's wish too.'

Even while Appaji was deliberating whether he should endorse Ramalinga Naidu or not, Gayatri entered, with Thirumalai in her arms. 'The Queen said that Thirumalai has been crying asking for Your Majesty. So Her Majesty asked me to leave the child with you,' she said, and put the child on my lap, and turned to leave, when Appaji stopped her.

'Stop, why did you search for this manuscript?' he asked.

'I didn't search for it, Prime Minister. I chanced upon it. The Queen Mother asked me to index the manuscripts in the library. That was something I enjoyed doing. While I was indexing the manuscripts, I stumbled upon this one. I recalled the Queen Mother expressing a desire that the Balakrishna idol be brought back from Udayagiri. So I brought the manuscript here. I had nothing else in mind when I brought the manuscript here.' She sounded confident and yet humble.

'All right, you may go,' I said to her. I felt she wasn't telling the truth about how she had found the manuscript. I was sure she hadn't found it accidentally, and that she had worked according to a plan.

I now knew why she had spent hours in the library. One more mystery remained. I had to find out why she roamed about in the Matanga Hill.

I looked at my son Thirumalai. He was playing with my diamond necklace. His smile was divine. His eyes were redrimmed, because he had been crying. I wiped the tears at the corner of his eyes.

After a long time, I asked Appaji what his opinion was.

'What am I to say? You have already made up your mind. General Ramalinga Naidu has also given his consent. But it is true that the soldiers are all tired. So let us leave after a few months.'

'You sound so unenthusiastic, Appaji. Can't you say it more cheerfully?'

'All right. I endorse you decision cheerfully,' said Appaji.

☙

That night, I couldn't sleep, and paced up and down the balcony. I noticed that the town was well-lit. But the street where the Balakrishna temple was located was dark. Every temple appointed a man, whose duty it was to check if there was oil in the lamps in the temple, and also to tease the wick. He received a salary from the temple. I presumed that the Balakrishna temple hadn't appointed anyone for the purpose. I must make sure they did, I told myself.

The darkness in the temple could be taken care of, once a man was appointed to ensure the lamps were kept burning. But who would light a lamp to dispel the darkness and gloom in my heart? Chinnadevi was the only one capable of lighting a lamp in my heart. And for Chinnadevi to become mine, Venkata Thathayya would have to return.

I was angry with myself, for thinking of Chinnadevi and not concentrating on my duties. My focus should be on defeating my enemies, and expanding my Empire. Duty came first and romantic attachment came next. I suppose God has arranged for this Udayagiri expedition, to remind me of this.

I shook off my thoughts of romance. War! War! War! That would be my focus for some time. I hardened my heart.

☙

Udayagiri had a strong fort and was on top of a hill. The path that led up to the fort was a very narrow one. The path was strewn with rocks, making it difficult for horses and elephants to climb the hill. I led my men up the hill and made them break the rocks that obstructed our path.

The paternal uncle of Prataparudra Gajapati, was in charge of the fort. After a fierce battle, we defeated him and captured the fort.

My first task was to look for the Balakrishna idol. What if the idol had been installed in some temple in the city? Wouldn't it be a sin to uproot it?

Fortunately for me, I didn't have to make such uncomfortable decisions. The idol was in the palace. It was a small idol of Lord Krishna as a child, crawling on all fours, with a ball of butter in one of His hands. I gave the idol to the priest and asked him to wrap it in a silk cloth. He then handed it over to our army generals, to whom I said, 'Take this idol safely to our capital.'

'Now that we have accomplished our mission, isn't it time to return?' asked Appaji.

'No, Appaji. We have more wars to wage. I plan to continue with my military expeditions. We have to capture all the forts belonging to the Kalinga kingdom and we have to advance towards Katak, the Kalinga capital. That is my aim.'

'Very well, let us do as you say,' said Appaji. 'Your Majesty, I have something to say to you in private. Will you please step aside?'

I went to the top of the fort.

'Look down, Your Majesty.'

I looked down and I saw the tents where the soldiers were resting.

'Look at the women there. They are the women servants who have accompanied the army, and you can see that girl Gayatri there.'

I had clearly instructed the women servants of the palace that none of them should accompany us on this campaign. And yet, Gayatri had come. She had disobeyed my orders and she was here without my knowledge.

Appaji gave me a contemptuous smile, which only annoyed me further. 'Bring her here,' I ordered.

Thirty-six

'I will send for that girl,' said Appaji.

I was furious with Gayatri. She did a lot of things without my knowledge.

I went to my tent and lay down on my bed. I knew that when one was angry, important decisions would have to be deferred. To keep my mind occupied, I turned to the manuscript that lay beside me. It was about governance and administration. Every day, I made some entries, based on what I thought were important for administration of a kingdom. I thought my descendants would find it useful.

As I thought of my descendants, my thoughts went to my little boy, whom I had left behind in Vijayanagar. What would he be doing now? He was perhaps having a stroll in the garden, with one of his little hands holding his grandmother's hand and the other holding his mother's hand. He would see the butterflies on the flowers. He would shake off the hands of his mother and grandmother and run after the butterflies. His mother and grandmother would laugh at his antics…

These pleasant thoughts soothed me, and so when Gayatri arrived, my anger against her had subsided. I couldn't be stern with her.

'Gayatri, I don't like what you have done. I had left specific instructions that no one from the palace was to accompany us. And yet you have come.'

'Your Majesty, I am a servant. Many serving girls have accompanied the army. I have come as a serving girl too.'

Appaji who was just entering, said, 'Don't try to be clever. Those who disobey a royal command are punished with death.

But because the Queen Mother is fond of you, I am prepared to excuse you. Go back to the capital now. You have an hour's time. Leave.'

When Appaji ordered her to leave, Gayatri fell at my feet and said, 'Your Majesty, please don't order me to go back. I have accompanied you to many war fronts. I am anxious to witness the Kalinga war. It is my only desire. I have kept myself alive only to witness your march against Katak, and to see the fall of Gajapati, the King of Kalinga.'

I was taken aback. Appaji was livid.

'Look here! You may have many desires. That does not mean that you can dictate to the Vijayanagar emperor on military matters. We haven't yet decided whether we should march against Katak or not. How can you decide what we should do?' Appaji said.

'Forgive me, Prime Minister. You must definitely march against Katak. Victory will certainly be yours. I swear on my mother, you will be successful,' said Gayatri.

Appaji gave her a wry smile. 'If wars were won on the basis of hope, then the Vijayanagar flag would have been flying all over the country long ago. Hope and belief are not to be confused with practicalities,' said Appaji. 'Your Majesty, we have received some information yesterday night.'

'What is it?'

'You know that Gajapati Prataparudra has the support of the generals known as Mahapatras. There are a total of sixteen Mahapatras. Each of them has a huge army at his disposal. They have all pledged their support to Gajapati. It will be difficult to defeat their combined strength.'

'Again, you must forgive me,' said Gayatri. 'We don't have to worry about any of those Mahapatras. We can advance upon the enemy. I swear there will be no danger from the Mahapatras.'

I had not expected Gayatri to speak so emphatically. Neither had Appaji.

'Appaji, we cannot advance upon Katak, based on assurances given by this girl. But I have already decided to march against Katak. You are a clever military strategist. You must start making preparations. Even if sixteen thousand Mahapatras oppose us, we will still be victorious!'

The best way to make me resolve to fight someone, is to tell me my chances of victory are slim. Appaji knew it and must have cursed himself for his discouraging words.

'As you please, Your Majesty,' he said, glared at Gayatri, and left.

There was an awkward silence for some time. Gayatri broke the silence. 'Your Majesty, do you remember what I always told you, when you asked me to tell you about my life?'

'Yes, I do. You would always say, "Your Majesty, I want you to be happy. I want to accomplish something for which I will need your help." Now what is it you wish to accomplish with my help?'

'This Kalinga war.'

She looked directly at me, without lowering her gaze. People who look one in the eye while speaking can be trusted. This is something I have learnt through experience.

'At least now, tell me who you are. Where are you from? Why are you so anxious that Gajapati should be defeated?'

For a long time she remained silent. Dance programmes were being organised to entertain the soldiers, and I could hear the music distinctly.

'If you accompany me after sunset tomorrow, I will show you something,' she said. 'Cover yourself with a cloak, so that no one will recognize you.'

I didn't know what to make of her words. Was she scheming

and devious? Or was she someone I could trust? I couldn't make up my mind, but after a few seconds I said, 'All right, I will come.'

Appaji was pacing up and down outside the tent, impatiently. As soon as Gayatri left, he came into my tent, and asked, 'What punishment are you going to give that girl?'

'The arguments in this case are far from complete. Tomorrow evening she is going to take me somewhere after sunset, to show me something. My judgment will be deferred until then.'

Appaji frowned. 'I will send an escort with you.'

'No. She has said we should go alone. Let me see what happens. And Appaji, you are not to send someone to shadow me.'

Appaji's anger was writ large on his face.

The next evening, I accompanied Gayatri. I had covered myself with a cloak, and so no one recognized me. Gayatri was dressed like a servant.

Milestones marking the boundaries indicated we had moved out of the town. The milestones gave details about the distance to the next town. The stones also had holes drilled in them. This was for the benefit of those who could not read. They could tell the distance by the number of holes.

Gayatri walked on in silence. I was about to ask where she was taking me, when she asked a passerby the way to the cremation ground.

He pointed the way.

I was shocked. 'Are we going to the cremation ground?'

'Yes, Your Majesty. I want to show you something there. It is an everyday occurrence. But let us see if we will get the opportunity to witness it today,' she said.

Presently, we reached the cremation ground, which was marked off by a huge wall. A guard stood outside. 'Is there going to be a Sati today?'

'Yes. There they are,' he said pointing to a funeral procession, and went away to attend to his duties.

A dead man was being brought in a palanquin. A young girl, with flowers in her hair, and wearing a lot of jewellery walked along. She was smiling, and looked cheerful. She was surrounded by many women, who were singing and dancing.

'That young girl is the dead man's widow,' whispered Gayatri.

I wasn't surprised. A woman giving up her life upon the death of her husband was not surprising. I had heard about many such women. They happily embraced death, because they would soon be united with their respective husbands.

'Do you know these people?' I asked Gayatri.

'No. They have nothing to do with me. I just brought you along, because I assumed you would never have witnessed a *sati* before,' she said.

I lost my temper. 'I only asked you to tell me your story. I didn't ask you to bring me to witness a sati.'

And yet, I couldn't bring myself to move away. My reluctance was attributable to the ghoulish satisfaction people usually have when they are witness to acts of cruelty.

We followed the procession into the cremation ground. A king should never visit a cremation ground. I decided that I would have to send for pundits well-versed in the *Sastras* and perform some purificatory rites.

I looked for a pyre, where the woman would be burnt alive. I found nothing. Gayatri guessed what I was looking for and said, 'There are many kinds of sati. This is one kind.'

Illumination from torches helped me see what was happening clearly.

A deep pit had been dug and two seats had been placed in the pit, facing each other. On one seat, the husband's body was placed. The widow of the dead man circumambulated the pit three times. She then took off all her jewellery and gave them to her relatives. They embraced her and bid her farewell. When she stood near the pit, my heart began to beat faster.

If she were burnt alive, they would pour lots of oil on the flame, so that her agony would soon end. But this…?

The girl herself was still cheerful.

Two people helped her enter the pit. She sat on the seat opposite her husband's body. The people outside the pit quickly covered the pit with sand and finally put two stones on top of the pit.

Buried alive!

Without knowing what I was doing, I clutched Gayatri's hand tightly. I had heard so many stories about satis, but now that I was face to face with one, I shuddered. How could one term this a religious belief? It was a cruel practice. And yet, although I was the Emperor, I could not bring about legislation which would interfere with the basic beliefs of the people, and their customs. My inability to do anything filled me with shame.

The people who had accompanied the girl turned back.

'Did you bring me here just to witness this?' I asked Gayatri.

'Yes, I did. My elder sister was subjected to such an act of cruelty,' she said, her voice choking with emotion.

I recalled that she had mentioned her sister in a conversation once. I remembered that she had said her sister was good at painting. But Gayatri hadn't told me anything else about herself.

'Bandham Lakshminarayana told me you belonged to the Kalinga royal family. Is that true?'

'Yes,' she admitted. 'And that is why my sister met with such a cruel fate…'

'You and I may think this is cruel. But the women who give

up their lives don't seem to think so. They are happy because they are going to be reunited with their husbands.'

'Maybe. Maybe if my sister had been married and had died after her husband's death, she too might have died happily…'

'What are you trying to say?'

'She was not married. She had no husband. But she was buried alive with a man who was not her husband…'

I was shocked. I thought Gayatri was crying. But when I looked at her, there were no tears in her eyes. There was a look of fierce hatred on her face.

'Your Majesty, if my sister had been married and had been either burnt alive or buried alive with her husband, she would have died happily. But she was not married at all. She was said to be the wife of a man she had nothing to do with and was buried alive with him. And because she did not die willingly, but cried and protested, the people stoned her.'

My blood boiled when I heard Gayatri narrate her sister's story.

'Who did that to her, Gayatri? Who was the one who perpetrated this cruelty on your sister?'

'Veerabhadran, the son of Prataparudra Gajapati!' said Gayatri.

Thirty-seven

There was complete silence. Everyone had left. And yet the thought of a girl buried alive and Gayatri's words that her sister had met with a similar fate, haunted me. I had the illusion that ghosts and demons were dancing and shouting all around me.

The guard came to us and said, 'Who are you waiting for?' and his words broke the grip which the scene of horror had on me.

'Let's go,' I said to Gayatri.

She followed me quietly.

The way to our military camp was crowded. Bullock carts were taking provisions for the troops. The sound of the bullocks' anklets and the light from the lamps under the carts brought me back to reality.

'It's getting late, Gayatri. Since I've been to the cremation ground, I have to have a bath. You too must bathe. Have your dinner and get some sleep. We will talk tomorrow,' I said.

Although I had asked Gayatri to get some sleep, I myself slept fitfully.

I couldn't meet Gayatri the next morning. I couldn't meet her in the evening either. Since the generals were discussing our march against Kalinga, I had to be present there.

Appaji kept repeating the same point. 'I would request you to reconsider you decision to march against Kalinga,' he said.

'Why, Appaji?' I asked.

'The King of Kalinga belongs to our religion. Like us, he too is keen on stopping the dominance of the Muslim kings in the South. Should we not see the enemy of an enemy as a friend?'

'If you will permit me, I have something to tell you,' said Minister Vadamalaiannan.

'We have assembled to have a discussion. Everyone is free to express his view,' said Appaji. But the tone of his voice indicated that he was not happy with Vadamalaiannan's interruption.

'It is not just my opinion. Ramalinga Naidu also feels the same way,' said Vadamalaiannan.

'Get to the point, my friend,' I said. Ever since Vadamalai's brother Haridasa had accompanied me on my Thiruvannamalai trip, I had struck up a friendship with Vadamalai.

'Gajapati is not keen on stopping Muslim dominance, as you seem to think. As a matter of fact, he is making arrangements to join hands with them to defeat us.'

'Who said so?' asked Appaji.

'Our spies,' said Vadamalaiannan. 'I have learnt from reliable sources that Gajapati and Qutub Shahi of Golconda have made a pact. Qutub Shahi's Army Chief Bijili Khan is now head of the Kalinga forces. Many other Muslims too have been appointed to important posts in the Kalinga army. If we do not rout them all once and for all, all the Bahmani Sultans will join hands against us.'

'Yes, Prime Minister. You have to look at it from that angle. An enemy's friend is an enemy,' said general Ramalinga Naidu.

'When you all feel this way, I must defer to your view,' said Appaji magnanimously.

၏

The shadows were lengthening, and I wanted to spend the evening outside my tent. I had my throne brought out and sat on it. I was relieved that everyone had come to an agreement about our further course of action.

I sent for Gayatri.

She paid her respects to me, and waited for my instructions. 'Sit down,' I said, and she sat on the ground.

'Now tell me the story you began yesterday, but didn't complete,' I said.

'I am sure you know that there have been a lot of differences among the members of the royal household of Kalinga.'

'To some extent.'

As far as I knew, although Gajapati's family resided in the same palace, each of them was inimically disposed towards the rest. That feeling of enmity began hundred years ago.

It was the fault of Kapilendra Deva, who established the rule of the Gajapati clan.

He had four wives, and through them he had eighteen sons and ten nephews. Even while he was alive, quarrels broke out about who should be the next king.

Kapilendra Deva was particularly fond of one of his sons. His name was Purushottama Deva. Kapilendra Deva wanted Purushottama to become the next king. In order that his wish should be fulfilled, he spent an entire night in the Puri temple, praying to Lord Jagannatha. The next morning, he came out of the temple, and announced that Lord Jagannatha had appeared in his dream and ordered that Purushottama should be the next king. No one knew how far this was true. But the ministers acquiesced to his decision without protest.

Purushottama Deva became the king. He spent most of his time fighting neighbouring kings, his brothers and his sisters' husbands. Gayatri was descended from one of his sisters.

After the demise of Purushottama Deva, his son Prataparudra Deva became the king. He was a very intelligent man. I had heard that he was the author of the work *Saraswati Vilasam*, and that it was based on the Dharma Sastras. I had also heard that every day, holy water from the Puri Jagannatha temple would be brought to him and only after he had had the holy water would he eat.

This was the extent of my knowledge. But I knew nothing about Prataparudra Deva's son Veerabhadran. I didn't know he was so cruel as to force a woman to become a sati.

'Go ahead,' I said to Gayatri.

'The father wanted unity in the family. But the son didn't want anyone except his father and mother to stay in the palace. He wanted everyone else to be thrown out. He suspected that everyone was ranged against him and was plotting against him. He especially disliked my father, my brother, my sister and me. He got rid of three of us. I was the only one to escape.'

Her eyes had an empty look in them. The horrific incidents in her life must have come to her mind…

'Veerabhadran had a trick to get rid of those he didn't like. He is an expert swordsman. He would challenge everyone to a sword fight. It is considered dishonourable to refuse to take up a challenge. So some accepted his challenge and fell prey to his sword. Others ran away from the palace, fearing for their lives. One day he challenged my father to a sword fight. My father was an old man. His eyesight was poor. My brother, who was only fifteen years old at the time, stopped my father, and told him that he would take my father's place. The duel took place in the palace courtyard. As we watched with bated breath, Veerabhadran felled my brother and we saw him fall down in a pool of blood. He died before our eyes. A young life snatched away…'

She couldn't talk for a while, because she was emotionally overwhelmed. She looked fierce, like a wounded tigress. I waited for her anger to subside and then said, 'Now tell me your sister's story.'

She narrated her sister's story:

'That was the time when Chaitanya Mahaprabhu was visiting Kalinga. He stayed in the capital, and he and his disciples spread their bhakti cult. Their songs were in simple language and even the uneducated could understand the songs. Chaitanya gave importance to the lower strata of society. Prataparudra had great regard for Chaitanya. Since Chaitanya refused to come to the palace, Prataparudra went to meet him. But Veerabhadran disliked Chaitanya's cult. My sister used to sing along with Chaitanya's disciples and so Veerabhadran disliked her. He tried to prevent her from attending Chaitanya's prayers. But she paid no heed to him.'

Even as Gayatri narrated her story, a few ministers and generals came to meet me, but seeing me talking to Gayatri, they left. They must have been annoyed. 'This is the time to discuss military strategy, and here we find the Emperor wasting time talking to this girl,' they must have said to themselves.

'So Veerabhadran burnt your sister alive,' I completed the story for Gayatri.

'If your Majesty is keen that I should cut my story short, I will do it,' she said. Not wanting to hurt her feelings, I said, 'No, no. Give me a detailed account.'

'My sister was a good artist. But she only painted pictures of Radha and Krishna. She hadn't done portraits of any human being, not even of Chaitanya. One day, Veerabhadran asked her to do a portrait of him. She refused. He tried to force himself upon her. But she escaped. Veerabhadran was waiting for an opportunity for revenge. At that time, war broke out between our kingdom and some ruler in Rajamahendravaram. Veerabhadran led our forces against him. As he returned with our wounded soldiers, he hatched a sinister plan to deal with my sister.'

'A plan to kill your sister?'

'Yes. One of his generals was mortally wounded. Veerabhadran promised that he would reward the general's family generously, if the general averred that he was married to my sister. The general agreed, and before he died, he told the generals that he wanted his wife to give up her life. Everyone believed that the general had told them the truth. My sister was dragged protesting to the cremation ground. People felt she should not refuse to die when her husband had died in battle, and when it had been his desire that she should give up her life. They abused her and threw stones at her. One of the army generals, who was my father's friend, told us about what had happened. My father did not live for long. When I had lost my entire family, I knew that I would be the next target of Veerabhadran. So I left my country, and even today, I am not certain I am safe.' She glanced round her as if she expected danger to be lurking in the shadows.

It was a starry night and I looked up at the sky. There was a strong breeze blowing and caused the curtains in the tents to flap.

Gayatri sat before me hugging her knees. How much tragedy this girl had witnessed! The flaming torches that lit the camp were dying down. But the fire that burned in her heart would never be put out, I told myself.

'Go on,' I said.

'I decided that I would join hands with the enemy of the Kalinga kingdom and bring down the Gajapatis. I didn't know how to go about it. A Telugu poet told me to go to Vijayanagar. He also told me that Saluva Narasimha had expressed his desire that the Gajapatis should be defeated and that he had recorded his wish in a palm leaf manuscript, which was preserved in the palace library in Vijayanagar. He told me to search for that manuscript and give it to you. That is why I took up employment in your palace. I wanted your dreams to be fulfilled first, before suggesting a campaign against Kalinga. I knew that until you married Chinnadevi, you wouldn't be happy. So I helped you as much as I could…'

I interrupted with a disappointed laugh. 'Love? Chinnadevi? I had heard of mirages. But until recently, I hadn't had first-hand experience of it!'

'Your Majesty mustn't sound so dejected. Very soon your dream will come true.'

'Let us not talk about my dream. Now you tell me what plans you have…'

'I want you to march against Kalinga, defeat Gajapati, imprison Veerabhadran, and bring him to Vijayanagar,' she said.

'And what happens after I bring him to Vijayanagar?'

'I will reveal the rest of my plan to you after you bring him to Vijayanagar.'

'All right. We have already decided to march against Katak tomorrow. But if I tell Appaji and the other ministers your story, they will have a hearty laugh…'

'Why?'

'Why won't they laugh? I marched against Bijapur because of Chinnadevi. Now I am going to march against Kalinga for your sake. I am the only Emperor of the Vijayanagar Empire to have marched clutching the apron strings of women!' I laughed. 'It's getting late. You have unburdened yourself. I hope that helps you get a good night's sleep.'

Gayatri expressed her gratitude by falling at my feet. She wiped the tears from her eyes, and prepared to leave.

'Wait,' I said.

She waited.

'You have told me what you were looking for in the library. But what were you looking for in the Matanga hill? Tell me,' I said.

She smiled at me and said, 'When you reach Kalinga, that mystery too will be cleared.' She then went away to her tent.

She had gone through a whole gamut of emotions—anger, sorrow, dejection—and now after a long time, I had seen a smile on her face, and I felt that no price was too big for that smile.

Thirty-eight

Since my ministers and I had already decided to march against Katak, the capital of Kalinga, I did not tell Appaji about Gayatri's request that Veerabhadran should be taken prisoner. There was no need for me to inform Appaji.

The Vijayanagar army surged ahead victoriously. The forts of Vinukonda, Kondaveedu, Bellamkonda, Devarakonda, Jallipalli, Anantagiri, Kambam Mettu fell into our hands easily. When we reached Pothanooru Simhadri, I ordered the erection of a victory pillar there.

All that remained now was for us to march against Katak. I inspected my army.

The last tent housed the men who tended to the wounded. The Italian, Nicholas was there, busy bandaging a soldier's wound. He didn't even notice me enter. I didn't want to disturb him and I moved on. Wherever I went, Nicholas followed me. I felt this was not just because of his love for the Vijayanagar Empire, but also because of his love for Gayatri.

In Gayatri's tent, I found her doing some sewing, along with a few other women. I was surprised. We never provided clothes to the soldiers or to the generals. They had to have their clothes stitched themselves, and at their expense.

So for whom was Gayatri making clothes? She could guess the question on my mind, and she said, 'This is for you.' She showed me what they had been doing.

It was a silk garment, with gold thread work on it. The sewing wasn't complete.

'How did you guess that I was a poor man, who didn't have even one good garment to wear?' I laughed.

'This garment is special. I want you to wear this after you win Katak.'

'You can arrange for the victory celebrations right away,' said Appaji, even as he entered the tent.

'What are you saying, Appaji?'

'I have good news, surprising news for you, Your Majesty. I had sent some spies to Katak to scout round for information. Do you know what they have told me?'

'What do they say?'

'They say that there is no resistance at all to us in the Kalinga capital. The gates to the fort are open. There are no soldiers on the ramparts. Anyone can enter or exit at will. There is no one there to fight against us…'

I was stunned. 'I can't believe this, Appaji,' I exclaimed.

Appaji felt it was beneath his dignity to discuss all this in the presence of Gayatri. 'Your Majesty, let us march with a small force to Katak. If the spies are right, then we will not need further reinforcements. If there is resistance, then we will send for the rest of our forces.'

'That's a good idea, Appaji,' I said. He left, very pleased with the turn of events.

I looked at Gayatri. I saw a mysterious smile on her face.

ೞ

When we marched towards Katak, Appaji, Vadamalaiannan and I headed the troops, while Gayatri followed us. Gayatri was clever. She knew that if she marched side by side with us, Appaji would be upset. So she kept a few steps behind us.

The spies were right. There was no resistance to us in Katak. The city was peaceful, and we could hear the strains of bhajans from temples.

We reached Gajapati's palace. Appaji and Vadamalaiannan, unsheathed their swords, and went in search of Gajapati. I followed Gayatri. But in room after room, we only found servant and guards, but of Gajapati's family, there was no sign.

Gayatri ran round looking for Gajapati. She questioned the servants. She stood outside a room for a few seconds, with tears in her eyes. 'This is the room my father, my sister, brother and I occupied,' she said, her voice breaking.

I peered into the room. Was this room a part of the tastefully decorated palace? What a mess the room was! It was obvious that it had not been swept for a long time. The cobwebs and the dust on the floor made it appear like a place that had not been cleaned for years. Many paintings lay scattered on the floor. They were paintings of Radha and Krishna, the divine lovers. They were the handiwork of Gayatri's sister, who was no more.

Although the floor was dirty, Gayatri sat on the floor, and cleaned the dust on the pictures with her saree. She hugged the paintings to her bosom and wept. But mingled with the tears was her rage, and I could sense it. She put back the paintings on the floor and turned to me. Her face was red like glowing embers.

She fell at my feet. I could feel her hands touching my feet and her hot tears drenching my feet.

She got up and said, 'Your Majesty, wherever Veerabhadran is, he must be captured. For my sake, for the sake of my sister, my brother, my father…'

'Silly girl,' I said and patted her back gently. I flicked the tear drops from the corner of her eyes. 'I will capture Veerabhadran, not just for your sake, your sister's sake, your brother's sake and your father's sake. I have to capture him, because he and his sons pose a danger and threat to my empire. Let us see where he is hiding…'

Gayatri turned back to have a last look at that room, even as we walked to the durbar hall. The hall was so beautiful, that for a minute I forgot all about wars and battles. I began to study the differences and similarities between Kalinga sculptures and Vijayanagar sculptures. I wanted my sculptors to borrow some of the ideas the Kalinga sculptors had used. Even as I indulged in aesthetic appreciation, Vadamalaiannan's voice broke into my thoughts. 'I have checked the northern wing of the palace. Neither Gajapati nor anyone from his family is there. There are some women in the kitchen but they don't seem to be able to speak any language except Odia. And I, as you know, am a Tamilian. I couldn't make out what they were saying...'

Appaji came in with his report. 'I have good news for you. Sixteen Mahapatras, owing allegiance to Gajapati, are now in a smaller palace towards the South. They want to surrender to you. They have sent word to their armies to come here to surrender to you. Since Gajapati, the ruler of Kalinga has himself left his capital, they see no reason to continue to fight you. That is why they have decided to surrender to you.'

I couldn't believe what Appaji was saying. 'Where are they? Ask them to come here.'

'I will call each of them individually,' said Appaji and sent word through a servant.

One of Prataparudra Gajapati's generals came in. He had a box in his hands. It must have been quite heavy. He brought the box to me, and laid it at my feet. He also placed his sword at my feet. 'I bow before you, Your Majesty. I am Narahari Mahapatra, the royal representative of Daranikonda.'

'What does the box contain?' I asked.

He opened the box for me. It was full of gold coins, jewels, and precious gems. On top of it all lay a letter. Following Narahari, another Mahapatra came in. He too placed treasures before me, and in his box too there was a letter. The third Mahapatra came in, the fourth followed and so on...

Each of the sixteen Mahapatras placed a box of coins and jewels before me and also a letter.

They were all surprised to find Gayatri there. They seemed to want to ask her where she had been all these days. Some of them even greeted her. All of them seemed to know Gayatri.

I picked out a letter from one of the boxes. It was written in Odia. Although I couldn't understand what was written, I could guess that all the letters probably expressed the same sentiments.

Narahari Mahapatra read out the letter in his box. 'This letter is addressed to me. All the sixteen of us here have received similar letters. This is what the letter says: "To Mahapatra, from Vijayanagar. We are grateful for all the help you have rendered so far. Here is a small gift for you. Please accept it." But the letter is unsigned.'

Another Mahapatra said, 'The letter that I received too is unsigned, and who sent it remains a mystery. We offered no help to the Vijayanagar Empire. We didn't promise any help either. A copy of this letter reached Gajapati too. He thought all the Mahapatras were plotting against him. He knew he could not fight without our support. So he has gone into hiding.'

I was astounded. Appaji was red faced. 'I never sent such a letter or any gifts to these men. No one I know has sent these. Who is responsible for this?'

I could see that we would have to debate this later and not in the presence of others.

'You may leave,' I said to the Mahapatras. 'I accept your surrender. I am not interested in capturing new territory. I only want peace with my neighbours. I do not want neighbouring countries to be hostile towards Vijayanagar. You may continue to rule over your respective territories. But you must pay taxes to the Vijayanagar Empire and also acknowledge our supremacy.'

'We are grateful to you, Your Majesty,' they said and prepared to leave, when Appaji stopped them. 'Wait,' he said. 'Where is Prataparudra Gajapati now?'

'We are told he is in the Kondapalli fort.'

'All right. You may leave now.'

An uneasy silence reigned. I looked at Gayatri. The expression on her face gave the game away. I recalled her confidence that the Mahapatras would offer no resistance.

'Gayatri, it was you wasn't it—the one who sent the Mahapatras those jewels and the letter?'

'Yes, Your Majesty. I knew the names of the Mahapatras and with the help of some of their servants, I had these letters and jewels delivered to them. Usually the Mahapatras stay in the capital. So getting the letters across to them and also to Gajapati was not difficult. I knew that Gajapati would do one of two things. Either he would kill all the Mahapatras, or he would run away, fearing a plot against him. I also knew that whichever of the two things happened, it would be to our advantage. That is why I told you not to worry about the Mahapatras…'

Appaji was livid. 'Now tell me, how did you get so many gold coins and jewellery and precious stones? Did you get them from the Vijayanagar treasury?'

He didn't actually ask her if she had stolen these things, but it was obvious that this was what he meant to ask.

'No, Prime Minister, When there are strict rules preventing the Emperor himself from opening the treasury chests, how could I?'

'Then how did you get all this gold?' I asked.

Gayatri smiled. 'Your Majesty once asked me what I was doing on Matanga Hill. I had heard the legend that when Ravana carried off Sita Devi, She threw down her jewels, and that these jewels lie hidden in the caves of the Matanga hill. While that may be just a myth, there is a belief that the rich have hidden some of their treasures in the caves in the hill. I went looking for the hidden treasures. I looked in all the caves, and I did find some treasure. That is what I sent over to the Mahapatras. Anyway, I should not have taken wealth that belonged to the Vijayanagar Empire. But I used it for the welfare of the Empire. And now the treasures have reached you…'

Appaji had been pacing up and down while Gayatri had been explaining. When she finished, he exploded: 'Shame! Disrespect! A victory is honourable only if we have fought for it. This kind of trickery is a blot on the Vijayanagar Empire.'

'Prime Minister, I don't think you should lose your temper over this. After all, we have to use every means possible to overcome our enemies—sometimes war, sometimes tricks. This is what we have been taught. This girl, by sowing the seeds of suspicion in the mind of our enemy, has helped us achieve victory. There is nothing to be ashamed of,' said Vadamalaiyannan.

Usually, Vadamalaiannan never argued with Appaji. But he knew that I had a soft spot for Gayatri, and so he spoke on her behalf.

Appaji glared at him. But he did not reply. He had nothing to say.

I held Appaji's hands and tried to mollify him. 'If we had fought, we would definitely have won, with you at the helm. There is no doubt about that, Appaji. But think of all the soldiers who would have died fighting. Think of how many elephants and horses we would have lost. Gayatri has achieved for us the desired result without any loss. Please be kind enough to forgive her,' I said.

My words calmed him down a bit, but he wasn't completely reconciled to Gayatri's method. 'When the Emperor himself has decided to forgive her, who am I to say anything? I am just a worm.'

'Please don't say such things, Appaji. There is something we have to do for this girl, to show our gratitude.'

'Oh, so we have to do something for her?'

'Yes, Appaji. There is a reason why she took so much trouble in this matter. She wants Prataparudra Gajapati's son to be captured. I will tell you her story some other time. But we are indebted to her and we must help fulfil her desire. So we must march against Kondapalli, where Gajapati is hiding.'

'Before Appaji could reply, a guard entered and said, 'Your Majesty, your mother has sent you a message from the capital.'

Thirty-nine

Although the guard had told me that there was a message from my mother, it took some time for the message to reach me.

'Where is the message?' I asked.

'I was told that there was a message for you. I told the man who was bringing the message to hurry up and I came here to inform you about the message,' said the guard.

I went up to the terrace. I could see my huge force of elephants and horses, but where was the messenger?

My thoughts went to my son—Thirumalai. I don't know the reason, but for some time now, I have been worrying about him. I have been worried, imagining that some harm might befall him. Sometimes, I imagine that he will go into the elephant stable and that he will be picked up by an elephant and dashed down. Sometimes, I imagine that he might peep over the parapet, and hurtle down. Sometimes, I worry about his horse riding lessons. What if the tutor puts him on a skittish horse and the horse throws the child down?

And the biggest worry of them all—what if my son were abducted, or killed by enemies? There could be so many enemies, ready to harm him. Why, even my step-brothers housed in Chandragiri could harm him!

Comforting thoughts, sweet thoughts are for some reason, slow to come. But frightening thoughts, rush into one's mind easily.

At last the messenger arrived. He handed over to me a rolled up silk cloth.

I read it and then said to Appaji, 'Nothing special. Just the sort of letter mothers write to their absent sons. Let me read it out to you.'

'To my dear Krishnan, blessings from your mother. I am told that you are on a conquering spree. I am proud of you. But it is so long since I saw you. This mother's heart aches to see you. Enough of wars. Come home soon. Your wife Thirumala Devi and your son Thirumalai, miss you too.'

I rolled up the missive and asked a servant to take it to my tent. There were two more lines in my mother's letter, but I didn't read these out to Appaji. There are some secrets which remain buried in our hearts, and I decided that the last two lines had to remain buried in my heart.

'The Queen Mother's feelings are natural,' said Appaji.

'A man in power has to make some sacrifices. One of them is to sometimes give up his desires,' I replied. 'Have you given up your desire for Chinnadevi? Isn't that your obsession all the time?' my conscience mocked me.

'Appaji, we have to march against Kondapalli. Please make arrangements,' I said.

Till then, Kumara Veeraiyya—Thirumala Devi's father and the King of Srirangapatnam, had been standing at some distance from me. Now he came close to me and said, 'I have information that Prataparudra Gajapati is reorganizing his forces. Bijili Khan, the general of the Golconda Sultan, is also with Gajapati. So we must march against them as soon as possible, without giving them much time to make plans against us.'

Appaji resented suggestions about wars from anyone except me. But since the person making the suggestion was my father-in-law, he remained silent. 'The planets are unfavourable to us. Let us wait for two more days, before we march against our enemies,' he said, and left.

Gayatri had remained silent during these exchanges, but I had a feeling she was looking at me suspiciously. She must have guessed that there was something more in my mother's letter, which I had kept from Appaji. I avoided looking at her.

I washed my hands and legs and went into the next room, which served as the puja room. The idols I used every day in Vijayanagar had been kept there. There were priests too, who had accompanied me, so that the daily worship of the idols would be according to the prescribed rules. The fragrance of sandal paste and of flowers was pleasant. Golden lamps had been lit, and bathed the room in a glow. The Vedic chants were alluring. I sat down with my hands folded.

Gayatri was a serving girl. So she too was there. She gave me a searching look.

For the next two days, she continued to give me a searching glance, whenever we met. She seemed to be saying, 'Tell me, Your Majesty. What else did your mother's letter say, besides the lines you read out to Appaji?' There was a look of pleading in her eyes. But I did not tell her about the last few lines in Mother's letter.

Since we had to wait for two more days before advancing upon Kondapalli, I tried to turn my thoughts in other directions. I decided to take a tour of the palace. When I reached the terrace, I saw clouds of smoke. I knew what that meant. My men had set fire to the city. This was a cruel practice, which I disapproved of—the practice of setting fire to a city we had captured. I had given clear instructions to my men that they were not to do this. But the soldiers of some kings who had offered me their help must have done this. How could anyone do this? It was the sort of thing done with no regard for the consequences. Wouldn't people who lost their houses and their belongings hate us? I ordered that the fire be put out at once.

I then went to the Jagannath temple. I worshipped Balarama, Krishna and Subhadra. I picked up some soil from the street which the famous chariot of the temple toured, and paid my respects to it.

My soldiers were sprinkling castor seeds all around the fort of Katak. I don't know when this practice began. I've asked many people about it. Appaji's theory is that it is to shame the enemy, but even he wasn't able to come up with a convincing explanation. Castor bean plant is a hardy plant and comes up quickly, and soon it will make the area look like a densely forested area. The purpose might be to conceal the fort from the eyes of enemies. That could be a plausible explanation. But castor seeds are very useful in Ayurvedic medicine and I was sorry to see them go to waste.

※

I went round inspecting all my forces, and when I reached the place where my horses were stationed, I found Nicholas there, doing something quite strange. He was cutting the hairs in the tails of the horses. Why was he doing this? Did my horses have some disease, and was this some sort of treatment? But why had Nicholas, who treated human beings, begun to treat horses? Every hair that had been cut off was at least a foot in length. Nicholas did not throw away any of them. Gayatri was beside him and as he snipped off the hairs, she took them carefully from him. I noticed that many of the horses had already lost the hair in their tails. I was very angry. I was fonder of my horses than of my elephants. And it is not just me. All Vijayanagar kings have had a fondness for horses. If you look at the temples we have built, you will know how much we love horses. In every temple, you will find horse sculptures, with the horses in galloping poses. How could Nicholas make my horses' tails look so ugly?

'Nicholas, what are you doing?' I asked.

Nicholas didn't stop what he was doing. He continued to snip the tips of the horses' tails, even as he answered. 'I thought you would have guessed. When soldiers have gaping wounds, the wounds have to be stitched up. Sometimes soldiers have to be operated upon. In all these cases, we use horse hair to put in the stitches. I had a stock of horse hairs, but I have run out of stock. That I why I am replenishing my stock,' he said.

Gayatri remained silent. But I noticed that she still continued to stare at me. I avoided her stare.

That evening, a dance performance was arranged to entertain the soldiers. I was told it was a Bhagavata Mela dance that they were going to witness. So I decided to watch too. Many members of the troupe were known to me. When the dancers took their positions on the stage, with their anklets jingling, my mind flew back to my first meeting with Chinnadevi.

When I came out of my reverie...

The facial expressions and gestures of the dancers suggested a man being tied up in a sack, and his being beaten up by government officials. What was this supposed to convey? Usually, stories from the Puranas formed the themes of Bhagavata Mela dances. But I couldn't recall any Purana story similar to the one being enacted.

'Stop!' I called out. 'This is not a Puranic story you are enacting. What is the source of this story?'

The head of the dance troupe said, 'Your Majesty, this is not a Puranic story. This is based on something that actually happened.'

The governor, who was in charge of the area the dancers were from, was called Sampetta Guruvaraja, and he handed down such harsh sentences to poor farmers. In fact, his punishments were even more severe than the one depicted in the dance. The dance troupe wanted to draw my attention to the governor's cruelty, and that was the reason for inclusion of this piece, he explained.

I had already had some reports about this governor. But as I heard the dancers talk of his cruelties, I was furious. 'I will put a full stop to all this right now,' I said. 'Gayatri, fetch me a palm leaf and also the royal seal.'

Gayatri brought me a palm leaf, and the royal seal, and gave it to Minister Kondamarasu. He wrote out my orders, affixed the royal seal, after which I also signed the order. It was only after I had done all this that peace returned to my mind.

'Please, let us have your usual dances,' I said to the troupe.

By the time the story of Prahlada had been enacted, it was well past midnight. It was a full moon day, and it was pleasant as I walked back to my tent. Someone was following me. I turned. It was Gayatri.

'What is it? Please tell me. Let me not see you conveying something through dance gestures too,' I said to her.

'Your Majesty, I think it is best that you return to the capital, as per your mother's wishes. Acharya Venkata Thathayya is going to visit Vijayanagar. So your mother is right in wanting you to be there, so that you can get his permission to release Chinnadevi from her vow,' she said.

'Oh, so you have read my letter, without my permission, have you?' I asked angrily.

'I didn't do so on purpose, Your Majesty. When I went to your tent to fetch the royal seal, I noticed the letter lying on the ground. Quite by accident I happened to read the last two lines of the letter. Why did you not mention those two lines of the letter? It is perhaps all right that you kept it from Appaji. But why did you not tell me?'

'I have to go to Kondapalli, capture Veerabhadran and hand him over to you. Everything else can wait.'

'Your regard for me...' she was choked with emotion and

couldn't continue. I noticed that she was crying. She composed herself and then said, 'Your Majesty, I am just one of your many subjects. The fulfillment of my vow and the capture of Veerabhadran will delight me, no doubt. But my wish can be fulfilled later. However, your love for Chinnadevi is more important. If your desire to marry her is fulfilled, imagine how happy you will be. Your joy is the joy of this huge Empire. If you are contented, then all your subjects will benefit. Please go to Vijayanagar. Talk to Venkata Thathayya. Let your dream come true.'

When Gayatri made such an emotional appeal to me, I could not refuse to return to Vijayanagar. Now was the moment when her vow was going to be fulfilled, and yet she was prepared to put that off, keeping in mind my happiness. 'All right. You too come with me,' I said.

When Appaji told me when we could start for Kondapalli, I told him there was a change in plans. I was going to return to Vijayanagar. 'Let Rayadeva Udayar's son Dhananjaya Udayar lead our army against Kondapalli,' I said.

'I don't know why you keep changing plans so often,' Appaji murmured, but he did not object to my choice of Dhananjaya Udayar. Just as I knew that Viswanatha Nayaka was destined for great things in Madurai, I knew that Dhananjaya Udayar was also destined for great things in Karnataka. Appaji too had the confidence that he would prove a great leader.

☙

When I entered the capital, I first made my way to my mother's palace. She was in the puja room, offering prayers, with Thirumala Devi seated on one side of her and my son Thirumalai seated on the other.

Thirumala Devi fell at my feet. I touched her shoulders and told her to get up. I noticed that my touch excited her mildly. She realised it too, and moved away at once and stood beside Gayatri.

Thirumalai walked towards me. How tall he had become!

But he hesitated. 'Thirumalai! Don't be scared. That is your father,' my mother said to him. 'It's three years since he saw you. He is unable to recognize you.'

'Yes, Mother. This has become a longer campaign than I had expected. And it is still not over. Gajapati Prataparudra and his son Veerabhadra are sheltering in the Kondpalli fort. I've sent an army to capture them.'

'Krishna, may I ask a favour of you?' my mother said.

'Certainly, Mother,' I said.

'Krishna, the Gajapatis may be our enemies. But they are great devotees. They have studied the scriptures; they have built many temples and have donated to many charitable causes…'

'And so?'

'Capture their kingdom, by all means. Make it a part of your empire. But…'

'But?'

'But don't treat Prataparudra and his son as you would your other enemies. You must not kill them.'

I looked at Gayatri. Her face had hardened.

Forty

The servants in mother's palace were busy. I could hear the puja bell being rung. Mother's pet parrot screeched in delight as it pecked at a guava fruit. In the garden, I could see a spotted deer gambolling. The whole world seemed to be happy. But why was it that I had to face one awkward situation after another?

I had rushed back to the capital to meet Acharya Venkata Thathayya. But Mother, instead of discussing his visit, had requested that I should not harm Prataparudra Gajapati. Gayatri was anxious to have her revenge on Veerabhadran, but mother's request had put paid to her plans.

Why did I have to face such problems?

Trying to change the topic, I said, 'Mother, I forgot to tell you. Chaitanya, the saint you have such regard for, is in Kalinga. I wanted to pay my respects to him, but I didn't have time to do so.'

But I soon realised that to have brought up the topic of Chaitanya was foolish. 'Chaitanya was born in Bengal. But it is only in Gajapati's kingdom that he enjoys complete freedom. Do you know Pratparudra has great regard for Chaitanya?' Mother said.

I began to wish I had not mentioned sage Chaitanya. 'Oh, does he?'

'Yes, Krishna, he does. Prataparudra made several attempts to invite sage Chaitanya to his palace. But Chaitanya said he would never visit the homes of the rich. One day, Prataparudra went to where Chaitanya was staying. Chaitanya was meditating at the time. Prataparudra fell at his feet. Chaitanya opened his eyes, and cried out in horror. Not because an Emperor had fallen at his feet, but because he had been touched by a man who was a slave to power and wealth. He refused to talk to the king. And it was only after much persuasion from his disciples, that Chaitanya accepted Prataparudra as his follower. Even today, when Chaitanya walks along the road singing his bhajans, Prataparudra accompanies him, without any footwear, and with his hands folded in all humility.'

As Mother told me about Prataparudra's devotion to Chaitanya, I watched Gayatri. At first she was shocked by mother's words. But now she smiled. She seemed to be a better actor than I was.

Mother continued: 'That is the reason for my request to you. You captured Udayagiri. The Balakrishna idol has returned to our temple. I thought you would stop with that. But you have advanced up to Katak. Please, Krishna, do not harm a great bhakta. Why are you silent, Krishna?'

'Prataparudra may be a good man, Mother. But he has a son called Veerabhadran. Veerabhadran is a cruel man. Ask Gayatri. She has been in Gajapati's palace for many years. She will tell you about Veerabhadran,' I said.

'What does Gayatri know? She is a young girl. Someone must have misled her. The son of a good man has to be good himself,' said my mother.

'How can we be sure of that, Mother? You are a good lady, and yet you gave birth to a wicked son like me,' I said.

'Are you a bad man?' Mother laughed. 'Don't try to change the topic. I asked you to promise that you would not harm Prataparudra. And you still haven't made that promise.'

I was anxious to talk about Venkata Thathayya. So in order to steer the conversation in that direction, I said, 'All right, Mother. I promise.'

'You must also promise not to hurt his son, the one you said was wicked,' Mother insisted.

Thirumalai was running around, and playing a game of hide and seek with his mother Thirumala Devi. I was embarrassed to talk about Chinnadevi, when Thirumala was around. So I lowered my voice, and said, 'You had asked me to come here for a specific reason. But you haven't spoken about that so far.'

'You mean about Venkata Thathayya. He is visiting Vaishnava temples in the South. He is expected to arrive here soon. That is why I sent word to you. Don't leave the capital for some more days.'

'All right, Mother,' I said, and picked up my son Thirumalai, and went out. Gayatri followed. We went out into the garden. Thirumalai ran off chasing a butterfly. 'Wait. I'll catch it for you,' said Gayatri to the child.

'You are disappointed, aren't you, Gayatri?' I asked.

'About what, Your Majesty?'

'You wanted to have your revenge on Veerabhadran. But my mother insists he shouldn't be harmed.'

'I only said he should be captured. I didn't say he should be killed, did I?'

'How will you have your revenge then?'

'I will shame him. He will never be able to live it down.'

'How do you plan to do that?'

'I will tell you at the appropriate time.'

I laughed. 'Gayatri, shall I tell you something? I have put down my thoughts on administration, my experiences, and I plan to compile all of these observations of mine together. And do you know what title I am going to give my compilation? It will be called "Will tell you at the appropriate time"! That seems to be the statement I have heard most often in my life.'

'I feel honoured, Your Majesty,' she laughed. 'Will you send word to your general not to kill Veerabhadran? I don't want him to be killed, but captured alive.'

'What concern for the enemy!' I teased. But I could see that hers was a sensible request. So I sent word to my general Dhananjaya.

After Gayatri left, I sent for Jangamaiah, and asked him to send some men to find out exactly where Venkata Thathayya was.

☙

The whole of that day was spent in meetings and consultations with my council of ministers. Since Appaji and I had been away for almost three years, they had made some temporary arrangements in our absence. We retained some of the arrangements. We rejected some of them. We also had to give our attention to some other things.

The most important of them was the work titled *Madura Vijayam*. It was written by Ganga Devi, the wife of Kumara Kampanna Deva, one of the earlier Vijayanagara kings, who had expanded our Empire.

When Kumara Kampanna Deva marched up to Rameswaram, and defeated the Madurai Sultan, Ganga Devi accompanied him. She wrote of her experiences in *Madura Vijayam*. The work was written in Sanskrit. She had given descriptions in Madura Vijayam of the havoc wrought by the Sultanate. The details given by her will bring tears to the eyes of any reader.

Poet Allasani Peddanna wanted to translate the work to Telugu and Kannada. I told him to go ahead.

We next took up a request from Ethirajan. His complaint was that many devadasis had been denied the privileges they were entitled to. We decided to investigate his complaint, and we also decided that devadasi families which had served in a temple for three generations were entitled to use a palanquin.

I had a suggestion to make. I wanted to end the practice of widows being burnt on the funeral pyres of their husbands. But

Appaji and the other ministers refused to accept my suggestion. After much deliberation, it was decided that if a widow wanted to commit sati, she could do so, but that if she didn't, she was not to be forced on to the pyre by anyone. However, I had misgivings about whether this order would be implemented.

At the end of a day of discussions and debates, Appaji said, 'We've spent the whole day discussing matters pertaining to women. Our Emperor simply melts when it comes to women!'

'So what? The one who gave birth to me is a woman; the one who gave birth to my heir is a woman. Half the population of our empire consists of women,' I said.

༺༻

When all the debates were over, and I could finally call it a day, it was rather late in the night. As I approached my bedroom, I could hear someone singing sweetly. It was Thirumala Devi singing a Purandara Dasa composition in praise of Lord Krishna. My son Thirumalai was resting on her shoulder, as she walked up and down the room, rocking him to sleep. Soon he was fast asleep.

'Thirumala, you have broken a tradition. You have uttered the name of your husband—Krishna,' I teased, as I entered.

She laughed, and whispered, 'The child is asleep.'

'Where are you going now?'

'I have to ask the nurse to take Thirumalai to his room.'

'No. Let him sleep in my room.' I put Thirumalai down on my cot, and wrapped him up in a silk blanket. Thirumala Devi was watching me without batting an eyelid.

'What are you staring at me for?' I asked.

'I used to think you wouldn't have any affection for this child of yours.'

'Don't be foolish, Thirumala. I adore him. Why did you think I wouldn't love him?'

'Well, he is not a child born of love. He was the result of your anger, your disappointment.'

'Oh, is that so? Then shall we have another child? This time without anger, or disappointment? This cot is spacious. Come on,' I said.

Thirumala Devi covered her ears with her hands, in shock. 'I have made a vow. This is a penance. I know you have given me a place in your heart. I also know that I don't own all of it. Let the other woman you love also come here. Please do not make such a suggestion. That can wait until she arrives,' Thirumala said. She then lay down on the smaller cot in the room.

I was angry with myself. Because of my love for Chinnadevi I was ruining the life of a young, beautiful woman. I began to doubt if I really loved Chinnadevi. The more elusive Chinnadevi became, the more I yearned for her, and I wondered if my determination to marry her was more a result of an attraction for something that seemed unattainable, rather than real love.

My thoughts made me uncomfortable, and to break free of this line of thought, I said, 'Thirumala, you sing well. This is the first time I have heard you sing.'

'When I was in Srirangapatnam, I learnt music. My music teachers belonged to the Thalapakkam Annamacharya family. Some members of that family are here, Your Majesty. They have a request to place before you.'

'Thalapakkam family? Why did you not tell me they were here?'

'You were busy. That's why I hadn't told you. I will bring them to you tomorrow morning,' she said, and turned over and promptly went to sleep. I couldn't sleep at once. For a long time, I kept looking at Thirumala Devi.

The next day, Thirumala Devi's music teachers met me. They were all over fifty years of age.

Annamacharya was a saint. For some years he had been King Saluva Narasimha's minister. He would not praise any deity except Lord Srinivasa of Tirumala. It is said that Saluva Narasimha asked him to sing a song in praise of his king, and that Annamacharya refused to do so, and left for Tirumala.

The visitors and I spoke about the saint for some time. The eldest of the visitors said, 'Your Majesty., we need your help.'

'Please tell me what I can do to help you,' I said.

'Many of Annmacharya's kritis have been recorded in copper plates. But only some are available now. Many remain locked up in the Tirumala temple. We would be happy, if you could get those copper plates for us.'

'That shouldn't be a problem. No one will refuse to hand over those plates to you.'

'The temple authorities have refused to open the room in which they are kept. They said that they cannot open the room without Venkata Thathayya's permission.'

'Venkata Thathayya is touring the South. When he returns…'

'No, Your Majesty. Thathayya is now in Tirupati. If you come to Tirupati, you can ask Thathayya.'

'Is he in Tirupati? On the sacred hills? I will leave tomorrow,' I said enthusiastically. 'Usually, after every military campaign, I visit the Tirumala hills and make offerings to Lord Srinivasa. I haven't done it after my latest campaign. I suppose this is God's way of reminding me that I have to thank him.'

The visitors went away very pleased. Needless to say, that I too was very happy. Yes, I, the silly, crazy fool was happy too.

Forty-one

It was decided that my mother, Thirumala Devi and my son Thirumalai would leave for Tirupati right away and that I would follow later with Vadamalaiannan and Ethirajan. Appaji was to stay back in the capital, and to ensure its security in our absence.

When Thirumala Devi and my son prepared to leave the palace for Tirupati, I came to the entrance to see them off. Thirumala Devi asked Appaji to bless the child.

He stepped back and would not pick up the child. Nor did he bless the child. 'Let Lord Srinivasa bless him. Of what use are the blessings of a mortal?'

Appaji had some conservative views. He was by nature suspicious. He would often doubt if a person had had his bath, and if he wasn't sure, he would keep his distance. That must be the reason for his reluctance to pick up Thirumalai, I told myself because he had never once picked up Thirumalai or played with him, and I sometimes wondered why.

༶

We had reached the foot of the Thirumala Hills. As we climbed the hill, Ethirajan chanted Sanskrit slokas, while Vadamalaiannan chanted verses from the Tamil *Divyaprabandham*. It was early morning and the sight of trees and greenery, the sight of birds and playful monkeys all served to remind us of the One who was responsible for it all.

At one point Vadamalaiannan said, 'Your Majesty, it's all right if you walk normally here.'

'That's what I've been doing. I haven't been walking differently, have I?'

'I suppose no one told you the significance of the hills. Look around you.'

I looked around.

'Do you see how black and shiny these rocks are?'

'I do.'

'It is believed that these rocks are Salagrama stones, which means they are Lord Vishnu Himself. So usually people walk on their knees, as a mark of respect to the Lord. Since you would find it difficult to…'

'It is always difficult to reach God,' I said, and began to crawl upwards on my knees. Ethirajan and Vadamalaiannan too began to climb up the same way. After we crossed the black Salagrama rocks, we began to walk upright. My knees were bleeding, and I had a crick in the back. But otherwise I felt no discomfort of any sort.

We reached the temple by noon. I bathed in the temple tank and then went to the temple. I was told that Thirumala Devi and Thirumalai had offered worship and had retired to the rest house behind the temple. Acharya Venkata Thathayya was staying in the math next to the rest house.

The men who had met me regarding Annamacharya's devotional compositions now met me outside the math. They told me that they had sought Venkata Thathayya's permission to open the room where the copper plates were kept. He had given them permission at once and so now they were on their way to the temple. By the grace of God, that had been sorted out.

When I entered the math, I found my mother and some others seated before the Acharya. Venkata Thathayya was giving a religious discourse. I paid my respects to him and sought his blessings.

'Sit down. I hear you have made significant donations to

Vaishnava temples. Right from the beginning, the Vijayanagar Empire has been a great source of support to the Vaishnava religion. If today such a large number of people are Vaishnavites, it is because of you,' Venkata Thathayya said to me.

Except my mother, everyone else addressed me as 'Your Majesty.' When Venkata Thathayya dispensed with such formality and addressed me in terms of familiarity, I was taken aback. But I realised that to a man of God royalty meant nothing.

Acharya Venkata Thathayya was more than seventy years of age. But his body was not that of an old man. I wondered how a man who fasted often and who walked long distances all over the country could be so strong. But then, a person's strength comes from his spiritual strength. It comes from God. I had been so immersed in my thoughts that I had not paid attention to what Venkata Thathayya was saying. I apologised to him.

He smiled. 'Your thoughts were elsewhere. Never mind. I wanted to come to your capital and place a request before you.'

'Request? Please don't use such words. You should command me, Acharya.'

'The Vaishnava religion has many groups, and I want to unite all of them.'

'If that is what you want, you will be able to accomplish it.'

'I will also need your support. I want you to announce that I am the only recognized leader of all Vaishnavas.'

'I will do it at once,' I said and consulted my ministers on how to go about this.

I looked at my mother. She signalled to me that I should do as per the Acharya's wish.

I passed my order in the presence of the Acharya. Minister Ayyapparasu read out my order:

'With respect to the Vaishnava temples in the Vijayanagar

Empire and those outside it, Acharya Venkata Thathayya will be the head of all of them. Vaishnavites of all persuasions should act according to his directions. In all Vishnu temples, he is entitled to be the first to receive the holy water.'

Venkata Thathayya then blessed everyone there. He had not noticed Ethirajan at first and when he did, he said, 'Ethiraja! It is years since I saw you. You forgot about your sister and became a soldier in the Sultan's army.'

'Swami, I didn't join the Sultan's army of my own volition. I was taken away and forced to fight in their army.'

I was glad that I now had an opportunity to broach the subject of Chinnadevi. But Mother had other plans. She said that she had many doubts pertaining to Vaishnavism and wanted clarifications from Venkata Thathayya.

I was furious. Was this the occasion for her to have her doubts clarified? She had promised me that she would ask the Acharya about Chinnadevi…

But I soon realized the reason for mother's questions. She waited for Thirumala Devi and the others to leave. She signalled to Gayatri to stay back. She gave me a meaningful glance.

I went into the adjacent room. But I asked the others in that room to leave and stood near the door, so that I could hear the conversation in the next room.

Eavesdropping is a shameful thing to do, and it is all the more shameful when a king does it. But when one is in love, nothing else matters. Ethics, justice, honour, prestige—all quietly make their exit. I am sure all young men in love know what I mean.

Venkata Thathayya gave Mother and Gayatri some holy water. He then asked my mother: 'What are your doubts?'

'Please forgive me. I wanted the others to leave. So I just used that as a ruse to get them out of the way. There is a personal matter I want to discuss with you.'

'What is it?'

'Since you mentioned Chinnadevi, I felt I could talk to you about it. My son Krishna is madly in love with that girl. But she is a dedicated devadasi of the Srivilliputur temple, and bears the conch and discus emblems on her arms.'

'I am the one who put the Vaishnavite emblems on her arms.'

'That is why you are the only one who can release her from her vow, so that she can marry my son.'

There was silence for a few seconds. That meant the Acharya was thinking over mother's proposition.

Finally he said in a stern voice, 'That is a thing of the past. That was your son's infatuation. Now he is an Emperor, and that girl is a servant of the math. She gives dance performances occasionally. But otherwise her life is dedicated to service. There is no use talking about her marriage.'

I was devastated.

'Acharya, you mustn't turn down my request. The future of the Vaishnava religion lies in your granting me my wish,' said my mother.

'What are you saying?' Venkata Thathayya asked in surprise. I too was puzzled.

'I have tried reasoning with my son. But his love for Chinnadevi is so strong, that he says that since it is the Vaishnava religion that stands in the way of his marrying Chinnadevi, he will convert to the Saiva religion.'

'What?'

I was shocked. I had never said anything of the sort to Mother. Nor had I entertained such thoughts. But here was my mother peddling a lie, and even threatening the Acharya! My mother who valued honesty, was telling a lie, because of her affection for me! I was moved. I had read about Yashoda's love for Krishna. I had read about Kausalya's affection for Rama. I had read about Kunti's concern for her sons. But I had never read of a mother who had lied for the sake of her son's happiness. How fortunate I was to be her son!

Acharya laughed. 'Your son will not convert. Don't worry.'

'I am really afraid that he will carry out his threat. You are a scholar and a religious leader. But you do not know how the present generation thinks. If they cannot have what they want, they will do something drastic,' said Mother.

Venkata Thathayya was silent again.

Mother continued: 'I am not worried so much about my son. It is the people I worry about.'

'Why should you worry about the people?'

'You yourself said a while ago, that because the king is a Vaishnavite, the people too are Vaishnavites. If the king were to become a Saivite, then they too will convert to Saivism. My worry is that such large scale conversions will take place when you are the undisputed Vaishnavite Acharya.'

I had never expected my mother to argue so brilliantly. I peeped into the room. Venkata Thathayya's eyes were closed, and he seemed to be deep in thought. After a few seconds he said, 'It is highly unlikely that your son will convert from the Vaishnava religion. Vijayanagar Emperors have all been Vaishnavites.' But he didn't sound so sure of it anymore.

'Again, you must forgive me. It is wrong to say that Vijayanagar Emperors have all been Vaishnavites. The early monarchs were Saivites. King Virupaksha was a Saivite too. And you know why he later converted to Vaishnavism.'

Acharya was silent again. He seemed to know the story of Virupaksha's conversion. I didn't.

I felt it was very wrong to blackmail such a great man. Yet

I was happy that Mother was lying so cleverly so that I could marry Chinnadevi. As I waited with bated breath for the Acharya's decision, he said, 'Nagalamba, send for your son.'

I entered trying to look like someone who was totally unaware of what had been going on. 'Ask Ethirajan to come here,' he said. Ethirajan came in and stood beside me.

'Your mother has been arguing with me for a long time,' Venkata Thathayya said to me. 'I agree to release Chinnadevi from her vow. I am doing this not because of your love for Chinnadevi, or because of your mother's arguments and pleas on your behalf. I am doing this only to keep the Vaishnava fold intact. I know that what I am doing is in contravention of all Sastraic rules, and yet I do it for the sake of the Vaishnava religion,' Venkata Thathayya said.

Tears rolled down from my eyes. I thanked him.

'But I have to lay down one condition. You must fetch that sword.'

'Sword? Which sword? And where is it?' I asked.

'The sword in the Srivilliputtur temple. Take Ethirajan with you. He will give you all the details.'

Forty-two

I took leave of Venkata Thathayya. He blessed me, and Thirumala Devi and our son Thirumalai.

'What is that sword the Acharya spoke of?' I asked Ethirajan.

'Since we will be travelling together to Srivilliputtur, I will tell you about it on the way,' said Ethirajan.

'Gayatri is responsible for spreading this disease.'

'What disease?'

'It is a strange disease. I will tell you about it later. Let us go to the temple again.'

The administrative officer of the temple showed me a platform. 'This is the platform on which we plan to install your bronze image. We were told that you wanted your image to be installed together with the Queen's. And now we can install your image, because the Queen is also here.'

I stared at the platform. True—the Queen was here. But it wasn't this queen I had had in mind, when I had said my image was to be installed with my consort's.

The sound of the temple bell reminded me that I was in a sacred place. Priests were reciting prayers. I made the sixteen kinds of donations prescribed by the sacred texts, and went to the Ranganayakalu pavilion. When Malik Kafur had invaded South India two hundred years ago, the processional idol of the Srirangam temple had been brought to Tirumala for safety. The idol was taken back only after the danger to the Srirangam temple had passed.

Although the Srirangam idol was no longer here in Tirumala, the pavilion had been sanctified by His presence there two hundred years ago. So we worshipped at the pavilion. After worship, we sat down in the courtyard of the temple. 'Mother, why did you frighten Venkata Thathayya that I would convert to Saivism? You even said our ancestors were Saivites. Is that true?'

'I thought you knew that story.' Mother then told me the story. It was a story passed on from generation to generation.

In the early years of the Vijayanagar Empire, King Virupaksha had to fight many of his relatives; he had to kill many people, before he could ascend the throne. It was said the ghosts of the slain people haunted the palace. Afraid that they would harm him, King Virupaksha moved out of the palace to another one. At that time he was a Saivite.

But two Vaishnavite scholars who visited Vijayanagar did not know that the king had moved to another palace. They saw the ghosts of the members of the royal family who had been killed. They saw the ghosts sit on the throne and behave like royals. Mistaking the ghosts for real people, the scholars gave a religious discourse on the Ramayana before them! When the ghosts heard the story of Rama for three days, they were released from their ghostly state. Before departing, the ghosts rewarded the scholars with lots of gold, and said that they had been liberated because they had heard the Ramayana.

The two scholars told King Virupaksha what had happened at the old palace. He was amazed to hear that the Ramayana had such powers. He asked the scholars to give a discourse on the Ramayana, so that he could listen too. At the end of the discourse, the king converted to the Vaishnava religion.

This could well be an apocryphal story, cooked up to spread Vaishnavism, but the fact remained that till the time of Virupaksha, Vijayanagar Kings had been Saivites, and that after his time, they became Vaishnavites.

Anyway, the important thing was that Mother, using this story, had made Venkata Thathayya change his mind.

Glad that our mission had met with success, we visited a few more temples, and returned to the capital.

⁂

That day, when I visited Thirumala Devi, she was watching the antics of her pet parrot. I felt there wasn't much difference between Thirumala and her parrot. The parrot was in a golden cage, but nevertheless it was a prisoner in a golden cage. So was Thirumala. She enjoyed the luxuries of life in the palace; she was honoured as the Queen. But wasn't she too a prisoner, in a sense? Hers was a lonely life. She was surrounded by wealth and power, but was without company. She was married, and yet lived the life of an ascetic.

'Krishna, Krishna,' screeched the parrot.

'How dare you call out my husband's name? Even I don't do that,' said Thirumala to her parrot, as she stuck her finger through the bars of the cage and tickled the bird.

'Rama, Rama,' the parrot now screeched.

'Excellent,' I said and clapped my hands in appreciation of the bird's smartness. Only then did Thirumala notice me. She smiled. 'Thirumala, show me your hand,' I said. I looked at her hand decorated with mehndi. 'I was afraid the parrot might have bitten your finger. It happened to me once. Be careful.'

'This is my pet. It will not hurt me. Even if it does bite me, I don't mind. Some pleasures in life are accompanied by pain.'

I could see what she was getting at.

'I am going to Srivilliputtur,' I said to her.

'I know, Your Majesty. Venkata Thathayya has asked you to bring a sword from there, hasn't he?' she asked. I could see her hesitation in talking about my Srivilliputtur trip, and to save her further embarrassment, I said, 'Not just because Venkata

Thathayya has asked me to. I am also going there because my happiness is at stake. I feel embarrassed to talk about it.'

'Why should you feel embarrassed, Your Majesty? I've told you several times and let me repeat it, this empire will be happy only if you are happy. Have a happy journey. Bring that sword from Srivilliputtur. I don't know what the mystery behind that sword is, but, I know that once you get the sword, you are going to marry Chinnadevi and live a happy life.'

Her face betrayed no sorrow or jealousy.

'Where is Thirumalai?' I asked.

'Now if you had built a small house like other people, it would be easy to find him. But you built the largest palace in South India. How will we find him easily? Who knows where the child is playing now?'

'A ceremony awaits him. Please tell his nurses to take good care of him.'

'What ceremony is that?'

'I will tell you at the appropriate time,' I said, and burst out laughing. That was Gayatri's favourite line! And now I had caught her disease too!

On my way back, I saw Appaji.

'I have made arrangements for your trip. Guards will follow you. I will give you your itinerary when you leave,' Appaji said.

Appaji had never approved of my love for Chinnadevi. So I was surprised that he had made arrangements for the Srivilliputtur trip. 'There is an auspicious day next week. Your Majesty can start on that day,' he said.

'On that auspicious day, there is something else I want to do,' I said.

'What is that?'

'I want to officially make Thirumalai the Crown Prince.'

'What's the hurry? Why can't it wait?'

I was furious. Here I was talking of something auspicious, and Appaji was objecting!

'Your Majesty, can I refrain from speaking the truth, because you won't like it? There is peace in the empire. If it becomes widely known that a child is on the throne, there could be threats from enemies. Your elder brother Bhujabala Narasimha made the same mistake. Luckily, the danger to the Empire passed, and you became the Emperor,' said Appaji.

'I haven't forgotten the past. But I want to officially announce that Thirumalai is the Crown Prince. I am going to put him on the throne, and then I am going to tour the southern parts of India as his representative. Please don't start making objections. I want your co-operation.'

'As you wish. But please tell the Queen Mother and also Vyasa Guru.'

For the last few days, Appaji and I have been at loggerheads. I don't know if he is right, or I am.

ൟ

As I proceeded to my mother's palace, I saw Nicholas approaching. These days, he too accompanies the royal physician, when the latter examines my mother.

'Nicholas, how is my mother?'

'She is fine. She will live to see her grandson married and will live to be a great-grandmother,' he said. 'What worries me are the superstitious beliefs of the people.'

'Not so loud. My mother believes that there is some logic behind every superstition. What is it that saddens you?'

'Yesterday, a man came to me for help, because his wife had gone into labour. He said he could not bring her to me. So I went to his house. But the woman locked herself up in her room, and refused to open the door. She said she would not be attended to by a man! Refusing my help, she died, and the baby died too. There is no hope for this country as long as people have such silly beliefs.'

'Nicholas, I suggest that you train women to be physicians, so that lives are not lost. Why don't you train Gayatri, to begin with?'

'Good suggestion,' said Nicholas and went on his way happily. He was glad because this gave him one more opportunity to be in Gayatri's company.

೧೨

I decided I would meet Vyasa Guru first. I went to his math at the head of a huge procession. My gifts to him were carried on the back of ten elephants. Hundreds of men and women followed with baskets of fruits and flowers and grains.

I told Vyasa Guru about my plans for Thirumalai's coronation.

'A very good idea,' he said. I also told him about my Srivilliputtur trip. Vyasa Guru blessed everyone, and then asked for a private audience with me.

'You have fought using a sword, haven't you?' he asked me.

'Several times.'

'Do you always use the same sword, or different ones for different battles?'

'Most of the time it is the same sword that I use. I prefer using one particular sword, because it has proved lucky for me.'

'Take that sword with you when you travel to Srivilliputtur.'

'But I am not going there to fight,' I protested.

'Please listen to me. Take that sword.'

'All right.'

Venkata Thathayya says, 'Fetch a sword.' Vyasa Guru says, 'Take a sword.' I couldn't fathom the reasons for either of these instructions.

Forty-three

My mother wasn't keen on Thirumalai's coronation.

'If Appaji doesn't approve of something, there must be a reason for it. Why don't you follow his advice?' she asked me.

'There is something that tells me that I should go ahead with this coronation,' I said.

'No, there is nothing to justify the coronation. It's just a whim on your part. I have a feeling that you shouldn't proceed with this coronation.'

'I suppose it is some meaningless fear that prompts you to say so.'

'You know what is best. Whether you go ahead with this coronation or not, all I pray for is the welfare of the child.'

'With your blessings, everything will go according to plan, Mother,' I said and moved away before she could raise any further objections.

The day before the coronation, a guard came in to announce that Nicholas sought an audience with me.

'Ask him to come in,' I said.

Nicholas seemed to be in a good mood, for he was smiling. But something seemed to tell me that it was not a genuine smile. It seemed the sort of smile one puts on to mask one's worries.

'Every time we meet, you tell me some frightening story. The last time it was about a young woman who refused treatment and died. Please don't give me some such story. Tomorrow is a great day. If you plan to tell me some sad story, let it wait. I don't want to hear it now.'

'I have brought some news for you, Your Majesty. It's about a fever.'

'Fever?'

'Yes. It started in one corner of the capital, and started spreading. It killed many. But now, thanks to my efforts, it is under control. We found the reason for the fever and stopped it spreading any further.'

'I am glad it is under control. Let me reward you for bringing me some good news,' I said, and took off my strand of pearls and gave it to him. 'You can give me all the details later on. You may leave now.'

'This pearl strand will look more beautiful on another person I know,' he said and smiled meaningfully.

I was glad to have some encouraging news on the eve of my son's coronation.

ಉ

The city of Vijayanagar came to life, shortly after midnight. Vedic chants and music rent the air. I went out to the balcony. I could see the fireworks that lit the sky. Thirumala Devi also joined me and watched the firework display.

'See how happy the people are for your son,' I said.

'Yes,' she replied.

I noticed that she looked anxious. 'You seem to be thinking of something,' I said.

'Yes, I was thinking of the plans for Lord Rama's coronation. The people of Ayodhya must have celebrated in the same way.'

'Stop, Thirumala. What a silly comparison. That coronation…' I didn't complete the sentence. I didn't want to talk of the stopping of Rama's coronation and the events that followed. It seemed inauspicious to do so when my son was going to be crowned.

'Please don't mistake me. I am worried that our son should

not be the target of evil eyes. Many of your ancestors had their coronation in Tirupati. We too could have had our son's coronation there, and it could have been a simple one.'

'Celebrating it in Tirupati is one thing, but to have a simple celebration is another. None of my ancestors ruled over such a huge empire. I am an unparalleled monarch. And my son, therefore, cannot have a simple coronation.'

A servant entered. 'The Prince is about to be given a ceremonial bath. The Queen Mother wants you both to be present there,' she said.

'We will be there,' I told her.

☙

Thirumalai was seated on a golden throne. There were 1008 pots of water, brought from three oceans and seven rivers. As each pot of water was poured over the child's head, Vedic mantras were chanted. Musical instruments were played. Flowers were showered on his head.

Thirumalai was enjoying himself. As each pot of water was poured over his head, he laughed delightedly.

I said to Kondamarasu who was beside me, 'Your men have done excellent work. This coronation has been arranged at such short notice, and yet they have managed to bring holy water from so many places.'

Kondamarasu whispered: 'Let me tell you a secret. But you must promise not to be angry. Not all the water was brought now. When Vyasa Guru was anointed, a lot of water was brought. Not all of it was used then. We didn't want to discard the unused water. So we preserved it in the palace and that is what is being used now.'

'How clever!'

The child was laughing with joy. They draped him in silk clothes. They adorned him with more jewels than he could hope to bear on his slender body. Vyasa Guru sprinkled sacred rice on the boy's head and turned to fetch the crown. Loud shouts praying for the welfare of the prince went up. Gayatri was behind the throne holding the royal umbrella above the child's head. Two women were fanning him. Every time the peacock feather fans brushed against him accidentally, Thirumalai laughed because of the tickling sensation.

All the members of the royal family sprinkled sacred rice on him. Thirumala Devi and I and all the ministers did so too. I stood beside Thirumalai and said, 'In two or three days, I am going on a tour of South India. I seek the blessings of all the elders here.'

'Long live the Emperor!' the courtiers called out.

I pointed to my son. 'Long live Emperor Thirumalai!' they shouted in approval.

Appaji told me that I would have to give gifts to all the dignitaries assembled there, each according to his status. I also announced many donations to temples, including to the Tirumala temple.

It was only then that I noticed Ethirajan. I wanted to give him a special gift. 'Appaji, I have a request. Some time ago, when I wanted to open Devaraya's treasure chest, you stopped me. There is a ruby strand in it, that rightfully belongs to Ethirajan. I wanted to give it to him. That is why I wanted to open the chest. That strand came into our possession with a curse. Let us give it away on this occasion. I want my son and his descendants to start ruling without a curse over them.'

'Krishna, I don't understand what this is all about,' said my mother. Appaji clearly disapproved.

Ethirajan said, 'Your Majesty. There is a rule that treasure chests belonging to previous kings should not be opened. Please do not break that convention. I have the prince's welfare in mind when I say this. Please do not go against established practice.'

I didn't wish to argue any further. 'As you please,' I said.

'You mustn't be angry with me, Your Majesty. What will I do with that ruby strand? I have neither wife nor children to whom I can pass it on,' Ethirajan said.

'You have a sister, don't you? She is going to be here soon. Don't forget that.'

'When she comes here, she is going to be the recipient of things that are a thousand times more valuable than that ruby strand.'

Dance and music performances began in the pavilion. The sound of the anklets of the dancers reminded me of Chinnadevi. The temple astrologer came to meet me. He looked concerned about something. 'He has something to say to you,' said Appaji.

'I fixed an extremely auspicious day for the coronation. And by God's grace everything went off well.' It was obvious that all this was a preamble to something else he wished to say. 'Get to the point quickly,' I said.

'It was only later that I also had a look at the country's horoscope. The horoscope of the ruler is different from that of the country. When I looked at the horoscope of the country, I found some disturbing things were about to happen.'

'There is no kingdom where disturbing things do not happen at some time or the other. There is always some remedy to unfavourable planetary positions. So what can we do now to rectify the situation?'

'Yes there is a precaution we can take. Let the prince not

spend the night in this palace. Let him not stay anywhere in the royal enclosure.'

Mother, who had been listening to the astrologer said, 'Krishna, he must be right. Thirumalai and I will spend the night in the Balakrishnan temple.'

'That temple is under renovation. It is dusty and dirty. Thirumalai might fall ill,' I objected.

'Shall I take the Prince to my house? My house is outside the royal enclosure. My sons and daughters- in-law will look after the Prince. And he will not lack any comforts there,' suggested Appaji.

Before I could reply, Mother said, 'That's a good idea.'

Had it been any other time, I would have criticized such superstitious beliefs. But even reformers do worry, when it comes to their own families and at the slightest hint of trouble, they abandon their reformist zeal.

'Please go ahead, Appaji,' I said.

That evening, I took my son on elephant-back to all the temples in the city and we offered special worship in all of them.

Ramaswamy temple, Balakrishna temple, Veerabhadra temple, Sasivakkalu Ganapati temple, Kadapakkalu Ganapati temple, Virupaksha temple, Kodandarama temple, Vittalaswami temple, Malyavanta Raghunatha temple—we visited all of them. We even worshipped at the Jain temples.

Our final stop was before the idol of Veera Narasimha. It was a five-foot-tall monolith. It had Goddeess Mahalakshmi seated on Narasimha's lap, with her right arm around his waist.

'It is only after the idol has been completed that a temple can be built for it. Maybe in your time you will build a temple for it,' I said to Thirumalai. I don't know if Thirumalai understood what I was saying, but he nodded his head in agreement. At the end of our temple tour, I sent Thirumalai to Appaji's house and returned to my palace.

※

Thirumala Devi was looking out of the window. I thought she was admiring the decorations in the streets. But when I looked at her face, I could see that she was worried about something.

'Worried again?' I asked.

'No. It's just that Thirumalai has never been away from me.'

'But every night, you send him away with the servant who looks after him and you sleep alone. So how is tonight different?'

'The thought that he was somewhere in the palace was comforting. This is the first time he is going to sleep outside the palace.'

'You are a queen. When he assumes charge as king, he will have to travel to many places; he will wage many wars. You will not be able to see him for months. Look at my mother. The days when she and I have been separated are more numerous than the days when we have been in the same place.'

She didn't seem convinced. She gave me a sad smile, and went to bed.

But for some reason, I couldn't sleep. It seemed as if Thirumala Devi's worry had transferred itself to me. It was only in the early hours of the next morning that I managed to get to sleep, but was soon woken by someone knocking on my door.

No one had ever woken me up like that before. Singers would sing; veena players would accompany them. And it is to the strains of music that I would wake every day. So I thought I must have imagined the noise at the door. But the knocking persisted. 'Your Majesty! Oh, Queen! Emperor!' I heard the cries distinctly.

I opened the door. A servant stood there. She was weeping

and could hardly communicate coherently. 'Your Majesty, Your Majesty…' she didn't stop crying, but conveyed to me the news she had brought.

'Is that true?' I shouted. 'Is it true?' I cried out again. Thirumala Devi gripped my hand hard.

The girl repeated the news she had brought. 'Oh my God! Thirumalai, my darling!' I cried, and ran out. I forgot that I was an Emperor, that I had to take control of my emotions. I ran on the streets of Vijayanagar like one possessed. Thirumala Devi was following me.

The citizens of Vijayanagar stared at me in astonishment. I paid no attention to anyone. I reached Appaji's palace, and ran in.

There, in the palace, lay my son Thirumalai, covered with a white blanket. He was dead. My darling son was dead!

Forty-four

I hugged Thirumalai, and wailed: 'Oh my darling Thirumalai, my dear son.' I was surprised at myself. I didn't know I had loved him so dearly.

Thirumala Devi, my mother and Gayatri were there too, sobbing. But I paid no heed to them. I, the king who had read a lot of philosophy, and should have learnt to take this loss in stride, wept uncontrollably. I hugged my son tightly, as if I feared they would take him away from me. This was the child who had been anointed with holy waters yesterday, and now he was drenched in my tears. Why had his fair skin turned dark? Why was the sprightly child of yesterday lying so still in my arms? How was it that the beautiful poem of yesterday now resembled the aimless scribbling of a mad man?

I could hear Appaji telling someone that the child had been sleeping next to him. 'I had my arms around him. Around midnight, I noticed that the child's body was hot. I could also hear him moaning. The prince had fever. I sent for the physician. But before he could arrive…'

Before the physician could arrive, death, which had seemed so far away from my son, had him in its coils. I looked up and saw servants and soldiers whispering to each other. They were pointing to Appaji and to the child and whispering. I was assailed by a terrible suspicion. I dropped my son, shook one of the soldiers and shouted: 'What were you whispering about? Tell me. What is it that you are trying to keep from me?'

He had never before stood in close proximity to me, and now when I shook him, he was terrified. 'I don't know anything, Your Majesty. It's something I overheard.'

'What did you overhear?'

'Your Majesty, I know nothing. People have been saying that Appaji, wanted to become the Emperor, and so he…'

I felt as if I had been struck by lightning. Appaji was standing beside the court astrologer. So he had hatched a plot to kill my son, and had taken the help of the astrologer.

'Appaji! You murderer!' I yelled, and attacked him. 'So this was why you wanted me to go to Srivilliputtur! So that is why you never once picked up my son or played with him! You arranged with the astrologer to say that staying in the palace would turn out to be inauspicious for my son. You plotted to bring him here to your palace, so that you could poison him. You…you…'

'Stop. Let him go' said Nicholas, and pushed me aside. 'Do you know how many hundreds have died of this fever? You don't even know what has afflicted your people. Your son has died of a fever, not because of poisoning. A fever has no respect for royalty. It afflicts a prince just as it does a commoner.' He stood shielding Appaji.

He continued: 'Your son has fallen victim to your superstitious beliefs. You used water fetched from rivers months ago. You poured several pots of water on the child's head. You didn't pause to think if it might affect his health in any way. I would have pointed it out to you. But then you would have said that I was a foreigner who did not understand your beliefs. Or you would have labelled me an atheist. That is why I had to be silent yesterday, during the coronation. Now look at what has happened.'

Nicholas's assistants had dipped Thirumalai's fingers in a pot containing some liquid. One of them came to Nicholas and said, 'This is not a case of poisoning. The child has died of fever.'

'Did you hear that, Your Majesty?' asked Nicholas. 'We

examine corpses to find out the cause of death. We can tell if a person has died of poisoning or of a fever.'

I was shaken by Nicholas' words. Before I could respond to him, my mother came up to me. She said to me in the fiercest possible tone: 'How dare you? Appaji was the one who saved your life. You owe your position and your life to him. He has served you sincerely all his life. How dare you accuse him of having murdered your son? Thirumala Devi is also devastated. We all are. But we haven't taken leave of our senses. I wish I had never given birth to a son like you.'

I retreated slowly, and dropped into a chair. I held my head in my hands and was silent. After a few minutes, I looked up and saw Father Louis there. 'Your Majesty. I am a citizen of Portugal. I should not speak against my country. But if at this time, I do not speak the truth, the God I worship will not forgive me,' he said.

I was confused. Father Louis continued: 'Governor Albuquerque wants the help of the Vijayanagar Empire to drive the Muslims away from Goa. We asked for your help several times, but your Prime Minister did not respond positively. So my government felt that we would first have to get rid of your Prime Minister. That is why our spies spread many rumours about your Prime Minister. This is one such rumour. Our men who are here told me about this plan.'

I turned and looked at Appaji. Tears streamed down his cheeks. I wanted to fall at his feet and beg for forgiveness. But I didn't. I was the Emperor of all the land from the banks of the Godavari to the banks of the Tamaraparani river in the extreme South. How could I admit that I had been wrong and how could I seek someone's forgiveness? My pride prevented me from doing the right thing.

I suppose Appaji could guess that I was caught between the

prodding of my conscience and my pride. He came up to me and said: 'Please forgive me, Your Majesty. I did many things that roused your suspicion.'

'Appaji, I…I…'

Appaji lowered his voice and said: 'Ssshhh! I know what you want to say. You are an Emperor. You mustn't apologise in public. Please don't apologise.' He then instructed the other ministers on what needed to be done.

In a trice Appaji forgot all the insults he had been subjected to, and went about discharging his duties. But I could not get back to normal so easily. I looked round and saw Thirumala Devi, my mother, Gayatri and Nicholas. I couldn't bear the pitiful look they gave me. I can deal with anger, but not pity.

I had one last look at Thirumalai. He was now on Thirumala Devi's lap. I pressed Appaji's hands, indicating to him that he should take care of everything. I couldn't bear to see my son's body being cremated.

I returned to my palace. I had run like a mad man when the news of my son's death had been brought to me. But now I was calm. I walked with measured tread, like one balancing a huge rock on his head.

I recalled a line from Bharthari's *Niti Satakam*. 'You cannot conquer Fate.'

In the days that followed, I took no notice of anything. I did not know what was happening in the palace, or in my empire, or even in my own family.

Poets assembled as usual. Dance and music programmes continued. Ambassadors from other countries, tradesmen, weddings, temple festivals—everything went on as usual.

I participated in all these. But I did so mechanically, without any involvement.

One day, after a meeting of all the ministers, Vadamalaiannan said to me, 'These days, the Prime Minster does not attend ministerial meetings. Have you noticed?'

I was taken aback. I hadn't noticed Appaji's absence. Had I been that indifferent to affairs of the state?

'Perhaps he is unwell. Did you enquire at his palace?'

'I did. I was told he was not in town. Maybe he is on a pilgrimage.'

I paced up and down, my hands behind my back. I had not paid attention to anything, because I knew Appaji would take care of everything. But now that he was not here, what was I to do?

'He left the day after it happened,' said Vadamalaiannan. I did not ask him what the 'it' meant. I knew he did not want to refer to the death of my son.

'Yes. Continue,' I said.

'Appaji was very sad. He said he had lost a five-year-old granddaughter, and a three-year-old grandson. He had doted on them. After their death, he always kept away from children. He was afraid that if he doted on any child, something might happen to the child. That is why he had not played with the Prince. But you mistook him. He was very sorry about this.'

I sighed.

'I will find out where Appaji has gone. By the way, Your Majesty will have to have a wedding gift ready. Two people, about to be married, will be here soon, seeking your best wishes.'

'Who are they?'

Vadamalaiannan just gave me a smile, but said nothing.

The suspense was soon over. The persons he had been talking about were Nicholas and Gayatri! I had expected this, of course. 'God bless you,' I said to them. Gayatri was blushing, and this was, in fact the first time I had seen her blushing!

'Appaji no longer mistrusts us. Ever since Nicholas cleared his name, he has been kind to us. And affectionate too. That is why he gave up his objection to our wedding.'

'Had he any objections to your marriage? You never told me about this.'

'We didn't want to complain against him. We were sure he would give his permission in course of time and we were prepared to wait. Since he is the Prime Minister and also minister-in-charge of the religious administrative department, we had sought his permission. He said that if I married a man of another religion, he would order that both of us should leave the Empire. And since that was also the law of the land, we couldn't protest. But ten days ago, he sent for me. "I am told that Rajput kings have given their daughters in marriage to Muslim kings. So I am no longer going to stand in the way of your marriage to Nicholas. Go ahead and marry him," he said.'

Gayatri was clearly delighted. Her happiness was infectious, and helped to lift my spirits. I opened my treasure chest and gave them lots of gifts.

'Gayatri, do you have any idea where Appaji is?'

'Didn't you know? He has gone to Kondapalli, and that too because of his affection for me. He has gone there to capture Veerabhadran. Dhananjaya Udayar has not been able to make much headway in the campaign. So Appaji has gone there to lead the forces himself. He told me he would bring Veerabhadran here.'

It was only then that I remembered Gayatri's wish to take Veerabhadran prisoner remained unfulfilled.

'I am very happy for you, Gayatri. Your dreams are all being realized one after another. When is your wedding?'

'Not for now, Your Majesty. It will have to wait.' She looked out and said, 'Please come in.'

Ethirajan entered.

'Go on, talk to the Emperor,' Gayatri said to Ethirajan.

He hesitated, and then said haltingly, 'After our return from Tirupati, I met my sister once. I told her that Venkata Thathayya had released her from the vow, and had asked you to fetch the sword from Sriviliputtur. She was overjoyed and is waiting for your arrival.'

I was ashamed of myself. I had forgotten all my duties as a king, because of my grief over my son's death. But how could I forget my beloved Chinnadevi, who was waiting for me?

'In your present frame of mind, you will not want to travel anywhere. Ethirajan and I will go to Srivilliputtur and fetch the sword,' Gayatri offered.

'No. I will go myself,' I said. I had been drifting aimlessly since my son's death. Now it seemed as if I had suddenly regained my enthusiasm and strength.

Forty-five

I perked up, when I thought of making a trip to Srivilliputtur to meet Chinnadevi. After my son Thirumalai's death, I had been steeped in sorrow. But now I felt as if someone had dragged me out of the morass of self-pity and sorrow. I felt energized. The thought that there was a woman waiting for me on the other side of the Krishna river, and that there was another woman here in this palace, who ached for my love, gave me strength. It no longer seemed as if the world was about to end.

'I am grateful to you for reminding me, Gayatri. Ethirajan and I will go to Srivilliputtur. It doesn't matter if Appaji isn't here. All my ministers are trustworthy. And there is no threat to the Empire from anyone as of now.'

'Please take enough men with you to ensure your safety, Your Majesty,' Gayatri said.

I looked into her eyes. She had come into my life unexpectedly, and now seemed an inextricable part of it.

'Your Majesty, please forgive me for what might seem to you my impertinence. When I first came to this palace as a servant, I only had thoughts of revenge on my mind. All I wanted to do was to take your help to capture Veerabhadran, so that I could avenge my family's death at his hands. I thought that involving myself in your personal matters would help me earn your goodwill. That is why I interfered in your personal affairs. But in course of time, my selfish motives disappeared. And for a long time now, my only desire has been to see your love materialise, and to see you live happily with Chinnadevi,' Gayatri said.

'Lord Srinivasa will definitely bless my love, and also help you attain your goal. Don't worry,' I said, and went to my mother's palace, to take leave of her.

We all labour under the delusion that even if we have erred, all we need to do is to feel contrite, when we realise our mistake, and that everything will be all right from then on. But this is self-delusional. Many days had passed since I had insulted Appaji, and had at once sought his forgiveness too. But my mother was still angry with me. She was cold towards me. Usually she welcomes me and regales me with stories from the Puranas. But today, she merely indicated that I should take a seat, but didn't utter a word of welcome.

But when I mentioned the Srivilliputtur trip, I noticed a slight softening of her features. She held my hands in hers and said, 'Take care. I gave you my word that I would get Chinnadevi married to you. But so much has happened since then, that I haven't been able to fulfil my promise to you. Let us hope I am able to now.'

Thirumala Devi gave me her best wishes for the journey. What a wonderful lady she was! She knew I was going in search of another woman, and yet she was cheerful! She brought me flowers that had adorned deities, and gave the flowers to me, and applied vermilion powder on my forehead.

Ethirajan and two others were to accompany me. I was taking Haridasa with me, because I wanted him to introduce me to Tamil poets. Although I had made it clear that I didn't want any ceremonial send-off, my soldiers had assembled to see me off. I wasn't in disguise, and so my people could recognize me, and they shouted: 'Long live the Emperor!'

I took my sword with me, as instructed by Vyasa Guru. I worshipped in all the temples in the capital. I first went to the Vittala temple. The temple had been built, but the deity had not been installed yet. Devotees had wanted to instal the deity from the Pandharpur temple here. But it is said that when the idol was brought here, the Lord said that he didn't like to be a part of such a huge, ornate temple, and that he preferred being in Pandharpur. And so the deity went back to Pandharpur. Since then the temple here had been without a deity. Once I returned from Srivilliputtur, I would have to install an idol in the temple.

Our first stop was Tirupati, where we worshipped Kalyana Venkateswara and Goddess Alamelu. Our next stop was Kalahasthi. From there we proceeded to Kanchipuram, where we worshipped at the Varadaraja temple. I had a gold covering made for the temple vimana. I worshipped at the Ekamabaresvara temple too. Haridasa introduced me to Mandala Purudar, author of *Choodamani Nigandu* and Kachi Gnanaprakasa, author of *Kachi Kalambagam*. Wherever I went I was surrounded by a crowd of people, and I couldn't have a private conversation with Ethirajan. At last when I managed to find myself alone with him, I asked him to tell me the story of the sword we were to fetch from Srivilliputtur.

'Your Majesty, do you remember that incident long ago—when there was an argument between two people about to be married and the revenue officer?'

I laughed bitterly. 'That was a turning point in my life. How can I ever forget that day?'

'Until the Vijayanagar soliders addressed you as "Your Majesty," I had thought you were a commoner like me. When I came to know you were of the royal family, I was furious. When I realized that you belonged to the family, with which I wanted no truck, and also that you were soon to be the Emperor, my fury knew no bounds. Until then, I had not objected to the love that had blossomed between my sister and you. I wanted to get my sister married to you. But…'

I sighed. 'I am an extremely unfortunate man.'

'No, Your Majesty. It is my sister and I who are unfortunate. Otherwise, would she not have been married to you long ago?'

We were now somewhere between Tiruvannamalai and Kanchipuram. Acting upon my order, a few guards kept up the rear, and they were in civilian clothes. Yet, many people recognized me and paid their respects to me. Many officials met me. 'I am now on a pilgrimage. I do not want to discuss matters of state. Please meet me later,' I said to them.

I remembered that this was the same route I had taken once, when I had travelled in disguise to capture the bandits who waylaid travellers. But how different the road looked now! It was broader, and the road was dotted with camps of guards, to instill fear in thieves and confidence in travellers. Rest houses too had been built, and all of this was Muthu's handiwork. I had had my doubts about whether I had made the right decision when I had put a sculptor in charge of administrative work. But I could see that I had made the right decision. I wanted to express my appreciation to Muthu and to Solai, but I felt this wasn't the time to do it.

As we made our way, Ethirajan continued with his story.

'For the next few months, I performed for any Bhagavata Mela troupe we came across. But I did not experience the peace of mind I had enjoyed in the original troupe.'

'And how was Chinnadevi at the time?'

'She was miserable, because of me. She said she couldn't forget you. "Why did you separate me from him? Is it his fault that he is a member of the royal family?" she asked. She either argued with me, or shed tears for you. I felt that as long as she was in a place close to Vijaynagar, she wouldn't change her mind. So I moved to Tamil territory. The Cholas and the Pandyas seem to have nurtured the arts better than we do now. Wherever we went, we could hear the strains of music and the jangle of the anklets of dancers.'

'After wandering all over Tamil Nadu, we finally reached Srivilliputtur. By then the bonds of affection between us were almost completely broken. We didn't talk to each other. If I asked Chinna a question, she would answer. But there was no conversation beyond that. One day, when I returned home, I saw that she had something in her hand, which she touched to her eyes, reverentially. She was also crying. Do you know what it was? It was something that belonged to you…'

'My ring. The ring that bears my royal emblem.'

Ethirajan was surprised. 'How did you guess?'

'Many days after I returned to the capital, I realized that I had left behind my ring with the royal emblem. I used to console myself with the thought that Chinnadevi would find it and treasure it.'

'I didn't know that she would preserve it as she would her own life. I was very angry that she was still thinking of you. So I…forgive me, Your Majesty…I…'

'You snatched it from her, and threw it away, I suppose.'

'Yes, Your Majesty,' Ethirajan admitted shamefacedly. 'It rolled out on to the road and was lost. I stormed into my room angrily, and Chinnadevi sobbed. After some time, I couldn't hear her sobbing. I thought she must have reconciled herself to the situation. But when I came out of my room, I saw that she wasn't there. On the floor, she had scratched a message for me: "Do not look for me." I panicked. I ran out on to the street and began to look for her. Some people said that they had noticed her proceeding towards the Cauvery river. I ran towards the river. The river was in spate then. As I ran towards the river, I saw a huge crowd in a small shelter on the way. When

I drew close to the crowd, I noticed that they were watching a dance programme. I didn't want to waste time there, because I wanted to find Chinnadevi. Even as I turned to leave, I noticed Chinnadevi there.'

'Was she dancing?'

'No, she was watching the dance. It was not a Bhagavata Mela dance. It was a Bharatanatyam performance. Chinnadevi was so absorbed in the dance, that she didn't even notice me standing beside her. She noticed me only when I touched her hand. I signalled to her that we should leave. "Wait for the dance to be over," she said. The dance concluded only around midnight. Chinna was silent on the way home. When we reached home, she wept and asked for my forgiveness. She had planned to commit suicide, by jumping into the Cauvery river. But she happened to watch the dance and she liked it so much, that she forgot all about the suicide and stayed on to watch the dance. It was only then that I realised her passion for dancing. The Bhagavata Mela has only male dancers, but Bharatanatyam was danced by women. So I felt that if Chinnadevi learnt Bharatanatyam, she would, in course of time, get so involved in the dance, that she would forget you…'

Before Ethirajan could compete his narration, we reached Tiruvannamalai. We were welcomed with temple honours. The temple had been famous even in Rajendra Chola's time, but it was not very big. I ordered that an eleven-tiered gopuram be built for the temple, and also ordered the construction of a thousand-pillar pavilion and a tank for the temple. I made the necessary financial provisions for all these additions to the temple. I was told that there were a total of three hundred and fifty sacred springs and ponds around the temple. I bathed in as many of them as I could; I worshipped in the caves that once upon a time had been inhabited by sages. The governors brought many gifts for me. It was only after we left Tiruvannamalai and travelled towards Chidambaram, that Ethirajan resumed the story.

☙

'The head of the dance troupe in Srirangam was a lady. She was a temple dancer,' continued Ethirajan. 'I asked my sister if she would like to learn Bharatanataym from this lady. She jumped at the opportunity. I felt this was the only way to make her forget you, and to divert her thoughts from you. The next day I met the lady who was in charge of the troupe. I requested her to accept Chinnadevi as a pupil. I told her about our having been a part of a Bhagavata Mela troupe.'

'Where will you go after you leave your sister with me?' the lady asked.

'Never mind where I go,' I said. Chinna cried when she heard that. She didn't want to be separated from me. The lady of the troupe, who was called Kamakshi Ammal said, "You said you could play the mridangam. Why don't you stay with our troupe and play for us?"'

'Kamakshi Ammal belonged to a village near Srivilliputtur. She was a devadasi attached to a small temple there. She took us to her village. My sister would clean the temple there. She would string flowers for the deity, light the lamps and so on. She also began to learn Bharatanatyam from Kamakshi. She was a quick learner. I was beginning to believe that my sister had a secure future. She would be a good dancer. Kamakshi Ammal said my sister would have to go and perform in neighbouring villages. Unfortunately, Kamakshi Ammal fell ill. So we couldn't go to any village. We were forced to stay back in her village. Chinnadevi and I had assumed that all the residents of the village were honourable, but we soon discovered that it was not so. One day, when Chinna was dancing in the temple, a drunkard made his way to the stage, and approached Chinna menacingly. She moved back in fear. I jumped on to the stage and pushed him down. We didn't complete the programme, but returned home. We learnt later that he was the richest man in the village and that he was also a wicked man. No one who had earned is enmity would be left unharmed by him. When we reached home my sister told Kamakshi Ammal what had happened.

'She said to my sister, "You will not be bothered by such men, once you are married." My sister protested and said, "No, no. I will not marry. I have already chosen the man I want to marry. I will never marry anyone else." Kamakshi Ammal said, "Don't worry. This is no ordinary marriage."'

'Yes, Your Majesty, it was a strange marriage,' said Ethirajan. It was when he got to this part of his narration, that we reached Chidambaram.

Forty-six

I worshipped Lord Nataraja and Goddess Sivakami. I made provisions for the repair of the Northern tower of the temple.

When I had time to rest—actually I shouldn't use the word 'rest,' because my mind was not at rest. My thoughts were about Chinnadevi, and about how soon I would be able to get that sword from Srivillipittur. It was only my body that I was able to give some rest to.

Haridasa came in and said, 'Thiruvarur Tattvaprakasa Swami has sent a message to you.'

Tattvaprakasa Swami was a great devotee of Lord Siva and he was also a poet. He was in charge of the Thiruvarur temple.

'What is his message to me?' I asked.

Haridasa laughed. 'It is bandied about that he sent this palm leaf to you through a parrot! But actually it was a messenger who brought it. Tattvaprakasa Swami has banned the temple priest from carrying out his duties at the temple. He has sworn on Your Majesty's name and the name of my brother Vadamalaiannan, that he will not allow the priest to perform the rituals at the temple.'

'Why drag me and Vadamalaiannan into this?' I asked.

'During the Thiruvarur chariot festival, it is customary for the priest to go to the neighbouring village called Velankudi, and cut a bitter gourd creeper there. The priest failed to do this. Hence he has been removed from service. Tattvaprakasa Swami just wants you to be informed of what has happened.'

'If Swami is of the view that the priest should be dismissed, then there must be a reason for it. Appoint a new priest for the temple.'

I made arrangements for all of Tattvaprakasa Swami's verses to be collected together. We then continued on our journey.

When I managed to be alone with Ethirajan, I asked him about the unusual wedding Chinnadevi had gone through. Here is what Ethirajan said. The following account is in Ethirajan's words:

༺༻

Kamakshi Ammal arranged for an unusual wedding for my sister Chinnadevi. There were more women in the crowd that had gathered to witness the wedding. But I managed to squeeze in. There was a lot of singing and laughter and noise in the temple, where the wedding was to take place. The nagaswaram was being played.

Everyone seemed to know what was going to take place. I was the only one in the dark. I knew Kamakshi Ammal could be relied upon not to do something that would make Chinnadevi unhappy. So I knew it wouldn't be a marriage Chinna would disapprove of. Yet, I was uneasy. I didn't know what Chinnadevi felt about the whole thing. She was dressed in bridal clothes and sat with her head bent, as any other demure bride.

'Make way for the priest,' called out someone. Everyone stepped aside and made way for the priest. The priest of the Durga temple came in. He looked quite fierce, but he seemed to be respected by the people.

He had a copper plate in his hands. There was something on the plate. I couldn't make out what it was. It was long, and was covered with a silk cloth. The priest removed the silk cloth, and I could see that it was a sword that had been concealed by the cloth.

'This sword is your husband,' the priest said.

I was shocked, and so was Chinnadevi.

'Don't be afraid. Once you go through this ritual, you become a slave of Goddess Durga. You become a divine bride. No man will dare touch you.'

Chinna looked up at me. It seemed as if she was seeking my opinion.

I indicated to her to go ahead. A wooden plank was placed beside Chinna. The sword was placed on it. The wedding mantras were recited, and the priest, who was the representative of the deity, tied the scared thread round Chinna's neck. Chinna picked up the sword and went round the fire seven times. After all the rituals connected with the wedding had been completed, Chinna danced in the temple.

We then took the sword and brought it home in a procession. We had all the celebrations that are a part of any wedding. That night, a bed was decorated with flowers, and Chinna was led to the nuptial bed, on which the sword was placed. Chinna had been fasting since morning, and she looked weak. I smiled reassuringly at her.

After she sat on the nuptial bed, she was given milk and fruits. The women who had escorted her to the room then left, after shutting the door.

I was waiting outside, and Kamakshi Ammal said to me, 'Don't worry. Hereafter your sister will be looked after by Goddess Durga.' She was very tired and went straight to bed.

But I couldn't go to sleep. I leaned against the wall of the room in which Chinna lay beside a sword. I slept fitfully. The thought of a sword beside my sister filled me with dread. She had already once threatened to jump into the Cauvery river and commit suicide. What if she killed herself with that sword?

I wiped the sweat from my face. It dawned. Nothing had happened as I had feared. Chinna was cheerful. She had risen early and had bathed. She was wearing new clothes. We took the sword in a procession to the temple and left it there. There were four other dancers, who were staying with Kamakshi Ammal. They too underwent a similar sword marriage. Having thus ensured the safety of her students, Kamakshi Ammal breathed her last a few days later.

But a few days after Kamakshi Ammal's death, Muthuraja was back, and he began to harass the girls. Some of them fell prey to temptation. One day Chinna suggested that we leave the village.

'Why? What has happened to make you suggest this?' I asked.

'I understand that Muthuraja plans to kidnap me. Our servant warned me to be careful.'

I thought for a bit. I was a strong man and it was true that I was good in warfare. But fighting in a king's army was different from pitting myself against a bunch of thugs in a remote village. I knew I could not defeat a group of dangerous men single-handedly. If I were killed, who would look after my sister? I felt the prudent thing to do would be for us to leave the village. That night, Chinna and I left. Chinna was holding my hand, and I could tell that she was terrified. The whole village was at peace. Why then were my sister and I alone in trouble? I was in anguish over our plight. But I didn't let on that I was scared or that I was miserable. I smiled, to infuse confidence in my sister.

We chanted the name of God, and slowly we made our way to Srivilliputtur. We reached Srivilliputtur the next morning. We didn't know whom we should turn to for help, for we knew no one there. The temple festival was on. As part of the celebrations, residents of the town were providing food to all visitors. So food was not a problem for Chinna and me. We also heard that Venkata Thathayya was visiting Srivilliputtur, and that too was encouraging news. I had heard about his greatness and scholarship. That night, after my sister and I met him at his math, we told him our story and of our travails. 'You may spend the night here, in our math,' he said.

The next morning, he asked Chinnadevi to have her bath and he then branded her arm with the conch and discus symbols-conch on the left and discus on the right arm.

'You lived in a small village. The ceremonial wedding you went through does have value. But that will not keep away a wicked man like Muthuraja. I will make you the devadasi of the Srivilliputtur Vadapatrasayee temple. This branding was done with that in mind. You can travel anywhere you want to, as the representative of this temple. You can dance in any temple. Even kings will be afraid to touch you. That is the power of these symbols.'

'Shall I remove the mangalsutra?'

'No. Let it remain. It indicates you are a married woman. So it offers further protection.'

After that, we travelled to many places, without any fear. Chinna was invited to dance in many temples. But as instructed by Acharya Venkata Thathayya, we did not stay in anyone's palace or house.

We received invitations from many temples in Vijayanagar. We hesitated and wondered if we should accept the invitations. But it was so long ago that you and Chinna had met and fallen in love. You had subsequently become the Emperor. So we felt that a visit to Vijayanagar would not rekindle old memories. But we were proved wrong. Chinna was troubled by the past, and she said, 'I am afraid I may break the commandment of Acharya Venkata Thathayya. I thought I had forgotten the events of the past. But they have come back to haunt me. Let us leave this place.'

To add to her fears, we learnt that you had watched her dance and that you had also started to make enquiries about Chinna. So we decided to leave at once. Your Majesty, my sister and I spent most of our time running away from someone. We packed our bags and left. But Fate was not going to be kind to us. We fell into the hands of a governor called Singapiran. He handed us over to the men of the Bijapur Sultan. Again, it was Venkata Thathayya who came to the rescue. He rescued us from the clutches of the Sultan's men and offered us shelter in his math. But I was forced to join the Sultan's army. And you know what happened after that, Your Majesty.

ॐ

Ethirajan completed his narration. Actually, he didn't give such a coherent account as the one I've given here. I have put his narration in some order, so that readers do not get confused.

Our journey towards Srivilliputtur continued and we visited the temples of Srirangam and later Azhagar Koil, where I donated a pearl studded crown and emerald pendant to the deity. We then came to Madurai Meenakshi temple. Here I donated diamond earrings, a diamond pendant, emerald earrings and a pearl nose ring. We were now nearing the village in which Ethirajan and Chinnadevi had stayed. 'There is one thing I do not understand,' I said to Ethirajan. 'Why did Acharya insist that we bring that sword?'

Ethirajan sighed.

'I hope we find the sword in that Durga temple. It's seven years since we left it there.'

Forty-seven

The road to the village in which Chinnadevi and Ethirajan had resided was quiet. A few of the village administrators met us, and welcomed me. But I could see that their welcome was a mere formality, and that they were not excited about my visit to their village.

'Why are you all so dull? This is the month of temple festival. Has it begun?'

'No. It hasn't. We are all hoping that your visit will help.'

It was a beautiful village. I was charmed by the greenery all round me, by the twittering of birds, and by the gentle caressing breeze. 'What was an empire beside all this? Of what use was romance or valour? Did one need the trappings of power and royalty? It would be better if I could throw away all of this and settle down under a tree in this village,' I told myself.

There was a huge crowd of women outside the temple. They had applied turmeric powder on their faces; they were clad in yellow sarees. Each of them had a sprig of neem in her hand. But the doors of the temple remained locked.

I summoned the priest, and said, 'Why are you keeping these people waiting? Why don't you open the doors?'

'The keys are with the trustee of the temple.'

'Where is he? Send for him.'

'The trustee is…is…Muthurasu.'

'Muthurasu?' Ethirajan asked in surprise.

'Yes, the same Muthurasu who was responsible for your flight from this village. His atrocities continue. Hearing of your visit to this village, he ran away, and is in hiding somewhere.'

I was very angry. 'Now tell me—what is more important?

The trustee's permission, or the temple rituals? Why didn't you break open the lock of the temple?'

The village chief said, 'I suggested that. But the villagers are afraid. Now that Your Majesty is here, he is in hiding. But after you leave, he will be back. That's what they are afraid of.'

'Don't worry. I know how to deal with him,' I told the villagers.

'Station some soldiers in the village. Take the help of the governor of this area. If Muthurasu dares to come here, then capture him and send him to the capital,' I instructed one of my ministers who was accompanying me.

In the meanwhile, many of the women had surrounded Ethirajan and were making enquiries about Chinnadevi. Ethirajan fielded their questions with aplomb. 'I told His Majesty about this temple, and requested him to worship at this temple before proceeding to Srivilliputtur,' he said. Ethirajan was already looked upon with respect by the villagers, because he was travelling with the Emperor. Now that they knew he was the one who had brought the Emperor to their village, he instantly became a hero in their eyes.

Now that they had my permission, the villagers brought a huge rock to break down the lock of the temple. When the lock broke open and the doors to the temple were opened, the villagers called out to the Goddess reverentially. Folk instruments were played. I was impressed by the innocence of the villagers and their deep devotion to God.

A priest put a copper pot on the ground, upside down. He then put a sword on it, after worshipping the sword. What was amazing was that he placed the sword upright on the upturned pot, and yet it didn't fall off. Haridasa explained that it would remain in that position for two hours, the priest would hold out his hands and the sword would drop into his hands.

Elsewhere a pit had been dug, and Haridasa informed me that it was called the pit of flowers. Inside the pit were pieces of wood from a tamarind tree. The wood had been lit, and on the glowing embers, men and women danced. Even eight and nine year old children danced on the embers. And yet not one of them had burns on their feet!

I had travelled all over my kingdom, before I ascended the throne. But most of my travels had been in cities, and I had not travelled much in the Tamil region. The temple bell was rung, and the sound broke into my thoughts, and reminded me of the purpose of my visit. I entered the temple, and Ethirajan and Haridasa followed. I worshipped the Goddess, who was fierce where the wicked were concerned, and kind where her devotees were concerned. But even as I worshipped, my eyes began to seek the sword. Where was that sword? There were lamps, pots of sandal paste, flaming torches to light the sanctum, vessels containing oil. But there was no sword there.

I asked the priest to wait outside the sanctum and I entered the sanctum. The priest was puzzled. He could see that I was looking for something, but he didn't know what it was. Ethirajan looked at me, almost as if he was seeking my permission to tell the priest about our mission. I signalled to him to go ahead. The priest came up to me and said, 'There is a room in the first corridor. That is where…'

'Let's go there,' I said.

We came out of the sanctum. The room the priest had referred to was in the first circumambulatory passage outside the sanctum. The priest opened the lock to the door. 'All the swords are kept here,' he said. 'But how can you tell which is the one you want?'

I hadn't cottoned on to the priest's mention of many swords, and it was only when we entered the room, that the import of his words struck me, for lined up there were at least sixty swords!

'Kamakshi Ammal, and others too used to perform sword marriages. And after the ceremony, they would bring the sword here to this temple, and all the swords would be kept in this room. So how will you find out which one is Chinnadevi's?' the priest asked me.

I was so disappointed, that life no longer held any meaning for me. I had journeyed so far, only to be thwarted again!

Ethriajan was inspecting the swords, and suddenly he exclaimed: 'This is the one,' and showed me a sword.

'How do you know this is the one?' I asked.

'Look at the anklet motif on it. My sister had this habit of sketching pictures of anklets. She would embroider anklets on cloth. On the night of the wedding, the sword was beside her in the room. She must have used some sharp object, a knife, perhaps, to etch an anklet motif on the sword. This must definitely be her sword.'

I was so relieved to hear Ethirajan's words, that I gave him a hug and we both shed tears of joy.

When we came out of the temple, we witnessed many weddings. It was an auspicious day, and so many people had decided to tie the knot. I thought of Gayatri, who had vowed not to marry, until my dream had been realised. I wrote to Gayatri at once: 'I've found the sword. Don't wait for me. Please marry Nicholas on an auspicious day.'

I handed over the sword to a soldier and asked him to take it to Vijayanagar at once.

'Why don't we leave for Vijayanagar too?' asked Ethirajan.

'Are you so anxious to see your sister wed?' I laughed. 'God has in mind a role for each of us. If he has made me come almost to the southern tip of the country, then it can't be just for the sake of this sword. Let us visit the other temples in this region, before we return.'

☙

When we reached Srivilliputtur…

Viswanathan had come there with his generals, in order to welcome me. This was my first meeting with him, after I had asked him to rule Madurai as my representative. I embraced Viswanathan, whose loyalty to the Vijayanagar Empire had been such, that he had imprisoned his father, who had turned traitor. I travelled all round the town in his company.

Viswanathan told me about how Srivilliputtur came into existence. A queen called Malli had been ruling the area. She had two sons—Villi and Kandan. Kandan was killed by a tiger. The queen was then advised to cut down the trees in the area, and establish a town there. And the town that thus came up was Srivilliputtur.

After worshipping Vadapatrasayee—the stone idol in the sanctum sanctorum, Andal, Periazhvar and Rangamannar—the processional deity, I went to the palace built by Viswanathan and rested there.

But I couldn't go to sleep. I tossed and turned. I then decided to listen to the story of Andal, which Haridasa narrated.

Vishnuchittar, who was also known as Periazhvar, lived in the time of the Pandya king Vallabhadeva. He chanced upon a little girl, whom he decided to adopt. He gave her the name Andal. Every day, she would wear the garlands intended for the deity of the Sriviliputtur temple. When her father discovered what she was doing, he was aghast. But the Lord Himself said he preferred the garlands that Andal had worn to the ones she hadn't. Andal's desire to wed Lord Naraayana himself was fulfilled at Srirangam. Her sojourn on this earth ended with her divine union with Lord Ranganatha.

'Even Periazhvar, who lived like a sage, was unable to part from his daughter, and he said: 'I brought her up like Goddess Mahalakshmi herself, but now the lotus-eyed-one has taken her away.'

Until then I had been lying down, listening to the story of Andal. Now I sat up and shouted joyfully: 'I've got it!'

Ethirajan, who was in the next room, heard my shouts of joys and came in. 'What have you found now, Your Majesty? We already have the sword,' he said.

Haridasa looked confused. 'After the Kalinga war, when I was on the way home, I worshipped at the Srikakulam Vishnu temple. That night, the Lord appeared in my dream and said: Write a poem about me in Telugu. There are so many stories about the Lord. I didn't know which of them I should write about. Anyway, I began to write down notes about various stories, and the morals of the stories. But now I know what He wants me to do. He wants me to write the story of Andal in Telugu.'

I began to write my epic poem. I gave it the title—*Amuktamalyada*. Amuktamalyada means the girl who offered garlands that she had worn and discarded.

Dawn had broken by the time I finished writing eighty-nine verses and completed the first chapter. I lay down on the bed. I could feel something on the bed. It was my sword. I moved it aside. I had felt tired and sleepy, but now again I found I could not sleep. Why had Vyasateertha directed me to take this sword along?

I wasn't going to fight anyone now. What was the need for this sword, I wondered. The answer to that question came in Dhanushkodi.

Forty-eight

I offered a nose ring, a belt studded with rubies, gold anklets, and a head ornament studded with nine precious gems to Andal. I arranged for the temple tank to be repaired and for a pavilion to be built in the middle of the tank, and resumed my journey.

Something interesting happened just as we were about to leave. A solider came on horseback, and brought a silver vessel, which he gave to Haridasa. Haridasa brought the vessel to me and said, 'This is food offered to the deity at Thirumaliruncholai. The temple authorities forgot to give it to you, when you worshipped at the temple. So they have made the offering again, especially for you. They have offered it to the deity and then sent it to you.'

I opened the vessel. Porridge made with jaggery and rice, with ghee dripping from it!

'Hmm. There are lakhs of people in the Vijayanagar Emire, who are so poor that they cannot afford even a glass of gruel. And yet, a soldier comes on horseback to give such a rich sweet to the Emperor. I will have some, because it comes from the temple,' I said, and ate a little. It was divine.

'This is not the usual porridge, Your Majesty. This is called akkaravadisal. In the case of the usual porridge, the rice is cooked in water. Here it is cooked in milk.'

I laughed. 'I too am a Vaishnavite, a devotee of Lord Vishnu. But I am not fortunate like you, I am unable to enjoy the richness of this sweet from the temple.'

'Your Majesty, the porridge from Thirumaliruncholai is special. Andal is said to have made 100 huge vessels of the porridge for Azhagar, the deity of the temple. She prayed to the Lord to eat all of it, and promised that if He did, She would make many more vessels of the porridge for Him. But she married Lord Ranganatha, before she could fulfill Her vow. And the Vaishnavite saint Ramanuja, who came centuries later, fulfilled her vow. So the porridge in this temple has a special significance.'

I realized I should be careful about what I said. I didn't want to say something that might offend the deities. And so I was silent in all the other temples we visited.

In Karivalamvandanallur, I worshipped Paalvanna Nathar, and then visited the Sankaranarayana temple. There I bathed in the sacred water known as Nagateertha, and I worshipped Sankaranarayana and Goddess Gomathi. Our next stop was Trikutachalam, where I bathed in the Akasha Ganga and also in the Kalyana Teertha of the Agastya hills. I ordered that a gopuram be built for the Agasteeswara temple. I worshipped the Lord at Gajendra Moksha. I made arrangements for the construction of a hall in the Nellaiappar temple, and then went to Vanamamalai. I witnessed the anointing of the deity with oil, and also worshipped His Consort—Srivaramangai, and proceeded to Kanyakumari. It is said that the nose ring of the goddess is so bright that it guides seafarers to the shore. How true!

Thirukkurungudi, Tiruchendur, Kanyakumari, and all the other Vaishnavite temples of the Pandya kingdom were on my list too, and I visited all of them. I then took a boat from Sethu to Dhanushkodi.

I was glad that I had worshipped at almost all the important pilgrim centres in South India.

The east coast has large sandy beaches. The west coast is rough, and is scattered with boulders. What a pleasant sight it is to see huge stretches of sand!

I kicked the sand, unearthing all kinds of shells in the process. I enjoyed my leisurely walk. All the catamarans had gone out to sea. It wasn't time for the fishermen to return. A few fishing nets were drying in the sun. In the distance I could see the huts of the fisherfolk. There was a smell of fish in the air.

I told the men following me to stay back and stop following me. I find these security forces as annoying as the silk robes I have to wear. The silk robes make me sweat and make me feel uncomfortable. The guards make me feel just as uncomfortable as my clothes.

I reached the waters alone, without the annoyance of security guards. A huge wave rose furiously, but once it crashed against the shore, it shrank and broke up, like a person, who has a huge ego to start with, but is chastened by experience.

I put my sword on the sand, and sat down on the sand, with my legs stretched out. Some waves tickled my feet. Some of them came up to my knees.

I was steeped in thought. Was there any purpose to my life? The wars I had fought, my victories—did they have any meaning, I asked myself.

Men of God, and recluses can have the luxury of such contemplation. Could someone like me have such a luxury, I asked myself, and smiled.

'Stop! Stop!' the cries broke into my thoughts.

I turned back and found a fisherwoman running towards me. She had a small vessel in her hands. Before she got to where I was sitting, my soldiers and generals had stopped her. 'Who do you think he is? He is the Emperor,' they said to her.

'Really?' she asked, her eyes dilating in surprise. 'I thought he was a traveller. I saw him sitting on the sand all alone. I thought he might be tired. So I brought some buttermilk for him.'

'How dare you? You and your filthy vessel of buttermilk! Go away,' said one of my generals.

'I have cleaned the vessel. It isn't filthy,' she argued.

'Don't stop her,' I ordered my men. I sounded so stern that they backed off.

To the woman I said, 'Give me the buttermilk. I will have it.'

'Your Majesty, I cleaned the vessel, before filling it with buttermilk. I've been watching you for a long time. I thought you were just an ordinary traveller. Now that I know that you are our Emperor, my happiness is even greater.'

'I'm happy too. Give me the buttermilk.'

She gave me the buttermilk. It was most refreshing!

'It was very tasty,' I said, and pulled off one of my bracelets and gave it to her.

'My buttermilk isn't that expensive, Your Majesty,' she said, proving that she could speak wittily. 'I feel honoured that the Emperor Krishnadevaraya drank buttermilk that I offered him. Now that is enough of a reward for me. This day will remain etched in my memory, and in the days to come, I will talk about it with my children and grandchildren.' She bowed before me and left.

I put the bracelet on. Had this been one of my generals, or a governor or a poet, he would have gladly accepted my gift. I have always noticed that when it comes to self-respect, it is the poorest of the poor who score high.

Her words kept echoing in my ears: 'I washed the vessel thoroughly, Your Majesty.' There was something about her words, that made me feel very uncomfortable.

I picked up my sword. The tip of the sword and the handle were a bit rough, and had a brownish hue. No, it was not rust. Despite the fact that after every battle, I cleaned my sword, yet, traces of blood remained and the brown particles I now noticed were nothing but dried drops of blood.

As I saw my sword and thought of the hundreds of people I had killed, I was reminded of Vyasa Guru's words: 'Krishna, your duties as a king are over. You have captured a lot of territory. You have expanded your empire. You have fought many wars. You have killed many people. Let the killings stop. Let not your sword be besmirched with blood any more.'

I had asked him why he insisted that I take my sword with me, when I wasn't going to a war. But he had insisted, and now I had the answer to my question. Here in Dhanushkodi, I had my answer. Vyasa Guru must have decided that my eyes should be opened here in Dhanushkodi. I walked up to the water, and dipped the sword in the salty water. I rubbed it again and again, until it gleamed and there was no trace of any blood on it. I put it in the scabbard, and walked back. My men were watching me, but they didn't dare ask me why I had cleaned my sword. Ethirajan said, 'If you had wanted the sword to be cleaned, you could have asked one of us to do it. Did you have to do it yourself?'

'A man has to wash away his sins. No one else can do it for him,' I replied.

We went back by boat to Sethu. I worshipped Kasi Visveswaran, Ramalingaswami, Sethumadhavan, and Goddess Paravatavardhini. I bathed in all the twenty-four sacred waters. It is believed that one will be blessed if one spends three nights there. So we spent three nights in Sethu. After offering ornaments to the Goddess, I began my return journey to my capital.

One the way back, we stopped at Gokarna, where I worshipped Lord Gokarna and Goddess Brihadambal, and proceeded to Srirangapatnam, where I worshipped at the temple of Lord Adiranga. My astrologers told me when it would be auspicious for me to enter my capital, and accordingly I made my entry into the capital. Vijayanagar was in a celebratory mood.

The place was milling with soldiers. Their shouts of praise for their Emperor rent the air. After worshipping at the Vittala and Virupaksha temples, I made my way to my mother's palace. I fell at my mother's feet and asked for her blessings. Thirumala Devi and Gayatri fell at my feet, and asked for my blessings.

Gayatri was beaming. I could tell by the mangal sutra round her neck that she was now married. 'Oh, so now you are Nicholas' wife, are you?' I asked.

'I was waiting for your message. The moment the messengers arrived, this girl didn't even wait to consult astrologers about an auspicious day for her wedding. She took four or five priests with her, and she got married right away in the Balakrishna temple. And these days, she doesn't pay attention either to Thirumala Devi or to me. She has no time for anyone except Nicholas,' Mother teased Gayatri.

'You have lost weight, Krishna,' my mother observed.

'Ah, just the observation I had been waiting for. Isn't this what all mothers say, when their children return after a long absence from home?'

'Yes, your son has lost weight,' Thirumala said to Mother.

'Thirumala, don't try to please your mother-in-law,' I said. 'Actually I had excellent food wherever I went, because I ate at temples and the food in temples is rich, with lots of ghee and butter and milk. I think I have put on weight.'

'Was your trip successful?' my mother asked.

'Yes, Mother. With your blessings, the purpose of my trip was fulfilled. I have brought the sword and it is now with Ethirajan. Has Acharya Venkata Thathayya arrived?'

My mother laughed. 'The Acharya doesn't know you are in a hurry. He is visiting one pilgrim centre after another on his way here. I know he has left Tirupati. But there is someone else who has arrived.'

'Who is it Mother?'

'Appaji.'

'Appaji? You mean the Kondapalli war is over and he is back?'

'You have been away so long, touring pilgrim centres in the South, that Appaji could have conquered all of North India in that time!' Mother said.

I now knew why the soldiers had been in such a jolly mood when I entered the city.

'He has not only conquered Kondapalli, but has also imprisoned Gajapatirudra's son—Veerabhadran.'

I looked at Gayatri. She was looking out of the window, as if she had nothing to do with the conversation between my mother and me.

'There are two things I want you to do, Krishna,' said my mother. 'You must take Appaji on a procession, on elephant back. You must also shower him with gold coins. That is the only way for you to make amends and to atone for your harsh words against him.'

'Yes, Mother, I will certainly honour him. And what is the other thing you want me to do?'

'It is something I have already told you. You mustn't treat Veerabhadran like an ordinary prisoner. I have told Appaji that he must be treated with respect and must have all facilities. I do not want my instructions to be countermanded.'

I wanted to say I wouldn't revoke her orders, but I couldn't say so. I just nodded my head in agreement.

As I had expected, Gayatri arrived a few minutes after I left my mother's palace.

'You heard what my mother said, didn't you?' I asked her.

'Yes, I did, Your Majesty.'

'My mother wants him to be treated respectfully. You want to kill him.'

'A small correction, Your Majesty.'
'And what is that?'
'I never said that I wanted to kill Veerabhadran. I only want to destroy his arrogance.'

'And how do you propose to do that? Please don't give me that usual answer that you are so fond of: I will tell you at the appropriate time. You cannot get away with that answer, because now is the time.'

'He thinks he is the best fencer around. If someone can defeat him, he will no longer be able to boast about his skills. He will be humbled.'

'Don't talk like a child, Gayatri. A man loses a sword fight, only if he dies, or if he is mortally wounded.'

'No, Your Majesty. Forgive me for contradicting you. We just have to find someone who can defeat him without hurting him.'

'Now where will you find someone who can do that? I can. But I am determined never to fight again. So that rules me out.'

'I have just the man. I've trained him, Your Majesty. Let me bring him,' she said and went out.

Forty-nine

'I'll fetch him,' said Gayatri, but she was gone a long time. I wasn't convinced that there was someone who could defeat the Kalinga Prince, Veerabhadran in a fencing match, and yet not kill him in the process. Had she been lying to me? Even as I was telling myself that she was quite capable of lying, I heard footsteps. But it was not Gayatri who was there, but Vadamalaiannan. Was this the man Gayatri said she had in mind? As far as I knew, Vadamalaiannan had never participated in any major war. He was also approaching fifty. It didn't seem likely that he would have the skill and energy to defeat a young man like Veerabhadran.

But in a minute Vadamalaiannan put an end to all this speculation. He was there in connection with something else. He had a palm leaf manuscript in his hands. 'I've organised all the literary works we brought with us, and I've put them in the library,' he said.

'What's that you have in your hands?'

'I just brought this along for you to read in your spare time.'

He handed me the manuscript. It was in Tamil. 'But I am not well-versed in Tamil,' I said.

'This is not difficult to follow. It's written in an easy style. This has been written by a king. I thought it would be encouraging for you to read something another king had written, before you start working on your Amuktamalyada.'

'Who is that king?'

'Remember we visited a place called Karivalamvandanallur? The place where we worshipped in the Paalvanna Nathar temple? Varatungarama Pandyan was the king who ruled in that region. He is the one who wrote this work. It is said that in his young days he wrote a work titled *Kokkogam*, based on Vatsyayana's *Kama Sutra*. But I wasn't sure if that information was correct. So I haven't brought that work. Instead I've brought this.'

'What is the title of this book. 'Thi-ru-k-...'' I tried reading the title.

'*Thirukkaruvai paditruppathu*,' he completed for me. 'That king became the disciple of a sage called Isana Muni, and from him the king obtained Siva deeksha. This work is in praise of the deity of that village. It is said that because the king sang these hundred verses in praise of the presiding deity of the village, he was cured of some disease.'

There was still no sign of Gayatri. What was keeping her?

I tried to read the manuscript Vadamalaiannan had given me. It was simple. I began to read a verse, when I heard footsteps. But when I looked up, I was taken aback. I had expected a man, but there stood before me a veiled woman!

'Who are you?' I asked sternly.

'Gayatri sent me. I am one capable of fighting Veerabhadran,' said a voice from behind the veil. It was a male voice. Was it a woman speaking in a male voice?

'Who are you?' I asked, even as I lifted up the veil. It was a man behind the veil! A young man. He was wearing the uniform of a soldier. He had a moustache. This…I looked closely at the man. 'Gayatri!' I shouted out. Yes, it was Gayatri. But she was disguised as a man, and she had been very cleverly disguised. Unless one knew her, one wouldn't be able to tell it was Gayatri.

'Yes, Your Majesty. It is I, Gayatri, your servant. Please bless me so that I win the fencing match against Veerabhadran,' she said, and fell at my feet.

'What foolishness, Gayatri! How can you defeat Veerabhadran? Have you had any training?'

'Yes, I have had training. When I was in the Kalinga palace, I had some training. And ever since I arrived in Vijayanagar, I have practised in my spare time. Many generals who were unhappy with the Gajapati king, left Kalinga and came to Vijayanagar. They are serving here in your palace. I approached one of them and asked him to help me hone my skills in fencing. But I have been training in secret. That is why I am dressed like a man. And this completely veiled look is to conceal the male attire!'

Gayatri was waiting for me to say something. But I paced up and down, and said nothing to her. What could I say to this girl, who was prepared to go to any extent to attain her goal? Should I praise her for her determination to avenge the death of her family at the hands of Veerabhadran? Or should I pity her for her foolhardiness? Should I worry because I was sure her experiment would end in disaster for her?

I stopped pacing and watched her keenly. 'So, you want to fight Veerabhadran, disguised as a man?'

'Yes, Your Majesty.'

'Does your husband Nicholas know of your plans?'

'No, he doesn't. I've kept my plans and my training from him too. I know he will stop me, afraid that I will be hurt in the match.'

'That's exactly what I think too.'

'Please do not be afraid, Your Majesty. Please don't stop me.'

'All right. Cover yourself with that veil, and follow me.'

'Where are we going?'

'To my mother's palace. You have to assure my mother that you will fight Veerabhadran, but will not kill him. She must trust you and then grant you permission to go ahead. That's important. My permission can wait.'

Gayatri didn't hesitate. She covered herself with the veil and followed me.

∽

When we arrived at my mother's palace, Thirumala Devi, who usually was beside my mother wasn't there. My mother was listening to one of her servants reading something. As I listened to the girl, I could tell she was reading from Nandi Thimmanna's *Parijatha Apaharanamu*. It was a work in Telugu. It was the story of Krishna's trip to Indraloka, to fetch the Parijata tree, to appease Satyabhama.

Nandi Thimanna belonged to Srirangaptnam. When my father-in-law brought his daughter Thirumala to Vijayanagar, he brought Thimanna along and left him behind in our palace. Thimmanna was a very intelligent man.

'Come in, Krishna. Sit down,' my mother welcomed me. She didn't take notice of the veiled woman beside me. 'I suppose you know that Thimmanna is referred to as "Nose" Thimanna. I used to think that was because he had a beaky nose. But I think that is not the reason for the nickname. This girl has been reading Thimanna's work to me. In one of the verses, he describes a girl's nose and it is a wonderful description. I think he acquired the nickname because of this description.'

I sighed.

This seemed to be a day for me to hear about one poet after another. A while ago, it was Varatungarama Pandya; now it was 'Nose' Thimmanna!

At this rate I would never get round to telling my mother about Gayatri. I edged closer to my mother and said, 'Mother, here is someone I want to introduce to you.'

Mother signalled to the servant to leave the room. She

then said, 'There is no one here. You may remove the veil, Gayatri.'

I wasn't shocked. My mother was so sharp, that one couldn't keep anything from her. But Gayatri didn't know this, and she was taken aback.

'Gayatri, come here and sit beside me,' my mother said to her. Gayatri then pulled back her veil, and paid respects to my mother.

'You look nice in these clothes, Gayatri. But it looks like the uniform that Vijayanagar soldiers wear. The uniform of a Kalinga solider is different, isn't it?'

Gayatri blinked back her tears. 'Forgive me. I should have told you about myself. It was wrong of me to have concealed a lot from you.'

'That doesn't matter, because I made it my duty to find out about you. The first day you came to me, I had a look at your palm and said you were not a servant, but belonged to a royal family. I asked my trusted spies to gather information about you. Don't think only kings have spies. Queens have spies too. I know you are a Kalinga princess. I also know you learnt fencing here in Vijayanagar, dressed in a man's clothes.'

'In that case, Mother, I suppose you also know that her sister and brother and father suffered at the hands of Veerabhadran,' I said.

'Yes, Krishna. I know that Appaji headed an army and marched to Penukonda, to capture Veerabhadran, because that's what Gayatri wanted. Appaji himself told me this.'

Gayatri was silent. I didn't know what to say to my mother either. 'Can you tell me why you are dressed as a man and why you have been learning to fight with a sword?' my mother asked Gayatri.

Before Gayatri could reply, I said, 'Veerabhadran thinks no

one can beat him in a sword fight. Gayatri is going to defeat him and humble him. She has been well-trained to take him on. All she needs is your permission to go ahead.'

'And I refuse to grant permission,' my mother said emphatically.

'Queen Mother!' gasped Gayatri.

But Mother ignored her and said to me: 'Krishna, Gajapati may be your enemy today. But that is just a temporary enmity. You have no idea how hard they have fought to safeguard our religion. If the Suryavamsa Gajapatis had not offered protection to the Neelachala temple, and supported saints like Ramananda, Vallabhacharya and Chaitanya Mahaprabhu, it is not just our empire, but the whole of South India which would have been destroyed. Have you not read of the atrocities committed by Malik Kafur? If you haven't, then please read the account given by Ganga Devi, the wife of Kumara Kampanna in her work *Madura Vijayam*.'

'But Mother…'

'No, Krishna. I would have stopped your march against Kalinga. But I didn't, because you had to do it. It was your duty as King. The King of Kalinga had foolishly entered into a treaty with the Bahmani Sultans. It was your duty to break up that relationship. But I cannot allow this girl to go ahead with her plan for vengeance against the Prince of Kalinga. Capturing him and then allowing this girl to hurt him is something I cannot allow.'

'Your Majesty, I will not kill him,' said Gayatri.

'You will have you revenge and you will kill him. That is what I am afraid of. That is why I have housed him in a palace and thrown a security net around him. How can you challenge a man to a sword fight and not kill him?'

'I can do it, Your Majesty,' said Gayatri. I had never noticed such a defiant tone in her words until then. And she was openly defying my mother!

'I am telling you that I do not want any harm to the prince's life and that I am sure you will harm him,' Mother said calmly.

'And I am saying that no harm will come to him,' said Gayatri.

'Is that so? All right, then. If Veerabhadran is killed in the fight, you must never meet me again.'

'All right, Your Majesty.'

'You must never enter this palace.'

'All right.'

'You must never meet the Emperor.'

'All right.'

'I would even go to the extent of saying that you should leave the Vijayanagar Empire. But your husband—Nicholas—is a good man. He treats the poor people of this empire, without taking any fees from them. His service is important to the Empire. Therefore I will not ask you to leave. But tell me, do you agree to the other three conditions?'

'Yes, Your Majesty,' said Gayatri.

ღ

Mahanavami was approaching and Vijayanagar was in a celebratory mood. I decided to send for Veerabhadran, so that the sword fight could be organized. I sent one of my ministers to him to ask him if he was prepared for a sword fight. The minister returned with the message that Veerabhadran was willing to participate in a fight.

A warrior will never turn away from a challenge. To do so would be a blow to his pride. And Veerabhadran had supreme confidence in his skills as a fencer. I knew he wouldn't refuse to fight. His reply was along expected lines.

A huge crowd assembled to watch the fight. Veerabhadran was brought in. When I saw him, I felt like Anjaneya, who upon seeing Ravana, said, 'How unfortunate that such a brave man refuses to tread the right path!'

Gayatri entered and she even walked like a man, so that no one would suspect it was a woman in man's clothing. Each of the fencers had a helper. It was the duty of each helper to check the sword of the opponent, to make sure it wasn't coated with poison. The helpers stepped in and checked the swords. The rule was that neither the fencers nor their helpers should engage in any conversation. And the crowds were not to shout or cheer. One should hear nothing but the clash of the swords.

For a while we could hear nothing but the clanging of the swords. From the way Gayatri wielded her sword, one could tell that she had trained hard. It even seemed as if Veerabhadran would lose. But Veerabhadran lifted his sword, to signal to Gayatri to stop. He walked towards me. 'O King, I have a doubt,' he said.

I was shocked. I was an Emperor, and yet he was calling me a king! But that was not the reason for my shock. He said he had a doubt. What could that be? Had he recognized Gayatri?

Fifty

The place earmarked for the sword fight between Veerabhadran and Gayatri was only thirty feet from where I was seated. But as Veerabhadran walked towards me, every step that he took, made me feel uneasy.

I wanted Gayatri to win the fight. But I also wanted Veerabhadran to be unhurt, as Gayatri had promised my mother. So naturally when Veerabhadran stopped the fencing match and said he had a request, I was nervous.

At least I was able to maintain a façade of calmness, which was more than I could say for the others assembled there, especially my ministers.

My father-in- law, Kumara Veeraiyya is beside me all the time, these days. He has become a self-appointed guardian to his son-in-law. Since he is an elderly man and since he is still mourning his grandson, I am deferential towards him and treat him with the same respect I show Appaji.

When he saw Veerabhadran walking towards me, he whispered: 'Your Majesty, whatever his wish might be, don't accede to it. How dare he address you as a king, when you are an Emperor? That is proof enough of his arrogance.'

'Don't worry. Leave this to me. I know how to deal with him,' I assured my father-in-law. Veerabhadran had now reached the place where I was seated. I wanted to address him as 'Prisoner.' But I felt it would be mean of me to retaliate to his gratuitous insult. I decided to be magnanimous. 'Yes, Prince. What do you want?'

'Oh, King, You have heard about the Gajapati dynasty to which I belong. We value our prestige and we are proud of our lineage…' he began. His pride angered Appaji, who said, 'Young man, the families of those seated here are just as eminent as yours. None here is inferior to you.'

'Patience, Appaji,' I calmed him down.

'Yes? What was it you wanted to say to me?' I asked Veerabhadran.

'In a war, when two armies clash, it is all right to fight anyone. But in a fencing match such as this one, it is important that the opponent also should be from a royal family. We do not fight those who are not from royal families. I don't care even if you think I am backing out of this fight because I am a coward. But I will not fight a commoner. I don't know who this person is, who has challenged me. So you must assure me, you must give me your word that he is of royal blood.'

He looked up at me expectantly; waiting for my reply.

'Don't worry. Your opponent is a prince too. The one who challenged you, the one who stands before you is from a royal family.'

Veerabhadran could tell from the tone of my voice that I was telling the truth. So he went back to resume the fight. Gayatri did not seem perturbed at all. She adjusted her turban and false moustache. I noticed it, but no one else seemed to have noticed it.

The next second a fierce fight began.

Every time Gayatri or Veerabhadran had a narrow escape, there were gasps from the audience. Once or twice, Gayatri managed to knock Veerabhadran's sword from his hands, but before it could hit the ground, he caught it and continued with the fighting. I was astounded by Gayatri's skillful wielding of the sword. Where had she learnt to fight so well?

I turned towards the area where the women from the royal family were seated. My mother was watching the fight keenly.

The fight was getting fiercer by the minute. Gayatri lost her balance a couple of times but managed to keep from falling to the ground.

Mother was keen that Veerabhadran should not be killed, but who was there to worry about Gayatri? I prayed to Lord Venkateswara to guard this girl who had known nothing but sorrow all her life.

Veerabhadran stepped back a little, as if he couldn't face Gayatri's onslaught. But suddenly, he began to fight ferociously. The tip of his sword got dangerously close to Gayatri's head, and just when I thought he was going to lop off her head, he knocked off her turban. Her long hair came uncoiled; her false moustache chose that moment to drop off too.

'Gayatri, is that you?' Veerabhadran shouted in shock.

'Yes, it is I,' Gayatri said and laughed like one possessed.

'Gayatri, no. Please stop.' That was Nicholas. Until then there had been no sound except the swish of the swords. But now there was a huge commotion amongst the spectators. 'Gayatri? Is that the girl who is a servant in the palace? The one who married the Italian?' People were asking excitedly, and were advancing towards the fighting ring. Soldiers had a difficult time keeping them in their seats.

Veerabhadran came to me, with his sword held aloft. 'You are unfit to call yourself a king,' he yelled. 'I made it clear I wouldn't fight one who was not of royal blood. Still, I wouldn't have minded even I had had to fight a man who was not royalty. But I am ashamed that I have been fighting with a woman. This is an insult to my family. I will never be able to live this down.' He then threw his sword into the air, and as it came hurtling down, he stood in its path, so that the falling sword pierced his heart, and Veerabhadran fell to the ground, bleeding profusely from his wound.

'Nicholas, attend to him immediately,' I shouted.

Nicholas, who had been questioning Gayatri about the fight, ran to Veerabhadran, and cradled his head on his lap. He then checked Veerabhadran's pulse, and with a sigh, he gently laid down Veerabhadran's head on the ground.

'It is too late, Your Majesty. Veerabhadran is dead. He was a very skilled fencer. He knew how to mortally wound himself; he knew how he could ensure his death. The sword has pierced his heart.'

The spectators were unnerved by what they had been witness to, and they began to leave the place. I could see my mother leaving the place angrily.

The blood from Veerabhadran's wound had spread on the ground beside him, and there lay the prince of Kalinga, his hands outstretched. Gayatri stood transfixed with horror.

'Tomorrow, Mahanavami celebrations begin. What an inauspicious start to the celebrations!' said a minister to another.

༄

I had never seen my mother so angry. And her anger was against Gaytri, who had been like a daughter to her.

Gayatri sought my mother's forgiveness repeatedly.

'Queen Mother, I did not disobey you. I fought very carefully, so as not to wound Veerabhadran. This was totally unexpected,' Gayatri said.

'I don't care if it was planned or not. You are responsible for bringing the Gajapati dynasty to an end. It is a dynasty that made huge contributions to temples and maths, and played a major role in protecting our religion. That is the dynasty you have now brought to an end. I had already made it clear that if something were to happen to the Kalinga prince, I would never see you again.

There is no change in what I said. Leave the palace at once. You should never enter this palace again. You should never meet my son again.' Mother had turned away from Gayatri, and her hand was pointing to the entrance.

I was taken aback by the magnitude of mother's anger. I knew she was a very devout woman. But was it fair to be unkind to Gayatri who had done nothing wrong? Was it necessary to care so much for Veerabhadran, simply because his family had patronised maths and had been liberal in its donations to temples? How could she forget that the Gajapatis had been the enemies of Vijayanagar for a long time and that even recently, they had joined hands with the Bahmani Sultans?

'Mother, I was witness to what happened. So were you. It is not Gayatri's fault.'

'Stop, Krishna. Don't argue with me. She was determined to have her revenge on Veerabhadran, and she has managed to. She should never have challenged that prince to a sword fight. He killed himself, only because he was ashamed to have fought with a woman.'

Nicholas was at his wit's end. He was wringing his hands in despair. Someone had just told him about Gayatri's promise to my mother and the reason for her disguise. He hadn't known until then that behind the gentle Gayatri that he knew, there lay a vengeful woman. But this did not seem to have detracted from his love for her in any way. I saw understanding in his eyes, as he looked at Gayatri.

Appaji was silent. He has very fond of Gayatri, but even he didn't dare argue with my mother. He came close to Gayatri and whispered to her: 'This is the anger of the righteous. It will soon pass. But for now, please do as the Queen Mother says.'

Gayatri wiped her tears and quietly exited the room.

Nicholas put his arm round her shoulders, and walked out of the room.

☙

I have been witness to many Mahanavami festivals. But this year's festival was soulless. Rituals were performed to cleanse the place, since a suicide had taken place there the previous day. Kings and vassals of the Vijavayanagar Empire gathered in Vijayanagar, ahead of the celebrations.

Every day I sat on the throne and received the gifts that were brought for me. I watched the horses and elephants that lined up before me. Huge skin instruments called murasu were carried on the back of bulls and were struck, producing resounding beats.

Hundreds of women danced with lamps in their hands. Soldiers marched past with flaming torches in their hands.

It seemed as if Thirumala Devi and even my mother had forgotten the incidents of the previous day, and were enjoying themselves. They laughed and clapped their hands. I too clapped my hands, but lifelessly, like a toy operated by someone.

On the last day of the festival, I sat on my golden throne. That was the only day on which I sat on that throne. There was a reason for this. It was a throne that had been in the family for generations. My ancestors had laid down many rules for the use of the throne. A king seated on this throne was not to utter lies. He was not to veer from the path of righteousness. He was not to hand down judgments that were in violation of the principles of justice.

Fortunately, nothing that challenged my principles occurred that day. Ramalinga Naidu, however, came to me with a complaint. 'There are a lot of Muslims in our army, and there are frequent clashes between our people and the Muslims. Do you think we should ask them to convert to our religion?'

'I thought you were a sensible man. But now I have to change my opinion. Our empire has the support of everyone, only because of the freedom we give to people, to choose their faith. Do you know something, Ramalingam? A general once made a suggestion similar to yours, to King Immadi Devaraya. Devaraya said to him: We are only paying them to use their bodies in fighting. We have not bought their souls. We have no right to control their souls. That is my argument too.'

'As you please, Your Majesty,' said Ramalingam.

Fortunately nothing exciting happened when I was seated on the golden throne. That evening, I alighted from it. I saw Ethirajan. I hadn't seen him for many days.

'Where were you all these days?' I asked him.

'It appears Acharya Venkata Thathayya will be here in a few days.'

'And so?'

'I thought Chinnadevi should be here, when Acharya visited. So I went to his math and have brought Chinna here.'

'Chinna? Has she arrived?' I asked, unable to contain my excitement.

'Yes, she is in my house. But, she is adamant on one count.'

'And what is that?'

'I will bring her to the palace tomorrow morning. Why don't you ask her yourself?

I couldn't sleep the whole of that night. I lay awake, waiting for daybreak.

Fifty-one

Midnight. A sudden roll of thunder. I remembered that it had been drizzling the previous evening.

I looked out of the window. Because of the rain that was lashing it, the city of Vijayanagar, which had worn a festive look the previous day, now looked like a bedraggled old man. I thought about the merchants who had set up stalls and the women who had been eager shoppers. Where were they sheltering from the rain?

I returned to my bed. Thirumala Devi was in the cot next to mine. She lay curled up like a child, and was fast asleep. Her face was innocent like a child's. I wondered how she would reconcile herself to Chinna being a part of my life. But I knew that no sacrifice was beyond her. In these five years of married life, except for that one night, when I forced her to yield to me, her life had been as empty as a desert. But she knew the secret of how to keep her sadness concealed. So she could handle any situation.

I dozed off, but got up when I heard some rustling. I woke up and found Thirumala Devi with a mosquito net in her hands. She draped it round my cot. 'I don't know where all the mosquitoes go in summer. And I don't know how they suddenly materialise in the rainy season,' she said with a pleasant smile.

'Just like life. One never knows when something good is going to happen or when something untoward is going to happen,' I said. 'Anyway, don't worry. There is no mosquito in the Vijayanagar Empire which will dare bite me. Besides, my skin is hard. I can bear even a tiger's bite. You are the gentle one. Hang a mosquito net round your cot too.'

'There is only one. Such thin nets are made in Bengal.

Someone brought them from there. You must have it. No mosquito will dare bite the Empress of Vijayanagar.'

I laughed. 'You have become very clever with your words. You too can sleep under my net. Come in,' I said.

'My cot is comfortable enough, Your Majesty,' she said. She sat down on her cot, facing me. She rested her elbows on her lap and cradled her chin in her hands.

She looked up at me, without raising her chin. The pressure of her fingers on her cheeks, had pushed up her plump cheeks and she looked very attractive. I watched her from inside the mosquito net. Every time the net swayed in the breeze, it seemed as if Thirumala Devi was swaying too. I found this funny, and burst out laughing. Thirumala Devi laughed too.

'I can see that my father's observation about you was right,' she said.

'What did he say? Did he warn you that a person bordering on lunacy was going to marry you and that you would have to be careful?'

'Not at all. My father has great regard for you.'

'What was it he said, then?'

'He said, "Our Emperor laughs a lot, and likes a sense of humour in others." I find that to be true,' said Thirumala Devi.

'This is just a façade,' I sighed. 'If the Emperor were sullen and irritable, then the ministers and my people will lose their zest for life. So I pretend that I am extremely happy. As to how I feel…'

I left the sentence unfinished. For a second, there was an awkward silence. Even without my expressing my feelings, Thirumala Devi understood how I felt. She stretched her hand, as if to comfort me by her touch. But she didn't touch me.

'Your Majesty. Please don't worry. Chinnadevi will definitely be with you soon.'

I wondered how she knew what I was thinking of.

'Ethirajan has promised to bring her here today,' I said.

'Chinnadevi will not come here,' said Thirumala Devi.

'Why not?' I asked angrily. I felt her words were inauspicious.

'She is very adamant on one count, Your Majesty.'

I recalled Ethirajan telling me something about her adamance. Thirumala Devi continued: 'When we heard that Chinnadevi was here in the capital, the Queen Mother and I sent for her.'

'Why?'

'In case there were any further hurdles to the marriage, your mother wanted to get them out of the way.'

I could see the reason for mother's gesture. She knew I was upset about her harshness with Gayatri. So she was hoping to mollify me.

'And what was Chinnadevi's reaction, when she was sent for?'

'She turned down your mother's request, very firmly, but respectfully. She says she will enter the palace, only if Thathayya tells her to.'

'Let us be patient.'

'That's not all. Because of the Mahanavami celebrations, Lakshmidhara and other artistes invited her to dance in our auditorium. But she turned down their request, and said she would come only if Acharya told her to.'

'There is no reason to worry. Venkata Thathayya has given me his word. All our problems will end as soon as he arrives.'

I could now see what Ethirajan had meant when he had mentioned Chinnadevi's obstinacy. Although I was happy that she was unwavering in her determination, I was also quite worried that there might be further delays.

☙

Although it was clear that Chinnadevi wasn't going to come, I didn't give up hope.

Every time the herald announced someone's arrival, I stood up to see if it was Chinnadevi who was entering. Every time there was a slight commotion at the entrance or the sound of a palanquin arriving, I peeped out from the balcony. I was picturing her getting down from a palanquin and walking towards me, with the bells in her anklets jangling.

Just as Mother wanted to pacify me, I too wanted to mollify my mother.

A victory procession had been arranged for Appaji. I seated him on an elephant and took him round the streets of Vijayanagar. I rode ahead of him on horseback, as if I were his guard.

I could hear people commenting on the regard I had for Appaji, and they were right in observing that I had great regard for him.

As we went round the streets, I hoped we would see Chinnadevi somewhere. My hands held the horse's bridle, but my eyes looked round to see if Chinnadevi could be spotted somewhere.

It wasn't raining heavily, but it continued to drizzle. So people still walked round with their umbrellas open. Arabian merchants were bargaining with shopkeepers. The chariot festival of the Durga temple was just two days away, and so the chariot was being decorated. As Appaji and I moved around the streets of the city, women welcomed Appaji with auspicious coloured water, which they then poured on to the streets. There was something almost poetic about the way the coloured water joined the rivulets of rain water and flowed along.

But Chinnadevi was nowhere in sight. I had no idea in which house Ethirajan resided. Perhaps upon being told that I was passing through, Chinnadevi had locked herself up in her house!

At the end of the procession, I took Appaji to my palace. I seated him on the gem-studded throne. Many poets read out poems they had composed in praise of Appaji. Appaji gave away all the gifts he received. He donated lands that belonged to him to various temples.

My mother was witness to all the celebrations and was pleased. 'What you have done will earn you God's grace, Krishna. He will fulfil all your desires,' she said.

At the end of the celebrations, I had a meeting with all my ministers. I could see that all of them were jealous of Appaji, because I had honoured him. They had expected that my anger against Appaji occasioned by my son's death would last. They had not expected that I would have a change of heart and honour Appaji.

The agenda for the meeting was a discussion of the damage caused by heavy rains all over the country and remedial measures to be taken.

But at the very outset of the meeting, Kondamarasu said, 'That girl from Kalinga killed the Kalinga prince…'

'Gayatri didn't do it on purpose,' interrupted Appaji. 'Even assuming she had, the Queen Mother has already punished her severely for it. There is no need for us to discuss her now.'

'Prime Minister, you mustn't be angry,' said Nadella Gopa. 'The Gajapati King Prataparudra Deva is very angry with us because of the death of his son, Veerabhadran. We captured the son but allowed the father to escape. Our spies say that he may seek the help of the Golconda Sultan, Qutub Shahi. There is the danger of our enemies joining hands to attack us…'

'I have made arrangements to forestall such an eventuality. At the appropriate time, I will tell you what those arrangements are,' said Appaji sternly.

I didn't want the arguments to get bitter. 'We are here to discuss the damage caused by the rains. Let Managalarasayya and Chellappa tell us about what relief operations we should and can undertake.'

The discussion now veered in that direction.

'The road from Udayagiri to Vijayanagar is the one that is most badly damaged. And what is most worrying is that Acharya Venkata Thathayya is taking that road towards Vijayanagaram.'

I was gripped by fear. But I didn't want to show my fear. 'Please arrange to bring the Acharya safely in a palanquin,' I said.

Immediately Kondamarasu said, 'That's the problem. He has vowed not to use a palanquin this month. He travels to all pilgrim centres on foot. We expect that he will be in the capital in another two or three days.'

At the end of the meeting, when Appaji and I were alone, I said, 'You said you had made some arrangements to ensure that Gajapati would not march against us. What are those arrangements?'

'You will be shocked if I tell you…'

'Never mind. Tell me what they are.'

'We imprisoned many people in Kondapalli. Many of them are women. And of them…'

'Yes?'

'One of the women prisoners is Pratapa Rudra's wife and the other is his daughter. That is two of the women prisoners happen to be the mother and sister of Veerabhadran. As long as we hold them hostage, Prataparudra will never dare to march against us. He knows what will happen to them if he were to march against us.'

I was amazed at Appaji's cleverness. But what would my mother's reaction be if she came to know of this?

As Kondamarasu had predicted, Acharya Venkata Thathayya arrived in the capital two days later. I was told that he was coming to the palace.

I could hear Vedic chants and musical instruments. Elephants trumpeted as if they too were welcoming him. Priests went to the entrance of the palace to welcome him and I ran ahead of them. And there I saw an emaciated, almost cadaverous Acharya Venkata Thathayya. He was being supported by two of his disciples. As a result of his fever, he could hardly walk.

'Carefully,' I said to his disciples. I was at my wit's end. I took him to my room and made him lie down on my cot. He could barely keep his eyes open. But he recognized me and raised his hands as if to bless me.

'Quick. Someone fetch Nicholas. Only that Italian can offer him some relief at once,' I said.

Acharya mumbled inaudibly. I couldn't make out what he was trying to say. I bent close to him to be able to hear him. 'What did you say, Swami?' I asked.

'No, not the Italian. I don't want to be touched by a foreigner,' said Venkata Thathayya.

He was unwilling to compromise on his orthodoxy, even when he was on the verge of death!

Fifty-two

I was alarmed when I saw the state Acharya Venkata Thathayya was in and I was shocked by his refusal to allow Nicholas to treat him.

'Swami, he has converted to our religion,' I said. But I don't think he understood what I was saying. He was losing consciousness and I wondered whether he was capable of comprehending what he saw or heard.

But I was proved wrong. He was conscious. 'No…There is nothing the matter with me… Don't worry,' he said in a barely audible voice.

My mother was beside me and was watching him anxiously. 'Krishna, don't do anything that goes against Acharya's wishes. Send for our royal physician,' she said to me. Turning to the Acharya, she asked, 'Swami, I hope you have no objection to that?'

He waved his hand slowly, to indicate that it was all right. He then summoned one of his disciples and said, 'I am told Chinnadevi is in the city. Fetch her.'

Both mother and I protested at once and said, 'Swami, that can wait. You must get better first.'

He gave us a wan smile. 'That sword…'

'I went to Srivilliputtur and fetched it. But this is not the time to talk about it,' I said.

He smiled and said, 'You have kept your word. I will make sure you and Chinnadevi marry. Should I not keep my word too?' And then he noticed that the disciple who was supposed to fetch Chinnadevi was still there. He signalled to him to leave.

The royal physician came and examined the Acharya. He then

took my mother aside and said, 'He has walked a long distance in the rains. He has very high fever. Your Majesty, I am afraid to treat him. Why don't you ask that young man Nicholas to treat him? He has discovered some new medicines.'

'Acharya is adamant that Nicholas should not touch him. Cast your anxiety on God and do your best.'

The physician had prepared some potion, which he made Acharya drink. But there didn't seem to be any significant improvement in his condition. He managed to open his eyes. It was obvious that he was looking for someone.

There! The person he was looking for was here! Chinnadevi—the one I had also been searching for.

It is a rule of nature that one's good looks dim with age. But my Chinnadevi was not bound by any rule of nature. She was as beautiful as she had been when I had met her four years ago in Acharya's math, on the banks of the Krishna river. I now saw in her face the same magnetic charm that I had seen four years ago.

She was shocked to see the state the Acharya was in. But she bowed at his feet and took his blessings. She then stood beside my mother.

She lifted up her eyes and looked at me. She stared at me for a few seconds. I saw in her eyes her prodigious love for me. I also saw sternness in her eyes, indicating her unwillingness to go against the rules.

The Acharya indicated to her, partly through his words, and partly through his gestures, that she should take her mangalsutra off and hand it to me.

She took off the mangalsutra and gave it to me. I could see that her hands were shaking.

Acharya then said to me, 'Take this mangalsutra and the sword you brought from Srivilliputtur to the cremation ground. Burn them on a funeral pyre. After you have set fire to them, have your bath and come to me. I have to perform a ritual. And after that, there will be nothing to keep you from marrying Chinnadevi.'

I took less time to carry out his instructions than he took to convey them! With the help of Appaji and other Ministers, I carried out his instructions. I had my bath, dressed in new clothes and ran back to the Acharya.

Outside the room in which he lay, priests had lit a fire and were performing some rituals. I suppose they were acting upon Acharya's instructions. When Thirumala Devi saw me, she hurried towards me.

'How is the Acharya?' I asked.

'He is unconscious. Your mother had no option but to send for Nicholas, and he is there attending on Acharya.'

An Emperor should never run, whatever situation he finds himself in. I had once run, for the sake of my son Thirumalai, and that had ended in disaster. So I did not display my agitation, but walked calmly towards the Acharya.

Nicholas had wrapped a thin silk cloth around his hand and was examining Acharya's pulse. He also lifted the Acharya's eyelids and had a look at his eyes.

He sighed and said to me, 'The Acharya is in a serious condition. All bodily functions have been compromised…In Siddha medicine…'

I lost my patience. 'I don't want any medical explanations. Just tell me what his condition is.'

'Bad. He is unlikely to survive. He may regain consciousness now and then and open his eyes.'

'Chinnadevi, come here. Stand by my side. When the Acharya opens his eyes, let him see us together.'

But Chinnadevi did not do as I asked her to. She said to my

mother: 'Acharya said one more ritual remained to be completed. Let him complete that. I am sure he will.'

I was disgusted with her.

'How could she be so adamant?' I asked myself. But at the same time, I was also proud of her unwavering determination. I could see that she felt that for our love to be strong, we would have to get Acharya's blessings.

What more could we do now? I was like one tossed into a lime kiln. Every fibre of my being was in agony. I felt like a leaf tossed about by the wind. I wasn't even aware that I had made my way to my room.

Thirumala Devi was there, like my shadow. She didn't know what she could say or do to comfort me.

Usually, if she happened to brush against me, she would jump away, as if she had touched a hot iron rod. But now, because of the gravity of the situation, she touched my shoulder gently and said, 'Your Majesty…' She said nothing more. But her eyes communicated her words: 'Don't lose heart. Everything will turn out all right.'

Thirumala Devi was a woman with an iron resolve. But I could guess that her heart was breaking because she was afraid my dream would be shattered. I didn't speak either. But I gave her hand a reassuring squeeze, as if to indicate that I was not worrying and that she was not to either.

The chariot of Goddess Durga was on the adjacent street.

Smoke from a ritual fire was wafting through my room. The smoke was becoming less dense by the minute, as if the fire was on the verge of going out any minute now. Since the rituals were taking place close to my room, I could hear the chants of the priests. They were repeating a line. I knew that this was the line that was repeated when a respected elder was on his deathbed.

So did this show that they no longer believed that Venkata Thathayya would survive?

No, No! He would live long! He would bring me and Chinnadevi together!

I went out of my room and said, 'Stop. Stop it at once.' Hearing my command, a servant ran to the priests to convey my command to them. A few minutes later one of Acharya's disciples came to meet me.

'Your Majesty, why did you ask for the ritual to be stopped?'

'Because it is inauspicious.'

'Please forgive me, Your Majesty. These are sacred mantras. If they are recited when a person is on his deathbed, then he will be liberated from the cycle of births and deaths.'

'Acharya Venkata Thathayya is a great spiritual leader. He will attain liberation even if he doesn't hear these mantras being recited. Who are you to say his end is at hand? Are you God?'

He didn't reply. He left the room without a word.

When I came back to my room, Jangamaiyya was waiting for me, with a scroll in his hands.

'Your Majesty, a letter for you.'

'Who is it from?'

'I don't know, Your Majesty. Someone brought it just now.'

I went into the room. I was in no mood to read a letter. It was probably from some general asking for horses for his unit. Or it must be an invitation from one of my vassals, seeking my blessings for a marriage in his family.

Or it must be one of my subjects writing to me about the drought in his village, and asking me to make arrangements to provide water to the villagers. I didn't care what the letter was about. I flung it across the room. The scroll had not been encased in a metal container. So the silk cloth came undone. And there it lay in a corner, like a sulking child that has been chided by its mother.

I didn't want to even look at it. I paced up and down my room. But despite myself, my eyes kept straying towards the silk cloth, and the handwriting looked familiar. And when I could no longer contain my curiosity, I picked up the scroll and began to read.

'Respectful Emperor. Your servant Gayatri's humble submission to you.'

When I read the first line of the letter, I was seized with excitement and read further.

'Your Majesty. Let me take leave of you.

For the last four years you have been like a brother to me. The Queen Mother treated me like her daughter.

I had complete independence in your palace. When I came to your palace from Kalinga, I was an orphan. I took up employment as a servant, who carried members of the royal family on her back. But soon I rose to a high position and enjoyed privileges denied to even ministers. Sometimes more importance was given to my words than to the words of Prime Minister Appaji. In contravention of all the rules of the land, I married Nicholas—the man I loved.

But I now realize that I do not deserve such respect.

I wanted you to marry Chinnadevi. I did my best to help you in this regard.

But why did I do all this?

With the selfish motive of having my revenge on Veerabhadran.

It is because of my vengeful nature that my efforts have proved futile. And because you cast your lot with me, success eludes you too.

Acharya Venkata Thathayya, who is here to join you and Chinnadevi in wedlock, has fallen ill at the crucial moment. He is battling death. Why has that happened? That too is because of my thirst for revenge.

Now is the time for me to atone for my sins.

I have helped you in small ways in the past. But what I am now going to do is bigger than anything I've done before.

Some people might say that what I am about to do now is superstitious folly. But this is my belief. My unshakeable belief. It is my belief in God.

Your Majesty, again, let me request you. Please bid this sister of yours farewell. Your mother said I was never to enter the palace again. Please tell her that I have never once disobeyed that order.

My regards to you again and again.

Gayatri.

Post script: How lucky I am to be three months pregnant!

Gayatri.'

What was she trying to say? What was Gayatri up to? My head reeled.

Even as I stood there confused, the sounds of celebration from the chariot festival of the Durga temple stopped suddenly. There was an eerie silence. The musical instruments had stopped too.

The next second, there was a huge uproar from the people.

Now I knew what Gayatri had done.

'Gayatri,' I screamed and ran out. Thirumala Devi, who didn't know what the letter contained, followed me.

I almost collided with the man who was running towards me. It was Nicholas. 'Your Majesty! It's a miracle. Acharya Venkata Thathayya has regained consciousness. He is sitting up. He is asking for you. Come at once. At once,' Nicholas said.

Fifty-three

I was caught on the horns of a dilemma.

Here was Nicholas telling me that Acharya Venkata Thathayya had regained consciousness and was asking for me. And there was Gayatri, ready to sacrifice her life. What should I do?

I decided that whatever the exigencies of a situation may be, the Acharya's summons would have to be given priority.

'Nicholas, go at once to the street on which the temple chariot is proceeding. Gayatri has made up her mind to do something terrible. She must be stopped. Go, go at once and stop her!' I said.

Nicholas was disturbed by my agitation, but he was puzzled, not knowing what I was talking about. But, nevertheless, he ran out.

Acharya was sitting up in bed, and he didn't look like someone who had been battling death a while ago. He seemed to be simply glowing with health. My mother, Thirumala Devi, Chinnadevi, Appaji and the other ministers were by his side, all of them smiling happily.

The Acharya pointed to a wooden seat beside him, and asked me to sit down.

I sat down.

'I had been thinking of how I could unite you and Chinnadevi in matrimony, and I came to this conclusion,' he began. 'I will perform *Pancha Samskaram*[23] for you. You will then become a Vaishnavite and you will be free to marry Chinnadevi, who has also been initiated into Vaishnavism in the same way.'

---

23. Pancha Samskaram: Five purification rituals, for those who follow Ramanujacharya's tradition

I knew I should pay attention to what he was saying, but my mind was in the street where the chariot procession was taking place.

Venkata Thathayya then explained what Pancha Samskaram meant. He picked up a silver conch and discus and heated them over a fire. They turned red-hot. He then branded my right shoulder with the discus and the left with the conch. He taught me the Vaishnava mantras.

He taught me how to conduct a daily worship of Lord Mahavishnu. He then said, 'I will also have to give you a new name, to indicate your initiation into Vaishnavism. You will be known as Ramanuja Dasan. From today, 'Ramanuja Dasan' shall be appended to your name.'

He called Chinnadevi and asked her to hold my hand. Thirumala Devi brought Chinna to me, and put Chinna's hands in mine. Chinnadevi fell at my feet, and no longer able to control her feelings, she embraced me, unmindful of the fact that there were so many people present there.

This was the embrace I had waited for, yearned for, for years. But now that I had what I had ached for, I was in no position to enjoy it.

'Acharya, you must forgive me. I will be back soon,' I said to Venkata Thathayya, and ran out.

☙

By the time I reached the street, it was all over. Those who had been pulling the chariot, those who had been playing musical instruments, and the thousands of people who had gathered to witness the chariot procession stood stunned.

I could hear people saying, 'She cried out that she wanted all of Emperor Krishnadevaraya's wishes to be fulfilled and then she threw herself under the wheels of the chariot.'

Gayatri was near the wheels of the chariot, with her head cradled on Nicholas' lap. Her blood was turning the ground crimson. A white cloth covered the lower portion of her body, to keep the gory sight from people.

Nicholas was sobbing. I couldn't even do that, because I felt emotionally numb.

Gayatri had written in her last letter to me: 'How lucky that I am now three months pregnant!'

There was a stupid superstitious belief that if a woman who was carrying her first child threw herself under the wheels of a chariot, her wishes would be fulfilled.

Gayatri had believed this would happen. And now, miraculously Acharya Venkata Thathayya had recovered. How could I call it a superstitious belief?

I could hear my mother's voice: 'You silly girl! I was angry when I told you I would never see you again. But now you have left, without ever seeing me again.'

Chinnadevi, Thirumala Devi, Appaji and the other ministers said many things. Gayatri was dead. Beyond that nothing else registered in my mind. I sweated profusely, like one who had had a nightmare.

☙

This story began with Gayatri. Let me end it with Gayatri.

What more can I write, when she has made the ultimate sacrifice that anyone can make? I can go on giving lifeless historical details.

I don't know if her words were sincere, or if she had a selfish motive for saying it, but she would often tell me that the only thing she sought was my happiness. Now she has departed from this world, and I am happy, thanks to her prayers.

Father Louis brings me a lot of international news. He told me that there lived a great prophet called Jesus Christ. He also told me that history is divided into the era before Christ and the era after him, and that this is how dates are arrived at. By that reckoning, this is the 1529th year after Christ. In terms of the Hindu almanac, this is the Saka year 1452.

Nagalapuram, the township that I established, and named after my mother, is now thriving, with many settlers.

Tall gopurams are being built for all the existing temples in the country. The practice of building thousand-pillared mandapas in temples and the practice of a separate shrine for the Goddess have come into vogue.

Nicholas has got over his sorrow, and he uses a combination of European, Siddha and Ayurvedic methods of treatment. He has established many hospitals across the country.

The sculptor Muthu doesn't like administration. So he has put another able general in charge of Thiruvannamalai, and has returned to Vijayanagar with his wife Solai. The dance hall that he and Bandham Lakshmi Narayana designed looks divine.

Ethirajan has become a follower of Venkata Thathayya and is touring the country visiting various pilgrim centres.

※

There have been many changes in my life too.

I have completed the work on Andal's life, *Amukta Malyada*. The last two verses praise Vishnu as the One with lotus eyes; the One who is praised by Parvati; the One holds a bow; the One whose feet glow because of the gems in the crowns of those who touch His feet with their heads, and this includes the three-eyed one Siva, Brahma, Indra the king of the celestials and others. When I completed those two verses and brought the work to a conclusion, I was more pleased than when I had conquered new territory.

Although I have written other works in Telugu, like *Madalasa Charitram*, *Rasamanjari* and *Usha Parinayam*, scholars think Amukta Malyada is my magnum opus. When scholars say that if one were to classify Telugu literary works into the five most seminal works, as has been done in the case of Tamil literature, then Amukta Malyada will certainly be one of them, I feel embarrassed. I am not sure if my work is really deserving of such praise, or whether it is being praised because it has been written by the Emperor. Only time will tell.

In Amukta Malyada, I have written several erotic verses, about Andal's love for Lord Ranganatha. Some people say that these verses are the result of my pining for Chinnadevi. Perhaps they are right!

My mother had wanted my elder brother's son and my younger brothers Rangan and Achyutan to be released from the Chandragiri fort. I complied with her wish, and I brought them to the capital. They said that they had no intention of turning against me. Since I have no sons, I have arranged for Achutaraya to be Emperor after me. My son-in-law Aliya Ramanuja and Prime Minister Appaji are to assist him in administration.

My life with my two wives is peaceful. The two of them are great friends, and respectfully call each other 'Elder sister.' I often tease them, and tell them that since women always like to hide their age, each wanted to refer to the other as the elder one. 'Now tell me, which of you is really the elder and which of you is younger?' I ask them.

But someone must have cast an evil eye on the camaraderie we three shared, and my domestic happiness was shattered by a woman. If I do not mention this, then I will be guilty of concealing history. So let me mention that too.

She is my third wife—Jaganmohini. She is the daughter of Gajapati Prataparudra. She is also called Tukka.

Appaji was right. Because his wife and daughter were our prisoners, Gajapati did not wage war against me. On the contrary, he wanted to make friends with me. He brought me gifts and had talks with me. He wanted to prove that his friendship with me was genuine, and so he offered to give his daughter Jaganmohini in marriage to me.

At first, I refused. But Appaji felt that for political reasons, it would be wise if I married her. My mother felt that I should not offend Prataparudra's feelings. So I married Jaganmohini. There are hundreds of girls—virgins, all of them—who live in the women's quarters of my palace. I have never so much as given them a glance. And yet the world says that they are all a part of my harem. I thought Jaganmohini could also be a part of the women's quarters, which was already home to many girls.

But Jaganmohini was unwilling to be part of such an arrangement. She began to abuse Thirumala Devi and Chinnadevi.

When the sculptor who had made images of Thirumala Devi, Chinnadevi and of me, brought the images to the palace to show them to me, Jagnamohini demanded that an image be made of her too.

I would have conceded her demand. But what kept me from doing so was the harshness of her words. 'Look at your other two wives. One of them is the daughter of an insignificant king. Another is a dancer. But I am the daughter of a famous Emperor,' she said. I was livid. I ordered her to leave the palace. Since my mother and Appaji knew how angry I was, they didn't intercede on her behalf.

Jaganmohini did not stay in Vijayanagar. She didn't go back to her father's capital—Cuttack. She stayed in Cumbum. Although she was arrogant, I have to admit that she was a learned woman.

Allasani Peddanna tells me that she has written a work called *Tukka Panchakam*. He says that the work consists of verses which capture the sorrow of a woman separated from her husband.

The images of me and of my two wives have been placed in the Tirupati Srinivasa temple. I trust they will be there for hundreds of years.

Gayatri had prayed for my happiness, and I must say that her prayer has been answered.

And yet, why is it that in a corner of my heart, there is an inexplicable sadness?

I often ask myself this question.

Why are you sad, Krishna?

Why am I like a man who has been served a feast, but while he is savouring it, a small stone in the rice spoils everything?

Why do your eyes mist over with tears, when you should be happy?

When you watch a dance, when you hear sweet music, when you see the lovely lotuses in the pond, when you climb up the Matanga hill, when you enjoy the evening breeze, when you laugh along with children, when you take your mother's blessing, when you smell the fragrance of flowers, when you worship in temples, when you fall at the feet of learned men, when you watch the women of the palace dance, when you read beautiful verses—why, Krishnadevaraya, do you shed tears at such times?

These tears are for that woman, who made such happiness possible.

These tears are for that princess who experienced great suffering in Katak, who came to Vijayanagar to wreak vengeance on her enemy. These tears are for that woman.

These tears are for that princess, who helped me marry the woman I loved. These tears are for the woman who sought nothing for herself, for the woman who departed in a flash, at lightning speed.

These tears are for that young woman, for my dear sister, for Gayatri.

Epilogue

Krishnadevaraya's heir was a son who was a year-and-a-half old. So Krishnadevaraya arranged for Achyutaraya, the son of his father's first wife to rule after him. When Krishnadevaraya died in 1530 C.E., Achyutaraya succeeded him. But, Krishnadevaraya's son-in-law Ramaraya also wanted a share in power. So he too was given some power. Taking advantage of such dissensions within the family, Prataparudra Gajapati and Adil Shah captured some portions of the Vijayanagar Empire.

In the last seven years of his rule, Achyutaraya turned into a tyrant. In Madurai, Thanjavur, and Gingee, the Nayak kings ruled. The Portuguese also established themselves in trade.

Achyutaraya was succeeded by his son Venkataraya. But within a year he was murdered by his maternal uncle Salakkaraju. Ramaraya defeated Salakkaraju, and put Sadasivaraya on the throne.

Sadasivaraya (1543-1572) was king only in name. Power was in the hands of Ramaraya and his younger brothers Thirumalai and Venkatadri. But through some of their actions, they incurred the wrath of the Muslim kings. So the Bahmani Sultans joined hands under the leadership of the Golconda Sultan—Qutubmeeran. The rival armies were stationed on either side of the Krishna river.

The Talikota war, which took place on January 23, 1565, changed the course of Indian history. The Vijayanagar army had 10 000 elephants, 37 000 horses and five lakh foot soldiers. But in spite of this, Ramaraya lost the war. Venkatadri died on the battlefield. Ramaraya was captured and beheaded. Thirumalaraya retreated. Sadasivaraya disappeared. The four Sultans entered

Vijayanagar. They camped there for five months, looting the city. They took away the treasures of the Vijayanagar Emperors on elephant back, and they needed five hundred elephants for this. They razed buildings and temples, and the capital was reduced to rubble. The dream that a strong Hindu Empire would flourish in South India was shattered.

Thirumalaraya shifted his capital to Penukonda and established a new dynasty called the Araveedu dynasty. This dynasty ruled for about 150 years. Some small kingdoms in the South, took the help of the Golconda Sultans, to completely destroy whatever was left of the Vijayanagar Empire. In the North, the Mughals became powerful. During the reign of Akbar, their empire expanded.

And then European powers came to India, followed by the East India Company, but that is more recent history.